Hello!

...couple of years ago I wrote a book called *The Cake Shop in* ...e *Garden* which instantly became a firm favourite with ...y readers. I created, arguably, my most gorgeous romantic ...o in Danny Wilde – slight pause for sighing – and, some- ...nes, a character is so strong that you just can't get them ...t of your head. In the back of my mind, Danny and Fay ...ld pop up every now and again, making me think of ...m and wonder what had happened to them.

...are very fortunate in having friends who own a narrow- ...on the Grand Union Canal in Costa del Keynes, right ...e place where *The Cake Shop in the Garden* was set. They ...arly invite us out for the day and we have a lovely time ...ir boat. I have terrible narrowboat envy.

...was one particular occasion when we were with them ...ade me think of how Fay and Danny's story would ...e. It was a magical moment and I knew then and ...t I had to write it.

...e you for choosing to read *Christmas Cakes &* ... *Nights*. I really hope that you enjoy it. If you do, ...ce a moment to review it on social media and share ...r friends. It makes all the difference! If you want to ...me about it on my author Facebook page or on Twitter, ...ry happy to see you there. I'm blessed with lovely, ...ve readers and we have a lot of fun. So grab yourself ...cake, kick back and enjoy another trip down the ...nion with old friends and meet some new ones too.

..., Carole :) xx

...s. As a little extra I've described my perfect Christmas for ...u at the back of this book – let me know what you think!

Also by Carole Matthews

Carole Matthews

Christmas Cakes & Mistletoe Nights

sphere

SPHERE

First published in Great Britain in 2017 by Sphere
This paperback edition published by Sphere in 2018

1 3 5 7 9 10 8 6 4 2

A CIP catalogue record for this book
is available from the British Library.

ISBN 978-0-7515-6029-9

Typeset in Sabon LT Std by Palimpsest Book Production Ltd,
Falkirk, Stirlingshire

Printed and bound in Great Britain by Clays Ltd, Elcograf S.p.A.

Papers used by Sphere are from well-managed forests
and other responsible sources.

Sphere
An imprint of
Little, Brown Book Group
Carmelite House
50 Victoria Embankment
London EC4Y 0DZ

An Hachette UK Company
www.hachette.co.uk

www.littlebrown.co.uk

To Karen and Kevin

We love our days out with you on your cheeky *Beaver*, getting shouty on prosecco and nearly getting off the wrong side into the Grand Union. What japes!

Thank you for the inspiration.

Chapter One

I watch a weeping willow dipping its branches into the canal, leaves ruffled by the breeze. Beneath it, a cow and her young calf are standing at the water's edge where the bank has been trampled flat by many hooves. Delicate, spiky-headed teasels, crisp and brown now after their summer flowering, harbour the last of the dragonflies. Behind, a lush meadow stretches away and, in the distance, the spire of an ancient church peeps above the tall trees that have already turned golden this year, parched after our long, hot summer. A couple of swans glide elegantly by. It looks as if it's been unchanged for hundreds of years. If I was an artist, I'd try to capture this scene in watercolour. But I'm not, so I take out my phone and snap a shot for posterity.

'Fay! Are you planning on doing anything with that windlass?'

Danny's shout brings me back to the present. 'Sorry!'

He's waiting at the entrance to the lock for me to leap into action and open the gates. Which I now do. 'I'm on it!'

I've run ahead of him so that this would all be quicker and then wasted the time by standing here daydreaming for five minutes. I finish closing the top lock. Diggery, our little Jack Russell cross, runs up and down barking his own instructions. He's wearing a skull-and-crossbones neckerchief today and looks very jaunty.

When I've finished my part, Danny steers *The Dreamcatcher* into the tight space, bumping the sides slightly as he does. *The Dreamcatcher* is a decent-sized narrowboat and takes some manoeuvring. Despite spending the last few months living on the canal together, we're still very much novices. There's no doubt that we're learning quickly, though. Every day seems to bring some new challenge or obstacle to overcome – I can now unblock a loo with a certain degree of competence, light a stubborn woodburner, and fill the water tanks without giving myself an impromptu shower. All of these things are life skills I didn't have a short time ago – or ever think that I'd need.

'No worries,' Danny says as he cruises past me on the boat and settles *The Dreamcatcher* into the lock. 'We're not in a hurry.' He jumps off the back of the boat onto the towpath and together we manhandle the heavy lock gates into place.

I tell you, I have arms like Popeye now after all this physical work. The canals are not for wimps. No gym membership needed for me!

'I was having a little daydream,' I admit as we work the lock, watching *The Dreamcatcher* rise on the turbulent water to the next level. 'This place is so lovely.'

Danny looks round and takes it all in. 'We can stay up here as long as you like. Hopefully, I can get some more work.'

And that's one of our main problems. The last of the gloriously hot summer has gone and we're well into the cooler days of autumn now. Christmas will soon be upon us and the seasonal work that's kept Danny busy on our travels is slowly starting to dry up as the days grow shorter and colder.

'There's enough to keep me busy on site for the next two or three weeks.' Danny's currently doing casual labouring on a building site, but as the weather worsens there'll be less available. 'But that's about it. They won't be taking on until after the new year. Maybe even spring, if we have a bad winter.'

His work has been bringing in some very welcome money, but only just enough to keep body and soul together.

'After that, I'm not so sure what will happen.' He turns his heart-warming smile on me. 'But something will come up. You don't need to worry about it.'

Yet, I do. I'm one of life's worriers. The fact that I'm here at all is nothing short of a miracle. I'd never done a reckless thing in all of my forty-two years – until, of course, I left behind everything that I know and hold dear to run away with Danny Wilde for an itinerant life on the water-ways of England. Even though I'm telling you this, I can still hardly come to terms with it myself. I waved goodbye to my old life, my friends, my family, my lovely little café in the garden without a backward glance. Well, not much of one. I could well be having a mid-life crisis but if I am, it feels really rather nice. Well, most of the time. It's only when I look at my bank balance that I get the collywobbles.

'We've got our love to keep us warm,' Danny says.

'And a dwindling supply of firewood.'

'I'll get some later,' he promises. 'It's on my never-ending list of Things To Do.'

Life on the canal, as we're both finding, certainly isn't all about sitting back with a glass of wine and watching the world go by. It's hard graft, that's for sure. But, now that I've done it, I wouldn't change a thing.

We're in Wales on the Llangollen branch of the Shropshire Union Canal. It's the most beautiful part of the country and the temptation to linger here is very strong. It's taken us six weeks or more to work our way up here and the journey has been truly wonderful. I've never tried anything remotely like this before and I'm fully embracing the free spirit that's slowly emerging from somewhere deep inside me.

Together we open the other gates, me huffing and puffing like an old train, Danny doing it with consummate ease.

'Come on, Digs,' Danny calls. 'Back on board or we'll leave you behind.'

Taking no chances, Diggery bounds onto the boat and sits by the tiller.

Expertly handled by Danny, *The Dreamcatcher* floats happily out of the lock. It's a sturdy boat, getting on a little in age and slightly scuffed around the edges – much like my good self. A few bits are patched up and held together with string, glue, an extra coat of paint and crossed fingers which will need some attention when we eventually find some spare cash.

I close the lock behind the boat and climb on board too. I stand proudly beside Danny while he takes control of the tiller and steers us back along our route. Even now, there are times when I look at him and can't believe that we're a couple.

'What?' he says as I gaze at his face. 'You're looking all moony.'

I laugh. 'I *am* all moony!'

'Glad to hear it, Ms Merryweather.' He puts his arm round my waist and draws me close. He smells of woodsmoke from firing up the stove this morning to take the chill off the boat.

I didn't think my jaded, middle-aged heart was capable of containing this much love. But it does. Danny's young – much younger than me – handsome, and the nicest man that you could meet, to boot. And he's mine.

What can I tell you about him? He's thirty-two – a full ten years my junior, though I have to say I'm the least likely cougar on the planet. He's tall, skinny and muscular all at once. He never looks better than when he's wearing a tight T-shirt and black jeans. His hair's jet black, cropped at the sides but flopping every which way on top. I look at it now and think that it could probably do with a cut. Despite living frugally on the boat, Danny still likes to go to a barber rather than have me taking to it with the kitchen scissors. Today, because of the cool morning, he's wearing a black beanie hat and a faded grey denim jacket. He hasn't shaved yet and he subconsciously keeps smoothing the shadow of stubble on his skin. Originally, he's from Ireland – near Belfast – and even though he's lived in England for years now, he still speaks with a soft, sexy accent that makes my heart go all silly. He has dark, mischievous eyes and they make not just my heart but everything else go silly too. Actually, just take it as read that I'm as lovestruck as it's possible to be.

Danny Wilde came into my life at a time when I felt I had so little to look forward to. I'd completely lost who Fay Merryweather actually was or the woman she'd once hoped to be. I'd been in a relationship of sorts with the same man for years but, if I'm completely honest, I wasn't really in love. Anthony and I were together out of habit more than any great passion. He was more keen on his golf clubs than he ever was on me. My stepmother – a wicked one as it turns out – and her extensive range of illnesses had dominated my life. I was Miranda's prime carer and, for my sins, she made sure that it was a role I filled 24/7. I'd been forced to give up my job because of it and ran a café from our home by the canal, Fay's Cakes, that had developed out of necessity rather than any fabulously ambitious business plan. My ad hoc selling of cakes from our ancient canal boat, the *Maid of Merryweather*, became a success despite my daily struggle to hold it all together. Before long, I added light lunches and teas and my business grew into the garden when we put a few tables out under the apple trees. Then I took over the dining room and we had even more tables, so I hired Lija Vilks, my ill-tempered Latvian assistant, to help me keep my head above water. Lija turned out to be the most foul-mouthed and fastidious employee anyone could have and I have no idea how I would ever have managed without her. She's as feisty as I'm timid, and as lovely as she is difficult, but she's fiercely loyal to me and, well – just fierce, actually. Beyond all else, her cakes are flipping amazing. A slice of her lemon drizzle makes me overlook all her shortcomings in the customer-care department.

Yet, despite loving running the café, I still felt that I wasn't in control of my own destiny. Anthony and Miranda were controlling my life. When they said jump, all I did was ask, 'How high?' I got up, baked cakes, made beds, cleaned floors, pandered to Miranda's needs, baked more cakes, ironed shirts and sheets, pandered to Anthony's needs, fell into bed exhausted. Then got up and did the same thing the very next day. I was bumping along the bottom of my existence and that's never a good feeling. I'm in my forties and I should have been in the prime of my life – yet I was going nowhere fast. Little did I know how that was all about to change. Now I'm still going nowhere fast, but for very different reasons!

Our life on *The Dreamcatcher* is as far out of the rat race as you can get. Now we work to live, not the other way round. Danny had escaped the corporate life, buying the boat on a whim and taking to the canals for a great adventure. He came to the café looking for casual work – much in the same way that he's doing now. While Lija and I managed to stay on top of the daily upkeep of Fay's

Cakes, the garden and repairs around the house were going to pot, so I found Danny some gardening and odd jobs that had been on my To Do list for ages, unaware that this seemingly small decision would turn my staid little life upside down.

Every morning, I thank my lucky stars that I did. If I'd decided that my fence could stay unpainted, my trees unpruned, then I could quite conceivably have drifted into marriage with Anthony and would have spent the rest of my life as a downtrodden golf widow with a husband who thought having sex once a month was being rampant. Instead, I fell madly in love, embarked on a whirlwind romance with my young and gorgeous gardener, left Anthony, gave up the café, and ran away to join Danny Wilde on his travels. Go, me!

I couldn't have acted any more out of character if I'd tried. Yet I'm so glad that I did. My new life is everything I'd hoped for and more. Danny and I have lived together in close quarters on the boat for a few months now and, so far, we've hardly had a cross word. Seriously, I have to pinch myself on a daily basis to check that it isn't all a beautiful dream.

There are days when I wonder what Danny sees in me. I'm not one of those young, trendy forty-somethings that you see in the magazines. I'm no Kate Moss or Gwyneth Paltrow. No one would ever mistake me for a style icon. I haven't even had my hair cut since I've been on the boat, so my low-maintenance bob has taken on a life of its own. I've got random waves and it's longer than I've worn it in years. I might even grow it intentionally. I've also lost quite a few of my . . . ahem . . . *curves* since I gave up the café for a life on the water. Less cake and more physical work has done wonders for my waistline. Though I do miss the fact that I don't have the opportunity to do as much baking now. I've got a tiny oven on the boat which isn't really suited to my signature three-tier monster Victoria sponges.

Danny and I have wandered, at a leisurely pace, almost two hundred miles across the canals of our green and pleasant land. We started outside my former home on the Grand Union Canal near Milton Keynes and since then have taken in Birmingham, parts of Staffordshire and Worcestershire, before heading up onto the Shropshire Union waterway. We've stopped where the mood or the work has taken us and have travelled far from home.

We're slowly wending our way up through miles and miles of open countryside towards the towering Pontcysyllte Aqueduct – a part of the canal that rises high above the landscape of Wales – which, by all accounts, is spectacular. The picturesque town of Llangollen is our ultimate destination and, as Danny said, we hope to moor near the town there for a short while and take a break. One of the problems with not having a permanent residential mooring is that we can only stay put in one place for two weeks at a time – at the most – and then the Canal & River Trust require us to move on.

'I'll put the kettle on,' I say. 'We could do with a cuppa after all that exertion.'

'Any biscuits?'

'There's only a few left, but I'll bake some fresh ones later.' Danny likes my homemade oat cookies baked with hazelnuts, grated apple and raisins. I make them with maple syrup instead of sugar in an attempt to keep them on the healthy side. I'm not entirely sure it works.

As I go to move, Danny grabs my hand. 'You are OK, aren't you?'

'I'm fine.'

'I thought you were a bit quiet this morning. I know that you miss Lija and Stan.'

'I do.' Like mad, if I'm honest.

Lija now owns the café outright and I fret about how she's managing to run the place. It's not that she isn't perfectly capable, but I know how much hard work it is to cope single-handed. I hope she doesn't start telling the customers to eff off. She does get very sweary. Words beginning with F are by far her favourites. She sprinkles her conversations liberally with them. Also, Lija can't quite compute the concept of the customer always being right, though I've tried to explain it to her on many occasions. She treats most of them as if they're necessary evils – and I try to point out that when you're running a business they sort of are. Even the tricky ones.

So she's not exactly everyone's cup of tea, so to speak. Although some adore her. Much as people adore Basil Fawlty. Stan, on the other hand, is completely loveable. My elderly and endearing neighbour lives in the cottage right next door to Canal House and very quickly became a surrogate father to me or, at the great age of ninety-three, more probably a surrogate grandfather. He's a delightful old boy and the hardest thing is not seeing him every day when he comes in to the café for his lunch and a chat. He sits at his favourite table down by the canal, under his favourite apple tree, in his favourite holey cardigan, and watches the world go by. Being apart from them both is the hardest thing about my new adventure and there's nothing I'd love more than to see them now.

Lija and Stan might not be related by blood, but they were always kinder to me than my own family ever were. It's fair to say that I had a troubled relationship with the woman I called Mum all my life – only to discover when she died that she wasn't my real mum at all. She was my father's second wife and took me on as a baby as my own mother had died. I had no idea of any of this until Miranda herself passed away. The sad thing is that it seems as if she never really considered me to be her daughter at all. You have no idea how sad that made me and I still know so little of my birth mother beyond her name.

I've got a sister too – or a half-sister if we're being pedantic. What can I tell you of Edie? Bless her. My dear sister is Troubled with a capital T. She was always Mum's favourite and I guess I know why now. When Mum – Miranda – died it was Edie who inherited everything. Despite me being the one to stay at home and care for her for years, Miranda decided to cut me out of her will. I didn't get a penny, or one iota of thanks, for all the love and attention I lavished on her. Edie – who'd scarpered to New York as soon as she was able – was handed it all on a platter.

Miranda could never get over the fact that my mother was always my father's first love and this, I suppose, was my punishment. To compound the damage, my sister kindly sold my home and the café from beneath me, cutting me completely adrift. If I'm looking for silver linings in this, it at least gave me the impetus to throw in my lot with Danny and leave them all behind. At that point, it seemed as if I had nothing left to lose.

Edie and I have made up, after a fashion. We're still speaking – just about – but I'm not sure that leopards ever change their spots and I no longer trust the relationship between us. When you've been hurt like that, and so cruelly, it's hard to think about that person without dwelling on what they've done. Before the dust had even settled, before I knew what would become of me or where I might live, Edie hightailed it back to New York to be with her married lover. She's still waiting for him to leave his wife – which is never going to happen – and I haven't seen her since. We have the occasional, strained conversation – where there's clearly a lot that goes unsaid – and I hope that will change in time. I feel that I've mostly forgiven her for all the horrible things she did – sort of. But in truth, it's Lija and Stan who I pine for.

I love Danny to pieces and would go to the end of the earth with him – not just a pleasant part of Wales. But there's still a nagging pull to my former home. The café and the house were mine for so long that it's hard to completely cut my ties. I worry about Lija and Stan. I talk regularly to them both when I can get a good phone signal – never a given on the boat. The internet connection is even worse, even though we have a dongle or dangle – or something like that – to assist. It still means that Skyping is usually out of the question. Hence I don't chat to them quite as much as I'd like. They both assure me that they're managing perfectly well without me, but that doesn't stop the longing. I love my life on *The Dreamcatcher* and my heart is definitely here with Danny, but I can't help but feel that a small yet significant part of it has been left behind.

Chapter Two

Later, we moor up for the night and the next few weeks, hopefully. Even on a Sunday when there are usually day trippers galore, this seems to be a quiet stretch of the canal and we've found a spot not too far from Danny's work so that he can walk to the building site in the morning. There's also a local pub nearby in case we want to wander along the towpath for a swift half later. However, Danny has stoked up the woodburner and there's a comforting warmth spreading through the cabin which will be very hard to leave. I think there's a bottle of cheap red wine in the cupboard so the lure of snuggling up on the sofa instead of venturing out into the cold might prove too strong. Diggery certainly looks comfortable cuddled up snoozing on one of the cushions. His nose twitches occasionally as the scent of cooking wafts his way.

The Crock-Pot has been on all day, turning some budget cuts of meat into a delicious stew. Danny is doing hard, physical labour at the moment and eats like a teenager. I've given up watching my carb intake as we have a big bowl of rice or potatoes every night to fill him up and, weak-willed woman that I am, I can't resist.

I open the side hatch and look out over the canal. Within seconds two ducks appear, looking for an easy dinner. I find them some pumpkin and sunflower seeds and they snaffle them up, gratefully.

Danny, out of the shower, comes to put his arms round my waist. 'Smells wonderful. What's cooking?'

'Fridge stew. I need to walk into the town centre tomorrow and get some supplies. We're out of almost everything.'

'I'll be paid in two days, so we're doing fine this week.'

'I wish I could do more,' I say. I've not found it as easy to get casual work as Danny has. Anything on offer short-term tends to be physical work – mainly on construction sites or heavy-duty gardening. I can't really try for shop work or waitressing as we're on the move too much. If we're staying put somewhere for more than a few days, I've been displaying a sign with the hope of selling some cakes to passing trade. Some days it's gone better than others and I have to balance baking enough with making sure that we don't have any left over. It worked reasonably well in the last days of summer, but it's not so good now that the weather has changed and there are very few people on the towpaths who are keen to stop and buy some home-made cake.

'You do what you can,' Danny says, pragmatically. 'You can't do any more.'

'There's only so much cooking and cleaning I can do,' I tell him.

'I know.' He gives me a squeeze.

The truth is that I'm quite lonely during the day when I'm not selling so many cakes and chatting to the people who stop to buy them. I'm not unhappy, but I just wish that there was someone I could talk to properly or a little job I could go to. When I ran the café we had people in and out all day and I miss the company. Plus Lija was always around and was endlessly entertaining. I miss her potty mouth and stroppy ways more than I can tell you. Stan always had a good story to tell too – he's seen a lot of the world in his day – and I worry that Lija isn't looking after him properly now I'm not there to nag her. She has what you might call a 'casual' approach to everything in life. Though she regularly assures me on the phone that she's very solicitous of Stan's needs.

As I've told you, I looked after my mum for years, when she was bedridden – mainly with imaginary sufferings – and it was tough, so tough. I never had a moment to myself or the time to even think about what I wanted from life. Yet, now that she's gone, that's left a gaping hole too. I feel slightly adrift and not just because we're wandering the waterways of England like nomads.

'I've lost you,' Danny says into my musings. 'Where have you gone?'

'Thinking,' I admit.

'About home?'

I nod. There's no use pretending. 'I do feel a bit home-sick.' If I didn't have all day by myself to think about it,

16

then, perhaps, I wouldn't be as bad. I have Diggery for company but – delight that he is – that's not quite the same as human conversation.

'This job will peter out soon.' Danny moves away from me and pulls the bottle of red from the cupboard and waves it at me, needlessly questioning my desire for a glass of wine. I nod. So, it's a night on the boat rather than at the pub. 'We can head back towards Milton Keynes then. If we don't linger too long anywhere, then we could be back in time for Christmas.'

Sometimes you forget just how long it takes to get anywhere by canal. Most of the time, we toddle along at walking pace and that makes a hundred miles seem like one hell of a distance.

'It's definitely doable,' he adds when he sees the sceptical look on my face.

'Christmas.' I sigh. 'That would be lovely. Lija would let us moor up on the jetty next to the *Maid of Merryweather*.' This old boat has a strong pull for me too. It was my darling dad's treasure and, as a girl, I used to spend as much time as possible with him on it. Edie and Miranda were distinctly less keen, so it was always a special place for me as I had Dad all to myself. We'd tinker about, polishing it, touching up the paintwork, and Dad would fiddle with the engine, losing hours just happily pottering. We had family holidays on it too which were always a mixed bag of emotions as I loved every minute of it, but Miranda and my sister would moan for England. They were both more five-star kind of women rather than canal fans. And then, when Dad died, I stopped using it on the canal. Until it was pressed into service again as a make-do shop, it sat in the water going nowhere and is now in a parlous state of repair due to lack of use and neglect. The boat was the only thing that came to me in Miranda's will and, for that, I'm so grateful – even though it needs a small fortune spending on it to bring it up to scratch. At least there is something of my past that is still tangible.

'I'm sure Lija would be delighted to have us back.' Danny grins. 'I bet she hides it well though.'

'Yes.' Lija's default setting is grumpy.

He pours us some wine and we both take a welcome glug.

'You could give her a call after dinner, if we've got a decent signal here.' He picks up his phone and checks it. 'Looks OK.'

I get a little thrill of excitement. Our first Christmas together on *The Dreamcatcher* and I can't wait. It would be so nice to be able to share that with Stan and Lija too. 'Are you sure we could do it?'

'Why not?' He shrugs. 'That was the whole idea of this lifestyle. To go where the mood takes us. Admittedly, it would be a lot easier if we won the lottery. But we shouldn't feel tied if we want to move on. Flexibility. That's our new watchword.'

'Have I told you today that I love you?'

'Only once or twice,' Danny says. 'There's room for more.'

We're still like a couple of lovebirds so, despite Danny working a physical job all day, he still finds plenty of energy to get physical at night time too. My love life until meeting him could, at best, be called pedestrian. Now I feel as if

I'm speeding along the outside lane of the motorway, engine revving. My previous long-term partner, Anthony, never made me feel wanted as a woman, so I'm a late starter in the passion stakes. I'm determined to make up for lost time though. Perhaps if I did have a full-time job, then I wouldn't be able to keep up with him. As it is, I'm having fun trying.

'Are you ready to eat now?'

'I'm starving.'

Danny sets the table and I dish up the casserole. Diggery wakes from his slumber at the sound of clanking cutlery and jumps down from his cushion. He'll circle us like a shark until we've finished eating, knowing that I'll put a little of the stew in his bowl when it's cooled down enough for him to eat.

The evenings are drawing in now and Danny runs the generator so that we can have the lights on without draining the battery. We have a solar panel on the top of the boat, but there's not enough sunshine around at the moment to make it much use. When we eat our supper, I always put a candle on the table for a bit of atmosphere. I never want to lose the feeling of romance that we have now. It's possible to keep that alive, isn't it? I know that it takes more than a pretty scented candle and a few well-aimed glasses of red, but the little things are important too.

We have a worn leather sofa in the main part of the cabin, the worst of its wrinkles and bare patches covered with a hand-crocheted shawl and two Union Jack scatter cushions. There's a multicoloured rag rug on the floor and the lovely woodburner tucked in the corner. The coffee table doubles as our dining room and that's about it. There's not much room for anything else. The galley kitchen is just about big enough to turn round in, but we have a little oven – something that Danny never really used – and I can rustle up most of what we need. There's a neat bathroom with a shower that functions well most of the time and a double cabin that houses our bed. There's another tiny cabin with a narrow, single bunk that's basically our cupboard-cum-dumping ground. That's pretty much home.

'Food's great,' Danny says, gratefully. 'You're a fine cook, Fay. I seriously lucked out when I moored up at your café.'

I laugh. 'Funny, but I think the same too.'

We finish our meal and Danny pushes our plates aside. 'I'll wash up in a minute,' he says, 'But first, come here.'

I cuddle up next to him and he puts his arm round me. Diggery gets in on the action too and forces a space between us to snuggle down. I rest my head on Danny's shoulder. Outside, the night is closing in.

'This is the life,' he says. 'Glad we did it?'

'Yes, of course.' It's not all plain sailing – literally; I've lost count of the times that I've dropped one of the ropes in the cut or left the windlass behind at a lock or chosen a spot to moor up that was right next to a wasps' nest. Yet I wouldn't change it for the world.

'No stress, no strains. No monthly targets to hit. No burning the midnight oil just to keep ahead.' He sighs contentedly. 'We are living the dream.'

'On *The Dreamcatcher*,' I point out.

'I see what you did there,' Danny teases.

I turn to him. 'I'm glad you persuaded me to run away with you.'

'Hmm. As far as I remember, you didn't take *too* much persuasion.' He starts to kiss me and, as always, everything else goes out of my head. He tastes of woodsmoke and red wine.

'Let's wash up later,' he murmurs against my neck.

'Much later,' I agree as Danny's fingers find the buttons of my blouse.

Diggery, disgruntled at being edged out, heads to his bed. Then my phone rings.

'Leave it,' Danny whispers as he makes short work of another button.

'Might be Lija.' I reach out for my mobile while trying to keep my lips on his. When I manage to grab my phone from the table, the display shows it is, indeed, my dear friend. 'It is.'

'Passion killer.' Danny sighs, resignedly. 'Take it. I'll go and wash up now.' However, there's a twinkle in his eye when he says, 'We'll resume this later.'

Quickly, I answer my phone before it cuts to voicemail, trying to button myself up as I do. 'Hello, lovely,' I say to Lija. Danny eases himself away from me, takes our dishes and heads towards the sink. I curl up on the sofa with my wine ready for a girly chat. 'How are you?'

'Not good,' Lija replies and I can hear the tension in her voice. 'Am out of head with worry.'

'Why? What's wrong?'

Unlike Lija, she sobs when she says, 'Is Stan.'

My heart nearly stops. My dear friend is ninety-three years old and I know that he can't last for ever, but how I've dreaded this phone call. Oh, Stan. My dear, dear Stan.

Chapter Three

'He is poorly, Fay,' Lija continues, clearly distraught. 'Very poorly.'

My paused heart kicks in again. I'd feared the worst, but it's not too late. Stan, thank heavens, is still with us. 'What's wrong with him?'

'It started with silly cold,' she tells me. 'Sniffle, sniffle, snot, all that. Now is worse. Doctor has been today. He is sick. Very sick.'

'Oh, my poor Stan.'

'He asked me not to tell you.'

'Of course he did.' Stan never likes to make a fuss about anything, and if Lija's in this state, I'm thinking that it must be quite bad.

'I cannot manage, Fay,' she says. 'I don't know what to do.' I can tell, even down the phone, that she sounds strained, on the edge. 'You will know how to help. Can you come?'

Danny is standing next to me now and puts his hand on my shoulder. I gather from his expression that he's overheard some of the conversation.

He nods to me. 'Go,' he says. 'We'll work it out. If you need to be there, then we'll manage somehow.'

I don't need any further encouragement. 'I'll be there as soon as I can,' I tell Lija. 'Don't worry. I'll look at the logistics of doing it right away and will let you know as soon as I can.' My car, not being much use to me on the canal, is still parked in Lija's drive – I can't even remember if the tax or insurance is still in date – so I'll have to go back on the train or bus or something. If I need to be with Stan, I'd even walk it.

'Hurry,' she says. 'I don't want him to do old man croaking it while I am here alone.'

That makes me smile despite the serious nature of our conversation. Lija is ever the pragmatist. 'I'll text you as soon as possible.'

'You will be here tomorrow?'

'I'll do my very best. You know that. We're in Wales.'

There is a pause from Lija's end.

'It's quite a long way,' I fill in.

'I know where fucking Wales is,' she grumbles. 'Was trying to get train timetable on laptop.'

'I'll do it. We've got a half-decent signal for once. I'll get the first train or bus that I can. I don't want to be away from Stan while he's unwell.' Lija will have a lot on her plate just running the café, she won't be able to spare the time to care for him properly.

'OK.' She sounds quite relieved.

'I love you,' I say. 'Hang on in there.'

'Thank you, Fay. Come quickly.' Lija's phone cuts off.

'We'll walk down to the pub,' Danny says. 'You'll get quicker Wi-Fi there. It will take an age to look up train timetables from here.'

'You don't mind if I abandon you to go back?'

'You need to be with Stan. Lija wouldn't have asked you unless it was serious. She must be really concerned about him.'

'I know what he's like. He won't want to cause a fuss or go into hospital, but it sounds as if he needs more than Lija is able to offer. Poor thing.' Stan has no other family to call on, so Lija and I are all that he has.

Danny and I quickly pull on our coats and, jumping off the boat, we head down the dark towpath to the pub, Danny's torch lighting the way. Diggery trots behind, disgruntled at being disturbed from his snooze and rather surprised by the speed of our purposeful strides in place of our usual meander.

The canalside pub is modern, busy and is doing a roaring trade in top-priced wine and dinners served on chunky wooden boards. We strip off our coats, assailed by the fuggy warmth after the sharp night air. Danny heads straight to the bar and buys us two halves of a local bitter and I find the quietest corner away from the hubbub of the bar to log into the internet. Soon, I'm on the right site even though my fingers are shaky. I scan the timetables, piecing together the logistics which are never made easy on these things. As I feared, the journey home isn't straight-forward. The route is a little complicated, requiring two buses and three quite tight changes of train. On the plus side, I can go tomorrow.

I jot down some notes on my phone. If all goes to plan and I make my connections on time, after a scant five hours I'll be back home. Your perspective changes completely when you live on the canal and you easily forget that hundreds of miles can be covered relatively easily on other less ponderous forms of transport.

'It's expensive,' I tell Danny. 'The last train is in peak time. Are you sure we can do it?' It's more money than we have to spare at the moment, but it's not an insurmountable sum.

'Take the last of the cash,' Danny says, as generous as ever. He knows that I wouldn't use our meagre savings if I didn't need to. 'It's not a problem. The only thing that matters is that you're there for Stan.'

I know that in the short time that Danny got to know him he grew to love Stan as much as I do. If you met him, then you'd love him too. Stan's an old-fashioned gentleman, the like of which you don't see enough of any more.

'What if I have to stay for a few weeks? Maybe longer?'

'Let's see how Stan is when you get there.'

'I'll miss you.' I stroke Danny's face and he catches my hand, holding the palm against his cheek.

'As soon as I can, I'll follow you. I'll see out this job and then head back on the canal. I'll bring *The Dreamcatcher* back to Milton Keynes. That was going to be our plan anyway. We can still have Christmas together.'

'I hope Stan will still be with us too.' For the first time, I let myself have a little cry.

Danny finds me a napkin from the bar so that I can blow my nose.

'He'll be fine,' he assures me. 'I'm sure he'll perk up the minute he sees Nurse Fay coming to his rescue.'

'This is awful. It makes me realise that he won't always be there. I can't bear the thought of it.' I have another blub into my napkin.

'Come on,' Danny says. 'Drink up. We'll go back to the boat so that you can start packing.'

We down our beer and Diggery wonders why we're leaving again when he's only just got comfortable. We pick our way along the towpath in the moonlight, the wind buffeting the trees, my hand squeezing Danny's fingers in mine.

On *The Dreamcatcher*, I fill my bag with essentials and it's late by the time we fall into bed. We make love slowly, a bit sadly and I hold Danny tight as he falls asleep afterwards. I can't bear to be away from Stan and yet I don't want to leave Danny either. My head's whirring with what ifs and the usual gentle movement of the boat on the water fails to soothe me to sleep. I lie there fretting all night and, by the time dawn breaks, my eyes are gritty with lack of sleep. Gently moving Danny's arm, which is thrown across me, I ease myself out of bed and prepare for the journey ahead.

Chapter Four

I catch my buses without a hitch and, miraculously, make all my train connections on time, getting fleeting glimpses of Chirk, Shrewsbury and Wolverhampton stations as I run from one platform to another. I thank the universe for looking after me. Sort of. Despite the ease of transfers, I spend the entire journey squashed between businessmen shouting into their phones, mums with scratchy toddlers and a slightly inebriated lady who tells me more than I need to know about her boyfriend's extensive range of peccadillos. By the end of the journey I wonder why she's with him at all, but then I'm the past master of staying in unsuitable relationships.

I arrive in Milton Keynes feeling tired and quite emotional. At the train station, the scheduled bus out to my village doesn't arrive – the first hiccup – so I quickly grab a slightly wilted sandwich and a terrible cup of tea in a cardboard cup from the nearest chain café which makes me realise why my customers were so keen on coming to Fay's Cakes. We did do very good tea and cake. I didn't have time to get anything else to eat on my travels and the days of any form of catering service on our railways have long since gone. So I sit and eat my sarnie that has seen better days on a granite bench which is covered in graffiti and chipped by the abuse of a hundred skateboards and wonder why the youth of today want to despoil their surroundings so.

I call Danny, but he's obviously still at work and doesn't pick up. I leave a message to say that I love him and that I'm almost back home.

Eventually, the next bus comes and I join the half a dozen other passengers who board. As soon as the driver finishes his conversation on his mobile, we bounce out of the city and into the countryside. It takes more than an hour to get to Whittan. It's not that far in distance, but the bus goes all around the houses before we get there. However, it's nice to see the area where I grew up through the grimy window and my heart starts to settle. By the time we reach Whittan I'm the only one left on the bus. I check the time and realise that it will be just about time for Stan's supper by the time I arrive, so I can take it to him.

The bus drops me off at the end of the main road, so I hitch on my backpack and balance myself with the two other bags I've got and set off towards the house. At the end of the lane that leads to my former home, Lija has changed the sign. It now reads THE CAFÉ IN THE GARDEN. Fay's Cakes, as it was, seems to be gone now. It's a much better name, no doubt, but it still makes my heart feel a little bit heavier. I'm coming home, but not to the place as I knew it. Now this is someone else's home and I have to remember that.

I carry on down the lane which is bordered on the right by hedgerows, beautiful in the summer, but now the leaves are falling and too soon they'll be bare. I pass Stan's cottage which is on the left before my old house. I stand outside Canal House and look up. It seems so familiar and so strange all at once. It's a big, square house. Not the most attractive you'll see, but it's the setting which lifts it to another level. 'Highly desirable' as the estate agent called it. The lane peters out beyond, so this is the last house. After that and in front of the property is nothing but wide open fields. I lift my bags and walk round to the back. This is definitely where the place comes into its own.

The long, secluded garden stretches right the way down to the Grand Union Canal. It's enclosed by high brick walls weathered by time and, in the summer, covered with honeysuckle, clematis and rambling roses. There's a small orchard of apple trees down by the canal and a jetty that my dad built to moor the *Maid of Merryweather*. I can just glimpse her nestled down by the canal bank and a chink of happiness edges into my weary body. The garden at this time of year is well past its best, but it still looks beautiful to me. Tears fill my eyes to see it again. It's such a lovely spot. And once I thought it was mine.

The ornate café tables that grace the lawn are empty now. The day too cool, the hour too late to accommodate any customers. Perhaps I can help Lija to put them all away for the winter while I'm here. She'll have no use of

29

them until next spring when the sun has some warmth again. I stop the sob in my throat before it has a chance to rise, but I can't deny that it's hard to think it no longer belongs to me.

Edie didn't want Canal House. Of course she didn't. As soon as she was old enough my sister upped sticks and skedaddled out of here as fast as she could. She hated this place, the canal, the countryside. Edie made her home in New York and came back here as infrequently as she could manage. She has never seen the beauty of the waterways, the joy of living somewhere remote. She's a townie through and through. So it shouldn't have been a surprise when she didn't want to live here after she inherited the house.

It was a grand gesture on Lija's part to take on the house and café. She bought it lock, stock and barrel. All the furniture and fittings have remained, so, on the surface, very little changed. Lija thought we could continue to run the business together, and perhaps we could have done so in different circumstances. However, no one reckoned on Danny Wilde coming into my life and encouraging poor, mousy, downtrodden Fay to become a roaring lion. Well, maybe that's pushing it a bit. I'm still more of a pussycat – but at least I know where my claws are now.

Edie promised me some money from the sale of the house but, of course, it has yet to materialise. Much like everything else that Edie promises. She gave me a few thousand pounds, supposedly to tide me over after making me homeless, and I expect that will be the end of it. That's already been blown on luxuries such as diesel for *The Dreamcatcher* and food for me, Danny and the dog. The half a million quid that Edie banked from the sale of the house has never been mentioned again. Funny that.

All this rationalising hasn't stopped my emotions from being all mixed up. I feel as if I'm home, yet it's no longer my home. My home is with Danny on *The Dreamcatcher* now, but the ties to this place are as strong as ever.

Turning away from the garden, I step onto the veranda, which is surrounded by a pretty ironwork trellis running the length of the house at the back, one of my favourite nooks. When it's covered with the rambling, lilac wisteria, there's no nicer place to sit.

Feeling more anxious than I should, I knock at the back door and Lija comes to open it. 'No need for to knock,' she snaps.

'I wasn't sure.'

She tsks at me. 'Stupid woman.'

I smile. Exactly the sort of homecoming I'd expected from my prickly friend. Dropping my bags, I hold open my arms and she steps into them. Lija is always pencil-thin, but when I hug her it feels as if there's nothing of her at all. Clearly, she isn't eating much of the gorgeous cake she makes.

She lets me hold her for a few moments – which is never a given – and then says, 'I will put kettle on.'

I let go of her and ease myself into one of the chairs at the big pine table that dominates the centre of the room. The kitchen, as usual, is filled with the scent of a cake or something baking in the oven and I'm instantly taken back to our time here together. 'That smells good.'

'Scones for tomorrow,' she says. 'Christmas afternoon tea.'

I nod my approval.

'You look tired,' Lija says.

'I'm knackered. It's quite a way back from deepest, darkest Wales.'

'Hmm.' Lija doesn't look at all impressed by the thought of Wales. 'Bad journey?'

'It was all right,' I say. 'Scruffy trains. Screaming toddlers. Sweaty businessmen. I'm just glad I could get back so quickly. How's Stan today?'

'Not good.' She glances at me and her face is grim. 'I have called doctor again.'

'Someone's coming out? Dr Ahmed?'

'Yeah. Could be one hour. Could be three.' She shakes her head at the unsatisfactory nature of the situation.

'I'll have a quick cuppa and then go over there. I'd like to be there to see what the doctor says.'

Lija hangs her head. 'I am sorry to call you. I did not know what else to do.'

'I'm glad you did.' Lija never looks like the healthiest person on the planet, but I'm quite alarmed by her appearance. She's tiny, frail and the colour of milk. Even in the height of summer, when my face was always a riotous mass of freckles, Lija stayed deathly white. But now she looks drawn and her eyes seem too deep in their sockets. 'Is everything else OK?'

'Yes.' Lija is instantly defensive. 'Why would not be?'

'I'm only asking.' She plonks a cup of tea down in front of me followed by a pleasingly large slice of Victoria sponge. There's no one bakes it quite like Lija. This cake would make Mary Berry proud. Next to the plate, she slaps down a fork and I have to stifle a smile. 'I have missed you.'

She softens slightly. 'Have missed you too.'

'Is the café busy?'

'Very much so,' she says, proudly.

'I want to hear all about it, but first I should quickly drink this and try your lovely cake before I go next door to Stan. I'm desperate to see him.'

'Do not be shocked, Fay,' Lija says flatly. 'Is not good.'

Chapter Five

I leave Lija to tend to her scones and I go round to Stan's house. I knock and, after what seems like an age, he shuffles to the door. As Lija warned me, he isn't looking good.

Lija's nickname for our dear neighbour is Stinky Stan – cruel but, in fairness to Lija, he doesn't always smell as fragrant as he might. But the poor old soul is ninety-three years old and manages entirely by himself. He's never been married and you can tell that he lacks a woman's touch in his life.

He was always quite dapper, if you ignored that his cardigan was never buttoned up quite right or there were a few random soup stains down his shirt. Now he looks every one of his ninety-odd years and he's almost bent double. It's heartbreaking to see. He's in his pyjamas and a rather scruffy dressing gown. It looks as if he hasn't shaved for days.

'My dear Fay,' he says when he sees me. 'What on earth are you doing here?'

'Lija called in the cavalry,' I tell him. 'I've come to look after you.'

'No, no, no,' he says. 'You can't do that.'

'I can. Now let me in, Stan, or we'll both catch our death on the doorstep.'

'Sorry,' he says. 'Very sorry.' He opens the door wide and I step inside.

'You shouldn't even be up,' I admonish. 'Why are you not tucked up in bed?' The tiny living room smells fuggy and stale. Lija had said that Stan had recently lost the cleaner who came in once a week and it's clear that he's not yet replaced her. When I look close, it's obvious that Stan is sleeping downstairs as there are rumpled blankets and sheets on the sofa.

He gestures at his makeshift bed, then shuffles ahead of me and sits back down.

'Lija says that the doctor's coming again this evening?'

'I don't like to bother him,' Stan says. 'They're under so much pressure these days. I'll be fine. Just a bit of a cold.'

My guess is that it's a damn sight more than that. 'Lija's given me some homemade chicken soup in a flask. Do you think you could manage a small bowl?' She tells me that he's hardly been eating at all.

'Well . . .'

'I'll heat it up for you and make a bit of toast too.' I've come prepared with half a loaf. 'You might fancy it when it's done.'

'I don't want you to go to any trouble.'

I plant a gentle kiss on his bristly cheek. 'It's no bother,

Stan. I'm glad that I could come. Looks like you need a bit of Fay Merryweather's TLC to me.'

He tries a tired smile, but it doesn't reach his eyes which are rheumy and dull. 'I don't suppose it would go amiss.'

He coughs and it sounds like he's about to lose a lung. The doctor can't get here soon enough for my liking. I pass him some tissues and, embarrassed, he wipes his mouth.

'You sit there while I make this for you.' I go through to the kitchen, another tiny room that's cramped despite just having a small cooker, sink and under-counter fridge. I struggle to find somewhere to put the flask down. I find a battered old pan and tip in the soup. It's still quite hot so it won't take a minute. I turn on the grill and there's so little heat coming out that I could probably toast this bread quicker with my breath.

While the toast is taking an age to brown, I prepare a tray that I find tucked down by the cooker. No wonder Stan used to prefer to come into the café every day for his meals. This is definitely not a cook's kitchen. I put out the bowl of chicken soup and a small slice of lightly browned toast and take it through to my patient. Pulling a little table towards him, I set the tray down.

'Oh, thank you,' Stan says. 'My favourite.'

'Eat what you can.'

But as Stan lifts the spoon, his hand shakes and he spills most of it.

'This has really taken it out of you,' I note. 'Here, let me help.'

I tuck the napkin into the neck of his top to save his pyjamas and slowly spoon-feed him the soup.

'Lovely,' he says. 'You are kind, Fay.'

'Nonsense. You'd do the same for me.'

Slowly, slowly, he manages to eat all the soup and half of the toast.

'Good job,' I tell him and take the tray away.

Stan sits back on the sofa, exhausted by the effort. 'How's that young man of yours?' he asks.

'Danny's great.' I have a moment where I go all dreamy and get a pang of longing for him. 'He'll be following me in a few weeks, I hope. He's bringing *The Dreamcatcher* back along the canal when his current job is finished. We were planning to head back this way, anyway. We thought it would be nice to spend Christmas here with you and Lija.'

'Ah, Christmas,' Stan says. 'It seems to come round quicker each year.'

'I'm quite excited,' I admit. 'My first Christmas with Danny.'

'You deserve to be happy,' Stan says with a weary smile. 'I'm so glad to see it.'

'Why don't I get you settled in bed upstairs? You can't stay here on the sofa. I'm here now. It would be better if you rested properly.'

'I don't like to be a bother.'

'It's no bother, Stan. Are there clean sheets on your bed?'

'No, but there are some in the airing cupboard.'

'You sit here for a bit longer then while I sort the bedroom out.' So I go upstairs and realise that I've never been up here before. It goes without saying that it's as compact as downstairs. There's one small double bedroom off a little square of landing and another box room that houses an ancient desk and chair and a bookcase bowing under the weight of hardback tomes. The bathroom is functional, but in need of an update. He could probably do with a bath with handles to help him get in and out or a walk-in shower. I open the only cupboard door and find the sheets. In Stan's room, I strip the bed and remake it so that it's nice and fresh. His clothes might sometimes lack a little laundry action, but his sheets are spotless. I open the window while I do it to allow the cold night air to freshen the room. There's a small window in here but it has a lovely view over the garden and the canal beyond. Back in the cupboard, I find clean pyjamas too.

When it's ready, I close the window and flick a small fan heater on to warm the room again. Can't have my patient getting chilly. With one last look round to check that I've done all I need to, I go downstairs to Stan and help to move him upstairs. The bathroom's up here, so he won't have far to go if he needs it.

'Can you manage to put these on?' I give him the pyjamas.

He nods. 'Might take me a while, but I'll get there.'

'I'll stand out on the landing, but shout if you need me.'

I can hear the bed squeaking and a bit of huffing and puffing as he struggles them on. I resist the urge to go and help him.

'Ready, Nurse Ratched,' Stan shouts.

'Cheeky! You've not lost your spark,' I laugh as I go back into the room. Stan's already swung himself into the bed so I tuck him in properly and tidy up the bedspread. 'That's better.'

Stan puts his hand on mine. 'Thank you, Fay. Lija's been a Trojan, but she's got a lot on her plate. She won't tell you, but I think she's having a hard time of it without you.'

'I haven't had the chance to talk to her properly yet, but we'll sit down later with a glass of wine.'

'You're a good girl,' Stan says, his eyes filling with tears. 'What would we do without you?'

Then the doorbell rings. 'I bet that's the doctor.'

Sure enough, it is. Our local GP, Dr Ahmed, is a treasure. He came out frequently – probably too often – to see my malingering mother. In fact, when he arrives, I get a moment of déjà vu. I've somehow slipped seamlessly back into my role of carer as if I've never been away.

'Hello, Fay,' he says. 'Good to see you again.'

'Yes.' Despite the circumstances.

'I'd heard that you'd moved on,' he remarks as we climb the stairs together.

'I've been travelling,' I tell him. 'On the canal. But I'm back to look after Stan.'

'Then he's a very lucky man,' Dr Ahmed says as we go into Stan's room. 'You've got the best nurse in the business, Mr Whitwell.'

'Oh, I know,' Stan says. 'I only hope I can afford her.'

'My home care package is very expensive,' I tease.

'Now,' Dr Ahmed says. 'Let's see what I can do for you.'

I step out onto the landing while he examines Stan and I hear them talking in low tones. When he's finished his examination, Dr Ahmed calls me to join them.

He puts his stethoscope away and turns to Stan. 'I'm

afraid that it's a bit more than a cold, Mr Whitwell. Seems to me as if you've got pneumonia.'

'Oh.' A look of fear crosses Stan's face and I take his hand. It's a terrible blow, but I can't say that I'm totally surprised. He's so poorly that I knew it must be something more serious than a heavy cold.

'I'd really like to get you admitted to hospital.' Dr Ahmed adjusts his glasses. 'Then we can monitor you properly.'

'I don't want to go into hospital,' Stan says, obviously shocked by the doctor's diagnosis. 'I don't like to be a bother.'

But I can see how scared Stan is and know that it's much more than that.

'Is it critical that he goes to hospital?' I ask the doctor. 'What if I were to stay here and nurse him?'

'Well, I've prescribed some stronger antibiotics,' Dr Ahmed says. 'I'll give him a dose now and, if you can get the rest of those tomorrow, they should make him feel more comfortable. I can come back and see how he's getting on in a day or two.'

'Would you be happier with that, Stan?'

'I would,' he says, relief washing over him.

'Then that's settled. You can stay where you are and I'll look after you.'

I show the doctor to the door. 'He's not a well man, Fay,' he says when Stan is safely out of earshot. 'If there's any deterioration at all, you must call an ambulance immediately and get him to hospital.'

'I will. Thank you.'

When he's gone, I tidy the living room and throw open

the back door to air downstairs. I take Stan's sheets from the sofa and bundle them ready to take to the house for washing.

When I go upstairs to see Stan, his wracking cough has subsided somewhat and he's dozing.

'I'm going to leave you for a bit, but you must call me if you need anything.' I put his mobile phone within reach. 'I'll be back in a short while.' I'm planning to sleep on the sofa tonight, so that I can be here for him.

'You're very kind, Fay,' he says, sleepily. 'I didn't want to go to hospital. Once you get in those places, you never come out again.'

'I'll do my best for you,' I reassure him.

'I know it's very selfish of me, old fool that I am, but it's good to have you back.'

I pat his papery, mottled hand. 'If I'm honest, it's good to be back.'

Stan's eyes droop and I gently kiss his forehead. 'See you later.'

Chapter Six

Back at the house, there's no sign of Lija in the kitchen. I drop the laundry in the utility room and remember to ask her if it's OK before I put a load of washing on. This no longer being my home will take some getting used to.

I hear a heartfelt expletive coming from the dining room and make my way in there. Lija is standing in front of an enormous real Christmas tree looking very cross and muttering 'Shitshitshit' to herself.

'Goodness me,' I say. 'That's one hell of a tree.'

'Fucking Christmas,' she complains. 'How did I know how big this would be? Huh? I went to forest and picked it out. It looked much smaller.'

'Perspective,' I say, helpfully. What may have looked tiny in the vast expanse of a wood is now, indeed, a giant even in this rather large dining room.

Lija glares at me.

'It looks amazing though,' I add quickly. 'Why are you putting it up so soon?'

'So café looking fucking festive.'

'Ah. Of course. Excellent idea.'

'Do not stand there like idiot.' Lija gestures at the boxes and boxes of baubles on the floor. 'Put balls on.'

I can see from Lija's initial attempts that tree-dressing is not high in her skill set. 'I'll do it for you, if you like. I've always loved putting the Christmas tree up.'

'You do it. I will learn.'

'All right.'

'Was Stinky Stan OK?' she asks.

'He's not so good,' I tell her. 'Dr Ahmed thinks it's pneumonia. I'm going to sleep on his sofa tonight so I can keep my eye on him. The doctor wanted him to go into hospital, but I could tell it was the last thing Stan wanted.'

'I asked him to move in here, but he would not. He could have Edie's old room. Maybe he will for you.'

'I'll ask. You wouldn't mind?'

She shrugs. 'No. He is nice old man. I like him around. Despite smell.'

Praise indeed coming from Lija. 'Can I put some laundry on later? I stripped his bed.'

'Yes. No need to ask.'

'It's your home now, Lija, and I'm a guest. It's only polite.'

'Guest? Pah!' she says.

I turn my attention to the monster Christmas tree. 'How on earth did you get this home?'

'Man in van.'

'Oh, that was kind.'

'Cost me twenty quids extra,' she grumbles. 'Not kind. Merry Christmas and all that.'

'Ah. Perhaps the whole festive spirit thing hasn't quite kicked in yet.' Now probably isn't the time to mention that there's a perfectly serviceable Christmas tree in the depths of the loft somewhere. That was always Anthony's department. Still, this looks an awful lot better than a fake one and the lovely pine scent filling the room is quite divine. There are more decorations up in the roof too, I'm sure. Perhaps I'll make it my mission to hunt them out. We could do up the living room and the hall as well, though Lija might have a small heart attack if I suggest it. Perhaps I'll see if I can find the decorations first.

I have a good root through the baubles that are to hand and decide on my scheme.

'Why so long?' Lija taps her foot impatiently.

'You can't just rush at it,' I explain. 'I'm thinking about what will go where and making a little plan in my head.'

'Make it quicker,' she instructs. 'I have things to do.'

'Relax, enjoy it,' I say. 'You only get to do this once a year. We should get in the mood. Have a glass of wine, a mince pie, put some Christmas songs on the iPod.'

'I have all of these things,' Lija says, loftily. 'Is this tradition?'

'In this house, yes.'

'OK.' She shrugs and disappears into the kitchen. While she's not looking, I quickly take off the ornaments that she has thrown at the tree in a haphazard manner. I'm sure we can do a little better than that.

I lift out some sparkly baubles in silver and white. It makes me smile. Not a jot of colour here at all. Lija's style is very much along the Goth lines. I don't think I've ever seen her wear anything other than black. If she could, I'm sure that Lija would have an entirely black Christmas tree too. Still, this will look very pretty. Monotone can be very stylish. Also, what it lacks in colour, it makes up for in sparkles. Something I never thought I'd credit Lija with. Perhaps there's an inner princess lurking in there somewhere after all.

A few minutes later, I'm draping the tree with the fairy lights when she stomps back in and slams a tray down. 'Mince pies. Wine. Music.'

'Great.'

She puts on the iPod. Michael Bublé croons away, strains of 'It's Beginning to Look a Lot Like Christmas' fill the room. Lija looks at me and grimaces.

'Go with it,' I tell her. 'He'll make you feel all Christmassy and mellow.'

'He makes me feel like puking,' she counters.

I laugh and finish putting the baubles in my hand on the tree, then help myself to a mince pie. I wondered whether being the proprietor of the business now would have softened Lija's approach to life and customer service in particular. It seems as if she's just as tetchy as ever.

'Am doing very well with Christmas afternoon tea bookings,' she says a little smugly, picking up some of the baubles and following my lead in placement, though not taking quite as much care as I am, I have to say.

'Your idea?'

She frowns. 'Of course. I am boss. Mince pies. Christmas cake. Crappy crackers. Paper hats. All of the shit.'

'Sounds lovely,' I tell her.

'We are very busy. I have had one or two supper club evenings on Friday and Saturday. Big hit. Menus from round world.'

'Sounds great.'

'I have plans. For future,' Lija says. 'Maybe I will move sofa and telly upstairs. Will be more cosy for one. I will buy more chairs and tables for living room. I can have another twelve covers for café. You like?'

'I love.' Though, for some reason, I feel a bit piqued. I should be happy that Lija is moving on without me. But there's the rub – Lija *is* moving on without me.

'I suppose you would like to work while you are here?' she asks with feigned nonchalance. If she's as busy as she sounds, I bet she's desperate for help.

'You suppose correctly.' I don't think Lija realises quite how strapped I am for money. Or maybe she does. 'I'll help in any way that I can. Instead of paying you bed and board, what if I work to earn my keep?'

'OK.' She lifts her wine glass and offers it up to me. I take mine and we clink them together. I'm graced with one of Lija's rare smiles. 'I am glad you are back, Fay.'

'Me too.'

'To Christmas,' Lija says. 'May my till ring like crazy Christmas bells.'

'To Christmas,' I echo. Though my message behind it may be a little different. We seal the toast with a swig of wine which hits the spot. I return to decorating the tree.

It's starting to take shape now and is looking all sparkly and festive. 'I thought it would be nice to have our Christmas here, if that's all right with you.'

'Sure.' If I'm not mistaken, I see Lija's face brighten, though it's hard to tell. Perhaps she's lonelier here than she lets on. I know that feeling only too well.

'And Danny?' she asks.

'He's coming back on *The Dreamcatcher*. It's going to take him a few weeks at least. You can't exactly put your foot to the floor on the canal. The water and the locks dictate the pace.'

'You put very funny look on your face when you speak of him.' She mimics my 'funny' face.

'I'm in love,' I tell her. 'What can I say? It's the most amazing feeling in the world.'

She tuts at me.

'Don't be cross with me. You know what Anthony was like.' The first love of Anthony's life was his golf club membership rather than me. 'It's taken me so long to find love that I'm going to enjoy every minute. The best thing I ever did was run away with Danny. So mock all you like, Ms Vilks. I hope, one day, that you'll find someone to light up your world.'

Lija looks as if I've slapped her.

'What? What have I said?'

'Nothing.' She puts down the Christmas tree baubles. 'You finish this. You are better than me. I have cake to bake.'

And, before I can say anything else, she stamps out.

Chapter Seven

I finish the tree and it looks fabulous. I make Lija come back into the room to admire it and I press another glass of wine on her as a peace offering. She seems less frosty than earlier and I don't like to spoil the mood by asking what had upset her.

'This will look lovely for your Christmas afternoon teas,' I offer. 'Very festive.'

She gives an approving nod. Lija's equivalent of running round naked doing a happy dance.

'I must get back to Stan,' I tell her as I check my watch. 'I've been gone too long.' I hope he's still having a nice sleep and hasn't missed me.

'I've put your bag in your old room. Is OK?'

'That's fine. Thank you for having me.'

'This will always be your home,' Lija says.

It's a lovely sentiment, but I'm not so sure if that's really the case. I feel as if I'm straddling a very strange line between long-term resident and temporary guest. 'I'll go and sort myself out, if you don't need me.'

'I will make Stan something to eat.'

'Thanks, Lija. He won't want much though.'

'I wasn't planning three courses plus coffee,' she snipes.

'I'll nip up to my room quickly. If that's OK with you?' She rolls her eyes which I take as a yes. So while Lija disappears into the kitchen again, I climb the stairs to my former bedroom.

I thought with Lija living here it would feel different, but it's all pretty much the same. It still smells the same, the carpet is still worn in the same places, the wallpaper is just as faded. I stand on the landing and inhale. There's the faint scent of Miranda's heavy perfume on the air – the ghost of her quite present.

'I hope you're proud of yourself, Mum,' I say into the air. I hope she can hear me. Yet her spitefully cutting me out of her will may have been the best thing she ever did for me. 'How do you like that, eh?'

I still want to trace my real mum – all I know about her is that she was called Jean Merryweather and that she died too young. While I've been on *The Dreamcatcher*, it's been impossible – our internet connection is variable, at best. But it's something that I want to pay more attention to. I want to know more about the woman who brought me into this world. I know my father loved her very much and thought he was doing the best for me when he married Miranda. Still, it's all water under the bridge now. Mum's gone, and Dad too. All I have left of them is the *Maid of Merryweather* which is why it's so very precious to me.

Going into my old room, I cross straight to the window. I remember sitting here looking out at *The Dreamcatcher* and longing to be with Danny Wilde who seemed so free and so unattainable. I look at the bed and think of the rare nights I spent with Anthony in here – Anthony snoring and dreaming of his next round of golf, me shrouded in my cover-all nightie; that seems like another lifetime, another person. How things have changed since then.

The night has drawn in now and the garden is in darkness. I can barely make out the canal that runs at the bottom. Momentarily, the clouds part and the moon shines on the water. I catch a brief glimpse of the *Maid of Merryweather* in the moonlight and my heart swells. I'll go down and have a look at the old girl tomorrow – see how she's faring. It would be my dearest wish to do her up one day, restoring her to her former glory. With the current state of my finances, that could be some way down the road.

I take the picture of my mum and dad out of my bag, glad that I threw it in on the top at the last minute, and set it on the dressing table. They're posing in front of the *Maid of Merryweather* with me in their arms as a babe. It's the only photograph I have of them together and I look at it fondly. They look happy, carefree and very much in love.

Still, I can't linger any longer, so quickly I grab my pyjamas and my wash bag. That will do. I can, at least, clean my teeth, then I can come back here for a shower in the morning. What I'd really like is to lie in a nice, hot bath and relax – one of the things that I do miss living on

The Dreamcatcher. But I haven't time for that now. I must get back to my patient.

Lija gives me a food parcel for Stan. There's a toasted, buttered teacake wrapped in foil plus a little dish of fresh fruit: some chilled grapes, slices of banana and a handful of juicy, out-of-season strawberries. A few little bits to tempt him to eat.

I take them gratefully and say, 'See you in the morning. You'll be OK by yourself?'

She tuts at me. 'Am not alone. I have Micky Bubble.'

'You'll learn to love him, I promise. Next year you'll have the *Christmas Countdown* app on your phone from June.'

'I think not,' she says haughtily.

I kiss her cheek and hurry out into the cold night to Stan's cottage. The downstairs is in darkness when I unlock the front door and I chide myself for not thinking to leave a welcoming light on. The place feels cool, damp – the ancient central heating system not making much of an impression. I'll light a fire in a minute, get the woodburner going to drive the chill away.

Climbing the stairs, I'm glad to see that Stan's light is on in his bedroom and he's sitting in bed, propped up by his pillow.

'How are you doing?' I ask.

He has a good old cough before he answers, but it doesn't sound quite so painful as before. 'Not too bad,' he wheezes.

'Did you have a bit of a sleep?'

'Yes,' he says. 'I've only just woken up.'

'Lija's sent some food, if you're feeling peckish. I've got

a teacake and some fresh fruit for you. Fancy some hot milk and honey?'

'Oh, lovely,' Stan says. 'My favourite.'

'I'll go and set it out for you. Back in a minute.' In the tiny kitchen, I get Stan's meal ready and then trip up the stairs again. I sit with him while he eats and am pleased to see that he manages it all, then I tidy up. In the living room I light the woodburner and, due to my new-found fire-lighting skills, it's soon roaring away.

'It's all cosy down there now,' I say to Stan. 'Do you want to come downstairs for a while? I can find something for us to watch on telly.'

'I'm comfortable here,' he says. 'I'm feeling quite sleepy again.'

'The more you can nap, the sooner you'll get better. Can I get you anything else?'

'No, I'm fine thank you, Fay. You don't have to stay, you know. I can manage.'

'I don't mind being here at all. I'd rather keep an eye on you. That's why I came back.' I settle in the chair next to his bed and, finally, let myself relax.

'You spent enough time looking after that mother of yours,' he says. 'I don't want you stuck here nursing me. Now it's your turn to live.'

'Oh, I've been doing plenty of that,' I assure him. 'I love being on the canal.'

'You're happy?'

'More than anyone should be.'

He smiles softly at me. 'I'll rest happy knowing that.'

'You're going nowhere, Stan. You'll get through this.'

'I'm turned ninety, Fay. Something's going to get me in the end.'

'Not on my watch.'

'I've had a good life,' he says. 'A *full* life. I've no regrets.' Then he smiles sadly. 'Well, not many.' He smooths the blanket over his striped pyjamas. 'It would have been nice to have had a daughter. Someone like you.'

'You were never tempted to marry?' In all the time I've known Stan, he's never mentioned anyone special.

'I came close,' he says. 'Have I never told you?'

I shake my head.

'I was engaged to the most beautiful girl. A real head-turner. Oh, you should have seen her, Fay. She had blonde hair that tumbled to her shoulders and the prettiest blue eyes. She was tiny and slender. When her hand was in mine I felt like the king of the world. I thought I was the luck-iest man alive. Her laugh could light up a room – any room. And she was mine.' He gives a light laugh. 'Audrey and I were childhood sweethearts and she wrote to me all through the war. Every single day. I'll swear those letters kept me alive.' He points to his chest of drawers. 'They're all in the drawer there. I read them from time to time.'

'Oh, Stan. What went wrong?'

'I lost her. She fell ill and slipped away from me before I even knew what was happening.' His face shows the pain that, even after all this time, must be close to the surface. 'The wedding was planned, everything in place. But it wasn't to be. We'd both survived the worst the Luftwaffe could do and yet a simple infection carried her from my arms. Sepsis, they said. Though I never did know what caused it.'

'That's terrible.' There's a lump in my throat and I can hardly get the words out. How awful to lose the love of your life like that. If anything happened to Danny, I don't think that I'd ever recover.

'I never loved again,' he says, surreptitiously wiping a tear from his eye. 'She was the one for me. No one else. That's why I'm not afraid of going. She'll be there waiting for me, my Audrey. I know it deep in my heart.'

I want to cry too now.

'I've made you sad.' Stan tuts. 'Silly me. You don't need me wittering on. I'm feeling sorry for myself.'

'Of course you're not. '

'She feels close sometimes,' he says. 'I turn and think that I catch a glimpse of her or there's a hint of her favourite scent on the breeze. It's comforting.' He gazes at the chair in the corner of the room and then smiles. My eyes follow his, but I see nothing.

'Time for you to settle down, Stan. I'll bring some water so that you can take your tablets.'

So I pop downstairs and grab a fresh glass of water. When I take it back into Stan's bedroom, he's already dozed off. I guess the tablets can wait until later as I'm sure he'll wake in the night. I watch him for a moment and my heart's filled with affection for him. I never knew my grandfather, but I hope that he would have been someone like Stan.

I cover him up properly and turn off his bedside light, then I tiptoe out and go back to the living room.

Chapter Eight

The fire has warmed the room now and it's feeling cosier. I close the curtains against the night and change into my pyjamas. I clean my teeth quickly in the kitchen and then make up my bed for the night with the cushions and blankets that are on the sofa.

When I'm settled, I FaceTime Danny. He picks up instantly. It's lovely to be able to see his handsome face and suddenly the distance between us disappears.

'I've been missing you,' he says.

'I miss you too.' More than I like to admit. Perhaps it's the conversation I've just had with Stan, but I feel close to tears. I wish he was here to hold me now. 'I've had a hectic day. This is the first chance I've had to call properly. I'm sorry.'

'No worries.' The sound of his soft Irish voice always soothes me. 'How's Stan doing?'

'Quite poorly. But he seems to have perked up a bit since

I arrived.' I pull one of the crocheted blankets round my shoulders for warmth.

'You have that way about you.'

I laugh. 'Flattery will get you anywhere.'

'I learned that quickly.'

'I've just had a really sad chat with him. I didn't realise that he'd been engaged, but his fiancée died. He was only young, but he never wanted anyone else.'

'Poor old boy.'

'He's so kind and has so much love to give. I can't bear the thought of him having spent his life mourning for her.' My throat tightens. 'I never want you to leave me.'

'I'm not planning to,' he teases.

'I know I'm being silly, but it made me realise that we need to seize the day. *Carpe diem* and all that.'

'I like the idea of being impetuous, and we've both had our moments.'

'Let's never stop being spontaneous or adventurous. You never know what's around the corner.'

'Well, I don't know if it's good news or bad news, but my job here has finished. I'm being laid off at the end of the week. I didn't see that coming quite so soon. It'll mean less money, but I can set off on Saturday and I'll be with you sooner than we thought.'

'It's good news for me. I can't wait to see you.'

'Digs and I are both pining for you. The dog's off his food.'

'Don't tell fibs. It's not even a day. I bet he hasn't even noticed I've gone yet.'

'We'll both be a shadow of our former selves by the time we get to you.'

'Well, there'll be plenty of cake waiting, that's for sure.' I hold the phone closer as if it's Danny I'm nestled against. 'I'm glad it's soon. It's horrible being away from you but, in a strange way, it's nice to be back too.'

'Is Lija pleased to see you?'

'In her own way.' We both chuckle at that. 'I helped her to put the Christmas tree up when I got here. The house is starting to look quite festive.' I can't wait for Christmas this year, to be spending it with Danny and the people I love most. I stifle a yawn. It's been a long day and it's catching up with me now.

'You must be exhausted,' Danny says. 'I'll say goodnight and let you get your beauty sleep.'

'Goodnight. I love you.'

'Love you too,' Danny says. 'The bed will feel big without you.'

I think of our tiny, cramped cabin on *The Dreamcatcher*. 'That bed will *never* feel big,' I giggle. 'But I'm sad that I'm not squashed up in it with you.'

'Hope you manage some sleep on your sofa.'

'I'm sure I will. Love you.'

'Love you too.' Danny blows me a kiss and we both hang up.

I fidget and fuss with my blankets and the cushion for my pillow until I'm reasonably comfortable. But, as soon as I feel my eyes grow heavy, I hear Stan start to cough convulsively. So I heave myself from my makeshift bed and go to see how he is.

'You don't sound so good, Stan.' But he can't even answer me, so I put on the bedside light and sit with him, rubbing his back until the awful spasms subside.

'I'll make you a drink, see if it will calm the coughing down.' In the kitchen I make up a hot lemon drink and add some extra honey. I put the rest of the water into a hot water bottle for him and take it back.

Stan's sitting up now and I plump his pillows for him. He sips the hot lemon gratefully and I give him his pills before slipping the hot water bottle under the covers. The heat of the fire is starting to warm the upstairs now too.

'Shall I read to you for a bit?'

He smiles wanly. 'I don't want to keep you awake.'

'I'm here now. I can at least be useful.' So I pick up Stan's book – a Bernard Cornwell novel – and start to read for him. He closes his eyes and listens. I read out the words slowly, soporifically, and soon I hear his breathing change.

I sit quietly and watch him as he sleeps. I can't bear to see him looking so frail, so vulnerable. It terrifies me to think that he won't always be in my life. He's family and I hate to see him suffer. I close the book and put it on his bedside table. Then I stroke his wispy hair and pull the cover over his arms so that he doesn't feel a chill.

Turning out the light again, I retreat to my own bed on the sofa but stay awake until dawn.

Chapter Nine

Just before seven, I check on Stan again and realise that I'm holding my breath when I pop my head round his bedroom door. He's still dozing, but opens his eyes when he hears me.

'Morning, Stan. I'm just going to nip over to the house to get something for breakfast. Would you like a cuppa now?'

'That would be lovely, Fay. Did you manage to sleep on the sofa?'

'Slept like a log,' I lie.

Before I leave, I sort Stan out with a cup of tea and his tablets, draw his curtains, stoke up the woodburner with some fresh logs – I'm going to keep that thing going 24/7 if it kills me – and then I step out into the frosty morning.

The grass is crisp and white. Cobwebs on the trees are draped between the branches like lace doilies. There are wisps of mist coming off the surface of the canal and drifting slowly up the garden. It looks so beautiful. Truly a winter wonderland, although I do hope the coming winter isn't too harsh. If the canal ices up then Danny might not be able to move *The Dreamcatcher* – or it will certainly slow his progress. I'm glad he's setting off sooner rather than later to come back.

Instead of turning towards the house, while I've got a few minutes to spare, I take the opportunity to walk down to see the *Maid of Merryweather*. The lawn crunches beneath my feet and I wish I was wearing a proper coat instead of just my thin hoodie. I fold my arms across myself to try to keep some warmth in.

The boat's sitting quietly on the water at the bottom of the garden, moored to the jetty my dad built many years ago. The narrowboat was always his pride and joy. Now it's mine too. At least Miranda had the good grace to leave me that in her will.

I've got the key to the door in my pocket so I climb on board and let myself in. The chill air cuts through me like a knife. It's a shock to find that it's colder in here than it is outside. The windows are running with condensation and the usual warm, comforting smell has gone. The air is damp, fetid. Oh, my poor old lady!

I make my way down the steps into the cabin. It's clear that there's been a pretty substantial leak in the roof. Some of the ceiling has come down and the floor is soaking wet. Obviously, Lija hasn't been near her since I left.

When I touch them, the cushions on the sofas are sodden too. It's going to take an age to dry her out and the refit is going to be even more extensive. If I don't do something to get her watertight again and stop the rot, then she's simply going to become beyond repair and will be lost to me for ever. I can't let that happen.

'Oh, Dad,' I say into the air, 'I'm so sorry. I will bring her back to life, I promise you.' And I can only hope that I find the means to do so soon. He'd be distraught if he could see the state that she's in. This is more than a narrowboat to me too, it's my only tangible link with Dad and with my real mum. Being on board usually lifts my spirits and reminds me of all the lovely times I spent with my dad on her, but now it's only causing sorrow.

I check the rest of the damage caused by the leak and it doesn't get better. The cupboards in the galley are swollen with water ingress and I can't even open the doors. They'll need to come out. The little shower room is full of black mould and, quite frankly, you could grow mushrooms on most of the surfaces they're so soggy.

With a heavy heart, I lock up again and trudge up the garden to the house. When I open the door, Lija is already in the kitchen.

'You look like shit,' Lija says.

'I didn't sleep,' I tell her. 'Stan's sofa wasn't as accommodating as I'd hoped.'

'How is Stan?'

'A bit better, I think. Still not out of the woods yet.'

She pulls a confused face. 'What woods?'

'It's a figure of speech. It means I'm still concerned about him.'

'Ah. Why did you not say that?'

As I'm on the verge of tears, I don't even try to explain

and Lija doesn't press the point. 'I thought I'd take him some breakfast.' There's already the scent of cooking bacon in the kitchen and it's making me feel hungry.

'Oven is full of bacon, sausage,' Lija says. 'Take what you need. Maybe scrambled egg is good?'

'I think that would be perfect.' I move to put the kettle on, then check myself. 'Do you mind if I make some tea?'

'Stop keep asking this and that,' she snaps. 'You will become annoying person.' She slams a plate of toast onto the table. I pinch a bit and earn myself a tut.

'Sorry, sorry.' I put the kettle on. 'Want one?'

Lija nods. 'Coffee. Give me plenty caffeine.'

While I wait for it to boil, I say, 'I didn't know that you'd started doing breakfast too.' Again, I feel piqued that everything is changing and I didn't know.

'One month ago. Is very busy. Full English. Eggs Benedict. My own granola. All of the things.'

'I'm very impressed. It must be a lot of hard work.' No wonder she looks tired and is even more tetchy than usual. 'You need help.' There was talk of one of Lija's friends doing a few days a week, but it never quite worked out.

'I have help.'

'You do? Who? Why didn't you tell me?' Even as I ask a bubbly teenager bursts into the kitchen from the dining room.

'Hiya!' she shouts. 'Lija said you were back. TOTALLY fabulous!' She throws herself at me and gives me a bear hug. 'OMG! You've been on a canal boat and EVERY-THING. I've never been on a canal boat. My brother was going to hire one for the day once, but he didn't. He went on the train to Brighton instead. It's lovely, Brighton. They have the most amazing chocolate shop. I haven't been though. Someone told me. It might have been my nan. Or I might have seen it on *Countryfile*. We only watch that because my nan likes it. Brighton's the country, right?'

Lija glowers. 'Meet Rainbow.'

'Hello,' I say, slightly nonplussed and still enveloped in her arms.

Rainbow is big and round with chubby cheeks like pink apples. She has huge blue eyes and blonde curls form some sort of mad halo round her head and then tumble down to her shoulders. It looks as if she's been modelled on a Cabbage Patch Kid. She's wearing the shortest, tightest black Lycra skirt I've ever seen and I think her blouse is at least two sizes too small. Every button is straining across her comely chest and it's a miracle that they don't pop open and take out someone's eye.

'I've only been here for four weeks and two days,' Rainbow chirps. 'All the people are so nice. Well, most of them. There was one woman, all designer and stuff and EVERYTHING and she wasn't nice.' Whenever she says EVERYTHING, her eyes go round and wide. 'But that's not unusual, is it? She had a HERMÈS handbag. I'd never seen one in real life before. I'd only ever seen one on, like, *TOWIE* or something.'

I have no idea what *TOWIE* is, but I'm not sure that it matters.

'OMG. I LOVE it here!' Rainbow does a face that says *Squeeeeee*.

'Great.' I'm not sure what else to say.

'Two full English for table five,' she trills over her shoulder at Lija. 'One with the bacon really, really crispy, no tomato. One with EVERYTHING. I like my bacon crispy too. Do you? My nan cuts the fat off for me because it's better for you like that. Even though I actually like the fat. That's the BEST bit.'

Finally, she lets go of me and I can breathe again. Then she swipes the pile of fresh toast off the kitchen table. 'Back in a jiff!' Rainbow bounces out of the kitchen.

'Saying nothing,' Lija instructs.

It takes me a moment to find words. 'She's very . . . er . . . bubbly.'

'Customers love her.'

'I can imagine.' She seems the most unlikely person for Lija to recruit, but she's certainly very jolly.

I'm not actually sure how to put this. 'She doesn't really seem like the type of person that you'd be naturally drawn to.'

'Were two applicants for job,' Lija grumbles. 'Other woman had body odour.'

'Ah. She seems really lovely though. Chatty.'

Lija gives a death stare after her new employee. 'Too fucking cheerful.'

Chapter Ten

I take Stan some scrambled eggs on toast. Just a little bit.
But he seems a lot brighter this morning. I haven't discussed
Lija's idea of him moving into Canal House while he's
poorly. To be honest, I think there's too much going on
there now. It's lovely that the atmosphere is bustling – even
at breakfast – but it's not conducive to recuperation from
illness. Stan needs lots of peace and quiet, plenty of rest
and TLC.

Instead, I'll just keep nipping backwards and forwards
as much as I can. In between visits, he can sleep, read, and
generally gather his strength again. Plus I want to give Lija
a hand too, even though she insists that she and Rainbow
can manage. In my view, it's way too much for two people
to cope with. Even when the café is closed, Lija still has
the baking to do. I bet she's putting in horrendously long
days. I know, because I once did the same.

I switch Stan's radio on for him. 'Sleep as much as you

can,' I tell him. 'That's the quickest way to get you up and about again. I'll find Anthony's electric razor for you. I'm sure he left one in the drawer at the house. You can have a shave then. It'll make you feel better.'

'I was quite liking my new hipster look,' Stan quips.

Bless him. I don't like to tell him he's more Worzel Gummidge than hipster. 'I'll run you a nice bath, if you think you can manage.'

'A little later,' Stan says. 'I feel tired after eating.'

'At least you've managed something though.' He's so different to how Miranda was as a patient. Stan's so grateful for anything you do. 'It's a lovely morning out there. Freezing cold, but it looks great.'

'The years go by so quickly,' Stan says. 'It only seems a minute ago since it was summer.'

'I'm glad we caught the last of the good weather on the canal. We were so lucky.' I make sure his curtains are drawn wide so that he can see out to the water. It's nice to watch the boats going past, the busy wildlife. 'I had some good news last night. Danny's coming back soon. His job finished sooner than we expected – which isn't so great. But I'm glad he'll be on his way. We wanted to be here with you and Lija for Christmas.'

'Lovely,' Stan says. 'It will be nice to have company.'

In the past he's joined me, Miranda and Anthony for Christmas lunch but it was never a very jolly affair. Miranda fully embraced the concept of 'Bah humbug' and Anthony was Scrooge personified. This year I vow it will be different. We're going to have a lovely Christmas if it kills me doing it. If we can manage it, I'd love to have Christmas Day lunch on *The Dreamcatcher*. Danny and I will have to give some thought to the logistics and I want to decorate her beautifully too.

I leave Stan to have another snooze and the rest of the day goes by in a blur. I help Lija and Rainbow in the café. There's a steady stream of customers and the Christmas afternoon tea is proving a particular hit. Even now, in early November, we have a full house. It seems that Lija has given the café a new lease of life – which is great – but I can't help but feel slightly saddened that my presence hasn't been more missed. This is most definitely her place now.

I quickly check on Stan at lunchtime and feed him some soup, then I spend the afternoon baking – cranberry and white chocolate muffins and a couple of Victoria sponges which I sprinkle with icing sugar through a stencil in the shape of a snowflake. Next thing, I turn round and it's already teatime. We're all in the kitchen, glad that the last of the customers has left for the day and doing the last of the washing up. I'm washing, Lija is drying and Rainbow is putting the dried dishes away while keeping up a constant stream of conversation that doesn't appear to require our input.

'I've seen her before,' she says to no one in particular. I think both Lija and I have tuned out the majority of it by now. 'At the pub. Not with the same bloke. This one's MUCH better. I think he knows my brother. They're both bikers. She works at the hairdresser's in whatsisname. I wish I'd had my nails done.' She checks her manicure and the resulting frown on her pretty, doll-like face and pout of her strawberry lips show that she finds it wanting. 'Did you see how much she ATE? OMG. All the cakes and scones and EVERYTHING.' Wide eyes. 'I wish I could shove it away like that. She's probably a size EIGHT when she's wet through. I hate that. A lot of blokes like big girls though, don't they? Our dog's on a diet. My nan gets him low-calorie food from the vet. Costs a FORTUNE.'

Lija has been on her feet now since first thing this morning. I don't think I've even seen her eat. She never looks the picture of rude health and, against the fulsome bounciness of Rainbow, she seems positively deathly.

I take the tea towel from Lija's hands. 'Sit down,' I instruct. 'You look dead on your feet. Rainbow and I can finish up here.'

For once, she doesn't argue and sits, gratefully, at the kitchen table. There's some quiche left over from lunch and I cut her a slice, put it on a plate and slide it towards her. She picks up a fork and, hesitantly, starts to eat it.

'Thank you, Fay.'

'I'm going to the movies tonight with my bezzie, Luna,' Rainbow continues, unabated. 'I don't know what we're watching. It's her turn to pick. I think something with Superman is on. Do you think he was a real person? You don't see men in tights now, do you? Not unless they're transgender or WHATEVER. I go to that gay and trans-gender club in Fenny even though I'm not gay or transgender. They don't seem to mind. Have you seen the price of popcorn? OMG! It's WELL expensive. We get the popcorn and a bucket of cola and EVERYTHING. That's what you go to the flicks for, right? I like those spicy cracker things that have cheese sauce on that's like custard, but they make Luna want to PUKE.' She makes noises like a cat puking. 'My nan says she can't understand why people these days can't sit through a film without eating and EVERYTHING. I don't even know if they had films when she was young. She's WELL old. They probably just had to watch telly and STUFF.'

I smile when I ask, 'Did they have electricity then?'

Rainbow gapes at me. 'Dunno. Do tellies even need electricity? I thought you just got Sky and NETFLIX?'

Lija's face is getting whiter and whiter. I'm not sure if it's with exhaustion or simmering anger.

'You can go now, Rainbow,' I say, diplomatically. 'I'll finish up for you.'

'I don't mind,' she says. 'I only need to be home in time for *Hollyoaks*. My nan watches *Gogglebox*, but Dad can't stand it. I liked it when the posh people who drank too much were on it. You don't see them now. Have they gone? Sometimes they do that but then there's a big fuss on TWITTER and they come back. They might get their own series and EVERYTHING.'

I take the stack of plates from her. 'It's fine. I'll do it.'

'I could set the tables for tomorrow, if you like. My nan's got real silver knives and forks that you have to polish all the time. ALL the time. She has a special cloth. I don't know where she gets them from. Who wants to do that? Except my nan, obvs. Nan likes IKEA. They've got EVERYTHING in there. You could LIVE in it! They don't say it like we do in Sweden. That's where IKEA comes from. They say it like ICKYIER or something. Like it's

ICKY. In Sweden they have chocolate called PLOP. I saw it on Facebook.'

'See you tomorrow, Rainbow.' While she's still talking, I slowly back her out of the door. At the last minute she grabs her coat from the hook and her handbag from the floor.

'Bye, Lija. Bye, Fay. Love you.' Rainbow holds her fingers up to form a heart. 'I can come in early in the morning, if you like. I get up at SIX to walk the dog, so it's not a problem. I've always been an early bird. The rest of my family would stay in bed ALL day if they could.'

When she steps outside, I close the back door quickly. She waves madly at me and I wave back. Then I turn to Lija and we both burst out laughing – a rare thing for my friend.

'Where on earth did you find her?' I say when we've stopped chuckling. 'She's adorable, but MAN can she talk.'

'Is like verbal diarrhoea. It pours from her all time in unstoppable torrent.'

'She seems very willing,' I note.

'I may kill her.' Lija puts her head in her hands.

I make more tea and sit down opposite my friend. I push a cup towards her. 'This feels like old times.'

She smiles wanly.

'It's great that you've got so many new ideas,' I venture. 'But this is a lot for you to take on.'

Lija says nothing.

'You're coping all right?'

A tight shrug. 'The bills are high and I want to pay off

my aunt.' Lija borrowed the money to buy Canal House from a dodgy aunt in Russia. 'I have to work long hours to do that.'

'I know. And I understand. But you look a bit peaky, if you don't mind me saying. I wouldn't like to see you work yourself into the ground while you're doing it. You'll end up like me.'

She risks another smile at that. 'You have done OK. For old lady.'

'Yes. I guess I have.' I touch her hand and she doesn't pull it away. 'Let me help you when I can though.'

'You are here,' she says. 'You are helping.'

I stifle the sigh that I'd like to vocalise. When Lija decides that she's not going to let you in, then nothing will change her mind. 'I'll go to see Stan, then I'm going to have a long, hot bath. If that's all right with you.'

She shoots me a look.

I hold up my hands. 'I know, I know. *Tu casa es mi casa* and EVERYTHING.' We both smile at that. 'I don't have to ask. I'm just being polite. It's my nature.'

'Is very annoying. Let me straighten out. You can use bath, toilet, milk in fridge, food in cupboard. You can have shower, lie in bed, sit on sofa, use garden and cooker. You can have sex up against wall. OK?'

'Yes, lovely. Thank you. I'm not sure that your last point is going to be an issue, but I do appreciate it, Lija.' I stand up and head for the door. 'After my bath, I'll make supper for you and we can sit and have a good catch-up together. I'm sure there's lots for you tell me.'

She looks a bit shifty. 'Not so much.'

71

'Then I can bore you to death with all my adventures on the canal.'

'Don't make it too smoochy,' she warns. 'I may be sick.' She mimics Rainbow's cat puking noises, then looks as if she might regret it.

With that, I go upstairs, run myself a nice, hot bath and use Lija's wild thyme and raspberry leaf bath soak without even asking her. So there.

Chapter Eleven

After my bath, I quickly check on Stan. He's more than happy listening to the radio and he eats the freshly made ham sandwich and small slice of lemon drizzle cake that I take him with a pleasing degree of enthusiasm. Lija's lovely baking will soon help to put roses back into his cheeks. I fuss round and tidy his bed while chatting to him, then rush back to Canal House in time to make our own tea.

I do miss this spacious kitchen. It's more like a sprawling farmhouse kitchen than one suited to a squat, red brick, 1920's house. My baking has certainly suffered since I've been on *The Dreamcatcher* with its one tiny oven. I have to be super organised to cook a roast dinner for two. There used to be nothing I liked better than doing a big batch bake for the café and seeing every surface covered with cakes, scones, quiches and whatever was on the menu that day. Now that's Lija's prerogative.

As I'm setting the kitchen table, Lija comes in. Her hair is freshly washed and she looks as if she's been in the shower. The oversized sweatshirt she's wearing only serves to accentuate just how thin she is.

'Very romantic,' she says.

I've cut some stems of clematis with their heavy seed heads and have put them in a jam jar on the table. 'I just wanted to make it nice.'

There's a wine box in the fridge and I pour us both a glass. 'Cheers.'

Lija clinks her glass against mine but doesn't drink. Then I make two fluffy cheese omelettes for us both and serve them up with a green salad.

'Healthy shit,' she says, taking a tentative bite. 'Good.'

'Thank you.' It's nice to relax with Lija. Takes me back to old times. Even though Danny and I have only been on the canal for a short time, it seems as if we've been gone for ever. 'Have you missed me?'

Lija shrugs and admits, reluctantly, 'Some.'

'Up until his illness has Stan been all right?'

'Sure,' she says. 'He is here all the time. Day in, day out. But is cool. I like him around. Despite occasional stinky smell.' She pushes her fork through her salad. 'He did not want to stay?'

'I didn't actually ask him yet,' I confess. 'At the moment, I think he needs a bit of peace and quiet. Until he's stronger, all the comings and goings might be a bit much for him.'

'And Rainbow.'

I laugh. 'I bet he loves Rainbow.'

Lija smiles too. 'He does. What's not to love? She is puppy, candyfloss, apples, blue sky.'

'Does she like him?'

'Rainbow likes everyone. She does not even notice he smells of wee and cabbage.'

'Oh, Lija, you are terrible.'

'Is true,' she insists.

There might be a modicum of fustiness about him. Sometimes. But, well, he's an old boy with no one to look after him properly. Suddenly, the thought of that brings tears to my eyes.

'Why you cry?' Lija asks sharply.

'Hay fever,' I say, wiping my eyes on my sleeve.

'Is November.'

'Must be these seed heads.' I nod at the clematis, but she doesn't look convinced. 'How are things with you and Ashley?' I ask to change the subject. When we left Lija was seeing a lovely young barman from the local pub, but she hasn't mentioned him recently. There are a few signs that there's been a man staying here – some trainers that I don't recognise in the hall, a hoodie on the hooks in the kitchen, some sporty-type deodorant in the bathroom. They're definitely not Lija's.

She shakes her head. 'No go. Was too nice.'

'Oh, that's a shame. I liked him. He seemed very sweet.'

Lija glowers at me in her own inimitable way. 'I am OK alone.'

'Better to be by yourself than with someone unsuitable.'

'Yeah. I know.' She stands up from the table and tidies

her plate away. I notice that she scrapes half of her omelette into the bin.

'You're young,' I offer. 'There'll be someone along soon. You wait and see.'

Flopping back into her seat like a surly teenager, Lija says, 'I don't want to talk about it. Mind your own business.'

Well, that's me told. I pour her some more wine. The warmth of the kitchen and the alcohol are making me feel sleepy. Plus I hardly slept a wink last night or the night before which doesn't help.

'How's Edie?' Lija asks. Purely because she now wants to change the subject rather than from any desire to know what my dear sister is up to, I'm sure.

'I haven't talked to her much,' I confess. 'Not since Danny and I started travelling. You know what it's like. I can hardly ever get a decent signal. The time difference doesn't help either.' I don't want me and Edie to be completely estranged. We are, after all, related by blood. Albeit just Dad's. But I still haven't entirely forgiven my sister for what she did and I don't want to become embroiled in her relationship difficulties with Brandon. She's been with her married lover for years now and, though he says he will leave his wife for Edie, I can't see it happening any time soon – nor would I want it to.

'I haven't even asked Edie what she's doing for Christmas this year.' Normally, Brandon is at home with his wife and children while Edie snatches a few crumbs of festive cheer wherever she can. Still, she's a big girl now and only she can extricate herself from the mess she's got herself into. She's not that fond of it when I tell her so, however.

Chapter Twelve

I find Anthony's electric razor still in the bathroom cabinet in the en suite in my old bedroom. Poor old Stan's looking quite bristly, which I know he'll hate, but he's not up to standing in front of the bathroom mirror long enough for a wet shave. For a moment, I stare at the razor – left here for the rare nights when Anthony deigned to stay over – and feel as if my relationship with him is all a bad dream now. How could I have stayed with a man to whom I was so interminably unsuited, and for so long? I think of Danny and how we fit together, hand in glove, and can't wait for him to come back on *The Dreamcatcher*.

Obviously, Lija hasn't chucked any of my stuff out yet. Thankfully. Money is tight and I'm not sure how I'd manage to pay for storage. On *The Dreamcatcher* we have one wardrobe and a tiny spare room that's at bursting point. End of. At some stage, I'll need to have a major clear out. If I'm honest, most of the stuff in this cupboard should go straight in the charity shop bag. The tie-dye maxi-skirt was a mistake when I bought it. I thought I might try to have a hippy phase but I never found the courage to. Maybe I could put some of it on eBay and call it vintage.

I go downstairs and find a carrier bag for the shaver. 'I'm going next door now,' I say to Lija. 'I'll be back in the morning.'

'I'll come over with you. I haven't seen Stinky Stan all day.'

So Lija and I put our coats on to walk over to Stan's cottage. The night has drawn in now and it's cold. The sharp sting of the weather reminds me that it won't be too long until Christmas and I'm already starting to feel a little bit festive. I have no idea what to buy Danny for Christmas. Living on a narrowboat you can't just buy stuff for the sake of it, but I'd like to surprise him with something.

'I have been neglecting garden,' Lija says as we stroll together.

'It never looks its best at this time of year. We can take the tables in while I'm here and store them in the garage. They're not robust enough to stand a winter outside.'

'There's always so much to think about,' Lija sighs.

'The joys of being a home and business owner,' I remind her. 'But you are enjoying it?'

'Maybe,' she says. 'I think I like it better when you ran it and I was just waitress.'

I laugh. 'You were *never* just a waitress!' She has the good grace to smile too. I give her a hug. 'Soon it will fit you like comfy slippers. I love the change of name,' I tell her. 'Sounds great.'

'You don't mind?'

'It's not Fay's Cakes any more. I think The Café in the Garden is much better.'

'Next year I will get a man in to do the garden.'

'Perhaps another Danny Wilde will come passing by,' I quip.

Lija just snorts.

'You've not been using the *Maid of Merryweather*?'

She shakes her head. 'It did not seem right. It is your boat. When the tourists stopped coming there was no need.'

It's true that we never got much passing trade after the end of September. The regulars who live on the canal are out and about, but the people who hire narrowboats tend not to be hardy enough to cope with standing out on the back of the boat or working the locks in all weathers. Not actually sure I'm that hardy myself, but I'm getting used to it.

'If you have *The Dreamcatcher*, you should sell it. Why need two boats?'

'I could never do that. I feel it's all that I have left of my parents. What I'd really love is to have the money to do her up. The poor old girl's a bit of a mess.' I don't tell Lija about the leak or quite how bad the *Maid of Merryweather* is as she'd feel terrible. I should get down there in the next few days to try to dry the boat out a bit, stop the worst of the rot before winter.

In Stan's house, we shout out 'Hello!' and I stoke up the fire with some logs while Lija takes the food parcel she's brought into the kitchen. Then we go upstairs to see our patient.

Stan's awake, sitting up in bed and reading. He puts his book to one side when we go in.

Lija flops down on the bed next to him. 'How are you, old man? Not dead yet?'

'Doing quite well,' he says, sounding more cheerful than when I first arrived. 'I feel there might be light at the end of the tunnel.'

'What tunnel?' Lija says, frowning.

'It's another figure of speech,' I explain.

Lija tuts and throws her hands in the air. 'Why are you people always saying stupid things?'

'Can you manage anything to eat?' I ask Stan. 'We've brought some nice bread and cheese.'

Stan shakes his head. 'I'm fine, Fay. Just resting is doing me a world of good.'

'Great. I'll put the kettle on though.'

'That would be nice.'

'Lija, can you read to Stan while I make the tea?'

She looks horrified. 'Read to him? The man is *ninety-five*, not five.'

'I'm not quite that decrepit,' Stan intervenes.

'But nearly,' Lija insists.

'I'm a mere youth of ninety-three.'

'You look a hundred,' Lija bats back. 'More.'

I hold up my hands. 'Entertain him with your sparkling conversation then. I'm going to make tea.'

'We will bring Rainbow next time. She will talk him to death.'

'My kind of nursing care tends to be more focused on keeping the patient alive,' I point out.

'You were looking after Miranda. She died.'

'Thanks for that candid observation.'

'You're doing a grand job,' Stan says.

'I don't think you are ill at all, old man. I think you like to lie in bed and be entertained by pretty ladies.'

Stan chuckles and it sets off a coughing spasm again, though his chest doesn't sound quite so weak as before. Hopefully, the antibiotics will have kicked in by now.

'Oh, it's a long, long time since that happened,' he says when he has recovered.

'I should think so.' Lija looks horrified. 'You are *seriously* old person.'

I leave Lija teasing Stan in her own inimitable way, but he does seem to lap it up, bless him.

When we've had tea together, Lija goes back to the house. I help Stan to run the razor round his chin and take off the worst of the bristles.

'You look better now,' I say. 'Not quite so bedraggled.'

He feels his smooth chin. 'I feel a million dollars,' he says. 'You're an angel.'

'A tired one.' I give a yawn. Last night's lack of sleep is catching up with me. 'I'll be on the sofa. If you need me, just holler.'

'You don't need to do this,' Stan says.

'I do.' I plant a kiss on his papery skin. 'Taken all your tablets?'

He nods.

'Sleep tight.'

Downstairs, I FaceTime Danny and even though it's late, he's still making his way back on *The Dreamcatcher*. I can hear the gentle thrum of the engine and the swish of the water down the phone line. He's standing on the back of the boat, hat pulled down, wrapped up against the cold, light on to enable him to pick his way down the canal in the dark. I wish I was there to snuggle up against him. He yawns sleepily, as do I.

'Call it a day,' I say. 'I don't want you to get exhausted and fall in or crash the boat.'

'I'll moor up shortly,' Danny agrees. 'I wanted to make some headway. Now that I'm on the way, I just want to be with you.'

'I like the sound of that,' I say, dreamily.

'I'll be back soon,' he says. 'Not long now.'

And, with that thought in my head, I lie on Stan's lumpy sofa and fall fast asleep.

Chapter Thirteen

The time seems to whizz by. The days are colder, shorter. Mist hangs over the garden for most of the morning. The golden confetti of fallen leaves covers the ground. Life in the café is busy every day. December will hit us before we know it.

In the kitchen we can hardly keep up with the constant stream of Christmas afternoon teas. The festive season is truly in full swing now and I'm sure it starts earlier every year – or is that an age thing? I don't think I've ever baked so many mince pies. I am a mince pie making machine! At this rate, I might never want to see another one again. I make cupcakes topped with coconut that looks like snow and others topped with chocolate fondant, decorated to look like reindeers. While I've got my Christmas baking mojo on, I try a new recipe – a white chocolate tray bake flavoured with cinnamon, nutmeg and orange – which I think will be a big hit. Lija stomps about, grumbling.

Rainbow continues to talk the hind legs off any passing donkey.

'My nan says that Blackpool and Paris have both got the SAME tower.' Rainbow stacks dainty sandwiches on a tiered stand. Brie and cranberry, turkey with sage stuffing, smoked salmon with creamed horseradish mayonnaise. We have twenty people booked in this afternoon – full capacity in the dining room – and we'll be busy, busy, busy. 'So why would you go to Paris? You need a passport and EVERYTHING. But Blackpool's in this country. At least I think it is. It's not anywhere else, is it? Is it, Fay, is it?'

'No,' I assure her. 'It's definitely in this country.'

'So why would you go? DUH? What has PARIS got that Blackpool hasn't?'

'The French,' I offer.

'Yeah. I suppose.' She eats one of the sandwiches with a thoughtful look on her face.

The good thing about Rainbow's conversations is that she rarely requires you to join in with them and, when you do, it's for minimal input. I carry on lifting mince pies out of the oven. They're golden brown, bubbling with mince-meat and smell wonderful. I'll put a couple aside for Stan.

Thankfully, he seems to be through the worst of his illness and is getting a little stronger every day. He's out of bed now and I've got him a walking frame to use. He hates it and it's awful to see him shuffling along when he was so sprightly, but I feel if we can get him through the winter then he'll be his old self by the spring again. Fingers – and everything else – crossed. He *has* to get better. I can't envisage a life without this dear old soul in it.

The best news of all is that Danny is getting ever closer on *The Dreamcatcher*. He should be here in the next few days and his arrival can't come soon enough. I feel as if I've lost a limb without him.

'Did unicorns ever exist? Like dinosaurs?' Rainbow asks, apropos of nothing. 'My mate Chelsey says they did. So could they, like, bring them back to life and EVERYTHING, like in *Jurassic Park*? Unicorn Land would be TOTALLY cool. They wouldn't eat you like the dinosaurs do. It would be all pink and SPARKLY. Can you get yellow unicorns?'

'I've never seen one,' I say drily, which is totally lost on Rainbow.

I'm slicing the Christmas cake for the afternoon tea when the back door opens. I don't think we're expecting anyone, so I turn to see who it is. Danny's standing there beaming widely.

My heart tries to jump out of my chest and I stand there, frozen, knife in hand, just staring at him. It reminds me of the first day that he came into my life when he walked into my kitchen and filled it with his strong, youthful presence. From that moment I was smitten and still am.

'Hey.' Danny winks at me. 'Surprise, surprise.'

All I can do is stand and shake. I want to do nothing more than hold him but, if I'm not careful, I feel that I might cry with joy and never stop.

'OMG!' Rainbow shouts. Our young friend has no such inhibitions. In a second she's across the room and launching herself at Danny.

'It's YOU!' She wraps her arms round him and plants

a wet kiss on his cheek. To say that he looks startled is an understatement. At his feet, Diggery barks for all he's worth. 'Fay showed me a photo of you and EVERYTHING. We didn't think you'd be back for DAYS! Did we, Fay?'

'No,' I agree, finally finding my voice. 'We thought you were still on the canal.'

He still hasn't taken his eyes from me. 'I thought I'd sneak in and give you a surprise.'

'Well, you FLIPPING did!' Rainbow says.

Gently, Danny unpeels her from him. 'I'm thinking that you must be Rainbow.'

'How did you know?' she gasps in amazement.

'I've heard a lot about you,' he says.

'OMG.' She lets him go and runs out of the room. 'This is IMMENSE. Lija! Lija! DANNY'S here!'

Then he turns to me and grins. 'Do you have a hug for me too?'

In a distinctly more decorous way, but with no less enthusiasm in my heart, I go to him and hold him tightly. It's going to be very hard to let him go and return to my mince pies for the rest of the day.

'I didn't realise that you were so close to home.' I stroke his cheek, still not quite believing that he's back so soon. 'You don't know how wonderful it is to see you.'

He winks. 'I can make a good guess.' From behind his back he produces a bunch of holly complete with luscious red berries. 'For you. I picked it along the way. Merry Christmas.'

Taking the holly from him, I say, 'Now the Christmas countdown can really start.' I bend and fuss Diggery's ears, sending him into a frenzy of joy. 'Hello, boy. I've missed you.' Then, to Danny, 'How did you get back here so quickly?'

'I've put in some long hours,' he says, and I see that he looks unusually tired. 'It will be good to stay still for a few days.'

'A few days.' I get a brief palpitation. 'I hope we'll be here longer than that?'

'Oh, yeah. Of course. We'll stay here until after Christmas, for sure.'

I was worried for a moment that Danny was keen to move on again, but I definitely want to be here until Stan's back to his old self. I don't give voice to my thoughts that this could be next spring.

'How's Stan?'

As always, he seems to read my mind. 'Better. Doing really well. I think we had a close shave there though,' I whisper. 'I'm glad I came back when I did.'

My concern is that we're still living on borrowed time. An illness like that at Stan's age can really knock you back.

Lija and Rainbow come back into the kitchen. Rainbow's little cheeks are pink with excitement. I think she's already in love with Danny. Even Lija smiles and she's been prickly all morning. She was holed up in the office tackling the mountain of paperwork that's built up – at my insistence. Whenever I ventured in to take her tea or biscuits, she snarled at me. She is, however, beaming at Danny.

'So you are back, Hot Stuff?'

'Yeah,' Danny says. 'Good to see you.'

Lija throws a glance at me. 'Maybe now she will stop

mooning round like kicked puppy.' She goes to lean against him and he slings an arm round her shoulders.

'What's it like being a businesswoman?'

'Too many bloody bills,' she complains.

'Fay says you're doing a great job.'

Lija shrugs, never finding it easy to accept praise.

'I can help you while I'm here too,' he says. 'Let me know if there are any odd jobs you need doing.'

'I have list.' She's grinning in quite an evil manner now.

'I might have known.'

Danny eats half a dozen mince pies while I make him tea and Rainbow continues to stare at him, lovestruck. For once, she seems at a loss for words.

'Can I steal this lovely lady away from you for an hour?' Danny asks Lija when he's finished his tea and demolished a good deal of the cakes. 'I moored *The Dreamcatcher* further down the canal and walked up the towpath.' He nods towards the direction he's come from. 'I'm going to head down to the next winding hole and turn the boat around. I thought I'd tie up at the jetty, if that's OK with you.'

'Sure.' Lija flicks a thumb in my direction. 'Do not be like her and ask for every single thing or I will have to kill you.'

'Fair enough,' Danny says.

'I've got some cherries to dip,' I remind Lija. As part of the afternoon tea we're serving cherries dipped in white chocolate and tiny silver dragées, plus I've baked gingerbread snowflakes and there are red velvet macarons ready to be piped with icing sugar buttons and fur to look like Santa's coat.

'I'll do that,' Lija says. 'Am sick of paperwork.'

'Are you sure?' But I'm already taking off my apron. The thought of being alone with Danny sends a thrill through me after weeks of enforced separation. 'I'll be back in time to serve the teas with you.'

'I should hope so,' Lija says. 'Don't make me send out search party.'

'I promise. Two at the latest.' That's when our first guests are booked in. I hang my apron on the hook behind the door and Danny takes my hand.

'Come on, Digs.'

'Laters!' Rainbow waves at us.

Together we walk out of the house into the bracing cold and take the towpath along the canal towards *The Dreamcatcher*.

Chapter Fourteen

'You don't know how good it feels to be on board again,' I say with a happy sigh as I climb into the cabin of our lovely narrowboat.

'Good to hear it.' Danny wastes no time in wrapping his arms round me and pulling me close.

'When I came back to the house it felt as if I was coming home then I realised that this is Lija's place now. She's changed how the café is run and the house is most definitely hers. No matter how much she tells me otherwise, I do feel slightly in the way. The place is familiar and strange all at the same time. But coming here, with you – and Diggery – this feels like home.'

Twining my hair in his fingers and kissing my neck, Danny whispers, 'I've missed you. God, you smell so good.' Probably the lingering scents of vanilla and strawberry jam from this morning's baking session. 'I could eat you.'

'I thought we were taking the boat down to the winding hole?'

'That can wait,' Danny says. 'Come to bed.'

I need no persuasion.

'Stay, Digs,' Danny instructs and our dear dog curls up into his basket with a slightly disgruntled look on his face.

Danny leads me to our tiny cabin and closes the curtains over the window. I think of the first night we spent together when we fell into bed in a frenzy of passion. This time we take our time, slowly undressing each other, savouring every moment. There's no less passion, but this way of reacquainting ourselves feels all the more delicious.

As he moves above me, tears spring to my eyes and Danny kisses them away. This man completes me and makes me feel whole again. Whatever happens, wherever we go in the world, I know beyond a shadow of a doubt that I'm meant to be with him and there's a contentment deep in my soul from knowing that.

Afterwards, we lie in bed entwined in each other's arms.

'We should do this more often,' Danny says. 'Steal some afternoon delight.'

I glance at my watch. 'We should, but the clock's ticking now and I have to get back to help Lija before too long.'

Danny props himself up on his elbow. 'She doesn't look her usual self,' he notes. 'Feisty as she is, the spark's not quite there, and she looks even more pasty than usual.'

'I know. I can't put my finger on it,' I tell him. 'You know that she normally swears like Catherine Tate's Nan, but she's hardly been offensive at all. For Lija.'

'Perhaps Rainbow's relentlessly positive nature is having a good effect on her.'

I laugh at that. 'I think she's actually one cupcake away from killing the poor girl.'

'So what is wrong?'

'I'm not sure. I've tried to chat to her about it, but you know what Lija's like – not very forthcoming when it comes to emotions. It could just be the stress of taking on the house and the café. It's not a small undertaking by any stretch of the imagination. Perhaps she's just realising that.'

'We'll help her all we can while we're here.'

I snuggle in closer to him. 'I want to stay around for a while, Danny.'

'I know,' he says. 'I'm happy to do that. It's not much fun standing on the back of the boat in all weathers. I thought my fingers were going to fall off yesterday they were so cold. I'm not quite one of the hardened canal folk yet,' he admits. 'We can hole up here for the winter.'

I let out the breath I didn't know I was holding.

'I'll walk into the city either later or in the morning to see if I can get some casual work,' he adds. 'I might have missed out on seasonal jobs now but, you never know, I could get lucky.'

He kisses me again and then we get up and dressed. Diggery greets us as if we've been lost to him for decades. I make some tea while Danny goes out to get *The Dreamcatcher*'s engine started. When the tea's brewed, I pull on my thick fleece jacket and go out onto the back of the boat. He's already untied the ropes and I sit beside him as he manoeuvres us away from the bank. Danny takes the tiller as we head towards the winding hole – a wider part of the canal where we can do a three-point turn with a boat this long – though I'm more than happy to steer now too.

The air is cold as it blows past us, even at the sedate pace of the boat. I snuggle deeper into my jacket and Danny perches next to me, putting his arm round me for warmth.

A few minutes later and we sail past the bottom of the garden. From the water, even in its winter garb, the house looks attractive – solid, steadfast. The sort of place that most people would feel lucky to own. Unbidden, I get a prickle of irritation towards my sister who had it all and sold it without a second thought, but I bite it down as I don't want my dark thoughts to spoil Danny's return.

Next, we're alongside the *Maid of Merryweather*. Her once bright paintwork is faded now. She looks like one of the many abandoned or neglected boats that you see dotted along the canal.

'The poor old girl's looking a bit sorry for herself,' Danny remarks. I told him on the phone about the leak and what a mess it had made inside.

'I know. It breaks my heart. I haven't had time to do much. The boat needs to be run and a dehumidifier or something put inside. She's so damp. I'm worried that if we get a harsh winter, she won't make it through.'

'I'll have a look at her later, see what I can do.'

'Thanks. I'd appreciate that. I'd feel terrible if we had to scrap her.'

'I'm sure it won't come to that.' He squeezes me. 'I know how much she means to you.'

We reach the winding hole and Danny stands to concentrate on completing the task of turning the boat while I look at the scenery on the canal. A bold heron stands by the bank ignoring our presence as it searches intently for its lunch. A double row of towering poplar trees flank the cycle path that runs parallel to the towpath. I wonder how long they've been standing there, as I remember them being as tall when I was a child. This is an amazing place to be able to make your home and I thank my lucky stars for it.

Danny turns the huge boat on a sixpence – skills honed by doing this day in and day out. Then we head back to the house and moor up on the jetty next to the *Maid of Merryweather*.

Chapter Fifteen

During the afternoon I help Rainbow to serve the Christmas afternoon teas while Lija holds the fort in the kitchen. We are a veritable flurry of Christmas cakes and cups of tea. The dining room is filled with happy chatter and it's lovely to see the Christmas decorations giving a festive glow to the room.

With a little direction from me, Danny ventures up into the loft and comes down with our old family Christmas tree followed by boxes and boxes overflowing with decorations hoarded from many a Christmas past. If Lija's agreeable, I'll put this tree up in the living room. There's a smaller tree, less than a metre high, that would fit in a tiny corner of *The Dreamcatcher* and I'll also pinch a few of the decorations to give the boat a festive makeover. While I fuss with the boxes, Danny goes next door to say hello to Stan.

I don't know where the afternoon goes, but soon the

happy customers are departing. We've made some Christmas cakes to sell and it's pleasing to see several of the clients departing with them boxed up and tucked under their arms. Rainbow and I go back into the kitchen to help Lija. While we're clearing everything away and preparing some goodies for tomorrow's onslaught, the door opens and Stan is standing there.

'Thought I'd bring a visitor,' Danny says.

'Hello!' Stan risks taking a hand off his frame to wave.

I'm amazed to see him doing so well and also glad to see that my patient is wrapped up warmly as it must have taken him an age to walk just the short distance from his cottage to the house. He's been pottering about at home, but is still a bit unsteady on his feet. I don't want the cold air getting on his chest, but I'm sure he's happy to be able to leave the cottage for a short while. Every day, I'm pleased to say, there's a bit more colour in his cheeks and he looks a little stronger.

'Look at you, out and about.' I give him a hug. Danny has treated him to a proper shave and it's taken years off him. 'You look *so* much better.' I've been helping to keep his bristles at bay with Anthony's old razor, but clearly Danny has better barbering skills.

'Cut-throat razor,' Danny says, proudly. 'My dad taught me to do it years ago. I've not lost the knack.'

'Brave of you to put that to the test, Stan!'

'I had every faith in him.'

'Ran you a nice bath too, didn't I, Stan?'

'Oh, yes,' Stan says. 'I feel great. A million dollars. I could run a marathon.'

'Maybe not today, Stan. Leave that till tomorrow.' I give him a wink. 'Sit yourself down. Cup of tea?'

'Oh, lovely,' Stan says.

'SELFIE!' Rainbow trills and positions herself next to Stan. 'This is when you take a picture of YOURSELF. Selfie,' she repeats slowly. 'I know that old people don't know that.' She holds the screen up and duck-pouts. Stan grins amiably. 'SAUSAGES!'

'Sausages,' Stan echoes.

One day I must tell Rainbow that Stan was a fighter pilot and after the war led expeditions to Nepal and the North Pole. She might like to know that he worked in the movies doing dangerous flying stunts and has even spent summers hunting for the Loch Ness monster. As much as she loves him and fusses over him, I think all she sees is the frail old man next door who never complains about anything, but there's so much more to him than that. And even thinking that makes me all teary again.

Rainbow clicks the camera button on the phone. Then she does the same with all of us, taking noticeably longer over the one with Danny. 'SNAPCHAT,' she declares and no one even asks.

We all sit together, a mash-up of people thrown together as a family. We eat the leftover sandwiches and cakes for our supper.

'OMG, I've got a twitchy eye,' Rainbow says. 'Look, look.' We all examine her twitchy eye.

'Those eyelashes are quite something,' I note. Not her own, of course. As is the fashion now, they're long, black fluttery things.

'My nan calls them spiders for lashes. I HATE spiders. I've got that agoraphobia. Once I woke up with one of my eyelashes on my pillow and thought it was a spider. OMG, I ACTUALLY died!'

I have to say she looks quite well on it.

'My nan says that wearing false eyelashes damages your eyesight, but I'm not so sure. That's like saying high heels damage your feet, right? Who'd believe THAT? When I look back at old pictures of me when I'm, like, five and WHATEVER, I look really WEIRD without false eyelashes. They should make them for kids. Girls, like, not boys. That would be WEIRD. Except if you were a boy who liked to wear make-up – that would be fine.'

She continues to machine-gun us on the subject of false eyelashes and many kinds of make-up until we all start to lose the will to live. Even Stan, who has only just pulled back from the breach.

'Shall we all decorate the tree together?' I jump in quickly when there's a slight pause where Rainbow breathes.

Rainbow is out of her seat and bouncing before I've finished the sentence. 'OMG, it's my FAVOURITE Christmas job. Though I like wrapping presents too. And opening them. OBVS! I'm a nervous Christmas present opener because, like, you never know what you're going to get and you might not like it. But then I LOVE a surprise too, so I'm always CONFLICTED.'

It's a dilemma I'd never previously considered and certainly have never had.

'I was going to go to the pub with Chelsey, but she's seeing that bloke I told you about. The one who looks like

LIAM from One Direction. But not really. Should have gone to SPECSAVERS! Hahaha. And I said, "He was going out with that girl who looks like her off Corrie, why would you want to see him?" And she said . . .'

Then she's off again and we all zone out. Stan still looks stunned and he likes a talker.

Lija opens a bottle of red and I say, 'Shall I make mulled wine with that?' It looks a bit cheap and cheerful, so it might liven it up.

She shrugs. 'Wine is wine.'

'It'll be nice. Christmassy.'

'I am sick of it already,' is her contribution and she stomps off into the living room.

'I'll go and put the tree up.' Danny follows her and Rainbow trots along in their wake, still talking.

I pour the bottle of red wine into the big saucepan, adding some water, sugar and, finally, splash in a good slug of brandy. Thankfully, we have some left over from soaking the Christmas cakes. I give Stan a little tot of it neat.

'Good for the heart,' I tell him, though I've no idea whether it is or not. A little tipple won't hurt.

Stan rubs his hands together. 'Oh, my favourite.' He smacks his lips together as he sips it.

While the wine is warming, I cut up an orange and add that, along with a couple of cinnamon sticks and a sprinkling of cloves to add a bit of spice.

'It smells lovely, Fay.'

'So you'll definitely join us for Christmas dinner this year?' I ask. 'You've nothing else planned?'

Stan shakes his head. 'How can I ever thank you for your kindness? I wouldn't be here if it wasn't for your care.'

'Nonsense. It's the least I could do.' I go to give him a hug.

'How can I possibly repay you?'

'No need,' I say. 'It's been my pleasure. You're a very good patient.'

'If I'd been lucky enough to have a daughter, I would have liked her to have been like you.' There are tears in his eyes as he speaks.

'Oh, Stan. That's a lovely thing to say.'

'I know that I'm not your dad, but I feel very paternal towards you. Does that sound silly?'

'It sounds very nice.' I plant a kiss on his now smooth cheek before I scurry back to the cooker to check that the wine is warmed through. Then I pour it into glasses. 'I'll take you into the living room and then I'll come back for this.'

'I can manage,' Stan says and I try not to dive in to help as he struggles to his feet, gripping his walking frame. I know that he values his independence and wants to do this on his own. Eventually, with a bit of huffing and puffing, he gives me the thumbs up. 'Good to go.'

In the living room, the Christmas tree of my childhood stands tall in the corner. In fairness, it's probably looking a little dated now, but it's still an imposing sight, stretching right up to the ceiling. The branches are covered in dark green and silver strands of tinsel with no attempt to make it look like a real tree as the current ones seem designed to be. Rainbow is opening all the boxes, as giddy as a five-year-old. She pulls out all the baubles, scattering them over the carpet.

'OMG! Look at these,' she says. 'They're like ANTIQUE and EVERYTHING!'

'They're *glass*,' I chip in, hoping that Rainbow gets the hint and won't continue to chuck them about with quite so much abandon. 'Mainly from the sixties.'

'OMG!' She holds them reverently now. 'That was WELL long ago. They're like VICTORIAN or something.'

'Well, Stan is ninety-three. That's positively medieval.'

We all laugh – except Rainbow, who is quite prepared to believe it. 'WOW. I've done history and EVERYTHING at school.'

'Who was on the throne when you were a lad then, Stan?' Danny jokes.

'Henry the Eighth,' he deadpans.

'OMG. Wait till I tell my nan. She loves Henry Eight. She follows him on TWITTER. He looks exactly like that Irish actor who drinks too much and falls over.'

Rainbow is WELL impressed. OBVS. I smile at her naivety.

While she gazes at Stan in awe, clearly wondering why he can be so very decrepit and still be alive, I hand out the wine. 'There's alcohol in this, Rainbow. Go easy,' I say in the style of an old person. She's seventeen and, as such, could probably drink me under the table.

Rainbow wrinkles her nose as she tastes it. 'Hot wine? RAD.'

'Lovely,' Stan says. 'My favourite.'

'Come on, let's get this tree dressed.'

'Squeeee!' Rainbow says.

'I'll put some music on.' Danny goes to the iPod dock.

'There's a Michael Bublé playlist,' I tell him.

'Lovely,' Stan says. 'My favourite.' His wine glass is drained and I think he might just say that to everything on offer this evening.

'Not Micky Bubble again,' Lija complains.

Despite that, we observe my favourite traditions. The Bublé goes on, the mince pies come out, the mulled wine flows and the decorations go on the tree. I have another glass of wine and, as I look round at my friends, my lover, as they laugh and joke together, I realise what a very lucky person I am.

Chapter Sixteen

I pass one or two baubles to Stan which he hangs on the lower branches that he's able to easily reach, but we've been dressing the tree for a while now and it's all a bit much. So he sits down to enjoy another glass or two of mulled wine instead. As he's not had a drink for some time, I keep the glasses small. I don't want him getting giddy and falling over.

Lija exudes extreme reluctance, but joins in anyway. I think I've ground her down in my determination to be festive. When I look at her closely though, I can see that she looks tired down to her bones and I go and take the baubles from her. 'Sit,' I instruct. 'You look all in. Have another glass of wine and then it's an early night for you. I don't want you collapsing on me before we even get to Christmas.'

For once, she doesn't even argue. 'I am tired,' she agrees quietly and sits down on the sofa next to Stan. She rests her head on his shoulder and Stan beams at me, his cheeks pink from the wine and the warmth of the room.

Danny is clearly glad to be back in this odd little fold. He cuddles me and kisses me as often as he can and I can't say that I'm complaining. I have a lifetime of cuddles to catch up on.

I study each decoration lovingly. Every year, as far back as I can remember, Miranda let me and Edie pick a new decoration for the tree. My sister and I would spend hours in the shop, money burning a hole in our hot little hands, trying to select the best one. I pick up a Hummel angel in china. She has a round, apple-cheeked face – much like Rainbow's – and she's hugging a Christmas tree. That year I went off piste and chose this to go on the mantelpiece. The little angel has survived the intervening years surprisingly well with only a tiny chip to the tree where Edie swiped it to the floor in a fit of pique over something trivial.

It makes me think of my sister. I really should call her. She doesn't even know that Danny and I are back at the house. If I have enough mulled wine, I'll steel myself to ring her.

'OMG! Look at these!' Rainbow holds out a collection of glass ornaments – different sizes of pine cones, all painted in gaudy colours, pink, blue, yellow and green.

'This really will be a rainbow tree,' I say.

'Squeeeee!' And Rainbow's off again.

I should imagine that this is what it's like to have children in the home at Christmas. Something that I've never experienced and, quite out of nowhere, that makes me really sad. Danny's young, but I'm rapidly approaching my sell-by date. What if he ever decides that he wants children? He'd make a really great dad and has the patience of a saint. I can't say that I've been overly careful with contraception in the past because Anthony and I made love only on high days and holidays. My birthdays and Christmas morning were always a given and, usually, New Year's Eve. Beyond that it was all very sporadic. His golfing calendar definitely took priority over our love life. When I think of how different it is with Danny – how I feel loved, treasured, desired – I know that Anthony and I were only going through the motions. It's probably as well that we never managed to have children. But I sort of feel differently now. There are emotions stirring inside me that have been dormant for so long.

As irritating as Rainbow can be, I do love having her around. Her silly comments, her unfailing enthusiasm for everything, her childish naivety. Perhaps in the same way that Stan said he feels paternal towards me, I'm feeling distinctly maternal towards Rainbow. Though I think her actual mum must be quite a few years younger than me.

Would it be too late for me to start now? Danny and I are just embarking on our lives together, still learning about each other. When would it be appropriate to introduce children into the mix? It's not something that I've had to consider before. Are children even conducive to life on the canal? I'm sure some people must manage it. Yet I have to face the fact that my equipment might not even be fully functioning any more – like the poor old *Maid of Merryweather*, my insides might be desperately in need of attention and renovation. So much to think about.

The tree takes much longer to dress than I imagine. The original lights are long gone, but I replaced them several years ago with ones that are still in the retro spirit – tiny flowers in an array of colours which Danny has looped over the branches. Due to the sheer number of decorations that have been accumulated over the years, the tree is positively laden down with a random assortment of baubles and bits.

Yet when it's all done the tree looks beautiful – all bright and colourful. There's a selection of fragile glass Santas with fulsome painted beards and slightly freaky blue eyes, which are playing different orchestra instruments. In among them are colourful twists of foil in purple and orange. There are scarlet knee-hugging elves that must have adorned every Christmas tree in that era – I think they were Edie's choice.

Finally, I pick the fairy out of her box. Her dress is rather raggy now and faded, her wings more than a little bent, the paint on her face fading. But this is one that Miranda made when she was a girl. Despite the fact that she was so terribly cruel to me in the end, I have a momentary rush of affection for the woman that she must have been before it went so sour. It's this time of the year that makes you think about those loved ones who aren't around any more. So I give the fairy a little hug and plant a kiss on her grubby plastic cheek.

'Can you do the honours?' I hand her to Danny.

He climbs the stepladder and places her gently on top, twisting one of the fairy lights so that she has a golden glow on her. That makes her look much better.

Finally, I stand back to admire it. Colourful, it certainly is. Tasteful, not so much.

Out of the corner of my eye, I see that Stan is yawning and say, 'Come on, Stan. Time for your bed.'

'Do you want me to take him home, Fay?' Danny offers.

'No, I'll do it. Can you put the empty boxes back in the loft for me?'

'Sure,' he says.

'I'll text my dad to come and get me,' Rainbow says. 'This has been the BEST.'

Poor girl is saving up for driving lessons – God help us – so her dad is currently her private taxi service. He drops her off at the end of the lane every morning on his way to work and picks her up in the evening when she's done. He seems to bear it all with good nature – according to Rainbow.

Danny whispers in my ear, 'Are you staying with Stan tonight?'

'I'll see if he's happy to manage by himself,' I answer. The thought of spending a night in a proper bed rather than scrunched up on a lumpy sofa is quite appealing. Having Danny in the bed too is a definite bonus.

I take Stan's arm and help him to his walking frame. 'Night, night, everyone,' he says. 'Thank you for a lovely evening.'

Swaddling him in his coat on the way, we head out into the cold night air. The sky is clear and bright, the stars sparkle like diamonds. We make our way slowly and gingerly along the path, Stan leaning heavily on his walking frame, me guiding his arm. 'Take care where you step,' I warn him. 'I don't want you to slip.'

We pause at the edge of the path and, on the breeze, I think I hear the light laugh of a young girl near to us. I stop short, straining to see if I can spot anyone lurking in the garden in the darkness, but I can't make out anyone.

'Did you hear that?'

Stan nods and pats my arm. 'No need to be afraid. It's only Audrey.'

'Your fiancée?'

'Yes. She feels very close to me at the moment.'

'Oh, Stan, you've made me shiver all over.' Even the hairs on the back of my neck are prickling. I still myself to see if I can pick up the sound again, but everything's as quiet as a churchyard.

'Don't be frightened, lovely. She's a great comfort to me.' He looks out into the garden too, towards the canal. 'I can't see her, not quite, but I know she's here.'

I think I see a shadow shift in my peripheral vision, but when I turn there's nothing there. Stan looks at the same spot and smiles softly.

'I'm never alone when she's near,' he continues. 'She still loves me. I'm young and vibrant in her eyes. Unchanged. She doesn't see this crumbling body. I haven't aged, as she hasn't.'

'Now you're going to make me cry.'

Stan chuckles. 'You don't have to worry about me, Fay. Whatever happens, I'll be fine. I've lived my life, and enjoyed it all – you still have so much of yours ahead of you.'

'I'm trying to embrace the new me,' I tell him.

'Good,' he says. 'And I don't want to see you sleeping

on my sofa tonight. You should be on *The Dreamcatcher* with that young man of yours.'

'I was going to talk to you about that.'

'There's nothing more to be said,' Stan insists. 'You've got me through the worst. I'll be fine by myself.'

'Shall I still bring your breakfast in the morning or do you want to come into the café if you can bear the hustle and bustle?'

'I love it,' Stan says. 'I've missed the company so much while I've been poorly. I like to think you all keep me young.'

I laugh. 'That's good to know. I think Rainbow makes me feel as old as the hills.' I take his arm again, trying not to glance back as we leave the garden and continue to pick our way along the path to Stan's front door. 'Let's get you inside. You have to be careful with that chest of yours.'

'There's still a bit of life left in me yet,' he says with a twinkle in his eye.

'I think that's the mulled wine talking,' I tease.

'Ah, yes. You're probably right,' he agrees. 'I do love it. My favourite.'

Chapter Seventeen

I pop back to the house to say goodnight to Lija. There's no one in the kitchen, so I assume that Rainbow's dad has come to collect her and Danny has gone back to the boat. I find Lija in the dining room setting up for tomorrow's service, in darkness except for the glow of the Christmas tree lights.

Taking a plate from her, I say gently, 'Stop that now. You've had a long day and you look tired.'

'Am fine.' She tugs the plate back.

'Rainbow and I will do it in the morning.'

She puts the plate down, reluctantly conceding defeat. I open my arms and, with only a slight hesitation, she steps towards me, letting me hug her bony frame. 'You'll be all right?'

'Sure.'

But something in me feels as if she wants me to stay. 'Danny and I can move back in with you if you want.'

'I don't want.'

'We're only at the bottom of the garden. If you need me for anything, you only have to call.'

'Please go now.' She pushes away from me. 'You are annoying.'

I sigh. 'I'm only trying to help, Lija.'

'You don't think I am strong?'

'Of course I do, but we're here for you. There's no need for you to struggle alone. I'm sorry that we left for so long.'

She shrugs. 'You did what you had to do.'

'And I've loved it,' I admit. 'But now we're back.'

'For how long? Days? Weeks? What?' She scuffs her toe on the floor.

'I don't know. Certainly until after Christmas. Probably until Stan's better and the weather's improved. I'll have to talk to Danny about it.'

I wonder if this is what the problem is. Does Lija want us to be here for longer? There's a certain attraction about being settled again. An itinerant lifestyle is all very well, but it certainly is difficult to make plans for the future.

'He's going to go into Milton Keynes tomorrow to see if he can get work. We'll know a bit more then. OK?'

She nods.

I kiss her cheek and she grimaces. 'I'll see you in the morning. First thing. If you're tired, have a lie-in. I can organise everything in the kitchen.'

'Thank you.'

'Chin up,' I say to her. 'I know it's exhausting – I've been there. But at least you're busy. The phone never stops ringing and you're having to turn people away. It'll probably be as dead as a doornail after Christmas, so we've got to make hay while the sun shines.'

She looks at me, nonplussed. 'I have no idea what you talk about. Sun, hay, whatever. Doornails. Speak fucking English.'

'Go to bed,' I insist. Then I turn her round and point her towards the stairs. 'I'll lock the back door after me.'

So she does what I say without arguing and I notice that her step is heavy as she climbs the stairs.

I lock up, as promised, collect a small box of Christmas decorations that I put aside to add a little festive sparkle to the boat, then go back down to *The Dreamcatcher*. Danny is sprawled out on the sofa and he's poured me a glass of wine.

'Another one?' I stretch out on the sofa next to him and snuggle into his arms. 'I won't want to get up in the morning and I told Lija I'll be in early.' Nevertheless, I pick it up and drink.

'Is she OK?'

I shake my head. 'I think she's worried about us leaving again.' I cuddle in closer and he strokes my hair. 'She did this for me – buying the house and everything.' I resist the urge to emphasise EVERYTHING as Rainbow does. 'Part of me feels bad that I'm not around for her now.'

'We'll work something out,' Danny says. 'But, you're right, it's late and we should go to bed. I'm too tired to do complex thinking.'

'I need to Skype Edie,' I tell him. 'I haven't contacted her for weeks.' Danny doesn't point out that she hasn't taken the time to contact me either. 'She doesn't even know that we're back here.'

'It will only wind you up.'

'I've had three glasses of wine – maybe more – I'm feeling quite mellow.'

He laughs. 'Your sister will soon knock that out of you.'

'Quite probably. I should see if she's around though.'

Danny stands up. 'I'll take Diggery out for a constitutional while you call her. Come on, boy.'

The dog jumps up to join him and, together, they drop off the boat onto the canal path and head off into the darkness.

With a weary sigh, I pull the laptop towards me. At least we've got a decent signal here. I text Edie to see if she's there and she is, so we both log on. Moments later, her face is on my screen. There's a cigarette in one hand, not unusually, a large glass of wine in the other. Her gorgeous auburn hair is twisted up into an untidy knot and she's not wearing any make-up – most unlike Edie. She's wearing a black V-neck jumper that looks as if it might belong to Brandon.

'Hello, stranger,' is her opening gambit and, already, I feel a little of my goodwill towards her drain away.

My sister is what you might call 'high-maintenance'. I do love her very much, but I quite often struggle to like her. Despite that, I miss her in my life. She's my only living relative, joined by my dad's blood, and I can't let her go.

'Hello, Edie. I know it's been a while. I'm sorry about that.'

'I'm sure you've been very busy,' she says, crisply.

'I have,' I concede. 'I wanted to call you to let you know that we're back at Canal House. For the time being. Stan was ill and I dashed back to look after him.'

'Oh.' That sort of takes the wind out of her sails. 'That's very noble of you. Ever the good Samaritan, Fay? Eh?' I don't acknowledge my sister's slight or rise to the bait, so Edie adds, 'He's OK now?'

'On the mend. Thankfully. It was touch and go. Pneumonia.'

'Not good in someone Stan's age.'

'No. I think he'll be all right, though. He's a bit more frail, a little more unsteady on his feet, but managing.'

A siren wails. The sounds of New York city are a back-drop to our call.

'Are you staying in the house?' She looks understandably sheepish when she asks.

'I slept on Stan's sofa while he was poorly, but Danny's just got back so we're both on *The Dreamcatcher* now.'

'Still head over heels in love?' She sounds slightly bitter.

'Yes.' I'm not going to lie to make her feel better. 'What about you? How are things with Brandon?' Edie circles the periphery of his life hoping for crumbs of his affection, but I generally keep that opinion to myself for the sake of peace.

'No change,' she admits. I largely blame the pallor of her skin, the permanent dark shadows under her eyes on Brandon's inability to commit to his marriage or to Edie. Not that I absolve her though. She's a grown-up and can make her own choices. She's the one who chooses to wait on the whims of a married man. 'I'm a bit bored, if I'm honest. I should get a job or something.'

I know from Edie's track record in recent times that she probably won't. I just hope she won't burn through the money she got from the sale of the house. I thought it might put her in a better position, but it seems to have made no difference. Whatever Edie has earned, she's always spent it – and more. She wanted a Kardashian lifestyle on a minion's money. Now she has a lot of money in the bank yet still no focus in life. How sad.

'I thought it would be fun having money,' she says, 'but all my friends are at work. The days are quite long by myself. I'm even tired of shopping.'

Things must be bad.

'How many handbags do you *really* need?' she sighs.

'You sound so fed up.' I try to be sympathetic as she seems to have completely lost her way and that breaks my heart.

'Yeah.' She takes a drag of her cigarette and blows out the smoke. 'Can't deny it.' I wonder if she regrets her decision to sell the house now.

'What are you doing for Christmas this year?' It's always a sore subject, but I can't ignore it. I don't want Edie to end up on her own again and wish she'd organise to spend the day with friends or something. 'It'll be here before we know it.'

She rolls her eyes and grimaces. 'Don't remind me.'

'We're planning on staying here all over the holiday period. Lija's mad busy in the café – which is great, but it's a lot of work for her. I'm helping out as best I can. Danny's going into the city tomorrow to see if he can pick up some casual work.'

'I don't know how you cope,' she says, 'living hand to mouth.'

'Yes. It's not something I'd choose.' I can't help the small, barbed comment but resist pointing out that it was entirely her manipulation that put me in this position. Still, my life is so much happier than Edie's, despite having to budget every penny. 'You could come over.'

She swigs her wine before answering. 'I need to be here for Brandon. You know that.'

In case he can sneak away from his wife and kids for an hour. It makes me sick, but I bite my tongue.

'I should go, Edie. We've got a busy day tomorrow. I just wanted a quick catch-up.'

'Don't leave it so long to call me.' Surprisingly, she fills up with tears. She cuts a lonely figure and I hate to see it. 'I miss you, sis.'

'Of course I won't. I miss you too. We're a bit more settled now. Better Wi-Fi and all that.'

'OK.' I see a tear roll down her cheek.

'You'll be all right, Edie,' I try to reassure her. 'It will all work out fine.'

'I wish I had your optimistic outlook, Fay,' she says. 'Anyway, I'm going to drown my sorrows now.' She holds up her glass again.

I don't tell her not to drink too much or dabble with any dodgy substances because I know she doesn't appreciate it. Or listen. All I can do is try to support her.

Logging out, I sit in the quiet of the narrowboat, listening to the peaceful silence. An owl hoots in the trees and the breeze rustles the leaves. Opening the door, I step out into the well deck and look up at the night sky. It's cold out here, enough to make me shiver, but the moon is full and the stars are bright. I hear Danny walking down the towpath – coming home to me. He's whistling softly to himself, Diggery at his heel, and my heart swells. I think that I'm truly the happiest person in the world. I have a beautiful man who loves me and, right now, I wouldn't be anywhere else.

Chapter Eighteen

In my head, I was going to jump up, all raring to go. In reality, I savour being in Danny's arms and we lie in bed far longer than we should. The milky winter sun dares to peep through the crack in the curtains. The few narrowboats that are on the move on this cold and frosty morning rock *The Dreamcatcher* gently in their wake and I think that I would be happy to stay here for ever.

Eventually, I manage to force myself to sit up, but still can't bring myself to leave the warmth of his side. So I pull back the curtains to sit and watch the ducks go past on the water. Some of them have a nibble at the weed growing on the bottom of the boat and it sounds as if they're knocking to get in.

'I'm going to walk into Milton Keynes this morning,' Danny says, sleepily. 'There must be a job for me somewhere.'

'I'd like to come with you, if I can. Can you wait for an hour or so? I want to make a good start on today's teas for Lija, but I might be able to skip out for a short while after that. There are a few bits that I need too.'

'That would be nice. We could maybe grab a coffee together.' He pulls me closer to him. 'It's a long time since we've been on a date.'

'I don't think we've *ever* been on one. Not properly.'

'Really? I should put that right then.'

I turn to look at him. 'I'm happy exactly the way we are,' I say. 'I wanted to tell you that.'

He smiles lovingly at me. 'Good. I feel just the same.'

'You think I'm silly, don't you?' I feel self-conscious now. 'But I've spent so long feeling unloved that I count my lucky stars every day that I'm with you.'

'All I can say is that you're easily pleased.'

'Far from it,' I say and kiss Danny again. I press my body along the length of his.

'Don't start that, young lady,' Danny says, mock sternly. 'You'll be late for work and Lija will come banging on the roof of the boat.'

That makes me giggle. 'She would too.'

Danny climbs out of bed, looking as reluctant as I do. This is our little sanctuary and, the longer we live here, the harder it is to leave. Plus the sight of his naked body, lean and muscular, is really doing nothing to turn my mind to my working day.

'I'll put the kettle on,' he says. 'You can have first dibs on the hot water.'

When he's gone, I lie for a moment in the heat of his sheets, enjoying the scent of him on the pillow. When I can linger no longer, I haul myself out of bed and feel for my slippers on the floor. We have central heating on the boat, but it's slightly temperamental and, however warm the rest of the cabin is, the floor is always cold. I guess that's the downside of having your bottom permanently sitting in water. It makes me have a great empathy for ducks.

In the tiny shower cubicle, I stand stock-still and let the water flow over me. Then I change places with Danny – resisting the urge to stay in there with him. After two cups of strong coffee, I leave him to go and tinker with the engine while I head to the house.

As I walk up the garden, the clouds have mustered and the sun is hiding behind them. It starts to drizzle. The sort of drizzle that soaks you right through. Lija is already busy in the kitchen when I get there. I shake the rain from my hair and step inside, letting the warmth envelop me. There truly is no more comforting scent than baking bread and it fills the air now, telling me that Lija has already been working for a while.

'I was going to get us up and running this morning,' I remind her. 'Rainbow and I can cope with the breakfast shift. You were supposed to be having a lie-in.'

'I could not sleep,' she says. 'Too much to do.'

Putting my apron on, I ask, 'Where do you want me to start then?'

'Sandwiches.' She points at the fresh loaves piled up on the worktop. 'Make sandwiches. Lots of them.' So I set to.

A while later Stan comes in for breakfast and Lija makes him some toast, then he totters off again, picking up quite a pace with his walking frame now. Comparatively.

More customers arrive for breakfast and Lija turns to

cooking their orders while Rainbow serves them. For the rest of the morning we work efficiently together, me buttering bread like a thing possessed, Lija making pastry for a cranberry, mincemeat and apple lattice pie, covering herself with a dusting of flour and muttering as she goes. Rainbow looks after the customers in her own inimitable style. While I listen to the rhythm of her chatter, I make a sticky gingerbread bundt cake in a mould that is shaped like a ring of Christmas trees. Later, I'll ice it and sprinkle the top with some pomegranate seeds. Then Rainbow arrives and we continue to work quietly – principally because we can't get a word in edgeways.

'OMG,' she says, curls bouncing in excitement. 'I've just realised that it's NEARLY Christmas. Nan bought me an advent calendar and I've got a chocolate every day and EVERYTHING.'

To mark the occasion she's turned up today in a dress with a skater skirt that's covered in smiley Santa faces and has pinned up a handful of her curls in a red, sequinned bow on top of her head. She looks like a mad elf doll.

'Look,' she beams proudly, pointing at the bow, 'EBAY!' She does a little dance on the spot. Lija rolls her eyes. Our customers will love it.

'What are we going to do for pressies? I'm SO not organised. Are we having a SECRET SANTA present here? Are we? Are we? We should. I mean not, like, a LOT. Like, ten quid or SOMETHING but we should. Shouldn't we? We should. Definitely should. The best bit about Christmas is the giving. Although, actually, the REAL best bit is receiving. I think Zoella said that. Or someone.'

I don't know who Zoella is, but I daren't ask as then I'd be told more about her than I ever need to know.

So Lija and I work quietly for another hour or more while Rainbow trills away happily about the joys of Christmas and so much more. When I've polished off the pile of loaves and have an equal and equivalent pile of sandwiches, I wipe my hair away from my forehead with my sleeve. 'I'm done,' I say to Lija. 'Do you mind if I run into the city for an hour with Danny? Can you cope with the lunch rush? I'll be back in time for the afternoon tea service.'

'We can manage fine,' Rainbow answers before Lija can. 'I'm so happy today that I feel I could rule the WORLD.'

And wouldn't that be a sparkly place.

Lija glowers at me. 'What she said.'

Rainbow bounces into the dining room. 'Try not to kill her before I get back,' I whisper. 'Promise me.'

'Promise.' Lija is somewhat grudging. 'But I have fingers crossed behind back.'

'I won't be long.'

The slightly off-key sound of Rainbow singing 'Santa Claus is Coming to Town' drifts from the other room.

'It will feel like it,' Lija says.

With that, I leave them both to it and go in search of Danny.

I find him standing inside the *Maid of Merryweather*, scratching his head. Diggery barks hello. I climb down into the cabin.

'She's in a bad way,' I note.

'Just wondering where to start,' he admits. 'Turning this round is going to need some serious work.'

'And some serious cash to pay for it.'

'Yeah. Ain't that life.'

The smell of damp is terrible. Gone is the warm, wonderful scent of wood, replaced by a musty, unpleasant stench. The carpet squelches.

'It's all going to have to come out. She needs to be taken back to the shell.'

'I know. Sooner rather than later too.'

Danny scratches his head again. 'This rain isn't helping.' We both look in despair at the steady trickle of water running down the inside of the walls. 'What we need is a crisp, dry winter rather than our usual soggy one.'

There are dark and very threatening clouds overhead. Fat droplets of water run down the windows of the boat, unrelenting. Looks as if the rain has set in for the day. 'I'll start chanting for better weather.'

'Do one for a lottery win while you're at it.' He pulls me into an embrace.

'I'm free now,' I say as I lean my head against him. 'For a couple of hours. I've made enough sandwiches to go twice round the world.'

'Hmm, what shall we do?' Danny says, eyes twinkling.

'The plan was that we walk into the city centre.'

'Ah, that.' He lets me go. 'Ever practical.'

'We won't be able to eat, let alone renovate the *Maid of Merryweather*, if you don't get a job.' Lija's paying me cash in hand on an hourly rate, but it won't be enough to keep us both.

'Never a truer word spoken. Let's head towards Milton Keynes shopping centre then. I'll see what's on offer at a couple of places I've picked out there. Google tells me that there's a boatyard nearby too and I need a few bits for *The Dreamcatcher*.' He glances out at the rain again – a steady downpour now. 'We'll have to take a brolly, it's really starting to tip it down.'

'I'm sure Lija would lend us her car if we don't want to get soaked through.' Mine is currently missing a wing due to an unfortunate mishap, so isn't roadworthy, and we've no money to repair that either. It's tucked down the far side of the garage and I haven't yet got round to checking if the road tax is still valid.

'I don't like to ask too many favours of her,' Danny says. 'Besides, we're outdoorsy, boaty types now. A little bit of rain won't hurt us.'

'I'd forgotten that.'

He grins at me. 'The walk will do us good. We can go down the towpath, see what's changed while we've been away.'

So we go back to *The Dreamcatcher*, put on our wet weather gear and make Diggery lie in his bed, which he's distinctly unimpressed by. Then, hand in hand, we head along the towpath to Milton Keynes in search of work and the luxurious solace of a cup of expensive coffee.

Chapter Nineteen

We walk up through Campbell Park – a beautiful green oasis that links the Grand Union Canal to the vast, modern shopping centre. It's currently deserted due to the rain which has upgraded itself from downpour to driving. Danny and I have our hoods up, our heads down as we march determinedly up the hill from the canal.

'This is awful,' he says. 'Was it forecast to be this bad?'

'I don't know,' I admit. 'Since we've not been on the move, I haven't checked the weather as closely.'

When we hit the shopping centre, I push back my hood and wipe away the strands of wet hair that frame my face.

Danny says, 'We'll go our separate ways. When you're done come back to the Caffè Nero on the corner and we can catch up there. If I've got good news, I might even shout you a blueberry muffin.'

'OK. How long do you think you'll be?'

'Not sure. Shall we touch base in an hour?'

I nod. I've got a few bits and bobs I need to pick up but it's not going to take me too long.

'Cool.' With one last kiss, he disappears into the throng of festive shoppers.

The shopping centre is looking amazing. In the main hall there's a festive display featuring a Santa's Christmas Express train, filled with giggling children as it chugs round a landscape of igloos populated by perky penguins and polar bears. Christmas songs chirp out of the speakers. I lean against the picket fence that surrounds it and watch the children, wide-eyed and innocent, wrapped up in padded coats and knitted hats. How lovely. Their laughter lifts my heart. Surely, they bring a magic to Christmas that most of us somehow manage to lose as adults? The fairy lights sparkle, the noses of the reindeer flash red, the fake snow falls in wisps. I get that yearning again, that funny, unfamiliar feeling in the pit of my stomach – the pull of maternal longing. I want to be doing this with my own child one day.

Eventually, I tear myself away and let myself be carried along by the crowd of bustling shoppers. Most are laden down with bags, gifts for their loved ones. I dip in and out of the shops picking up what I need for the boat, and then I buy a few small gifts for Rainbow, Danny, Lija and Stan. Not much as my money won't stretch to extravagance. But I want to do what I can to make this a very special Christmas. It's been a difficult few years and we all deserve a celebration just for surviving.

An hour later and I've got all that I need for the time being. I text Danny and he replies that he has a few more shops to try and that he'll be another half-hour or more

126

yet. I tell him that I'll head back to Caffè Nero to wait. So I do, taking time to do some window shopping as I go, admiring the glitzy festive displays.

In the café, I order a cappuccino and find a table where I can watch the world go by. I gladly slip off my damp, steaming coat and try to rearrange my hair into some sort of style that won't frighten small children. I'm not sure I manage it.

Settling into my chair, I breathe a sigh of relief. Living on the canal has made me ill-prepared for all the hurly-burly of the shopping centre at Christmas time. Still, the coffee's lovely – a real treat, as, for once, it's made by someone else – and I enjoy sipping it through the froth. I'm sitting daydreaming and nursing my cup to me when a voice beside me says, 'Hello, Fay.'

It takes me a moment to place it. Which is really quite ridiculous when you think about it. 'Hello,' I answer. 'Fancy bumping into you.'

Anthony, my ex-partner, is standing there, red-faced and sweating. 'Doing a bit of Christmas shopping.' He flicks a thumb towards the mayhem outside the window. 'It's madness out there. Jolly hard work. Needed a bit of a boost.' He glances at the cup of cappuccino in his hand. 'Mind if I join you?'

I only hesitate slightly before I say, 'Be my guest.'

Anthony, it seems, doesn't notice my momentary reluctance and drops into the seat opposite me. For a second I wish I looked less ragged and that Anthony had caught me all dolled up to the nines. Then I realise that was *very* unlikely to ever happen and, now that I think about

127

it, I don't give a rat's arse what I look like to Anthony.

'I thought you were still off enjoying a life on the ocean wave.' He laughs at his own quip.

'We were,' I agree. 'I came back because Stan was poorly and I've been looking after him.'

'Oh no. Hope the old boy's all right now?'

'Yes, he's fine. Thank you.'

'Must be on his last legs though,' Anthony says, dabbing at the sweat on his brow with his paper napkin. 'Can't be far off getting his telegram from Her Maj.'

I look at him and wonder what I ever saw in him. There are days when I still feel as if I'm punching above my weight being with Danny – he could be with someone younger, more beautiful – but he chose me. Raggy hair, comely bottom and all. Yet I stare at Anthony and wonder how I could have been content to settle with someone like him.

'Stan's ninety-three and I'm hoping he's got a few more years yet. He's recovering nicely.' Thank God.

'You'll be on your way again soon, then?'

'We've not decided yet. We might stay put for a little while. If Danny can find work.'

Anthony frowns at the mention of Danny's name.

'Ah.' He busies himself stirring his coffee. 'Things going well there?'

I'm not certain I want to be getting onto this ground with my ex, but I say politely, 'Yes. Fine.'

'I'm not with Deborah any more,' he volunteers.

While we were still, supposedly, together, Anthony took up with a brunette bombshell from his handbell-ringing troupe, the Village Belles. She was as blowsy as I am mousy.

No wonder he had his head turned. But then I could hardly complain about his infidelity as my heart had already been given to Danny. And my body. Just the once. I try to hide my smile as I remember that wanton night and what a revelation it was to me.

I press my lips together. 'I'm so sorry to hear that.'

He shakes his head. 'It was for the best. She was too flighty for me.'

'Oh.'

There's a bitter little laugh before he says, 'She left me for the solicitor who was finalising her divorce. I thought she had to have a lot of meetings with him, but the whole thing had been quite acrimonious and, well, I'm very trusting by nature.'

I try not to laugh at that.

'He has a yacht in Southsea marina,' Anthony continues, 'the solicitor. A small one. Still, that apparently top-trumps membership of Woburn Golf Club.' He bristles at the thought and I can't help but smile. Some things don't change. He's as pompous and priggish as ever he was.

'I'm sorry to hear that.'

'It's only the Village Belles that are keeping me sane. My lovely ladies never let me down.'

I don't point out that, very briefly, Deborah the Deceitful was one of those ladies.

'We're entering our first competition this year,' he adds. 'National. Well, only in England. However, it would be a big one to land for our first foray into the competitive world of handbell championships. I have ambitions to be on the international circuit, but we'll have to see how we go.'

'I see. You've replaced Deborah?'

'Of course. With an older lady. One not prone to hysteria.'

'Lovely.'

'There's no one else in my personal life yet.' He fails to meet my eye when he says that. 'I had a go at one of those dating sites, but no joy.'

'That's seems to be the best bet, these days. Keep going.' I try to be encouraging. 'There'll be someone out there for you, I'm sure.'

'I might advertise for a young lover like yours.' He clearly can't resist a jibe.

'I can highly recommend it,' I say, calmly. Surely I'm allowed a dig or two as well. 'He'll be along in just a minute, in fact. You can say hello.'

Anthony bolts down his coffee. 'Must be going. Lots to do.'

'It's been nice to see you, Anthony.'

He stands up and fusses with the packages he has. Then he looks directly at me. 'You and I rubbed along quite nicely,' he says. 'If you ever change your mind, I'd be prepared to take you back.'

Once again, I try to smother my smile but there's a little shard of sadness in my heart for him. I think of how I feel about Danny – the love, the passion, the friendship, the laughter, the respect – and know that if I die tomorrow then I'd die happy as I know what true love feels like.

'Things would be different,' Anthony says, bashful now. 'You could take up golf. I'd be happy to introduce you as a member. If you had some lessons, of course.'

'Of course.'

'Well.' Anthony puffs up his chest. 'It's been good to see you, Fay.'

'It was good to see you too. Merry Christmas, Anthony.'

As he turns to leave, he adds, almost as an afterthought, 'If you ever wanted to take up handbell ringing – and you did once express an interest – then you'd be more than welcome in the Village Belles. As a beginner. You'd fit right in.'

'I'm sure I would.' The old Fay, perhaps, I think. But not the new me.

As he holds up a hand and walks away, I realise that Anthony really doesn't know me any more and probably never did.

Chapter Twenty

When Danny comes in ten minutes later, he throws himself into the seat next to me and plants a kiss on my cheek. Then he says, 'You look deep in thought.'

'I just had a coffee with Anthony.'

'Wow,' Danny says. '*The* Anthony?'

'The very same.'

'How did that go?'

'Weird,' I admit. 'Very weird. I find it hard to believe that I spent so many years with that man. It felt as if it was another lifetime, as if I didn't really know who he was at all.'

'Things change. People do.'

'Anthony hadn't changed at all. Or maybe he'd got even worse.' I shake my head. 'He said he'd take me back, if I ever changed my mind. We could play golf together and I could take up handbell ringing.'

Danny laughs and says, 'I can just see you playing at next year's canal festival. Actually, no I can't.'

'Good!'

'I'd better look after you then, if you have another offer.'

'I'm sure you don't have *too* much to worry about on that front,' I tease. 'I actually felt really sorry for him. Pity, really. It didn't work out with him and the lovely Deborah. Which is a shame. I'm sure he loved her. He's on his own again now.'

'He'll be fine, Fay,' Danny reassures me. 'People like that always are. You have to stop worrying about everyone. Anthony had his chance with you and messed it up. You're both different people now.'

'I know. It's hard to cut myself off completely when he was a part of my life for so long.'

Danny smiles at me. 'And that's why you're you.'

But he's right. I have more things to worry about than my ex being lonely. I put any thoughts of Anthony aside. 'How did the job hunting go?'

He shrugs. 'Not that great. Most of the seasonal posts have been taken. I've got a couple of application forms, though.' He brandishes them at me. 'One of them is for a trendy shop selling jeans. I wouldn't mind that.'

'You do wear denim very well,' I tell him.

'I'd probably be more at home in a jeans shop than at Marks and Spencers. They'd have to keep me in the back-room there.'

'You'll find something,' I reassure him. 'You're quite the most resourceful person I've ever met.' I fish for my purse. 'Let me get you a coffee.'

Danny jumps up. 'I'll go. Want another?'

'Please.'

'I'll see if we can run to a couple of treats too.'

I smile at him. 'Let's go mad.'

'Yeah,' he agrees. 'It is nearly Christmas, after all.'

So we enjoy our coffee together and Danny gets us two Christmas pastries studded with pistachios and cranberries and drizzled with white chocolate. I snap a quick photo to show Lija as a version of these would be fab for our café too. Then I stop short as I realise I called it 'our' café. It's not mine any more, it's hers.

'We should go.' Danny picks at the last few crumbs of his cake. 'Lija will think we've got lost.'

'It's going to be busy today.'

'If she doesn't need me, then I'll walk up to the boat-yard at Great Linford and see if they need a spare pair of hands. Lots of people put their boats in for repairs and repainting over the winter months and I'm a dab hand with both a spanner and a paintbrush, so you never know.'

We finish up and head out of the shopping centre, which is even busier than when we arrived. If people are tight for money, then there's no sign of it here.

The rain, still as heavy, is outdoing our umbrella and it makes us hurry. When we reach *The Dreamcatcher*, Danny kisses me and says, 'I'll carry on to the boatyard.'

'You'll be like a drowned rat when you get there. Why not dry off now and go tomorrow instead?'

'I want to strike while the iron's hot,' he says. 'I won't be long.'

'OK.' I watch as Danny, shoulders hunched, strides away down the towpath. I jump onto *The Dreamcatcher* and

Diggery goes into a frenzy, having cruelly been left alone for almost two hours. I bend down and cuddle him until he's calmed down. Then I dry my hair and, this time, do manage to tame it into respectability before I go to work.

Chapter Twenty-One

Diggery comes to work with me too. I couldn't bear to leave him by himself all afternoon. Those big brown eyes were looking at me in a very accusatory manner. Though he's not allowed in the kitchen while we're working, he can lie in the shelter of the veranda and watch the rain. We walk up the garden together and I'm glad that I've kept my boots on. The grass is absolutely sodden and big puddles are forming. Some of the path has disappeared beneath them. I can't remember it being this bad in a long time. 'This isn't much fun is it, lad?'

Digs barks his agreement.

I check the drive and that's starting to get pretty water-logged too. I don't want our customers to get their feet wet, but I can't think what else I can do for them. They'll have to pick their way through the puddles. When I get in I'll round up some umbrellas and I can rush out to greet people and keep them covered.

When I've settled Diggery by the back door, I go into the kitchen and slip off my boots. Rainbow and Lija are working away.

'OMG.' Rainbow shakes her curls indignantly. 'Wet or what? It's TOTALLY raining like TARANTULAS.'

'Tarantulas?'

'Torrential,' Lija translates.

'Oh. I don't know about making sandwiches,' I say, 'I think we need to build an ark.'

'That's when the unicorns drowned when Neil or WHATEVER wouldn't let them on the ship thingy,' Rainbow informs me. 'My nan told me.'

Lija and I exchange a glance. No idea.

'Have you checked upstairs for leaks?' I ask her. 'The roof has needed attention for years.'

'No,' she says.

'I'll get Danny to look up in the loft when he's back. You might need a bucket or two up there to catch the drips.'

I hunt out the umbrellas – there are still a few in the understairs cupboard that belonged to Miranda, and an old one of mine too. After that I check the dining room. Everything's nice and cosy in there. The Christmas tree lights are on and shining brightly. Rainbow has finished setting the tables and there's a silver Christmas cracker by each plate. The tables have a floral arrangement in the centre studded with silver and white pine cones. Pausing for just a few moments, I stand still and take a few deep breaths. Life rushes by at such a pace that it's sometimes difficult to stop and be in the moment. This looks lovely and Lija should be really proud of herself.

'A car's pulled up outside,' Lija shouts.

The first of our customers. Four elderly ladies. That's my brief meditation over with. I dash back to the kitchen and grab the biggest brolly. 'I'll go and escort them in.'

Outside, the rain is coming down like stair rods. Diggery is lying with his head resting on his paws, staring dolefully at the weather. He jumps up when he sees me. 'Stay here, boy. I won't be a minute.' But he ignores me completely and trots along at my heels.

The customers are tentatively opening their car door when they arrive and I hold the brolly up for them. It seems as though they've come already armed. 'I can hold this for you while you put your own umbrellas up.'

'I've had my hair done this morning, especially,' one lady says. 'I don't want to spoil it.'

I think how much nicer it would be if we had a crisp frost, a few wisps of gently falling snow. Torrential rain – or tarantula rain as I should now call it – never makes it feel festive. Still, I manage to get all of the ladies inside without too much damage to their hairstyles. After that, there's a steady flow of customers and the dining room is mad busy all afternoon. Rainbow holds the fort on service, while I dash in and out to help people out of their cars. The thing that worries me most is that there's no let-up at all. I've never seen the level of the canal this high and there are now rivulets of water running down the lane towards the house. Worrying. I haven't had time to check on Stan yet and I missed him at lunchtime as Rainbow took his soup round to him. So when I've escorted one group of customers inside, I nip back to his cottage while I'm togged up for the rain.

'All OK in here?' I ask.

'Snug as a bug in a rug,' Stan says, beaming. He's sitting in front of the log burner, which is roaring away, blanket over his knees. He's watching a black and white film on his television.

'Good. Don't you be venturing out in this weather. It's dreadful. I don't want you taking a tumble or getting wet through. The lane's like a stream.'

'I'm happy here. When this is finished,' he gestures at the film, 'I've got a good book and the radio. Sounds as if this part of the country is bearing the brunt of the weather. There are flood warnings all over the place.'

'Batten down the hatches, I think they're right for once. This shows no sign of letting up. I'll be back later with your supper.'

'Smashing.'

'But call me if you need anything.' I put his phone next to him. 'Anything at all.'

'Right-ho.'

I'm reluctant to leave him, though I have to say that he looks quite cosy. I glance down the garden as I make my way back and see the *Maid of Merryweather* looking very sorry for herself. We should get a tarpaulin or something to cover her. Though goodness only knows how much that would cost. I'll talk to Danny and see if he has any bright ideas. That roof could disintegrate entirely if this carries on.

The rest of the day speeds by, even though a couple of tables call to cancel due to the worsening weather which, at least, gives us a five-minute breather. When they're finished with their teas, I escort the customers back to their cars as they've finished, getting more concerned by the rising water all the time. As we're clearing up, Danny returns. He's soaked through to the skin. He stands and drips on the doormat.

'It's terrible out there,' he says. 'This rain is just getting heavier and heavier. Even the canal is overflowing in places. I've never seen that before. The sluice gates must be struggling to handle the volume of water.'

'I've been taking customers out to their cars all afternoon. The lane is really flooded.'

'Have you looked at the weather forecast?'

'We haven't had a chance,' I admit. 'But Stan said there were severe flood warnings for this area.'

'Great.'

Lija pulls her iPad towards her and taps away. 'Weather warning. Blah, blah, blah.' She turns the screen towards us. 'Bad shit all over.'

When I look at it over her shoulder, I can see that her assessment is fairly accurate.

'I wanted you to check in the loft, Danny,' I say. 'I'm worried there might be a couple of leaks.'

'I'll do that now.' He shrugs off his wet coat and kicks off his muddy boots, then heads upstairs.

'I'm sure we've got some wellies somewhere. I'll see if I can dig them out. We might be needing them at this rate.'

'I've got pink polka dot WELLIES,' Rainbow says. 'For festivals and WHATEVER. At home. In the cupboard. They're SO cute, I don't like getting them wet. In fact, I haven't ever got them wet. NEVER. LOL!'

140

With a bit of hunting, I find three pairs of wellies and dish them out. 'I'll go out and check on the lane,' I say.

'I will come with you.' Lija follows in my wake.

'I'll put the kettle on!' Rainbow calls after us.

Lija and I walk out of the garden, each step creating its own puddle. When we get to the drive, it's a disturbing sight that greets us. Rivers of water cascade down either side of the lane, they're carving their way down the drive and towards the house.

Lija's face is grim. 'Not good.'

'No.' I can only agree.

Even as we stand and watch, it's getting worse. Soon we're up to our ankles in water in some places. It's creeping towards the garage and, even worse, the house.

'Has flooded like this before?'

'No. Well, maybe once when I was a child. I seem to remember the bottom half of the garden being under water. I don't think I've ever seen the lane like this before though.' They've built a small estate of executive houses just across the road, so whether that's affected how the run-off water flows and it's channelled it towards us, I don't know. However, I do know that whatever's caused this, it's not good news for us.

Lija looks at me worriedly. 'What can we do?'

'I'm not sure. Let's go and have a talk to Danny.'

He comes into the kitchen as we do. 'Not good.' He shakes his head. 'There's half a dozen leaks upstairs already.'

'Shit,' Lija mutters.

'Have you got some buckets or big pans?' he asks.

'I will find them,' Lija says.

'There are buckets in the garage,' I tell him. 'Come outside. It will give you a chance to look at what's happening out there too.'

We all troop out again, even Rainbow who is TOTALLY not keen to get her hair wet. She hogs an umbrella to herself.

Danny blows out a worried breath and scratches his chin. 'OK. Let's round up what buckets and stuff we've got. If the rain eases off anytime soon, then we'll be all right. But if it keeps lashing it down, then we need to be prepared for the worst.'

We all head into the garage and the water follows us. Fighting our way through the cobwebs, Danny and I rummage about on the shelves at the back until we find the buckets we so need. We pass them to Lija and Rainbow. There are a couple of big paint kettles too. I wish I'd had a good sort out of this mess years ago. It was something I meant to get round to, but never did. I love the comforting, woody, musty smell in here – it reminds me of times spent with my dad. All his tools are still here and, at this moment, I'm so grateful for that. Danny is still going through the shelves piled with screwdrivers, hammers and goodness knows what else to see what might come in useful.

'There's some plastic sheeting.' I find it on one of the wooden racks. 'Hopefully, we won't need it, but I'll keep it to hand.' I have another look in case there's some big enough to cover the boat, but no such luck.

'OMG! MAJOR!' Rainbow exclaims. 'A bucket that MATCHES my wellies. Well, not THESE ones, OBVS, but the ones I've got at home. RESULT.'

I have no idea when or how a pink bucket found its way into Dad's garage, but clearly it's making Rainbow happy. 'I think maybe you should call your dad, Rainbow.' I lean on a spade, wondering if we could dig some sort of a trench with it to divert the water. 'If this gets any worse, he's going to struggle to get here to pick you up at all.'

'I'll stay,' she says. 'I'm not going to leave you like this, am I? DUH! I want to help.'

I'm not sure whether Rainbow will be a help or a hindrance, but there's no doubt we could do with an extra pair of hands and some cheery chatter.

'That's great. Thank you.'

'I'm like family and EVERYTHING,' she asserts. 'We sink, we sink TOGETHER.'

In truth, I was hoping for something a little more positive than that from her.

'We've got LOADS of cake too,' she reminds us. 'All our teeth might fall out, but we're not going to STARVE! LOL.'

'Let's take what we've got back to the house,' Danny says. 'We can lay it all out on the veranda. Then I'll go up into the loft to try to catch all the leaks before they do too much damage.'

'Good plan.' I squeeze Lija's shoulders. 'See, it's not too bad.' And I cross my fingers behind my back while I say it.

Chapter Twenty-Two

The water continues to rise, slowly but surely. Danny takes some of the buckets into the loft.

'I've managed to catch the worst of the leaks,' he says when he comes back down. 'For now. But if this doesn't let up, we could be fighting a losing battle.'

Lija says nothing, but grows a little paler.

'I thought we could take some of the stone from the rockery in the front garden and lay it out on the drive to try to divert the water away from the house.'

'It's worth a go,' Danny says. 'Anything is.'

The rockery was once Miranda's pride and joy, but when she took to her bed, sadly, it became overgrown. It's now more weed than plants. I used to have a token attempt at clearing it once in a while, but it's obvious that Lija hasn't touched it since I left. It looks even worse in the winter when the pretty, colourful alpine flowers are all dead and there's nothing but soil and brown, soggy remnants of plants.

'OMG. This is like being with ACTUAL Bear Grylls or SOMETHING,' Rainbow trills, clearly not quite appreciating the gravity of the situation. 'I can help. I got my Survival Badge in the Guides and EVERYTHING.'

'What did you have to do for that?' I ask, hoping that there might be something we can glean from her knowledge.

'I can't remember,' she says, after much eye-rolling. 'But I'm pretty sure I had to take my nail varnish off for it. RAD!'

'Did you camp?'

She thinks again. 'Nah. I'd have remembered that. I'm not that keen on nature. My nan says that more people get killed by COWS than by cars. Fancy that. I hate cows. But you only see them if you go into a field. So I don't go into fields. DUH! Did you know that you can kill someone if you drop an EGG off the top of the Empire State Building?'

'Your nan said,' Lija and I chorus.

Rainbow looks stunned. 'How did you know? OMG. You're like psychic and EVERYTHING.'

One day I would like to meet Rainbow's nana. But today we have slightly more pressing problems.

So we all gear up again and traipse outside. It's getting dark now and we work by the light from the garage. Danny hefts the stone from the rockery and we manhandle it as best we can into the drive, forming it into a line that curves away from the wall of the house and heads towards the garden. Soaked through, we take a breather from our toil. Rainbow looks half-drowned and her curls hang in rats' tails. All credit to her, she's worked like a Trojan.

For a while our little wall of rockery stones sways away the majority of the water and it looks as if my plan might work. But then, to our collective dismay, the water begins to find its way through any gaps in the stones and, soon, the muddy water is on either side of our rather ineffectual attempt at a barrier.

'Fuck,' Lija mutters.

I couldn't agree more.

'I'll take the car and go into town,' Danny says. 'The DIY sheds will still be open. I'll get as many sandbags as I can for flood defences.'

Lija digs into her pockets and then throws him the keys. 'You have money?'

'Enough,' he says.

'Be careful, the lane looks almost impassable,' I warn. The rivulets of water are certainly gathering in strength.

'I'll be fine,' he assures me. 'I'll try not to be too long.'

'What can we do while you're gone?'

'Move all that you can upstairs. Get anything valuable out of the way. Just in case. I'm hoping it won't come to that, but best to be prepared.'

'What about Stan?'

'I'll see how his cottage is doing as I go out. If it looks like he'll need them, I'll get him some sandbags too. He's a bit higher than us though, so he should be OK.'

'God, this is awful.'

Danny kisses me goodbye. 'See you as soon as I can.'

He jumps into the car, backs out of the drive and turns into the lane. The water is almost up to the sills, so he drives slowly. Even so, the wake from the movement washes the water over the stones, rendering all our good work futile.

'Oh, BUM,' Rainbow mutters and we all go back inside.

We spend the next hour carrying all the furniture that we can lift upstairs. We stack the chairs on top of the tables in the dining room and roll up all of the rugs that we can.

'What will we do about tomorrow's customers?' Lija says. 'Shall I ring round and cancel them?'

I chew at my lip. 'Let's wait for a while. We're all dry for now. Fingers crossed that it stays that way.'

As we're finishing moving the small items, I hear Lija's car in the drive. Danny is back. He's been gone much longer than I'd hoped and I rush into the kitchen to greet him.

'It's like Armageddon out there,' he says, looking drawn. 'I struggled to get back. Loads of the roads are flooded and the traffic is backing up now.'

'Oh, God.'

'I know. We're not the only ones up to our eyeballs in water.'

'Did you get some sandbags?'

He nods. 'Not as many as I wanted though. It looks like there's been a run on them and there were only a few left. I grabbed as many as I could and filled the car boot with as many packs of sand as I could manage too.'

Some of my panic ebbs away. 'That's a relief.'

'Not really.' His face is dark. 'Come and look at this.'

I slip on my boots and, taking my hand, he leads me outside. Carefully, we pick our way down the garden in

147

the gloom. The water has risen much further since I last looked and the canal has burst its banks. The bottom half of the lawn is completely under water and two ducks scoot about on its turbulent surface. Both *The Dreamcatcher* and the *Maid of Merryweather* are straining at their moorings. We'll have a good paddle to get back onto them.

'We'll have to move the boats, but it will have to wait,' Danny says. 'Hopefully, they'll hold for now. I think we're going to need these sandbags sooner rather than later.'

'All hands to the pump again.'

I take Stan a quick sandwich to tide him over and check that he's OK. The water is halfway up my wellingtons, but Stan has a solid garden wall which seems to be holding off the water, channelling it – for better or worse – towards Canal House. I tell him of our progress. 'It's still terrible out there, but Danny's brought sandbags to fill and stuff. We're going to get cracking now.'

'Can I help?' Stan says.

'No, love. You just sit tight. This is a bit of an ad hoc dinner, but I'll try to bring you something warm later.'

'Don't think about me,' he insists. 'Just protect yourselves and the house.'

'Will do.'

When I get back, Lija, Rainbow and Danny are filling sandbags under the shelter of the veranda and I join them. In better circumstances it might feel a bit like playing on the beach like we did when we were kids, but now it's just hard graft. It takes us an hour and still the water is rising. We lug them to the side of the house and Danny manoeuvres Lija's car so we can work by the light of the headlights. The water is still lapping at the sills and I'm not sure how we'll save the car from going under. We heave the sandbags into place, forming a low wall in an effort to divert the water away from the house and channel it down the garden. It's taller than our effort with the rockery stones and has fewer gaps. I keep my fingers crossed.

By some miracle, it works and the little river turns in a more friendly direction. We all stand and watch it, breathing a collective sigh of relief. It's getting late now – it must be ten o'clock – and we're all bone-tired.

'Time for tea!' Rainbow says. 'Yay!' Even she doesn't have the usual amount of enthusiasm in her voice.

We troop back into the kitchen, pulling off our boots and throwing our wet coats on the floor. I'll put the clothes dryer up in the utility room in a minute. But not now. First, I need some sustenance.

Lija wanders out of the kitchen and into the other room. I hear her cry out and bolt in after her, Danny hot on my heels.

She's standing in a puddle on the dining room floor. 'Is coming up through floorboards,' she wails. 'What to do now?'

'Oh, shit.' Danny runs a hand through his wet hair. The water is dirty and putrid. The smell is awful. 'Let's stack the tables against the far wall and take the chairs upstairs.' We all swing into action again, stacking and shifting until the main floor of the dining room is clear. The water is still seeping in, ominously. Soon the floor will be completely awash.

'I'll get what brooms we have. Can we sweep the water towards the French doors?'

'We need a pump,' Danny says. 'The ground must be completely saturated. I'm not sure that we're going to be able to stop this.'

'I've got a mop too.'

'Towels,' Lija says. 'I will get towels.'

So I boot and suit again and leg it to the garage where there's a choice of three brooms. I grab them all and bring them back, snatching the mop and bucket on my way. Danny and Rainbow are piling towels on the floor while Lija runs upstairs to find more.

'Here's the mop and bucket.' Rainbow takes it from me and sets to.

I go into the living room as no one's checked in here yet and, to my absolute dismay, the carpet in there is sodden too. My heart drops to my welly boots. Bloody hell. What now? I feel as if we're being assaulted on all sides. We're used to inclement weather in England, but this is beyond a joke. The rain is of biblical proportions and is coming at us from all sides – through the roofs, the walls and now the floor.

'Danny!'

He comes running. I stamp on the floor to show how squelchy it is. Water oozes round my boot.

He shakes his head, at a loss. 'We can't do anything in here other than save the furniture.'

'There's a pile of bricks behind the garage. Shall we bring some in so that we can put the sofa and chairs up on them? That might do it.'

'Good idea. I'll come with you. Rainbow and Lija can carry on mopping up in the dining room.'

So we head out into the deluge again and find the pile of bricks. We load up and haul them back into the house. When we've got a dozen or more, we stack them up and with much grunting and grumbling and some help from Lija and Rainbow, we lift the sofa onto the bricks. While they return to mopping and bailing out, Danny and I tackle the chairs in a similar manner.

'Is the kitchen the same?' Danny asks.

'Not yet. We'll have to keep our fingers crossed that it doesn't affect that too.'

'It's bound to,' is his conclusion and, in the next hour, he's proved right.

Chapter Twenty-Three

We're all exhausted when first light comes creeping through the window. The only good news that I can give you is that the rain has finally abated with the coming of the dawn. We're all sitting at the kitchen table, worn out. None of us went to bed or even grabbed a few winks and now I can hardly keep my eyes open. Exhaustion has given way to despair. We've worked together all night to keep the flood water under control. And we managed it. Sort of.

Currently, we're still sitting with our feet in an inch of water. The kitchen has quarry tiles on the floor and the water came in through those too but, thankfully, they should be all right when they dry out. However, the damage to the kitchen cupboards is much worse. The water will have soaked into the base boards and they'll need to be replaced, if not all the cupboards. The carpet in the living room is ruined, but I think we've salvaged the furniture.

It smells damp and terrible in there. The dining room floorboards will probably need replacing, but will hold for now if we can somehow dry them out. The water covered the skirting boards so they'll need renewing in all of the downstairs rooms too. I guess we'll have to wait for the view of the insurance assessor. Then a shard of terror strikes my heart.

'You are insured, aren't you, Lija?'

She nods her head. 'You think I am fool?'

'I was worried for a moment. It's easy to overlook these things.'

'I will call them.'

'Let me do it for you,' I say. 'You look shattered. Why don't you go and lie down for a bit? There's not much else we can do now.'

'I have to call all customers and cancel.' She looks close to tears.

I put my hand on her arm. 'We should be up and running by the end of the week. We'll all pitch in. It's not as bad as it looks.'

Rainbow, who has been strangely quiet, stands up and says, 'Tea. We all need more tea.'

'I'll second that,' Danny says.

She bustles about making tea and she piles some leftover cake on a plate – which is a great idea as I think every one of us is too tired to consider making anything else for breakfast. Even toast seems a step too far.

When Rainbow sits down again, we all sip our tea and tuck into slightly stale Victoria sponge for breakfast. As we missed dinner last night, it tastes flipping wonderful.

'I'll go back to *The Dreamcatcher*,' Danny says. 'I'll have a quick shower. I feel like I stink to high heaven.'

We probably all do. The water that comes up in a flood definitely isn't of the clear and sparkling variety. There was stuff floating in it that I couldn't bear to examine too closely.

'After that, I'll go into town and order some extra sand and bags to be delivered in case there's any more rain,' he adds. 'We only just had enough last night. I think without them it could have been a whole lot worse.'

He's probably right, but it's hard to look on the bright side at the moment.

'I'll help Lija here,' I say. 'I'll squeeze in a shower when we're done.'

'I'll have a look at the *Maid of Merryweather* before I go. See if she's sustained any more water damage.'

I'm sure she will have and that makes my heart even more sad. He pushes away from the table, gives me a stubbly kiss and then heads off.

'OMG,' Rainbow says when he's gone. 'I'm such a SKANK.' She sniffs at herself. 'Well ripe! POO. I bet this is what the ZOMBIES on *The Walking Dead* smell like. Zombies are DEAD but, like, not really DEAD.' She rolls her eyes, wondering at the mystery of zombies.

'You know that zombies aren't real,' I tell her.

'SERIOUSLY?'

'I'm pretty sure that *The Walking Dead* isn't a documentary.'

'Hahaha,' she laughs. 'Try telling RICK GRIMES that!'

'Zombies aside, I can't thank you enough. You've worked so hard,' I tell her. 'You've been great. We couldn't have managed without you.'

'Thank you,' Lija says. 'You are gold star employee.'

Rainbow beams with pride. 'OMG.' She's gone all giggly. 'This must be what it's like to get an OSCAR and EVERYTHING.'

Thankfully, she doesn't feel the need to launch into an acceptance speech.

'Do you want to call your dad soon to come and collect you? He'll probably be able to get through all right now.' Though we've yet to check the lane. I should go to look in on Stan too but, if he's managed to sleep, I don't want to wake him too early.

'Nah,' she says. 'I'll stay here and clean up. If that's all right?'

'It would be very kind of you,' I say. 'Go and have a lie down for an hour. I don't want you keeling over.'

'Cheers,' she says and bounces out of the room.

Despite the dark hours of the night, Rainbow is a bright spot. She makes me smile.

'What you grinning at?' Lija snarls.

'Oh, Rainbow. She's fun to have around.'

'Is bloody annoying,' she bats back.

'Don't say that. She's been a great help.'

Lija's expression says that she reluctantly agrees.

'I don't want you to worry,' I tell her. 'We'll soon be up and running again. This is just a little hiccup.'

She snorts.

'Look outside.' The sun is trying its level best to break through the clouds. 'It could be a lovely day. I'm sure the worst is over now.'

Lija glares at me, eyes bright with tears. 'Worst is not fucking over, Fay Optimist.' She wrings her hands and the tears run down her cheeks. 'I am up duff with baby.'

Chapter Twenty-Four

'When? How? What happened?' I'm trying to stop my chin hitting the rather soggy floor.

'How you think?' Lija gives me her trademark scowl. 'Usual way. Shagshagshag.'

'But who with?'

'Man on canal boat. Like Danny, but total shit.'

'Oh.'

'We did it here on table. Many times.'

I take my elbows off said table.

'While I was baking cupcakes,' she wails. 'I had buttercream where buttercream should not be.'

I didn't really need that image. 'Where is he now?'

'Gone.' She shrugs. 'Long gone. Good riddance to bad rubbish.' Lija puts her head in her hands. 'Shit. Now *I* am making silly sayings.'

'You loved him?'

Lija snorts. 'What is love?'

'Oh, Lija.' I go to hug her, but she holds up a hand.

'No hugging,' she snaps.

'Well. There's only one thing for it, then.' I revert to the typical British response in times of crisis. 'I think this requires more tea.' I make another pot even though I've just had three cups and all my insides are glugging with it.

I'm trying to stay calm for both of us, but my mind is whirring, whirring. I hadn't seen this one coming at all. Lija hasn't been quite herself since I've been here, but I thought it was because she was under pressure from running the café and paying the mortgage. I never imagined that she'd be pregnant. Neither did she, it seems.

When I've poured us out two more cups, Lija nurses hers to her chest. I feel that I daren't ask anything more.

'He was here two weeks, maybe three,' she says when she has finally managed to compose herself. 'All dreadlocks, torn T-shirts and six-pack.' She makes another disdainful noise. 'He fixed fence. Mowed lawn. Usual stuff.'

'He sounds nice.' Just like Danny. Apart from the dreadlocks.

I get The Look. 'You are unbelievable.'

'You didn't even mention him to me.' I feel slightly put out by that as I thought we talked about everything. Well, in the way that Lija does. 'What's his name?'

'Mog.'

'Short for?'

Lija frowns. 'Mog.'

'Oh, cool. Do you know where he is now?'

'Of course not.' Then she bursts into tears again. 'He

said he needed to move on and went. Just like that.' She clicks her fingers crossly.

'You've not got a mobile number for him?'

She nods, then wipes her nose on the back of her hand. 'He is not answering.'

Despite her previous protest, I move round to her side of the table and put my arms round her thin shoulders. She doesn't object. I give her the clean tissue from my pocket. 'Don't cry. Don't cry. It will be all right.'

'How?' she cries. 'I have no money. No man. No family. How will be all right?'

'You have us,' I remind her. 'We'll help.'

'You are off on boat. How will that help?'

'I don't know,' I admit. 'Not yet. It's a lot to take in. But we'll work something out.'

She cries some more. 'What I am going to do?'

'You're absolutely sure that you're pregnant?'

'Of course. Have done dozen tests,' she spits. 'Maybe more. All say same thing.'

'You didn't use any . . . er . . . *protection*?' I mouth the last word.

Lija shoots me a death stare. 'I am not stupid woman.'

I suppose these things aren't foolproof. 'Accidents happen,' I offer meekly.

'Yes. They fucking do,' Lija snaps.

'You've not seen a doctor yet?' She shakes her head. 'We'll have to sort that out then. Do you know how far gone you are?'

'Eleven weeks. Or twelve. Not sure.'

So it was literally just after Danny and I had left. I

wonder why she didn't tell me? She told me that it hadn't worked out with Ashley – who seemed so nice – for whatever reason, but she didn't say a word about anyone else. Perhaps she was feeling lonely and vulnerable as it's not like Lija to be taken in so easily.

'The baby is *definitely* Mog's?'

'Of course. Who else?'

'Ashley's?' I venture hesitantly.

Lija's shoulders sag. 'Is Mog's. We had one shag, *one* – maybe two – without condom.'

'Oh, Lija.'

'Do not "Oh, Lija",' she mimics. 'I know. I know. I missed two, three periods, but tried to ignore it.' She holds up a hand. 'Denial, whatever. Is very nice place to be.'

'So how long have you known?'

'Just before you came back.'

Yet she kept it to herself. Bless. She must have been terrified. I have to ask another tricky question, although I'm sure that I already know the answer. 'You're definitely planning on keeping the baby?'

'Yes! Is baby. *My* baby. How can I do anything else?'

'I only wanted to check that you'd considered other options. There's still time.'

'I am *keeping* baby.' Her little face is set in grim determination which makes me smile.

'Good to hear it,' I say. 'All we need to do now then is make a plan.'

She risks a teary smile. 'I like sound of plan. But is terrible time. I have café to run, loan to repay.'

'There's never a good time to have a baby.' I try to sound

160

reassuring. 'If you thought about all the pros and cons, then you'd never do it.' Though I'd rather Lija was in a settled relationship with a regular income, I'm sure we'll be able to work something out. People do, don't they? She's not the first young woman to find herself in this situation and I'm sure she won't be the last. 'This isn't the best of circumstances . . .'

'Huh. Tell me about it, wise woman.'

'But we'll get through it. Somehow.' She looks sceptical. 'We will. And there'll be no more lifting rockery stones or sofas for you, young lady.' I can't believe she did that in her condition. Part of her may well still be in denial about what the future holds. 'You've not told Stan or Rainbow yet?'

'No.'

At that moment, Rainbow bounces back into the kitchen. 'You've not told me what?'

I look at Lija for approval to spill the beans and she nods. 'Lija's going to have a baby.'

'OMG!!! Squeeeeeee!' Rainbow squeaks, even though the words are hardly out of my mouth. She does a little happy dance on the spot, jumping up and down, making her boobs and her curls bob alarmingly. 'AWESOME!! A baby! A FREAKING baby! Can I babysit? Can I babysit? Can I be Auntie Rainbow? Can I? Can I? I've never been anyone's auntie before! OMG! It's going to be a girl, I know it. AWESOME. I can buy her unicorn slippers and stuff from *Frozen* and EVERYTHING. We can put make-up on together! OMG! This is going to be AMAZING.' Rainbow runs round the kitchen fanning herself and then she remembers to hug Lija, who looks quite startled.

'Well, someone's happy,' I say. 'Think you could risk doing a little celebrating yourself?'

Lija tries a weak laugh and snot bubbles come out of her nose. However, her eyes are brighter and some of the strain has gone from her face. Rainbow contains her excitement enough to have a group hug and, despite my best assurances, I wonder exactly how we are going to cope with this.

Chapter Twenty-Five

I call the insurance company for Lija who will only speak to me after she's confirmed that I can sort this out for her. After that I contact the local doctors' surgery to register her. They tell me that she can download a form from their website and drop it in. I make an appointment for her. Rainbow is phoning round, explaining to the customers what has happened and trying to rebook their afternoon teas for next week when, by the love of God, we'll be up and running again.

Lija is still sitting at the kitchen table looking as if she's been poleaxed. I'm glad to be giving her good news. 'The insurance company are going to arrange for de-humidifiers and something that circulates air to dry the place out. They should be delivered later today and the assessor will be with us this afternoon too.' Can't beat that for service. I check my list. 'Plus you're booked in with the doctor next week for your first check-up.' I feel a flutter of excitement for her. A baby at Canal House. It's a long, long time since that happened. In fact, Edie was the last little one and it will be so nice to have a child here again. Then I realise that I very much sound like I'm planning on staying.

'Thank you, Fay.' In a rare burst of gratitude, she says, 'I do not know how I would manage without you.'

'Well, you won't have to.'

'Seems very real now I have said it out loud,' she admits. Her hand goes to her stomach and she strokes it. There's very little evidence of a bump, or I would have noticed, but there'll be one there soon enough.

'Shall we tell, Stan? I'm sure he'll be thrilled. It will give him a nice boost.'

'OK. Cat is out of bag as English person would say.'

I laugh at that. 'Do you want to come with me while I take him his breakfast?' I've already made up a little feast in the lunch box for him. I'm hoping that Stan has slept peacefully through the flooding and that he's been safe and sound in his house.

She pushes away from the table and puts her coat on. I hate the way she looks so drawn and burdened with worry. I link my arm through hers and we head towards Stan's house. The cold air makes us both wince and Lija pulls her coat tighter. The ground is still sodden and I have everything crossed that there's no more rain or we'll be in big trouble again. Surely, there can't be any more rain in the sky. It feels as if we've had a year's worth overnight. Thankfully, the forecast is for dry weather, but the temperatures are dropping steadily. If this freezes, then it will be like a skating rink out here. Just perfect for a ninety-three-year-old man and a pregnant lady.

I hold Lija more tightly and she turns to me, a tear rolling down her cheek.

'This is your first baby,' I say. 'You should be enjoying the experience. You need to be relaxing, not stressing.'

'Yes, excellent idea,' she says disdainfully, brushing aside her tear.

'Perhaps we could find a pregnancy yoga class for you?'

She looks at me, horrified. 'Fuck off.'

Ah, that's the Lija I know and love.

'You'll have to stop swearing when you have a baby,' I say. 'You don't want his or her first word to be a four-letter one. Unless it's Mama.'

Lija bites back another expletive with a 'Grrrr'. There's fear in her eyes when she adds, 'Everything will be different.'

'It will,' I agree with an excited squeeze of her arm. 'But in a good way.'

I shout a tentative 'Hello!' to Stan. Loud enough for him to hear, but not too loud in case he's still asleep. When he shouts back, I go and put the kettle on. I know it sounds silly, but every day that he's here feels like a bonus. I'm finding it hard to relax and accept that Stan is actually much better now.

Lija sets out his breakfast on a tray – a little bowl of fruit, two warm croissants with a pot of strawberry jam and some unsalted butter. I add a cup of tea and then we climb the stairs together.

Stan is sitting up in bed reading, a multicoloured

shawl draped around his shoulders. He's drawn the curtains and I look out of the window to check the damage to his garden. It doesn't look too bad. The water has obviously come halfway up Stan's garden too, given the line of weeds and detritus it's dumped, but has receded now.

I take his book from him and place the tray across his knees. Lija perches on the end of his bed. 'Nice warm croissants, old man.'

'Lovely,' he says. 'My favourite.'

'You survived the storm intact?' I ask. 'No leaks or anything?'

Stan shakes his head. 'Not as far as I'm aware. I was as snug as a bug in a rug, but it sounded terrible out there,' he notes as he tucks in. 'Everything all right with your house and the boats?'

'Not so great,' I admit. 'I haven't yet had a chance to check the boats, but Danny's down there now. Hopefully, they're OK. We did, however, spend all night clearing up in the house.' I can't stifle the yawn that comes. 'There was water everywhere, coming up through the floor even. We had a right night of it.'

'Oh, goodness,' Stan says. 'I nearly got up in the wee small hours to come over to see what was happening. The rain sounded biblical. I was very worried about how you were all coping.'

'I'm glad you didn't. You might have been swept away into the canal. Still, it can all be mended and the insurance company have it in hand now. They've been great. We've had to cancel the customers for the next few days, but we're hoping that the café will be up and running again as soon as possible. So long as we don't have any more rain.'

Stan reaches out a bony hand to Lija and I'm heartened to see that she takes it without flinching. 'You poor girl. No wonder you look so exhausted.'

I realise that I have yet to tell him about Lija's announcement and must do so straight away. 'Well . . . that's not the only reason Lija's tired. We also have some better news.' I give an encouraging nod, prompting her.

For a minute I think Lija's going to keep her lips sealed but then she looks at me uncertainly and blurts out, 'Am having bloody baby.'

'A baby?' Stan says in awe.

'Yes. Screaming, pooing baby.'

Now Stan tears up and starts me off again. Stan and I have a good blub. I pass him a clean handkerchief from his bedside table and he dabs his eyes.

'Everyone is crying,' Lija complains, crying. 'Stop it.'

'That's wonderful news,' Stan says. 'Wonderful. I do like a baby.'

'You will be sort of grandad, I suppose,' Lija says, grudgingly. 'Yes?'

'Oh, yes.' Stan looks thrilled. 'I should say so.'

'You'll be excellent grandad material, Stan.' I squeeze his hand.

'I never thought I'd see the day.' He is beside himself with joy. 'And when can we expect this lovely new arrival?'

Lija shrugs. 'I do not know. I will have to check with doctor. Next spring?'

'A spring baby,' Stan says. 'How lovely. I didn't even know you had a boyfriend. Did I miss something?'

'I do *not* have boyfriend,' she snaps. 'Is *big* problem.'

'Is *small* problem,' I correct. 'We'll sort it out.'

Lija tuts.

'It's very modern,' Stan says. 'Was it that nice boy Mog? I liked him.'

'You like everyone, old man!'

'You liked him too,' Stan observes. 'I might miss a lot, but I didn't miss that.'

Lija shuts up.

'He might come back,' I offer.

'He won't,' she snaps.

There's no point arguing. Even if he does by some chance come back, he may not be interested in his new-found status of impending parenthood.

I take Stan's tray now that he's finished with his breakfast. 'I'll send Danny up to give you a bath and a shave soon. Even though we're in a bit of a mess, do you want to come to the house for lunch today?'

'I could do with a little walk,' Stan says. 'Stretch my legs. If it's not too much trouble.'

'I'll come for you. It will depend on whether all the water has gone from the kitchen floor. But, all being well, we'll see you later then. Make sure you put some sturdy shoes on. Wellies if you've got them.'

'Very well done, Lija,' Stan says. 'Clever girl.'

'Nothing clever about finding yourself with bun in oven,' she mutters crossly.

Her turn of phrase makes me smile. Lija has obviously

decided if you can't beat them, join them. Then she stomps downstairs after me, swearing under her breath.

As we head back to the house, I ask, 'Can you do without me for an hour? I could do with going to go back to *The Dreamcatcher* to freshen up.'

'Yeah. Sure.'

'I won't be long. As soon as I'm back we'll start on the cleaning. I don't want you touching anything heavy.'

'I will sit here and cry.'

Kissing her forehead, I say, 'I don't want you to do that either. Try to relax. Go and have a little lie down or a nice bath. I'll be back before you know it.'

'Maybe I will do some mummy yoga,' she sneers.

'Great idea.' I grin at her, glad that she's getting her spark back.

I don't recognise some of the words that follow me as I walk down the garden. Some of them I do. Ouch. We're definitely going to have to work on her language or she's going to have the worst potty-mouthed kid on the planet.

Chapter Twenty-Six

Danny is coming out of the shower, towel low round his hips. I resist the urge to relieve him of it. He musses his wet hair. That's him styled for the day.

'Was everything all right here?'

'Yeah,' he says. 'Amazingly so. We've got a tight little ship. There don't seem to be any leaks at all.'

'And the *Maid of Merryweather*?'

He frowns at me. 'She hasn't fared so well.'

I sigh. 'Shall we go and examine the damage now?'

'Have your shower first. You look all in.'

'No doubt I smell of swamp water too.'

'And I thought it was Chanel No 5.' He grabs me round the waist and kisses me. 'You still feel good even though you smell like Stig of the Dump.'

'You and your Irish charm.'

'It's not going to get me anywhere today, right?'

'Absolutely. I'm going straight back up to the house to

help Lija clear up. The sooner we do that, the sooner we can book the customers in again. Assuming they'll risk rebooking. It's awful to have to let down people who want to enjoy their Christmas celebrations.'

'I'm sure they'll understand. People often rally round when this sort of thing happens. We can't be the only ones affected. I'll walk into town and see what sort of damage has been done there. I'll order some more sand and bags too – just in case.'

'God, I hope we won't need them. It's such a shame. Lija has been so busy. The Christmas afternoon teas are selling like a dream and were putting some much-needed cash in the bank. She'll need it even more now. As if the flood isn't enough to cope with.'

He looks puzzled and then I remember I still haven't told Danny of her bombshell. 'You missed out on one little development,' I tell him. 'When you left this morning, she told me that she's going to have a baby.'

'Ah,' Danny says. 'That explains a lot.'

'I knew she was keeping something to herself.'

'Is she pleased?'

'Not really. She wants the baby, but I think she's terrified too. There's no father around. He's someone from the canal, but he's long gone now. I guess it didn't work out as well as it did for you and me.'

'Poor Lija. She is going to keep the baby though?'

'Yes. She seems determined about that. She's going to need a lot of help.' I wait for him to chip in, but he doesn't. His forehead wrinkles as he looks deep in thought. 'I'm worried about leaving Stan too. I thought if we could stay until after Christmas then he'd be doing all right by then. She's yet to see the doctor, but we think the baby's due in spring sometime and that's when Lija's going to need me most.'

'Then I guess we'll be around here for a while.'

I hug him tightly and enjoy the feeling of his damp skin. 'I hoped that you'd say that.'

'She's family. What else can we do?'

'I want to do all I can to support her.'

'To be honest,' he says, 'I'm enjoying being back here. We can put roots down. I know it was my plan – *our* plan – to travel the waterways of Great Britain, but we can put that on hold.'

'I've loved our travelling too, but this is my home. I know that the house and café now belong to Lija, but I still feel emotionally tied to them. I couldn't bear to see her fail.'

He strokes my hair. 'I don't want you worrying either. You've had enough of that. We'll work something out.'

'Do I tell you enough how fabulous you are?'

'Yeah,' he says. 'But you can always tell me more. All we have to do now is ask Lija if she doesn't mind us living here at the bottom of her garden.'

'I'm sure she'll be overjoyed.'

'How will we tell?' he teases.

I laugh. 'Maybe her pregnancy will make her more emotional.'

'In a happy way, I hope. Otherwise, we'll have to hide all the knives.' Then Danny slaps my rump. 'Shower.'

'Have you left me any hot water?'

'Plenty. When you're done, we'll check out your boat too.'

So I strip off in our tiny bathroom and let the water run over me. There's nothing quite so reviving as a hot shower. Other than eight fabulous hours of sleep, of course.

When I'm dressed again, Danny and I walk along the jetty – which still has water lapping at its boards – to the *Maid of Merryweather* to survey how badly she's fared in the deluge. Diggery comes with us, trotting at Danny's heels. The water in the canal is caramel-coloured and even murkier than usual. It's moving quickly and Digs barks at two ducks that shoot by on the current. I think if they could give him the finger they would.

The level of the water in the cut has settled again now and, though it's still high, it's no longer burst over its bank or creeping up the garden. The jetty, however, is treacherous. One slip and we'd both be in the drink. Danny holds my hand as we gingerly walk along it.

We climb onto the *Maid of Merryweather* and Danny unlocks the cabin door. The sight that greets me is utterly heartbreaking. The bottom of the boat is entirely filled with water. How she's still afloat I don't know. I honestly think that there's more water in here than there is in the canal. We step down into it. The temperature of the freezing water seeps through my welly boots, turning my feet to ice in an instant. The rug and one of the cushions are floating in it. Part of the roof has sagged and there's water still dripping through even though it's long stopped raining. She's in an even worse state now than she was before.

173

'This is terrible.' I look around in dismay and feel close to tears again. Seriously, my eyeballs are going to fall out if I do any more crying. I wipe my cheeks on my fleece. 'Poor old girl.' I stroke the cupboard next to me and the wood feels all soggy. 'Is she going to have to be scrapped?'

'I don't know,' Danny admits. 'I thought I'd take a walk down to the boatyard and ask if they've got a pump we could borrow. They must have come across this before. I'm sure someone there will be able to advise us as well.'

She probably needs to be taken out of the water and put into dry dock if we've any chance of stopping the rot, but that's ruinously expensive and, currently, way beyond our reach. 'I hope we can save her.'

He pulls me to him. 'Me too.'

'I'm not going to get depressed about it now,' I say, trying to shake off my mood. 'Lija's troubles are far worse than mine. She needs me to be strong and positive.'

'We won't give up on the *Maid* though. Not yet.'

There's not much I can do here now, so I gird my loins and say, 'I'd better get back. There's a lot to do at the house.'

'I'll get going into town too, but I won't hang about. I'll come straight back to help you.'

'I'm sure when we get the dehumidifiers and whatever, then it will dry out quickly.' I wonder if the insurance company would notice if we brought them down here, but then I think that the *Maid of Merryweather* is far beyond dehumidifier stage.

174

Chapter Twenty-Seven

'Danny says that he's happy to stay here to help out,' I tell Lija and, instantly, I see some of the strain disappear from her young, troubled face.

'I am pleased,' she says.

'It will depend on him getting a job, of course. But that shouldn't be a problem. He's quite resourceful.'

'Good.'

'He's thrilled about the baby, you know.' Then I wonder if that's really true. In actual fact, he's said very little about it. Perhaps he's simply got more than enough on his plate to handle.

We set to with the cleaning. I won't let Lija do any of the heavy work, but Rainbow – bless her cotton socks – gets stuck in.

'OMG, this is EXACTLY like aerobics and EVERYTHING.' Rainbow whooshes the mop about. 'My nan's mad on exercise. She's on at me to go to Zumba with her, but I'm, like, TALK TO THE HAND, NANA!' She pauses to strike the pose of the gesture. 'Me and exercise are NOT mates! OMG, I'd properly DIE! I don't think you need to do exercising until you're about FORTY or something – like, really OLD – when everything goes slack and WHATEVER.' She carries on chattering and I zone out.

By lunchtime we've made good progress and the rooms still look damp, but we've cleared up from the worst of the flood water. Rainbow and I have thrown the rugs out into the garden and Danny will have to take them to the tip. It looks as if the floors will have to come up and the carpets need to be replaced. Even if they dry out, I'm sure they'll pong. The skirting boards are definitely beyond salvage too and some of the plaster will need patching. That's my assessment, anyway, as neither the assessor from the insurance company nor the promised dehumidifier or fans have turned up. I ring them and sit for half an hour listening to Bryan Adams singing 'Everything I Do' on a loop while on hold. Then I give up.

As the insurance company aren't playing ball, I go and get Stan. Lija's taken some soup out of the freezer and is warming it up. As the label has fallen off we're not entirely sure what it is, but it's vaguely carrot-coloured. We haven't made any fresh bread and yesterday's is feeling a bit stale, so she slices it thinly and puts it under the grill with some grated cheese on top to perk it up. The day is bright, crisp and there's very little evidence left of the devastation of yesterday. I don't know where all the water came from and I'm not exactly sure where it's gone either. Only a distinct tidemark of debris shows any evidence of where the water came up to in the garden.

Stan's all wrapped up in his overcoat. 'Do you want to sit out on the veranda to eat your lunch? You'll be sheltered there and I'm sure you're fed up of being stuck indoors.' I know how much he likes to sit outside in the summer. 'You're not to stay out too long though.'

'That would be lovely.'

So I settle him in the corner of the veranda at one of the little wrought iron tables and Lija brings him his soup.

'Looking better, old man,' she says.

'I'm feeling great. I could run a marathon!'

'Yeah,' Lija snorts. 'You could have fucking heart attack and die.'

'Flipping heart attack,' I correct.

'Fucking heart attack,' she insists.

'Flipping.'

'Fucking.'

I fold my arms to show that I mean business. 'Flipping, flipping, *flipping.*'

Lija holds up hers in surrender. 'Flipping, flipping, *flipping,*' she mimics.

I consider that progress.

'The soup's roasted sweet potato and carrot,' I tell Stan. I vaguely seem to remember Lija saying that she'd recently made a batch of that. 'Probably.'

'Oh,' he says. 'My favourite.' Then he winks at me. 'Probably.'

Whatever the flavour might be, I'm glad to see that he tucks in with relish. I sit beside him with my own soup and we eat in companionable silence. Even at this time of year, I still love the garden. Though a patio heater or a fire pit might improve the experience considerably.

Rainbow joins us. 'OMG. That was EPIC!'

'You've done a great job,' I tell her. 'Thank you.'

'No worries. I'm, like, one of the team and EVERTHING. It was, like, completely RAD staying over, like, camping and WHATEVER. Except I've got YESTERDAY'S pants on. AARGH! RANK! Dad's going to come and get me tonight though. My nan misses me when I'm not at home.'

I can imagine that. No matter what's going on, it's always sunny in Rainbow's world.

'You never talk about your mum.'

'She's gone,' Rainbow says. 'Not dead or nothing. She lives in Norfolk which Nan says is TOTALLY like being dead.'

'I'm sorry, I didn't know.'

Rainbow shrugs. 'She left my dad for another bloke. I don't remember it. I was only five. I can't even think what Mum looks like now unless I look at a photo of her and my dad hides those. I've got one that he doesn't know about. I keep it in a shoe at the back of my wardrobe, but it's all creased and whatever now. It probably doesn't even look like her any more.'

That makes me want to cry and I have to bite the tears down. But I feel them brim up on my lashes.

'Don't cry,' Rainbow says. 'It's all properly good. Really. There's just me and my dad and my nan. And my brother. And the dog. But that's cool. We all get on BRILLIANTLY.'

'Your dad never remarried?'

'Nah. He's REALLY old. I think he's like THIRTY-SEVEN or something.'

'Right.' Even Stan smiles at that. 'How old's your nana then?'

'*Well* ancient. She's nearly sixty. SIXTY. We're going to have a party next year for her – a proper BIG one – as she might not live much longer. OBVS.' She eats her soup with her little rosebud mouth. 'I hope she does though because she's really COOL. I tell her EVERYTHING. She's more like a mum than a nana. Well, I think so. Dad says she lets me get away with BLUE MURDER. I've no idea what that means.'

'You've never tried to contact your mum?'

'Nah. Dad would go MENTAL. Besides, she knows where I am. We still live in the same house and all that. She never even sends a birthday card or ANYTHING.' Rainbow's shrug says that the ways of the world are a mystery to her. 'Anyway, must get back to work.'

She bounces off.

'What a lovely young woman,' Stan says.

'Yes, isn't she?' I feel sad for Rainbow and for the mother who abandoned her. How much are they both missing out on? Stan finishes his lunch and I tidy up the bowls. 'Ready to go back home now? I don't want you getting cold.'

'I'll take myself,' he says. 'I can't have you running after me all the time, you've got enough to do.'

'The drive is still muddy. I don't want you falling.'

'I've got my stick.' He waves it at me. I note that Stan abandoned the walking frame as soon as he was able to. 'I'll take my time. Slowly, slowly.'

'I'll come and watch you until you get to the lane.' So I help him up and then follow him across the garden. True to his word, Stan goes at a snail's pace and I stand at the corner of the house and watch until he turns into the lane and towards his gate. He balances on his stick while he raises a hand and waves.

I go back inside and get on the phone again to the insurance company. Half an hour later, I've heard Tony Hadley singing 'True' more times than is good for anyone and have heard a robotic voice tell me that my call is important to them when, quite clearly, it isn't.

Then I talk to a young man called Sunil who politely tells me that Lija's last payment wasn't collected due to 'insufficient funds' in her bank account and that he's terribly sorry but the house isn't actually covered by their poxy insurance.

I try remonstrating with him. As far as I know Lija never had a letter or any communication about this and was labouring under the misapprehension that all was hunky-dory. Sunil might be polite, but he's also immovable. He insists that Lija had been informed. I hang up in frustration. It seems as if her protection has let her down once more.

Chapter Twenty-Eight

I sit on the stairs, head in hands, and wonder how I'm going to break this to Lija. She'll be devastated and I can't think of a way to wrap it up so that it sounds any better than it is.

When I finally summon up the courage to go back into the kitchen, Lija is busy wiping down the work surfaces.

I decide to go straight in, tell it like it is. 'I've got bad news, Lija.'

She pauses in her scrubbing. 'More?' One eyebrow raises. 'Don't tell me.'

'The insurance company say that the house isn't covered. It seems as if the last payment bounced.'

Lija's usually pale face goes deathly white.

'You didn't know?'

She shakes her head. I guess the letter could be some-where buried in the pile of paper she's been ignoring, but I think better of mentioning it. Lija takes a moment before she can speak and, when she does, her voice is shaky. 'What now?'

'Now it's down to us,' I say sadly. 'We'll have to rent some dehumidifiers. We need to get this place open again and fast. I'll put them on my credit card.' And keep my fingers crossed that we can find the money to pay for them when the bill comes in. 'I'll sort it out. I don't want you to worry.'

'Of course not,' she says sarcastically. 'I will put it right out of mind.'

She throws down the scrubbing brush and stomps upstairs. I shout 'Lija' after her but she completely ignores me. Her bedroom door slams. Probably best if I leave her alone for a little while, though my heart is breaking for her.

As it is, Lija comes down an hour later. Her eyes are red and swollen from crying, but neither of us mention it. I go to hug her, but she stiffens and backs away, so I let it go. I hand her the broom and she heads into the dining room without speaking.

When Danny comes back he, at least, has something good to tell us. 'Sorry I've been so long. Did you get my text?'

I admit that I haven't even checked my phone and I didn't hear it bing. 'No, I didn't.'

'I got a job,' he says. 'At the boatyard. I stayed down there helping them out. They're inundated with work at the moment and one of their guys has cut his hand badly. He's been signed off for a month. So his misfortune is my lucky break. They said they might keep me on even when he comes back they're so busy. I've just got to prove myself.'

'That's fantastic news. I'm sure you'll do fine.'

'It's a great boatyard. I asked them about the *Maid of Merryweather* too and they've said that if I can get her down there, I can put her into one of their old dry docks for the rest of the winter. She'll be out of the water then and undercover.'

'Really? They offered to do that? For nothing?'

'Yeah, but we'll buy all the stuff to repair her from them, so it goes both ways.'

'I can't believe they're being so kind.'

'I told them we were between a rock and a hard place. These guys are dedicated to the canal. They knew your dad and the *Maid*. They don't want to see a good boat lost any more than we do. Nevertheless, it's a very magnanimous gesture.'

'I'll say. I'm so grateful to them.'

Danny brandishes a bottle of wine. 'Thought we'd celebrate later. We need something to raise a glass to.'

'I think I'll need a drink tonight.'

'How's it going here?'

'Not so well.' I lower my voice. 'Lija hadn't paid the last instalment on her household insurance, so they're not honouring the policy. They say they wrote to let her know the payment had bounced but she seemed to be unaware of it.' I think of the mounting pile of admin again. 'Poor love is devastated.' I throw a glance towards the dining room. 'She's not a happy bunny. I've left her alone for a bit.'

'So, it's down to us?'

'Yes. I said we'd get in some dehumidifiers. We've done a pretty good job of clearing up. Rainbow has been a total star. There's some repair work needed but, if you don't look too closely, it will pass muster. It's even more important for us to reopen quickly to get some money in.'

'I'll head straight back into town, if you want me to. I'll have a quick ring round before I set off. I'm sure I can track one down.'

'That would be great. I'll give you my credit card. There's probably less on it than there is on yours.'

'Mine is pretty maxed out.'

I grimace. 'Mine too.'

Danny looks serious. 'We're getting really low on funds. Worryingly so.' He scratches his head. 'We could give up this idea of the itinerant lifestyle for the time being and I could try to get a job back in London. I've not been out of it too long. I still have contacts.'

'Hopefully, it won't come to that. I don't want you to go back to that. You hated it so much.'

'I know. It would feel like selling my soul again, but I can't think of another option. My talents are limited.'

I grin at him despite the gravity of our situation. 'I wouldn't say that.'

He manages a smile back. 'In certain areas,' he corrects. Then he's serious once more. 'Heading back into the City again might be worth it as a temporary measure. I can earn much more doing that and this house is going to take some serious money to put right.'

'That was always my worry when I lived here and now

poor Lija has inherited it from me.' She mustn't have had a survey done when she bought the house or it would surely have flagged up some of the remedial work that was so desperately needed.

'She'll be fine,' he says. 'She's not doing this on her own. We've got her back.'

'I know you'd enjoy working at the boatyard.'

'I would but that's not the be all and end all. The pay's not great and we need the cash right now.'

'I could get a job too.'

'Lija needs you here and she's paying you what she can. Let's see how it all pans out after Christmas. Everything else can be put on hold. Our priority is to open again.'

I wrap my arms round him. 'You're a very kind person.'

'Let me go and sort out a dehumidifier before the stores close. Then we'll go back to *The Dreamcatcher* and get rip-roaringly drunk.'

'On one bottle?'

His sigh acknowledges our alcohol-based shortcomings. 'We'll do our best. If one bottle isn't enough, we'll get drunk on love.'

'Sounds like a plan to me.'

When he leaves, I watch him making his way down the garden and then I go into the dining room. I find Lija curled up in the corner, crying.

'Oh, Lija. Don't cry, love. Hush now.' I sit down beside her, even though the floor is still quite damp, and take her in my arms. 'This isn't the end of the world. We'll sort it out, I'm sure. Danny's on the phone now trying to find a dehumidifier to hire. If he can get one, he'll go straight

185

into town to collect it. He'll be able to fix things like the skirting boards. It isn't insurmountable.'

But she doesn't stop crying. She just sobs in my arms. I've never seen her like this before. All her resilience has gone. So we sit on the floor together and I rock her until the tears eventually subside.

Chapter Twenty-Nine

Danny comes back with a monster-sized dehumidifier which he and I manhandle into the dining room with the help of Rainbow. When we switch it on it makes the noise of a large aeroplane taking off. I hope Lija has some earplugs as she's going to need them.

'OMG,' Rainbow says. 'Totally deafening or WHAT?'

We close the door on it and I cross my fingers, hoping that it does its job quickly and efficiently, even though the whirring din makes me feel as if we're standing on the end of a runway.

Lija returns from giving Stan his tea and, a few minutes later, Rainbow's dad comes for her and she gives us all a kiss and a squeeze before she goes, waving as she does.

Danny grins. 'She's a gem.'

'Would be nicer if she was *very quiet* gem,' Lija grumbles.

'We couldn't have managed without her,' I point out. If

she was my employee, I'd give her a bonus or a day or two off in lieu. Though, in fairness, Rainbow never seems to want to be away from here.

I don't like to leave Lija alone, so when Rainbow's gone, Danny and I stay and have supper with her. The cupboards are looking distinctly bare, but there are plenty of eggs so I whip up a few omelettes and grate a nub of blue cheese into them for some bite. To be honest, I don't think any of us are hungry. We're so tired we've gone beyond it.

Yet when I put the omelettes on the table, we all make a valiant stab at them. To help the meal along, we crack open the bottle of wine and I pour Lija a small glass. I know she shouldn't be drinking during pregnancy but she was knocking it back like it was going out of fashion the other night. I will talk to her about it, but now's really not the time. Poor girl has enough on her plate without me nagging her. I did notice that she's gone from smoking to vaping, and she's hardly doing that either, so that's another improvement. I think.

After we've finished, we sit there quite pleased with the result of our day's work but wondering exactly what happens next. I make coffee and we toss some ideas around, but nothing really fruitful comes of it. We're all too shattered to think and even a shot of caffeine fails to perk us up.

When Lija starts to yawn, I take that as our cue to leave. I'd stay here, but the bedrooms are too damp and leaky. Luckily, Lija's room has fared better than the others. We've had a fan heater running in there with the windows open to try to air it and take the chill off as this ancient central heating isn't the most efficient. I run upstairs to check how it is and all seems OK. Then I pop into what was my bedroom but there's still a steady drip in there that's half-filled a bucket today. I pick it up and throw the water out of the window, letting it run down the roof of the veranda to the garden, then position the bucket under the leak again. With one last check on the whirring dehumidifier, we're set to leave.

I kiss Lija goodnight and fret about her as Danny and I head back to *The Dreamcatcher*. It's cosy on here as Danny left the woodburner running. Diggery goes berserk when he sees us, as usual. I feel all my muscles relax when I climb on board and I hadn't realised just how tense I was. It's good to be home. The cold night can press in at the windows all it likes, the rain can try to beat us down, but in here we're safe and warm.

'Let's have another glass of wine,' Danny says. 'I'm too wired to sleep yet.' So he throws a couple of logs on the burner and opens another bottle. We curl up on the sofa together and one glass leads to two. I snuggle into him.

'You haven't said much about Lija's baby.' I top up Danny's glass again.

'I'm pleased for her,' he says. 'It's just going to be tough, that's all.'

'I know. But there's never a perfect time to have a baby. If anyone ever thought through the implications and waited until the ideal time, the human race would die out.'

'It would be nice if the guy was still around. That would help.' He raises an eyebrow. 'We're going to have to step in and do a lot for her.'

189

'I don't mind that. Do you?'

'No. I'd rather we were doing it for our own kid, though.'

I sit up at that. 'Really?'

'I haven't thought about it much in the past, but it's been on my mind recently. I'd like to be a dad one day.'

'You'd be a great father.' I can see Danny being cut from the mould of my own dad and that's no bad thing.

'I know we've never talked about having a family, but it would be good for us, wouldn't it?'

'It would be fabulous,' I agree. 'I didn't think it would ever happen. I'm ancient and my ovaries are probably like shrivelled up raisins. And we're as poor as church mice.'

'You just said that there's never a perfect time.'

'You're right.' Even through the haze of wine, I get a thrill of excitement. 'A baby Wilde-Merryweather. Wouldn't that be a thing? What if I'm too old? Could we even do it?'

Danny laughs. 'We should try *very* hard.' Then he takes my wine from my hand and kisses me deeply and my body aches for him. His strong hands stray under my shirt and I'm already lost. 'Starting right now.'

When we've kissed and kissed and kissed, he throws the rug and the cushions onto the floor. Still entwined, we tumble after them and make love on the rug, hot from the heat of the fire and our passion. We've been careful with our contraception so far, but not tonight. Tonight we're raw, wanton. It might be madness, but we both seem to want it. As he moves above me, face soft in pleasure, it reminds me of the first time we were together and I delight in his firm body and press his hips into mine.

When we're sated, Danny pulls the blanket over us and we fall asleep in each other's arms in the warm glow of our love and the fire. Diggery comes to nestle against my feet. I know that my back will give me merry hell in the morning from sleeping on the floor of the boat but, for now, I'm in seventh heaven.

Chapter Thirty

A week later and the café is open for business as usual. The diary is full with bookings and the mince-pie making machine – me – is cranking them out at full throttle. We're running the industrial-sized dehumidifier all night and that seems to be keeping the worst of the damp at bay. It still makes a horrendous racket though, so Lija is going to bed with cotton wool in her ears and, during the day when we have customers here, Danny and I wrestle it into the other room. I'm emptying litres and litres of water out of it every morning and I wonder how much longer we'll need it because it will have to go back soon due to the cost. It's over fifty quid a day to rent, but the upside is that's it's drying the place out like a dream.

Today, the frost is hard, the air freezing and it's a job to rouse myself from sleep. When I finally manage to sit up and look out of the window of the boat, the canal has thin patches of ice on the surface. The first time this year.

The overhanging trees are drooping low over the water, heavy with icicles. Lacy white cobwebs grace our windows. Even with the heating and the log burner going at full tilt, *The Dreamcatcher* is feeling chilly. I run out of the shower, shivering, and then make myself a quick piece of toast so that I can get cracking with baking as soon as I head up to the house.

Danny has been taken on at the boatyard and is loving it, even though it's hard, physical work. He's been getting up before six and walking along the towpath into work. At night he's not coming home until after seven or even later. This morning, he's going to try to take the *Maid of Merryweather* down into their boat dock. We've had no more rain since the deluge of last week, but the temperatures have dropped dramatically – the needle is barely above zero – and the weathermen are making ominous noises about snow.

It's still quite dark, dawn only just peeping over the horizon, and I stifle a yawn when I stand on the jetty with Diggery to watch Danny tinkering with her engine.

'Jump on the back and have a go at starting her, Fay,' he says, hands covered with oil. 'See what she does.'

What she does when I turn the key is cough, splutter and generally make a right old fuss. What she doesn't do is start. It's clear that our old lady isn't impressed at being so rudely roused from her lengthy slumber. I can't remember the last time she was moved in earnest.

'Come on, lovely,' I urge. 'You can do it.' Yet, disappointingly, the engine falters and dies once more.

Danny fiddles some more, then he shouts up. 'Give her another turn.'

This time she seems a bit more robust. Like Stan getting over his pneumonia, she sounds a bit rattly but steady. With one almighty cough, she conks out again. I hear Danny mutter, darkly.

'One last try,' he says. 'Then I'll have to see if we can get her towed.' He delves into the engine again, then shouts, 'Turn her over, Fay.'

I keep my fingers crossed as I turn the key and, despite a few wheezes, she sparks into life. After a few stutters and some alarming puffs of black smoke, the engine note settles and I do believe we've cracked it this time.

'Good girl.' I pat her side. 'I knew you could do it.'

Danny climbs onto the back with me, looking pleased with himself. 'I have the magic touch.'

'It works on all middle-aged ladies,' I assure him. 'Well done.'

He glances at his watch. 'Have you got time to cruise her to the boat dock?'

I shouldn't really as I know we have a lot on today and Lija will already be tapping her foot impatiently, but I can't resist the opportunity to cruise the *Maid* once more. I'll just have to face Lija's wrath. 'Oh, go on. I will.'

'Gently, gently,' he says. 'Don't rush her.'

So I ease the boat carefully away from the jetty. Diggery runs up and down barking, then jumps on board at the last minute. The thin ice creaks, cracks and parts for us. I keep the engine just above idling and we drift into the canal, inching our way forward.

'Nice work,' Danny says and leans back on the taff rail

behind us while I make micro-adjustments with the tiller. He slings a comforting arm round my shoulder.

The sun is venturing over the horizon now, reluctantly inching its way into the sky. The hoar frost takes on a lemon sheen as its rays reach out. I take my phone out and snap a photo as it would make a perfect Christmas card.

'This is beautiful.' I feel quite teary that the *Maid of Merryweather* is moving again, and through this magical landscape. I hope that this isn't her last journey and that Danny is able to repair her when we have the money. It feels as if we're taking her to the hospital for some major surgery – which she might pull through or might not. If it is to be her last journey, then it's a very lovely one.

Dad would hate to see the state that she's in but at least we're trying to salvage her. The boat is listing to one side slightly and feels fragile. I'd better not bump the lock as we go into it or she might break apart.

'She's doing all right,' Danny reassures me. 'There's plenty of life left in the old girl yet.'

'Like me,' I tease.

'Hmm,' he murmurs, gently kissing my neck. 'That was very unseemly behaviour for a lady of a certain age last night.'

I laugh. 'There's plenty more where that came from.'

'Glad to hear it, Ms Merryweather.' He pulls me to him and some of the chill of the day disappears.

There are a few new houses that have been built down by the canal. A row of pretty stone cottages. I peep inside as I pass by – a good view afforded by my elevated position.

They're all looking ready for Christmas with trees and lights in the windows. It makes me realise that I've still so much to do but there seem to be so many other things to think about. I could do with putting Christmas off for another month or two – I might just be ready then. But don't we always feel the same?

We negotiate the lock without incident, the only boat on the water at this hour, and a short while later arrive at the boatyard. With my heart in my mouth, I ease her into the boat dock. From here she'll be lifted to one of the covered dry docks so that she'll be protected from the elements for the rest of the winter. It's very kind of them to accommodate the *Maid of Merryweather* as I'm sure space is at a premium at this time of year. No wonder Danny is working all hours to show his gratitude.

I take a photo of the *Maid of Merryweather* for posterity. 'You'll be all right here,' I whisper to her. 'You'll be home before you know it.'

There's no one here yet but us, so Danny unlocks the Portakabin office and makes us a cup of tea. I drink from the chipped mug and my hands start to thaw out.

'I'd better get back,' I say as soon as I've drained the dregs. 'We've got a full house today.'

'I'll see you later.' Danny kisses me and I can tell that he's already itching to get to work.

I ruffle Diggery's ears and set off along the canal, humming the opening bars of 'White Christmas' as I go.

Chapter Thirty-One

When I get to the house, it's clear that Lija is not feeling festive but is very frazzled. She gives me a dark look for being late as I burst through the door, letting in a blast of cold air.

While I'm hurriedly tying my apron on, I say, 'Sorry, sorry, sorry. Danny and I had to get the *Maid of Merryweather* out of the water and down to the boat dock. I knew you'd understand.'

'Fucking canal,' Lija mutters into her scone mix.

If that's the worst of her anger, then I'll take it. I stand by her side and get stuck straight into preparing our cakes and sandwiches for the day. Rainbow is dispatched to give Stan his breakfast while we crack on.

I'd love to tell you that Lija's blooming in her pregnancy, but she isn't. She looks drawn and tired. Her face is as white as a sheet and she's got purple smudges beneath her eyes. I just want to give her a cuddle, but she's so prickly today that I daren't risk it. She'd probably take my head off.

Instead, I concentrate on making mince pies, then trays of cranberry-flavoured macarons. Lija makes gingerbread stars and we ice them with feathery designs and decorate them with silver dragées. She crashes and bangs the trays, yet, through it all, she hardly says a word.

Rainbow, of course, is blissfully unaware of the tension in the room. She puts on the Christmas music and cranks it up. Lija visibly winces. Singing away, Rainbow sets all the tables and prepares the cake stands.

Mid-morning, I can bear Lija's ill temper no longer and risk asking, 'Is everything OK?'

'Fucking Christmas,' Lija complains.

'I'm not sure that's the traditional sentiment.'

She gives me The Look again.

'It will be lovely,' I assure her. 'We'll all be here together.'

'Huh.'

That's not cutting it either. 'I'll do everything,' I tell her. Though I can hardly admit that I haven't made much in the way of plans yet. We're so busy that by the time Christmas comes we'll all just be fit to fall in a heap. Still, Lija doesn't need to know that. 'All you have to do is be here and put your feet up. I don't want you to lift a finger.'

She puts down the knife she's holding, quite emphatically, and turns to me. 'I am not keeping baby.'

'What?'

'I. Am. Not. Keeping. Baby.'

'Why? Why?' I feel as if she's knocked the stuffing out of me. 'Look, I know it's scary, Lija, but we can do it. Together. You won't be on your own.'

'Is my responsibility,' she says, tightly. 'No one else's.'

'I know that. Of course I do. You were so determined that you were going to keep the baby. What's changed?'

'This.' She looks round her. 'All this. I can hardly manage now. How will I cope with child on hip?'

'We'll all muck in.'

'*Muck in?*' She looks at me disdainfully.

'It means that we'll all pull together.'

'I *know* meaning. This is not problem. What when you go home to *The Dreamcatcher*? Who will "muck in" then? I will be alone. This is problem. What if you decide you might like to wander off again?'

'We won't. I promise. Danny has already said that he'd even look for a job in the City if we need the money.'

'Money,' she snorts. 'Don't even get me started on money. Is all pay, pay, pay. How will I have money for child?'

'This must seem insurmountable, but it isn't. We'll be your family. We'll be here for you. Danny is fully on board.'

'Now,' she snorts. 'What about down the road? When do you want your own life back? When child is one, two? Sooner than that?'

'We *want* to be involved. It will be lovely to have a child here.'

'I must do this alone or not at all. You saying nice things is not solution.'

'This is probably your hormones. You'll be in turmoil at the moment. It's no wonder that you feel vulnerable. If you won't listen to me, I urge you to go to the doctor and talk it through.'

'No.'

I go to speak again, but she puts her hand up to stop me.

199

'My mind is made up.' She snatches her knife again. 'Make sandwiches. This is your job. Not babysitter. Not nurse.'

'Think about it, carefully,' I beg. 'Don't rush into this, Lija. Take your time.'

'I do not *have* time.' She looks down at the tiny bump that's forming. She had a doctor's appointment booked this week which she cancelled, citing being too busy to take time away from the café. Now I wonder if it was something else. 'I have had many sleepless nights since flood. It was stupid to think I could be mother. I am stupid girl, in stupid situation. My decision is made.'

With that she resumes chopping, ferociously, and I can think of nothing that I can say to persuade her otherwise.

Chapter Thirty-Two

The alarm goes off and I reach out in the darkness to find it and shut it up. Beside me, Danny groans.

'It can't be morning yet,' he complains.

It's five o'clock and I risk a peek out of the window. There's a full moon and I can see that it's another hard frost outside. This winter is shaping up to be one of the coldest we've had for years and I'm grateful that we've actually got central heating on *The Dreamcatcher*, albeit a bit patchy in its efficiency. I nestle deeper into the duvet.

'Let's not go to work today,' I murmur. 'Let's stay here and make love all day.'

'Sounds very tempting.' Danny snuggles in closer. 'But we've had the credit card bill in for the dehumidifier and we don't have enough cash in the bank to pay for it.'

The noisy thing has gone back to the hire company now and it was worth every penny as it dried out the house a treat – at a cost though.

'Besides,' he adds, 'my boss might get a bit funny if I start to take duvet days.'

'I'd rather face your boss than Lija with a cake fork.'

'She's still no better?'

'No. Like a bear with a sore head. And a sore paw. And a sore EVERYTHING, as Rainbow would say. Lija's still absolutely adamant that she can't keep the baby, but she's very tight-lipped on the subject. I can't get her to open up to me at all. There's an appointment on the wall calendar for next week, but she hasn't told me what it's for. I'm dreading the worst.'

'You think it's for an abortion?'

'I hope not.' My heart is heavy when I think about it. 'I'll go with her, obviously. If that's what she wants, I'll support her. But I wish she'd trust us to be there for her.'

'Would you, in her situation? What if something happens to us? She'll be left, literally, holding the baby.'

'You think she's doing the right thing?'

'No,' he says. 'Though I can understand why she feels like that.'

'Why is life always so difficult?' I mutter.

Danny holds me tight. 'I'll bring you a cuppa in bed. That'll make you feel better.'

'Ah, tea,' I say. 'The universal cure for all ills.'

Reluctantly, he eases away from me and slides out of bed. Diggery instantly moves into his place, clearly relishing the warm spot.

Danny slips on his jeans and runs a hand through his hair. Working at the boatyard is dirty work and he's taken to having his shower when he comes home as the luxury of two showers a day is too hard on our water consumption.

I love to hear the sound of him pottering about in the galley and I lie there drifting in and out of sleep as he does. He brings me my tea back.

'It's really icy out there. The canal is frozen over. I'm glad we're not moving the boat at the moment. I'm not sure we'd even get out. We were lucky that we took the *Maid* to the yard yesterday.' Danny strokes my hair, tenderly. 'Be careful when you walk up the garden or on the towpath. It'll be treacherous underfoot.'

'You be careful too.'

He leans over and kisses me, his lips lingering. He pulls away with a reluctant sigh. 'I'd better go. There are boats to be stripped down, engines to be fiddled with.' He clicks his fingers at the dog. 'Are you coming too, boy?'

Diggery whimpers slightly as he leaves the warmth of the bed, but as soon as he drops to Danny's feet he's keen to get going.

'I'll stay late again tonight,' he says. 'Are you OK with that?'

'Yeah. I'll hang about at the house and keep Lija company. I don't like her to be by herself at the moment. When she's on her own, she's got too much time to think. That's a big house to rattle round in too.' I should know.

'The minute we've got Christmas out of the way and some money in the bank, I'll look at doing some repairs for her. That roof definitely needs attention sooner rather than later. If it snows, we're stuffed.'

'I love you,' I tell him.

'Love you too,' he says. 'Don't go falling back to sleep or Lija will have your guts for garters.'

I manage to rouse myself and stand in the shower, letting the hot water revive me. A few spots of scarlet blood in the water tell me that I've started my period and I am crushed with disappointment. I know it's silly of me, but after our night of passion where Danny and I were a little bit reckless, I had secretly hoped that we might have made a baby. I harboured the feeling that I had. Looks as if it's not to be. Anyway, at my great age, an absence of periods is probably more likely to signify the onset of menopause rather than a pregnancy.

Still, I shake myself down and tell myself there's no good brooding on it. You have to work with the cards that life deals you. I'm in love and have someone who loves me. I never thought I'd even have that not too long ago.

We've a lot to do today and I'm in the kitchen at the house for seven o'clock. Lija is already there, the oven up and running. The scent of vanilla is comforting on this cold day.

'Brrr,' I say as I close the door behind me. 'You don't want to be venturing out in that today. *The Dreamcatcher* is completely frozen in and the veranda's like a skating rink.' I pull off my coat and throw it on the hook. 'You're an early bird.'

'No sleep,' she says wearily.

Tentatively, I put my arms round her and she doesn't shrug me off. 'You look knackered. Take it easy today. Let me and Rainbow do the running around.'

'I can manage.'

'You don't have to. We're here. You don't get any extra points for being superwoman.' She sags slightly in my arms and I take that as compliance. 'Let's sit and take five together. We don't do that much any more. I'll make us some tea and toast.'

She sits without further protest and I make the promised breakfast. We sit and eat together, but there's not much chat. Lija looks as if she has the weight of the world on her shoulders and I wonder if she's thinking of the looming date on the calendar. I don't have the courage to raise the subject. I'm worried she'll think that I'm nagging her and will clam up even more. I'll just gently support her today even though she seems hell-bent on dealing with this alone.

Unusually, Rainbow is late to work. It's gone nine when she bursts through the door. 'OMG! Sorry I'm late. Flipping TRAFFIC! There are cars ALL OVER the place.' She does some sort of mad gesture with her hands. 'In ditches, hedges, fields and EVERYTHING. My dad skidded and slithered all the way here. He says people forget how to drive when there's ice on the road. I've never heard such LANGUAGE! I didn't know that my dad knew so many bad words. It took FOR EVER.' She pulls off a beanie hat and shakes the exuberance back into her curls. 'Still, I got here. PHEW! My nan says that in the olden days, when she was a girl, people used to skate on canals and whatever. MEGA! I bet we could skate on the canal today if we had any skates or something. COOL!'

She throws her coat and hat at the hooks and, miraculously, they land perfectly. She whips up her apron, ties it on and shouts, 'Rainbow Hesketh ready for business!'

That makes us both laugh.

'What?' She looks bemused.

'You never fail to cheer this place up,' I tell her.

'My nan says I have to be careful because I'm not everyone's cup of tea.'

'Well, you're certainly ours.'

'COOL.' She beams at us. 'What shall I start on?' she asks, ever willing. 'Sandwiches, cakes, whatever.'

Lija had tried out a recipe for stollen muffins bursting with diced marzipan, toasted almonds, sultanas, pistachio nuts and dried cherries – giving the classic German bake a contemporary twist. They were a big hit, so we're baking those again and they come out of the oven smelling of cinnamon and festive wonderfulness.

I make half a dozen chocolate logs, filled with *dulce de leche*, double cream and ginger, drizzled with white chocolate, decorated with sugar paste holly leaves. One calorie-laden cake that definitely goes straight to the waistline. But it's Christmas. Dieting is for January.

'I should start on the savouries,' Lija says, pushing herself away from the table. On the menu today are smoked salmon sandwiches with cream cheese studded with capers and sharpened with lemon zest, plus the usual turkey and cranberry with home-made clementine and fig stuffing. For the vegetarians we're trying chestnut and cranberry falafels with grated red cabbage and coriander in little wholemeal pitta pockets. Lija is making mini chicken and ham pies with chopped apricots and sage. No wonder our customers keep coming back for more.

She sighs. 'Another busy day ahead.'

I pat her hand. 'We'll get through it.'

Before we know it, the doors are open, our customers are arriving and it's all hands to the pump. The pies, sandwiches and cakes go out, the empty plates come back in a never-ending blur. It's six o'clock again by the time we draw breath and it's dark outside. The temperature hasn't hovered much above freezing all day and I do hope the ancient boiler keeps going all winter as the last thing we need is another unexpected big bill.

Rainbow is tidying up in the dining room now that the last of the customers has gone and, by some miracle, she's still bouncy and singing. Lija and I less so. I'm clearing up in the kitchen. My legs are aching, my feet throbbing. I don't think I've sat down since first thing. Neither has Lija, when it was my intention for her to take things easy. She looks dog tired, but we're very nearly done for the day. My brain is foggy from lack of tea and food in general. Despite our busy kitchen laden with food, I haven't even had time for a snatched sarnie.

Lija is sitting at the table, making a list for tomorrow so that we're ready for the onslaught again. As Christmas creeps ever closer, this isn't going to become any easier. I was hoping to get myself organised, but I think I'll do it all in a last-minute blast. It will probably work just as well.

'We're low on butter,' I tell her. 'I used up the last scrapings earlier.'

'Is plenty in the garage freezer,' she says.

'I'll go and get some.' I put down my J-cloth.

'I will go.'

'Check what else we're low on. We might need another run to Costco before Christmas.' As we're so busy, we're using up our store cupboard supplies at a rate of knots. 'Shall I come with you?'

The Look. 'I. Can. Manage.'

'OK. OK.' I grin at her. 'Ms Independent.'

She finishes her list, slips on her coat and heads towards the door.

I look down at her ballet pumps. 'You'll need your boots on.'

'Am going to garage, not up mountain.'

'It's slippy out there.'

'Whatever,' she throws over her shoulder.

'Be careful!'

I watch her slide as she steps onto the veranda and shake my head. Sometimes, that girl just won't be told. She rights herself and marches off towards the garage, head down, skinny arms pulling her coat around her.

Chapter Thirty-Three

I'm just turning back to my task when I hear a scream. She's fallen. Of course she has. I mutter a curse, and, not taking my own advice, rush outside, slithering as I go. At the end of the path, Lija is lying on the ground, holding her back.

'Are you OK?'

'Is stupid question,' she barks. 'I am on floor!'

'I mean are you hurting anywhere?' I put my arms out to help her up and she grabs onto me, but winces in pain. 'Did you go down heavily?'

She nods, tears in her eyes. 'I didn't see ice in dark.'

'Can you hold on to me?'

Lija takes hold of my arms and, between us, we manage to get her upright again. Sort of. She's bent over double, hands on her lower back.

'You'll probably have some nasty bruises tomorrow. Can you walk?'

I take her weight on my shoulder and Lija puts one foot in front of the other, but it's clear that it's a huge effort. She's limping badly, but I don't think it's her ankle. The pain seems to be radiating from her back which must have taken the brunt of the fall.

'Fuckfuckfuck,' she chunters under her breath as we make our way back to the kitchen. I don't think this is the moment to encourage her to say 'Flipflipflip' instead.

'Rainbow!' I shout as we get back indoors. She comes running.

'OMG! What happened?'

'She's had a fall,' I say, tightly. 'Pull a chair out and help me to get her coat off.'

Rainbow does as she's told without fuss. Together we strip off Lija's coat and try to help her towards a chair.

Lija pushes us off her. 'I am fine. I am fine.'

'I don't think you are,' Rainbow says, softly. 'You're bleeding.'

Sure enough, there's an alarmingly large bloodstain on the back of Lija's jeans. It's seeped through to her coat too, which I'd missed as, like most of Lija's wardrobe, it's black. My heart jumps to my mouth. The baby.

'Call an ambulance,' I tell Rainbow.

Lija opens her mouth.

'Don't say a word,' I instruct and she stays silent. 'You're going to hospital. Like it or not.'

Rainbow talks into her phone and then hangs up. 'Done. They'll be here in about fifteen minutes. Weather permitting.'

That's good news, but it's still going to feel like the longest fifteen minutes of my life.

We sit Lija down and I cuddle her. 'Hang on. They'll be with you soon.'

'I should go to bathroom and clean myself.'

'I don't want you tackling the stairs in case it makes things worse. Can you hold on?'

She nods and then sits grim-faced until we hear the sound of the ambulance coming down the lane, which isn't fifteen minutes, it's over an hour.

Eventually, when Rainbow has made two further phone calls stressing that we have an emergency, a couple of cheery women paramedics arrive, moan about the weather and then examine Lija all over.

'You've had a nasty tumble there, love,' one of them says. 'We'd best take you in. You can get checked over properly then.'

Lija doesn't protest when they bring a wheelchair and gently help her into it. I wrap my coat round her shoulders then grab my old gardening fleece from the hook and wear that myself.

'Can you lock up after us, Rainbow? I'm going to go with her.'

'Yeah, sure. Don't worry about nothing. I'm on the case. I'll take Stan his tea too and tell him what's happened.'

'Thank you. You're a love.'

'No worries. Hope everything's going to be OK.' Even Rainbow's usually sunny face is wearing a grim expression.

'I'm sure it will be.' But I'm not sure at all.

So they put Lija into the ambulance and I climb in beside her. As we set off, she clutches my hand.

'I do not want to lose my baby,' she weeps. 'Do not let them take my baby.'

'It'll be fine,' I say through gritted teeth. 'It'll all be absolutely fine.'

And, bumping down the lane, feeling every jolt as if it's magnified a million times, we head off to the hospital.

Chapter Thirty-Four

The A&E department is horrendously busy even at this hour. As it's December, it's mainly full of drunks who've had way too much Christmas spirit – probably at office parties – and I don't know how the staff bear it. They must be glad to see the back of Christmas. Despite the scrum, Lija is quickly taken through to a cubicle to see a doctor. I stay with her, holding her hand, until the young doctor arrives. He has a lovely calm air about him and I can see Lija relax visibly.

'Now then,' he says. 'I hear you've been doing some impromptu ice skating.'

'Was very stupid,' Lija says tearfully.

'Well, let's see what the damage is. I'm sure it's worse than it looks.'

I can only hope that he's right. While the doctor examines her, I step outside the cubicle. In the corridor, I call Danny.

'Hey,' he says. 'I'm going to be here late tonight. Still up to my elbows in grease. Don't cook for me.'

'I'm at the hospital,' I tell him. 'Lija's had a fall. She slipped on the ice.'

'Is she all right?' Even down the poor phone line, I can hear the concern in his voice.

'I hope so. She landed heavily on her back and started bleeding. We're worried that she's losing the baby.'

'Oh no. How is she coping?'

'She's tearful. Hoping that it's a false alarm.'

'Poor Lija. Do you want me to finish up here and go back to the house?'

'Rainbow's taking care of everything. Bless her, she's a good girl.'

'Just call me if you need me. Keep me posted. I'll leave as soon as I know you're coming back.'

However, I don't get back until much, much later. They keep Lija in hospital overnight for observation and we have a long wait for a bed. She is terrified.

'You'll be fine,' I assure her. 'The doctor said this was just a precaution. There's been no more bleeding. Better to lie here for a while than to come home and be worried.' I stroke her hair.

'I thought that I would be a very bad mother,' she sniffles. 'But now I do not want to lose my baby, Fay. I've been foolish.'

'All of this is a shock,' I sympathise. 'First, finding out that you're pregnant, then all the stuff with the house and the flood. It's enough to bring anyone to the end of their tether.'

'I cannot do it by myself,' she says. 'I need you, Fay. But what are you to me? Nice friend, yes. That is all. You are not even my sister.'

'It's probably pertinent to point out that you're a lot closer to me than my *actual* sister.'

'She is *total* cow,' Lija readily agrees.

We both laugh. 'We're an odd little family – you, me, Danny, Stan and now Rainbow – but we'll make it work for us. Danny and I are both really excited about your baby. We'll be the best auntie and uncle he or she could have.'

'You are kind person.'

'Have you told your family in Latvia yet?'

She shakes her head. 'I have not been in touch for many years. I moved here to get away. I do not want to go back there.'

'You might feel differently when the baby's born.'

'I must make preparations,' she says. 'No longer can I hide head in sand.'

'Let's get Christmas over with first and then we can really set to.'

She smiles a little at that.

'Try to have a good night's sleep. I'll be back first thing in the morning with some toiletries and clean clothes. I'll keep my phone on all night too. Ring me if there's anything you need or even if you just want a chat. I'll probably be awake worrying about you, anyway.'

'OK,' she says, still gripping onto my hand.

'I'll stay if you want me to.'

'Go. Go. I will be fine.'

215

So I kiss her forehead and head for home. I call a taxi and text Danny to say that I'm on my way. I take care as I walk down the garden to the boat as it's still freezing out here and we don't want another trip to A&E tonight.

When I climb aboard *The Dreamcatcher* I feel my soul settle. It's been a difficult night and I hope beyond hope that Lija's baby is going to be fine and that all she has to show for her ordeal is some cracking bruises. The cabin is warm and the kettle is already boiling. When Danny sees me, he opens his arms and I walk straight into them.

He strokes my hair. 'You look all in.'

'It's been a stressful few hours, but I think she's all right now.'

'The baby?'

'We'll have to wait and see. They're going to watch her overnight and give her an ultrasound scan in the morning. I hope to God everything's going to be OK.'

'Me too.'

He makes us tea and we sit on the sofa nursing it quietly, both of us lost in our thoughts – my mind still on Lija and the baby in the hospital.

Eventually, I turn to Danny. 'Penny for them.'

He sighs. 'I've been thinking that I should go down to London this weekend, pick up with some old contacts, see if there's any work around.'

'But you love being at the boatyard.'

'It's great,' he admits. 'However, what I earn isn't going to keep both of us and help Lija out with the baby.'

'You hated your old job. You hated what it did to you.' When I first met Danny he'd escaped from his City job

– call it burnout, or what you will. He felt it was destroying him and needed to get out. He was drinking heavily, dabbling with all manner of dodgy substances, living life in the fast lane and it was taking him to places that, morally, he wasn't happy with. I don't want him going back to that. 'We live in our happy little bubble here on the canal. It would feel like real life encroaching again.'

'I could earn more in a couple of months than I would in a year here. It's worth thinking about. It would be more cost effective if I stayed down there in the week and came home at weekends.'

'That sounds like a dreadful idea.' I hold him tighter. 'We'll need you here.'

'Hmm,' he says. 'How much do you need me?'

I laugh. 'A lot.'

So he kisses me and takes my sadness away. We make love in our snuggly little bed in our cosy cabin. The cold winter frost has breathed all over the windows, but it can't touch us in here. In here we're safe and warm, protected from the world. And I never want that to change.

Chapter Thirty-Five

The next day, our dear Rainbow steps up to the plate and takes control of the café while I go sliding down the country lanes and into the city to collect Lija from the hospital.

I find her sitting waiting for me in the reception. 'Are you OK?'

'I have had ultrasound scan and have been given a date for my baby.' She reels off a date. 'It seems very real now.'

'The baby's not harmed?'

'No. She is fine.'

'A little girl?'

Lija nods proudly and I clap my hands with delight which extracts a reluctant smile from my friend.

'The doctor says I must rest for few days.'

'I'll make sure that you do. Come on, let's get you home.' So I help her to the car and we drive back at a very sedate pace.

'You will not make Jenson Button worried,' Lija notes.

'I don't want to jiggle you and these lanes are lethal.'

She rolls her eyes, but doesn't make any further complaint. I crank the heating up in the car. Can't have her getting cold either. The sun hasn't even bothered to come out today. The sky is milky and a chill mist hangs low over the water and the garden.

At Canal House, Lija clings on to me as we walk to the kitchen and we both tense when we pass the spot where she slipped yesterday.

'Sensible shoes for you from now on,' I note.

'You are going to get on my nerves,' Lija snaps back.

Good to see that she's feeling better.

Rainbow is so excited to see us that she does a little dance. Her boobs and her curls bounce with joy. She's Diggery in human form. I'd texted her from the hospital to let her know that Lija was doing OK.

'OMG!' she shouts. 'You're back.'

'Yes, and we're going to look after her. Pull out a chair, Rainbow.' Lija sits down and I take her coat. 'Rainbow and I can manage perfectly well today. You should go and have a lie down.'

'I will.'

No protest. That's progress.

'Some brunch?'

Lija nods, gratefully.

We've got an hour or so until our first afternoon tea service and Rainbow has done a fantastic job of getting everything ready. Piles of sarnies on trays are stacked on the work surface. Today's cakes are good to go. We have

Christmas brownies topped with crushed amaretti biscuits, a sugared glacé cherry and a tiny chocolate truffle, plus a light honey and saffron Christmas cake. I could do with a slice of that myself. 'What would you like?'

'Bacon sandwich,' Lija says brightly. 'Am eating for two now.'

'One bacon buttie coming up.' Lija sits quietly listening to Rainbow's chatter while I go about making it.

'We can think about NAMES,' Rainbow says. 'What are you going to call her? GLITTER is a nice name.'

'I am not calling flipping baby *Glitter*,' Lija retorts.

'Sparkle?'

'No.'

'Twinkle?'

'No.'

'Moonbeam?'

'No.'

'Bubbles? Ocean? Sunshine?'

'No. No. No.'

A few minutes later, as I put Lija's bacon sandwich on the table and the name issue is still unresolved, the back door swings open, letting in an icy blast. All our heads swivel in unison. To say that you could knock me down with a feather is an understatement.

Our visitor stands there, arms aloft, and shouts, 'Surprise!'

It certainly is. We all look at our unexpected guest, stunned.

'Well, say something!'

'Omigod,' I say, borrowing from Rainbow.

'That will do for now.' My sister walks into the kitchen and wraps her arms round me. 'I thought I'd come for Christmas.'

'Wow,' is all I can manage. 'Wow.'

Edie is looking thinner than ever. She's wearing a white wrap coat – designer, no doubt – and red leather boots with heels as thin as needles. The suitcase at her feet is red leather too. Even I know the handbag over her arm would have cost more than I earn in a month – probably two. My sister always looks glossy, but there's something brittle about her too. Whatever the opposite of soft and cuddly is, that's Edie.

'You don't look pleased to see me,' Edie notes. 'Is this a bad time or something?'

'Your timing is impeccable.' As usual. 'Of course I'm pleased to see you. A phone call or text would have been nice though.'

'Spur of the moment,' Edie says, picking up one of Lija's bacon sarnies. My friend's face darkens. 'You know I like to be impulsive.'

I do. Only too well.

She flops down into a seat and proceeds to nibble at the bacon, discarding the bap. 'I'm knackered. Jet lag is exhausting. I'm a woman not in my own time zone.'

I pour her some tea and she inspects it disdainfully. 'I'm a coffee only girl.' She wrinkles her nose. 'That's what comes of living in New York. I've gone native.' Edie fluffs her long, auburn hair and strips off her white coat. She looks round for somewhere to hang it and, finding our cloakroom facilities lacking, she hands it to Rainbow.

Without complaint, Rainbow rushes off to the coat pegs. 'Any more bacon?'

Gritting my teeth, I put some more bacon under the grill. I should be pleased to see her, shouldn't I? My own true family member coming all this way to see me for Christmas. Yet I can't bring myself to say that I am. Instead, I ask, 'Where are you staying?'

'*Here,*' she says, looking at me as if I'm mad for even asking the question.

'In *Lija's* house?' I'm sure that even my thick-skinned sister will pick up the undertone in that. She was the one who inherited this house and then couldn't wait to get rid of it. She sold the only home she'd ever known from under her own feet. And mine. Lija was the one who stepped in to save it.

'Oh.' Edie looks slightly put out. She turns to Lija. 'That's OK, isn't it?'

'No,' Lija says.

Edie looks as if she's been slapped. I have to hide my smile. Lija's never one to beat about the bush. Even before the house debacle, there's never been any love lost between her and my sister.

'We've had a flood,' I interject before they start squaring up to each other. 'The roof's leaking and there are buckets everywhere upstairs catching drips. Your old bedroom is probably the worst affected.'

'So where are *you* staying?' my sister demands.

'On *The Dreamcatcher*. That's where I live.'

'Oh.' Edie takes a moment to compute that. 'That's where *I'll* stay then.'

I let out a laugh. 'Seriously? Have you any idea of the size of our spare cabin?' Not to mention that it's loaded up with our own stuff.

'What else can I do?'

'Check in to a hotel?' Though even I realise that at this, the busiest time of the year, there may not be any room left at the inn.

Edie looks aghast. 'You want me to spend Christmas in a hotel?'

'You're more than welcome to come and look at the room on the boat, but I'm sure you'll change your mind once you see it.' I glance at her designer suitcase. I've no idea where that thing will go.

'It'll be fine,' Edie says, breezily. 'I'm very adaptable.'

I hear my inward groan, but hope that I've not let it out. My sister is the most awkward and demanding person I know.

'I'll get Lija settled in bed and then I'll take you down there.'

'What's wrong with her?' Edie asks as if Lija's not there.

'It's a long story,' I explain. 'I'll fill you in later.'

Chapter Thirty-Six

'You are kidding me?' Edie says. She's standing at the door to our spare – and very tiny – cabin.

'I told you it was small.' It's also currently rammed full with stuff that we don't know what else to do with.

'Where will I put my case?' Edie looks aghast. 'Do you have a luggage room?'

I laugh. 'No. Of course not. This isn't the Ritz. What you see is what you get.'

She shakes her hair vehemently. 'I can't stay here.'

I shrug. 'And you can't stay with Lija either.'

'You asked me to come,' Edie reminds me. 'On the phone. You said "Come for Christmas".' She puts on a whiney voice. 'Now I'm here. Where did you think I was going to sleep?'

I have to admit that I didn't give it too much thought as I imagined hell would have to freeze over before Edie *actually* came for Christmas. 'I don't know,' I confess. 'If you'd given me some warning, I might have had a plan.' As it is, I don't. 'There are a few nice hotels in Milton Keynes which might still have some vacant rooms.' I keep my fingers crossed behind my back. 'Do you want me to call round for you?'

'No, no,' she says hastily. 'It will be nicer to stay with you. I came here so that I could have a family Christmas.' She glances disdainfully at the cabin again. 'Even if it isn't what I'm used to.'

The phrase 'Beggars can't be choosers' isn't far from my lips.

'You're going to move all this stuff out?'

'Well.' I look round at it. 'I suppose so.' Though quite where I'm going to put it, I'm not sure. The wardrobes in my old room are still full of my belongings and I hate to ask Lija for more storage space, but I'm not sure what else I can do. I think she'd rather have some of our excess baggage than Edie herself. 'Are you really certain that this is your best option?'

'I always used to love our holidays on the *Maid of Merryweather*.' She hugs me. 'It will be just like old times.'

For the record, Edie was like Miranda: she hated every moment she spent on the narrowboat.

'It'll be fun,' Edie says.

It won't. I can tell you that now. I'm not sure where this swift turnaround has come from either but, in the spirit of Christmas and familial bonds, I decide that Edie can stay and we'll make the best of it.

'I'd better get settled in,' she says, eyeing my piles of junk that currently grace the small, single cabin bed in a disdainful manner. 'I need to wash the flight away. Can I have a shower?'

'Yes, but you need to be quick. We have to ration water as it is, so no lingering in there. There's no en suite either. You'll have to share the one shower with us.'

She looks truly horrified. 'You're not selling this to me.'

'I'm not actually trying to,' I point out. 'I'm sharing the realities of canal living.'

'Joy,' Edie says, sarcastically.

For now, I scoop up an armful of spare clothing – mainly our waterproof gear – and, while Edie watches on, dump it on the bed in our cabin.

'Would you like to put the kettle on?' I say as sweetly as I can manage. 'There's no room service here either.'

'There's no need to be facetious, Fay,' my sister retorts but flounces into the galley and starts banging around in the cupboards.

Without her in the way, I move the rest of our gear out. The bed in here is very small – more like a bunk – and it's a good job that Edie is petite. I think her feet would hang over the end if it wasn't built into the wall. She'll have to keep her case on the bed when she wants to move around, and put it on the floor at night. That's how tight a squeeze it is. There's one long, thin cupboard and another one that's built over the bottom of the bed. There's storage under the bunk too, but that's rammed with tools for keeping the boat running and general maintenance so we can't farm those out.

I can't see Edie lasting long with us and, with all her money, I can't see why she would want to stay in such cramped conditions. She could book into a penthouse or something. It's nice that she wants to come back and spend a family Christmas with us for once – I can't remember when last she did that, but I'm also annoyed that with everything else going on she didn't think to give me any notice of her plans. The world always has to work round what Edie wants. Clearly, she had some romantic vision of what her return home would be like, but it's not to be.

Feeling less than gracious, I find some clean sheets and make the bed up for her. When I've done it, I look at my handiwork and am absolutely sure that she'd be happier in a hotel. The whistle on the kettle starts to blow so I smooth the duvet down and go to join her.

We sit by the warmth of the fire, nursing cups of tea. Edie has taken off the white coat again and has laid it across the only chair. Diggery is eyeing it as a possible cosy place to curl up. That would look great covered in dog hair. I'm sure Edie wouldn't mind at all.

'Come here, Digs.' I pat my knee, trying to avoid disaster. Obligingly, he jumps onto my lap.

Edie grimaces.

'He sleeps in your room,' I tease.

'He'd better bloody not.'

I think *The Dreamcatcher* is looking very pretty in its Christmas clothing. I've strung some fairy lights around the picture frames, along the top of the galley cupboards and outside in the well deck. The little tree that was in the loft has been squeezed into the corner of the sitting area. Some of my favourite old decorations grace its branches and I'm sure that Edie must recognise them from our childhood. If she does, she makes no comment.

I sigh. 'What *are* you doing back, Edie?'

'I told you. I thought it would be a nice surprise for me to be here for Christmas.'

I'm pretty sure that it's not simply a desire to spend Christmas with her nearest and dearest that has driven her across the ocean. I'm her only relative, of course. Technically, a half-sister. And it's fair to say that relations between us are somewhat strained. Perhaps she hopes this will smooth over the ripples.

'What's Brandon doing for Christmas?' I also know full well that this will have a bearing on Edie's decision to be here. Perhaps, as usual, he'll be spending it within the bosom of his family. He has, in the past, flown them all to Mauritius or Bali or somewhere equally exotic for the holiday period, while declaring undying love for Edie and his reluctance to spend any more time than necessary with his wife. A likely story.

'Brandon and I are going through a difficult time,' she says tightly.

'Oh.' That pulls me up short. 'You didn't mention it.'

'I don't tell you everything, Fay,' she snaps. 'I find you very judgemental.'

'Have you finally realised that he's never going to leave his wife for you?'

She turns and regards me with cool eyes. 'That's exactly the sort of comment I can do without.'

'I'm trying to be supportive, Edie. I'd love nothing more than for you to leave Brandon and move on. Then you'd have a chance of finding someone who's free to love you.'

'How *very* Mills and Boon,' she says.

'I mean it. Wouldn't you like a partner who could be with you all the time? You could settle down, have children?'

'Live on a knackered old boat?'

I don't take the bait. 'We love it on here,' I tell her. 'I know it's not everyone's cup of tea.' The cold weather is testing us sorely. We've yet to try to get out of the ice to pump out the loo and we can't last for much longer. That time will come even sooner with three of us on board. Oh joy. I haven't even told Danny yet that we've got a lodger. At least it will only be for a few weeks until after Christmas.

'I couldn't live in close proximity with anyone,' she announces.

'Well, at least you have the money to buy yourself a nice place.'

Edie snorts. 'It's a fortune for a shoebox in New York.'

'You could live somewhere else,' I suggest. 'Couldn't you? Now you're not so tied to Brandon.'

'Oh, I'm still tied to him,' Edie says, grimly. 'In ways that you couldn't begin to understand.'

And, though I try my level best to press her further, her lips are firmly sealed.

229

Chapter Thirty-Seven

Lija sleeps for the whole of the afternoon while Rainbow and I hold fort in the café. Despite our beautiful Christmas tree and all the lovely songs extolling the virtues of the season, I have lost my festive mood. I want to crash and bash things. I want to tell Andy Williams who's crooning 'The Most Wonderful Time of the Year' that he really has no idea!

Thank goodness Rainbow, with her preternaturally cheerful disposition, is oblivious to my black humour.

I left Edie on the boat sorting out her stuff and huffing and puffing at the inadequacy of our living arrangements and treating me as if she was doing me a favour by staying on *The Dreamcatcher*. I tell you, I was a hair's breadth away from ringing the nearest Premier Inn for her.

'OMG!' Rainbow says. 'Did you see *Celebrity Love Island* last night? Did you? Did you? That Kelly thingy, the one with the blonde dreads that was going out with that bloke from the band. You know the one. She snogged the face of David Do-Dah who used to be in *Holby City*. Or do I mean *Casualty*?'

I have no idea. 'We don't have a television on the boat, Rainbow.'

'OMG! No telly? How do you even manage?'

Even if we did have a telly, I still wouldn't have a clue who these people are that Rainbow chatters on about. I like to think I'd be watching worthy documentaries on BBC Two and old films starring Gene Kelly.

Rainbow is still aghast. 'What do you do all evening?'

I don't tell her that Danny and I read together or talk long into the night or make love. As Rainbow would say, 'TMI!' Though quite how that will pan out now that Edie is sharing our small space is anyone's guess.

'My nan says that I'll get SQUARE eyes from watching too much telly. Is that even possible? I've never seen anyone with square eyes and, like, LOADS of people watch telly now. LOADS.'

'Do you ever read a book?'

'Noooooooo!' Rainbow says as if I've asked her if she's planning to go to the moon sometime soon. I think I might add one to her Christmas present.

'Whatsername from *Geordie Shore*'s written one,' she says. 'I bet it's BRILLIANT. She's a right laugh, she is. I LOVE her.'

That should be the one then. I make a mental note.

'I'd LOVE to write a book. OMG! That would be AMAZEBALLS. Me, an AUTHOR. I could go on book tours and EVERYTHING. But I haven't done anything to write about. My nan says that EVERYONE'S got a book in them. I don't think I have. Though I could write a novel about mascara and EVERYTHING. I know about THAT.'

And on she goes. When I take Stan his tea, I'm feeling no better.

He's downstairs now and happily pottering about, no longer poorly enough to be spending his days in bed. On the surface, it looks like business as usual. Yet if I catch a glimpse of him while he thinks I'm not watching, then he's more frail, moves a little more slowly, is slightly unsteady on his feet. He lets me in and sits back down on his sofa, cosy in front of a roaring fire. He puts the film he's watching on pause.

'Do you want supper on your lap or at the table?' I ask.

'On my lap,' he says with a grin. 'I'm feeling rather decadent.'

'And why not?' I fix his meal in the tiny kitchen and carry it through to him. I take the lid off the little casserole pot and, as I put his tea tray down in front of him, say, 'Irish stew and a bit of soda bread.'

'Lovely.' Stan's eyes brighten. 'My favourite.'

The stew's been cooking all afternoon in the bottom of the oven and it smells mouth-wateringly good. I'll be taking some back to the boat for our dinner too.

I sit down next to him while he tucks in. 'We've got a visitor, Stan.'

He looks at me, quizzically.

'Edie's back.'

'Ah. The return of the prodigal sister.'

'Quite. I'm not exactly planning on killing a fatted calf to celebrate though. I'm struggling to try not to kill *her*.'

'Still not forgiven her for all her misdemeanours?'

'I guess not.' A lifetime of small misdemeanours, culminating in one great big one, is taking some getting over – even for me who is generally considered one of life's pushovers.

'I hope she makes it up to you.' He shakes his head. 'Poor Edie. She's a very misguided young lady.'

'That's one word for it,' I agree. Then I sigh. 'I want to love her, Stan, but she drives me bonkers. Now she's inveigled her way into living on the boat with me.' And I've still yet to tell Danny. 'Lija's refusing to have her in the house – and I can hardly blame her. How on earth will we cope?'

'She could stay here, if I had the room.'

'I wouldn't inflict her on you, Stan. She's a nightmare. You'd be on the sofa and she'd take your bed.'

He chuckles. 'You said she's been the same since she was a child.'

'I know. There'll never be any changing her.'

He pats my knee. 'You got all the nice genes, Fay. Be glad of that.'

'I just wish my sister wouldn't take advantage of it.'

'Don't let her come between you and Danny,' he warns. 'She's can be a troublemaker, that sister of yours. Keep a close eye on her.'

'I intend to.'

'I wish I could be of more help to you all. I'll be glad when it's spring again and I can come round to the café when I like and sit in the garden by the canal. I hate it that this cold weather is keeping me inside.'

'It'll be here before we know it. The baby too.'

'How's our lovely Lija doing?' he asks. 'I've been very worried about her.'

'She's fine,' I tell him. 'A bit traumatised. But they hope that the baby's going to be all right. It's looking OK, at the moment. Lija's been told to rest and she *actually* went to bed when we got back and didn't argue with me at all.'

'Perhaps she's growing up,' Stan says. 'She's lucky that she's got you to help her.'

'The baby's going to be a little girl,' I confide.

'How wonderful. Audrey and I would have loved to have a daughter.' He wipes a tear from his eye.

'I'm going to try to mollycoddle her so that she has a lovely pregnancy,' I say. 'If she'll let me.'

'Good luck with that one.' Stan puts his knife and fork down, wipes his mouth.

'Was that nice?'

'Delicious,' he says, appreciatively. 'You do look after me well.'

I take his tray and then kiss his cheek.

'I'd better be going. I'm hoping that Edie hasn't sunk *The Dreamcatcher* in my absence. Or sold it.' I wouldn't put anything past her.

Chapter Thirty-Eight

Danny comes home later. I hear the thump of his boots in the well deck before I see him and Diggery jumps down from the sofa to greet him. Edie, hogging the fire, turns to look what the noise is.

Danny's in the cabin door before I can head him off and explain.

'Hello,' he says when he sees Edie. 'This is an unexpected pleasure.'

For both of 'us, I want to add. I could also debate the word 'pleasure'.

'Here for Christmas,' she says. 'Sort of. I hope you don't mind me squeezing into your love nest.'

'No,' Danny says and almost sounds convincing. He looks weary and I can't help but wish that it was just the two of us.

'Hello, love. Long day?'

'Yeah.' He looks all in. 'I'd kiss you but I'm filthy.'

235

As Edie's here, I don't point out that I rather like the sound of a bit of filthy kissing. Instead, I ask, 'Do you want a shower before supper?'

'I need a good scrub down. I've been sanding crud off the bottom of a boat all day. I'm covered in paint, bitumen, weeds and probably duck poo.'

Edie wrinkles her nose. I don't suppose Brandon ever got his hands dirty in his life. My blood might not yet be boiling, but it's clearly at a slow simmer.

I borrowed a bottle of wine from Lija to smooth over the fact that Edie's here, but my sister is already tucking into it and there might not be any left for us if she carries on at the rate she's glugging it. 'I've had some Irish stew on the go all afternoon. That'll put a spring back in your step.'

'A taste of the old country,' he jokes. 'Smells great. Give me ten minutes.'

I follow him through to our cabin and close the door behind us. We squash together in the tiny space next to the bed. Danny leans against the wall and raises his eyebrows.

'I'm sorry,' I whisper. 'I've been meaning to text you all day, but I've had *so* much on.'

'What on earth is she doing here?'

'She turned up this morning. Completely out of the blue. I'd only just brought Lija home from the hospital.'

'Lija's OK?'

'Yes. Weepy. Tired. But otherwise she and the baby are unharmed.' I keep my fingers crossed as I say it.

'Thank goodness for that.'

'She won't let Edie stay at the house and I don't blame her. So it looks as if we're stuck with her.'

Danny lets out a weary sigh.

'I know. But she's my sister.'

'I can't forget what she did to you. The woman is a complete nightmare.'

'I know. I know. What can I do?'

'You could tell her to sling her hook. Most normal people would.'

'Do you want her to go? I'll tell her if you do.'

Danny softens and pulls me into his arms. He smells of burnt paint and there are black specks of bitumen stuck all over his face. He is, indeed, utterly filthy and I couldn't care less. All I need is to be in his arms and everything else in the world seems better.

'It's Christmas,' I remind him. 'Where would she go?'

'A hotel?'

'I've suggested that. She says that she wants to stay with us and have a family Christmas.'

He snorts. 'And you believe her?'

Now it's my turn to sigh. 'I'd like to.'

'She can stay until the new year,' he says, firmly. 'Then she has to find somewhere else. If she starts any messing about, then she'll have me to answer to. I'm immune to her charms.'

I know that she can twist me round her little finger. She used to do it to Dad too. He'd be horrified if he could see some of the things she gets up to now.

'We'll make the best of it,' he says. 'She's family.'

I kiss him. 'You're a lovely man.' Then I leave him to his shower and go to wrest the bottle from my sister before she swigs the lot.

Chapter Thirty-Nine

Dinner is a slightly strained affair. There's not much room in the cabin and Edie is perched awkwardly on the only chair. Even the warm glow of the Christmas lights fail to thaw the frosty atmosphere.

I offer Edie some bread. 'No carbs for me.' She screws up her face as if I'm offering her neat poison.

Clearly, even in the depths of a British winter, Edie would prefer to be eating edamame bean salad or something. Well, if she wants that, then she'll have to cook for herself. Danny is working at a hard, physical job and needs man-sized food.

After dinner, I wash up and, thankfully, Danny finds another bottle of wine in the depths of the cupboards – one I'd forgotten about. We share this one and, after a glass or two, I'm feeling distinctly more mellow.

The wine has loosened Edie's tongue too. 'I'm feeling so adrift,' she says. 'My life hasn't really panned out as I'd expected.'

'You've made bad choices,' Danny says. 'We all have. Now you need to sort yourself out.'

'If only it were so easy.' She tucks her knees under her and regards Danny through heavy-lidded eyes. If she starts flirting with him, I will, so help me God, kill her with my bare hands. 'I don't know what to do next.'

'I do,' I say. 'The wine has all gone. It's time we went to bed. Danny and I have both got a busy day ahead.'

'While I have more time on my hands than I know what to do with,' Edie finishes, tartly.

Danny locks up the cabin for the night and instructs Diggery to stay in his bed.

'I was thinking of Skyping some friends in New York,' Edie says.

'It's late. Go to bed.'

She holds up her hands. 'OK. OK. Your house. Your rules.'

'Yes.'

She tuts as she unfolds herself off the sofa. 'Night, night.' Then the sulky look goes from her face and is replaced by Lost Little Girl. 'Thank you both for having me. It really means a lot.'

'You're welcome.' I hug her and when I feel how thin she is, my heart softens. The trouble with Edie is that it's hard to stay mad at her for long. 'You can use the bathroom first.'

Edie heads off to her cabin and when we're by ourselves Danny says, 'That was fun.'

'Don't. It's going to be a tricky Christmas if it's like this. I feel as if I'm walking on eggshells with her.'

A few moments later, Danny and I go to our cabin and I hear Edie moving about in her own room, muttering. She bumps into the wall a few times and the resulting curses turn the air blue. I sit on the bed, head in hands. I thought she would be in the bathroom by now, but no. It takes a good ten minutes more before she heads there.

'She'll be in there for ages,' I complain.

'Hmm,' Danny says. 'How on earth can we amuse ourselves while we wait?' He slides a hand round my waist and lowers me to the bed.

'We can't,' I whisper. 'She's in the next room. She'll hear *everything*.' The walls are like paper and any movement rocks the boat. 'She'll *know*.'

'Then you'll have to be very, very quiet.' Before I can protest further, he strips off my clothes and his own, both stifling our giggles. His body is above me. 'Lie very still,' he breathes.

'Danny . . .'

'Ah!' He holds a finger to my lips to shush me. 'No talking.'

He moves, his skin against my skin, slowly, slowly, kissing me down from my face, my neck, my breasts, over my stomach and down, down. When a pleasurable moan escapes my lips, he puts a pillow over my face and we giggle some more.

Then he slides inside and moves torturously slowly, so as not to rock the boat. When I come, I swear that I try to be as quiet as a church mouse.

But Edie bangs on the wall and shouts. 'I can hear you! I can hear *everything*!'

240

Chapter Forty

In the morning, as I lie in Danny's arms, he says, 'I'm thinking of going into London at the weekend, if the boatyard can spare me. I'm going to hook up with some old contacts and see what's available, put my face around.'

I hold him tighter. 'I don't want you to.'

'I'm not that keen either,' he admits. 'But, if I can get a job, it would only be short term. I promise. I want to go in, hit it, stash some cash behind us and dive out again before it destroys my soul.'

'Getting *The Dreamcatcher* was your new start away from that life,' I remind him. 'I know how much you hated it.'

'I loathed every second,' he agrees. 'Lija's going to need our help, though, and our credit card bills are climbing steadily.'

I sigh and burrow down. 'Why is life always so complicated?'

'At the moment, we're always fighting fires. If I can bag a short-term contract, it will help us to get ahead of the game.'

'Swear to me that you won't get sucked into that life again.' It worries me that Danny might discover that life is too quiet and settled for him here. I know that he used to be quite the party animal and why not? He's young and there's still a laddish streak inside him that he's buried since he's been on the canal. Maybe it needs to resurface every now and again. I deflect my concerns by adding, 'I'd rather be poor than have you ground down by your job.'

For the first time in our relationship, I'm anxious.

'I know.' He eases away from me. 'I'll just put my toe in the water. I'd do it for six months max. It would be worth it for the money. I'll call Henry later.'

That's one of Danny's old colleagues. I met him briefly at the canal festival in the summer along with his partner Laura and another friend, Sienna. I hated them all, instantly. They were young, beautiful, moneyed, city-slick and supremely confident. All that I am not. My stomach tightens at the memory.

Sienna's name tells you all that you need to know about her. She's slender, pretty and successful – legs that go up to her armpits, and teeth from a toothpaste advert. Her long, glossy blonde hair is a marketing man's dream and she has a penchant for minimal clothing. She and Danny have 'history' and when I first clapped eyes on her, it was the first time in my life that I experienced raw, green-eyed jealousy. He said that they never had a relationship as such but used to sleep together if they stayed over in the same hotel whenever they were working away. I suspect that Sienna may well have wanted more. Even now the thought of it makes me feel slightly sick. If I close my eyes, I can picture them together and that's not an image I want. I've never had casual sex in my rather dull life and it terrifies me that, if Danny gets back in with that crowd, he might want that buzz again.

'However, now we have our current jobs to go to,' he says. 'Can't stay here snuggling up all day with you.'

I can't even promise him a day in bed at the weekend as we're both working seven days a week in the final push to Christmas. 'It would be nice though.'

'Yeah.' He flicks a thumb towards Edie's cabin. 'But our new lodger might complain if we stay in bed all day.'

I sigh. I expect our new lodger will complain about many, many things during her short stay here. Perhaps one night in her tiny, single bunk will have her frantically phoning round hotels this morning.

Danny and I get dressed. In the galley we stand leaning against the counter while we eat a couple of slices of toast and throw down some tea, whispering to each other so as not to disturb our guest. Poor Diggery has no idea why he's being shushed so much.

On the jetty, Danny takes me in his arms and kisses me. It seems strange that there's a yawning gap now where my dad's narrowboat used to be moored. 'Have you made any progress on the *Maid of Merryweather*?'

'Nah,' Danny says. 'Too busy. Not enough cash.'

'Same old story.'

He shrugs. 'We'll do it one day. For now, she's sheltered and dry.'

'For which I'm very grateful.'

'How grateful?' he teases, stealing another kiss.

It's a bitterly cold morning, the wind cutting through us like a knife. The sky is white, ominously heavy with the threat of snow that's been forecast for days now. The trees along the canal are mere shadows in the grey light of dawn. I shiver and Danny pulls me closer. The only plus side with the weather is that at least it's not raining.

'I'll see you later.' Danny kisses my nose and, with one last squeeze, breaks away, ready to head off along the canal.

'Have a good day.'

He clicks for Diggery and sets off at a stride, hands stuffed in his pockets against the cold. I watch him go and think that I could not love this man more. When he's out of sight, I turn and head towards the house.

Lija is at the kitchen table nursing a black coffee.

'How are you feeling today?' I hang my coat and try to shake the cold from my bones.

'Like shit,' she says.

'Rainbow and I can cope,' I say. 'Go back to bed for a couple of hours.'

She looks like she might be about to crack but, instead, she shakes her head. 'We are too busy.'

'Sit here and supervise, then. I don't want you rushing about today.' My fears about the baby remain unspoken. 'We'll find you some sitting-down jobs to do. You could decorate the macarons and stuff.'

'I cannot sit down for next six months,' Lija points out.

'I know. But you can sit down for the new few days.

Until everything's settled again. That's what the doctor ordered. I'm only following instructions.'

She gives me a slow and resigned smile. 'Better get baking with the mince pies then, bossy woman.'

I tie on my apron. After the Christmas rush dies down, I realise that I might need to find another job. I'm not sure that Lija will be able to pay me and we wouldn't want to have to let Rainbow go as she's pure gold. Yet the truth of the matter is that I'm never happier than when I'm here in my old kitchen baking. It feels as if it's where I'm meant to be. Perhaps if we're staying around for a while, I can help Lija to develop the business further. Then I remember the baby on the way and that Lija is going to have her hands more than full. Any business plans may well have to go on hold.

One moment I feel that we can all handle this new edition with ease – after all, women have babies every second of the day, the world over, and have always managed – the next moment I feel struck with terror at the enormity of it all and I can only imagine how much turmoil Lija's emotions must be in.

'You have gone quiet.' Lija shoots me a suspicious look.

'Just thinking,' I say hastily. I need to be her rock through all this and not have a wobble myself. 'Mince pies first?'

She nods.

As the first batch are going in, Rainbow arrives.

'Oh, man,' she says. 'It's totally FREEZEBALLS out there!' The beanie hat comes off and unleashes the exuberance of her curls. 'I seriously can't wait for global warming then we won't have cold mornings or have to go abroad on holiday and EVERYTHING. My nana said that 1976 was the last decent summer we had and that's, like, HUNDREDS of years ago. I wasn't even born, so I hardly remember it AT ALL. Where do you want me to start?'

'Morning, Rainbow.' I like a person who's breathless with excitement before they even begin their day. 'Do you fancy making the sandwiches?'

'My nana told me that some duchess or duke or SOMETHING invented sandwiches in the olden days. Probably 1976 or WHATEVER. If I was a duchess or duke or royalty, there's NO WAY I'd ever eat SANDWICHES. I'd go to Nando's EVERY DAY.' Without pausing for breath, she adds, 'Usual stuff?'

I nod and she cracks on with the task in hand. For no one's benefit but her own, she does it with a commentary about last night's soaps and reality shows while singing along to the Christmas songs on the radio. Lija rolls her eyes, but there's the hint of a smile on her face.

Stan nips in for breakfast and listens to Rainbow as she tells him about the latest happenings in the *Big Brother* house.

'I don't think they were really DOING IT,' she says over her shoulder to her confidant. 'They were under the duvet and, like, MOVING.' She indicates the specific type of moving up and down with her hand, grimacing as she does. 'But who'd do IT on TELLY? That's RANK!'

Stan bears it with a stoicism born of years of experience and nods his head when he thinks it might be required.

Around eleven o'clock the back door opens, letting in

a blast of wintery air. 'I don't suppose that the kettle's on,' Edie says.

'No,' I answer. 'But you're more than welcome to come in and make some tea for us all.'

'Oh,' she says. And, clearly unable to find a valid argument against it, my sister puts the kettle on and makes us tea.

We take a quick break and all sit around the table.

'How did you sleep?' I ask.

'Fine, once you two had stopped shagging,' she complains.

'Edie!' I feel myself flush.

'Well, you did ask. I thought you were going to be at it all night, for Christ's sake.'

Lija's expression tells me that she's quite impressed by what she's hearing and, in a rarely seen reversal of roles, I glare at her.

Edie flicks her hair. 'Actually, I hardly slept at all. That bunk bed thing is like a kid's bed and the mattress is totally concrete.' She rubs her back, theatrically. 'I'm going to need a chiropractor. Ducks quacking woke me,' she complains. 'I hate the countryside. I'm used to the sounds of the city.'

'Move to hotel,' Lija says flatly.

Edie throws her a disdainful look. 'I'm here to have Christmas with my family. If that's all right with you.'

'Then stop moaning,' is Lija's verdict. Edie looks as if she's been slapped.

I hide my smile behind my coffee cup.

'If you've not got anything better to do with yourself,

you can help us,' I say. 'Lija's taking it easy after she slipped on the ice.' I realise that I haven't told Edie that she's pregnant. Still, she doesn't need to know right now. 'It's shaken her up.'

'I am not shaken up,' Lija protests.

'You are,' I insist and she falls silent.

'Kitchen stuff really isn't my bag.' Edie pouts. 'I wouldn't know where to start.'

'Then you can learn. What else were you planning to do?' Edie looks blank for a second too long and I say, 'Excellent. That's settled then.'

I usher Lija off to bed for a rest and then give Edie a few tasks that won't strain her too much. Even someone unused to the ways of catering work can butter bread and set a table, surely?

We all have another push on making the food for the Christmas afternoon teas. Our first customers will be arriving soon and I show Edie how we like the tables set and instruct her on filling the three-tier cake stands with our lovely seasonal goodies. Today's special is a Black Forest cheesecake which has been lavishly decorated with choc-olate curls sprayed with edible gold. Very decadent. We've a full house booked again today and are going to be busy.

Edie works quietly, if a little sullenly, and I have to tell her off for eating as much as she puts on the plates even though she's supposedly a carb-free zone. But she does it – if not exactly with good grace.

Chapter Forty-One

In an economy drive, I bring the leftover cheese sandwiches back to the boat and bake them with some stock and single cream that was also going begging after today's service. It makes a sort of savoury bread and butter pudding. I'm sure Nigella would have some wonderfully exotic name for it. I've christened it cheesy bake.

Edie turns her nose up at it. 'I don't think I've ever seen so many carbs and calories on a plate.'

'Put your complaints in writing to the management,' I say.

'I could just eat the veg.' Edie pushes it away from her broccoli.

'If you want lobster and prawns every night, you're booked in to the wrong gaff,' Danny adds. 'Money's tight.'

'It's lovely,' Edie says crisply as she forks a morsel

into her mouth, turning up her nose as she does. 'I just won't be able to get into any of my clothes in a fortnight.'

We both ignore her, but the shine has been taken off my lovely make-do dinner.

'I called Henry today,' Danny says when we've finished our meal. 'I'm going to catch up with them all at the weekend. See what's on offer. I'll go down straight after work on Saturday, do a bit of networking and will be back in time for work on Sunday.'

'You're staying over?'

'I'll crash at Henry's place. Or with Sienna.'

My stomach turns to ice at the mention of her name. 'Oh.'

'It's cool,' he says. 'If I go there and back overnight, then I won't miss any pay.'

That's very good of him and I don't want to raise my concerns about him staying with the lovely, pouting Sienna – especially not in front of Edie. I don't want her to think there are any cracks in our relationship. There aren't. Are there?

'You could come,' he says. 'But we'll probably end up in a shouty, overpriced bar and you'd hate it. I expect you don't want to leave Lija at the moment, in case there's an emergency.'

'No,' I agree.

'What's the deal with Lija?' Edie tuts. 'Everyone's handling her with kid gloves.'

I don't know why I'm not keen to reveal Lija's condition to my sister, but I'm not and there you have it. Still, we can't keep it a secret for much longer. I take a deep breath and say, 'She's having a baby.'

'Christ on a bike.' Edie nearly splutters her food out. 'Lija is?'

'Yes. Next spring.'

'I can't believe it.' My sister looks stunned. 'Who's the father?'

'That's kind of a moot point,' I explain. 'He's not around any more.' I glance at Danny when I add, 'We're planning to stay on and help her out.'

'She's bloody well going to need it.' Edie puts her plate aside, food largely untouched. 'Who'd have thought that Lija of all people would be stupid enough to get herself up the duff?'

'I'm delighted for her,' I retort in defence of my friend. 'It will be lovely to have a baby around the house. It's been too long.'

'Yeah, wonderful,' Edie says. 'A howling kid, dirty nappies, tits like cow's udders.' She shudders.

I take it that Edie isn't feeling very maternal, but keep my own counsel.

'She'll be a terrible mother,' Edie continues.

'I actually think that it will be the making of her. You don't know Lija like I do.' Edie still looks sceptical. I slip my hand into Danny's and squeeze. 'Well, we're both very much looking forward to it.'

'Yeah. I second that.'

Edie pouts and then Danny, unsuccessfully, tries to stifle a yawn.

My sister holds up her hand. 'Please don't be saying

that you need an early night, you two. I couldn't bear it. I'm not lying on my own in that cramped cabin and kiddie cot listening to your shagfest.'

'We can supply you with earplugs,' Danny says.

'No one should have to listen to their sister having sex,' Edie counters.

Danny grins at me. 'I think your sister makes great sex noises.'

'Bleurgh. TMI,' she complains. 'This boat is so claustrophobic. You haven't even got a telly. That's positively primitive. We could go out to the pub or something?'

'It's cosy in here.' I snuggle closer to Danny. This is the time of day that I love the best. The log burner is roaring away, the curtains are closed against the cold night pressing in, Diggery is curled up next to us snoring gently. The man of my dreams is at my side. The twinkly Christmas tree lights add a magical element. A glass of wine would absolutely complete the picture, but Edie has slugged all that back. 'Besides, we haven't got any money to go to the pub. Unless it's your shout?'

I don't want to keep banging on about it, but I wish that Edie would start to appreciate our situation. I've never been a money-oriented person, but it makes a big difference when you haven't got any – at all – and your sister is frittering away pots of cash. She could help us out if she wanted to. However, you know what Edie's like by now. She's so selfish that she wouldn't even think of it. Perhaps I'm going to have to summon up the courage to sit her down properly and raise the matter with her. She did promise me half of the money from the sale of the house but, of course, it has never materialised.

'I'm bored,' she complains. 'There's nothing to do here.'

'You've been back for a day, Edie. I thought the idea of this festive holiday was that you were going to bask in the bosom of your family.'

'I miss New York.' She sighs like a sullen teenager.

'You could have a wild night in the fleshpots of Milton Keynes. Probably. But you'd need to count us out.'

Edie cocks an ear. 'Listen to that.'

'What? I can't hear anything.'

'Exactly. Nothing. Not a bloody sound.' An owl hoots. 'Well, apart from that. And a hooting frigging owl doesn't cut it. It's as quiet as a grave.'

'It's *peaceful*.'

She snorts.

'I'm sure it will take you a few days to adjust, but try to go with the flow. You've only got to put up with it for a few weeks and then you can head right back to the bright city lights and party central.'

Edie hugs a cushion and starts to pick at the embroidery with her long, perfectly manicured nails. 'What shall we do then?'

'We've got some jigsaws and board games.'

'You're kidding me. That reminds me of the holidays we had when we were kids. And not in a good way. It would be me, you, Mum and Dad squashed on that bloody skanky old boat.' She's referring to the *Maid of Merryweather* who might be skanky now but was beautiful in her heyday when we took all of our family holidays on her. 'We'd sit looking out at the pissing down rain. Mum and I would hate every minute while you and Dad were in your element.'

'Nothing much has changed then.'

'Were we even happy as kids?' she asks. 'I barely remember it really. I was always Mum's favourite and you were Dad's.'

We know why now.

'Good God, now I'm getting maudlin as well as bored. What do you do to distract yourselves? Apart from have hot sex?'

I ignore the jibe and say, 'Sometimes we read.'

'I haven't read a book since I left school,' Edie confesses. 'I don't intend to start now.'

'Oh, Edie.'

'I flick through *Vogue* at the hairdresser's. Does that count?'

Danny yawns again. 'I do need an early night,' he says. 'I've had a busy day today and I've got the same tomorrow.'

'Me too,' I agree.

'So it's just me drifting around aimlessly?'

'You could help us at the café while you're here,' I suggest. 'I'm sure Lija wouldn't mind. You seemed to enjoy it today.'

'Enjoying it might be a bit of a stretch,' she counters. 'I didn't want to gouge my own eyes out though.'

I'll settle for that. 'I'll have a word with Lija and see what she thinks.'

'I *am* on holiday,' Edie reminds me, sharply.

'On holiday from what?' I ask. 'You don't actually *do* anything.'

'There's no talking to you when you're in this kind of mood,' she snaps. And with that she stomps off to bed.

Danny and I exchange a glance and then start to laugh. 'Come on,' he says. 'Let's go and make this boat rock.' So we do. Lots. And Edie doesn't say a thing.

Chapter Forty-Two

The following Saturday I kiss Danny with my stomach in knots. He's going into London tonight straight from the boatyard to 'have a few drinks' with his old colleagues and is not coming back until tomorrow. I should be pleased for him. It will do him good to let his hair down for the night. I keep telling myself that. Instead, I'm wracked with nerves and want to cling on to him and ask him not to go. But, of course, I don't.

I work in the café all day with Lija and Rainbow. Edie stays out of the way on the boat. We've been skirting round each other for the last few days. Dinner time on the boat is strained and I've no idea what she's up to during the day. I think we're both starting to wonder why she came over at all.

We have yet another busy day at the café and it's good to see that the business is on a sound footing. We still have the repairs from the flood to contend with after Christmas but, for now, everything to do with the café is back on track. Which is a welcome relief as everything else seems to be in a state of flux.

The last of the customers has just gone and we're tidying up. Rainbow is singing along to Wham's 'Last Christmas' when Edie comes through the kitchen door. She's all dressed up in the fancy white coat.

'Hello.' I finish wiping the plate in my hands. 'Going somewhere nice?'

'I thought we could hit the shops,' she says. 'Just you and me. While Danny's out partying in London.' I don't miss the slight barb in her tone. 'We could have some cocktails too.' Perhaps she can sense my hesitation as she adds, 'I've been stuck on that boat all day. I need to get out.'

I don't bother to point out that I've been on my feet since seven o'clock this morning and what *I* really need is a jolly good sit-down.

'Let's do it,' Edie urges. 'For me.'

I put down my tea towel. Resistance is futile. Plus I can't cope with Edie sulking all night. 'Fine. I'll need to get changed and feed Diggery.'

'That will take aaaages,' she whines. 'Come as you are.'

That's nice. Edie in a designer outfit, me in my waitressing white blouse and black trousers. But, frankly, I'm too tired to argue. With my sister in full regalia, who'll be looking at me anyway?

'Do you mind if I leave now?' I ask Lija.

'Is fine.' She's glowering at Edie though. 'I'll feed dog.'

'Fab,' Edie says. 'I'll call a cab.'

'Can you take Stan his supper later too?' I hate to ask another favour of Lija when I want her to be resting.

'I'm going round to Stan's tonight,' Rainbow says. 'I'll take him his tea. We're going to watch *The Muppet Christmas Carol* together. He's TOTALLY never seen it! How can that even be? He's ninety-WHATEVER.' Even her curls are indignant. 'I've got popcorn and EVERYTHING. I've brought big fluffy socks for us both.'

'He'll be in for a lovely evening,' I say with a smile.

'My nan says it's not properly Christmas until you've watched it.'

'She's a wise woman.'

Edie taps her foot. 'Are we going or what?'

At this moment, I'd rather join Rainbow and Stan watching the Muppets' festive celebration, but I take off my apron and slip on my coat.

Her phone pings. 'That's the taxi.'

'Wish me luck,' I mouth to Lija and Rainbow as I leave.

Chapter Forty-Three

The shopping centre is heaving. It's six o'clock by the time we get there and the crowds aren't showing any signs of abating. Many of the big stores are open round the clock and I wonder who really needs to be buying tinsel at two in the morning.

'I haven't done *any* Christmas shopping yet.' Edie takes my arm.

'I've done a few bits, but they're token gestures this year. Just little bits and bobs.'

'What do you want as a present?'

'I don't know. Nothing really. There's no space to keep anything on the boat.'

'What about a *great* handbag?'

'Edie, does my current lifestyle look as if I need a "great" handbag?'

'I suppose not,' she says, sniffily. 'It wouldn't hurt to look though.'

So she drags me to a very posh designer store. The vast window is filled with sparkling plastic icicles with one artfully placed white leather bag in the middle. Inside, many of the handbags are locked in glass cases. An entire wall of the shop features just a handful of bags.

'Oh, I *love* this store,' Edie coos. 'Don't you?'

'I've never been in it before.'

She dashes here and there, stroking the bags that aren't under lock and key. 'Look, Fay. Look.'

I look. They all seem ruinously expensive. And impractical. Though I must admit that they're certainly more attractive than the supermarket Bag for Life I normally tote around.

'Which is your favourite? Would you like one?'

'It would be wasted on me, Edie. If I had that kind of money, I'd spend it on the boat.' Or on Lija. Or on buying food.

She rolls her eyes at me. 'Well, I'm going to treat myself. I can't help it.' Edie picks up one of the pristine white leather bags, the same as the one that graces the display in the window, and caresses it like an adored pet.

Ridiculous. I'd spill coffee or red wine on that thing on its first outing. I stand and try not to scowl.

'It's not just a handbag,' she intones. 'It's a work of art.'

'It's very nice.' I don't even ask her how much it is.

She waggles the bag at me in a tempting manner. 'Are you sure you won't?'

I shake my head. 'No, thank you.' Is my sister really so utterly insensitive? I feel as if she's rubbing my nose in the fact that she is the one with all of Miranda's money and I am not.

'Suit yourself,' she says. Then Edie flounces with her purchase to the cash desk and flashes her credit card to pay. It's beautifully wrapped and put into one of those fancy paper carrier bags that's probably worth more than my own handbag. Edie breezes out of the shop, clearly on cloud nine. I'm pleased for her. If that's what she wants.

Actually, scratch that. I'm not. I'm seething.

'Let's get a cocktail to celebrate,' she says, clutching her carrier bag to her. 'Is there anywhere decent to get a drink in this dump?'

I bite my tongue and steer Edie to the nearest bar. The place is too busy, the music too loud. We perch on uncomfortable bar stools at a table in the window. Edie puts her carrier bag on the stool next to her, mouthing a silent 'squeeeee' as she does.

We peruse the cocktail menu, yet I see nothing but red mist. The waitress comes and is dressed in a sexy Santa outfit. She looks as if she wants to kill herself. She stands with her pad poised, unsmiling. Edie trills off her order. I close the menu and say, 'I'll have the same.'

Edie is all a-shiver with excitement and when the cocktails come, she gulps hers down and orders another straight away.

'Cosmopolitans are my favourite,' she says. 'I go to this really hip bar in Manhattan all the time. You should come over sometime. We'll paint New York red!'

I can't think of anything worse. Sipping my drink

slowly – which I now know is a cosmopolitan – I let the strong bite of alcohol hit my throat with each mouthful.

'Where next?' she says.

'I'm not sure I really have the appetite for shopping,' I admit. 'I should go back to the boat and leave you to it.'

She pouts at me. 'You're such a spoilsport, Fay. What's happened to you? You used to be such fun.'

'I didn't, Edie. You were always the fun one. I was the quiet one that never shone.'

She shrugs her shoulders. 'Well, it doesn't always have to be like that. You can change. People do.'

'I've found, generally, that they don't.'

My sister fixes me with a stare. 'Meaning?'

I don't know whether it's the alcohol that's emboldening me, but in for a penny, in for a pound. 'You promised that you'd share Miranda's money with me. Before you went back to New York. That's exactly what you said. You said you wanted us to get back to where we were.'

Now Edie's face has darkened, the shine of excitement gone. 'And handing the money over to you will achieve that?'

'Some of it,' I stress. 'You know that Miranda didn't treat me fairly.'

'I got the house. You got that wretched boat you love so much.'

'Exactly. You banked over half a million pounds and I got a leaky narrowboat – which I do love dearly – but it's going to cost a fortune to make it fit to go on the water again.'

'That's hardly my fault, is it?'

'Danny's in London right now trying to get a job back in a world he hates, just to try to prop up our finances. We want to be able to help Lija too when the baby comes. We're on the breadline, Edie, and you're buying designer *fucking* handbags.'

Edie looks as if I've struck her. Whether my message has hit home or whether it's the unaccustomed expletive, I don't know. Then she flushes and says, 'I haven't told you everything, Fay.'

My blood runs cold when I reply, 'Perhaps you better had.'

Chapter Forty-Four

The surly Santa waitress brings us more cocktails, even though I'm pretty sure we didn't order any more. Still, I'm grateful for the numbing powers of the alcohol.

Edie and I sit in silence, doing our best to ignore the hubbub surrounding us, while she gathers her thoughts.

'Well?' I say when there's nothing forthcoming for what feels like five minutes or more.

My sister sighs and runs a hand through her glossy blonde hair. Her throat is tight when she says, 'I haven't got any of the money left.' She stirs her cocktail in order to avoid my eyes. 'Well, not much of it.'

I'm so gobsmacked that I struggle to form words. I struggle to form thoughts. I feel as if this cosmopolitan is woefully inadequate. I am a person in shock and need, at least, a double brandy. When I do finally manage to find my voice, I splutter, 'How? How can that possibly be?'

She takes a slug of her cocktail and tries to look

nonchalant, but I can see that her hand is trembling. When, eventually, she looks at me, she says, 'I handed most of it over to Brandon.'

I try to digest that, but words fail me.

'He said he'd invest it for me,' she continues. 'And he has. With a start-up software company whose stock has plummeted. It's all but gone.'

'Half a million pounds?'

'Mostly. Before Brandon got his hands on it, I bought a lot of handbags and shoes too. Designer ones.' Her eyes challenge me. We're both aware of the crisp carrier bag on the chair next to us bearing yet another one. 'Some of it I snorted up my nose and some of it I glugged down my throat. I have developed quite the taste for champagne and cocktails.'

I can feel pressure building in my head and I really, really want to slap my sister's silly face. I want to slap her more than I've ever wanted to slap anyone in my life. 'There's no chance of getting it back?'

She shrugs, but I can tell that she's not feeling as casual as she's trying to portray. 'A miracle could happen, I suppose.'

'But it's unlikely.'

Edie nods.

My heart is racing and my breath wavers when I exhale. 'How could you be so stupid?' So very, very stupid.

'It's easy for you to ask that,' she spits back. 'You with your perfect little life and your cute boyfriend and your cute dog, playing house in your cute boat. How dare you judge me?'

'I've worked hard for this,' I tell her. 'As well you know.

I was the one who put in hours and hours at the café to try and grow it into a decent business. I was the one who waited on Miranda – *your* mother – hand and foot. Where were you when she was ill? Swanning about with your married lover, that's where. Then when you were left everything you behaved like the grasping spoiled brat that you are.' Now my sister does look as if I've punched her in the face, but I'm not finished yet. 'You were handed a fortune on a plate – an *absolute* fortune – and, in turn, you handed it all over to Brandon without question?'

When she finds her voice, she stutters, 'I . . . I . . . I trusted him. He told me it was a sure-fire thing, that I'd make my money back a million times over.' Her expression is bleak. 'I thought I'd be rich. What a fool.'

I can hardly bear to look at her any more, let alone speak to her. I'm not sure what else I can say, so it's probably best if I shut my mouth now. I've probably said too much already and the only words that are still on my tongue are ones that I'll regret saying.

'That's why I can't stay in a hotel. That's why I have to stay *here*.' She says 'here' in the same tone as you would 'shit hole'. 'I can't even pay my rent, so I've lost my apartment. I handed back the keys as I left. I gave everything else away to my friends. I have nothing but what I brought back.' She stares out of the window at the crowds of Christmas shoppers. All of them happy, smiling, oblivious to the unfolding heartbreak of our family drama.

Edie puts the insolent expression on her face that she mastered when she was fifteen. 'I'm not here for Christmas, dear sister. I'm back for good.'

Chapter Forty-Five

Our shopping trip, needless to say, is abandoned. Edie texts for a cab and we ride home in it in silence. I leave her to pick up the bill for the cocktails and the taxi.

When we get back, I stomp down the garden to *The Dreamcatcher*, Edie trailing in my wake. On the boat, my sanctuary, I crash about with the kettle, making tea.

Edie stands there looking forlorn. 'I've upset you,' she says. 'What can I do?'

Spinning to look at her, I spit out, 'Upset me?' I hold my hand to my head. 'Upset me? That doesn't even come close. You have absolutely no idea, Edie, do you?'

For once, she does look properly penitent. 'How can I put this right?'

Hands on hips, I face her squarely. 'You can get your money back and share it fairly with me. That's what you can do.'

I see her gulp. 'You know that's not possible. I'm entirely dependent on Brandon. I wish I wasn't.'

I snort my disdain.

'I'd do anything to be able to fix this,' she insists.

Then I don't really know how deep inside it comes from, but all the anger that I've been pushing down for so long suddenly surfaces. It's clearly been bottled up for too long as a rush of bile floods my throat. The dam bursts and all the hurt that I've suffered at Edie's hands comes out in an unstoppable torrent. My head is reeling, my heart hammering with the force of my ire. 'Get out,' I say, coldly. 'Pack your things and get out now. I never want to see you again.'

Edie's face drains of colour. 'You don't mean that, Fay.'

'I do,' I assure her. 'I absolutely do. I've never meant anything more in my life.'

'Where am I to go?'

I fold my arms across my chest, forming a barrier between us. 'I don't know and I don't care.'

'But it's coming up to Christmas. We were going to have a nice family time together.'

'Well, I'm sorry, Edie, but that's really not going to happen.' I have never felt more determined not to be swayed by my sister's wheedling.

'This is because Danny's away,' she presses on. 'You're missing him. You'll feel better when he's back.'

'No, Edie. It's because you've treated me like shit for most of my life and it stops now.'

'You're my sister,' she pleads. 'You mean *everything* to me.'

'You have the most terrible way of showing it.' We stand

and stare at each other, both of us hurting in our own way. I feel the fight go out of me but, in its place, there's a steely resolve. 'I'm going to go up to the house to see Lija. When I come back, I want you gone.'

'Don't, Fay. Let's talk. I'll make you a cup of tea. You'll feel better when I explain everything. Perhaps Brandon will get the money back. It happens. The markets go up and down all the time. Software is a very good thing to be in. He said so.'

Though I'm still shaking inside, my voice is calm, controlled, when I say, 'I've heard enough, Edie. Just go.'

I put down the kettle, that I hadn't even realised I was still holding, and then I stride to the door and jump off the boat onto the jetty. I march up to the house, my unsteady breaths making clouds in the cold night air.

Chapter Forty-Six

Lija is in the kitchen when I get to the house. She has her coat on.

'I've just had the most almighty row with Edie,' I say without preamble. 'I've told her to leave.'

Lija purses her lips. 'Good.'

I notice that my hands are shaking and I feel like I've got post-traumatic stress or something. I so rarely get cross that it feels all wrong in my body, as if it doesn't quite know how to process it. 'I want to get very spectacularly drunk.'

'Excellent idea,' she says.

'You're not joining me. You're pregnant.'

'I will inhale fumes.'

'What have you got?'

Lija shrugs. 'Wine. Vodka.'

'Both,' I say. 'I'll have both.'

'OK.' She goes to the kitchen cupboard where she keeps her booze stash and grabs two bottles.

'Anyway, where are you going at this time of night?'

'I am heading to Stinky Stan's. Rainbow is already round there. I made serious mistake of telling her that I haven't seen *The Muppet Christmas Carol* either.' She rolls her eyes and, despite my anger, I can't help but smile.

'Well, it looks like I'm coming too. Is there room for a small one?'

'Of course.'

Surely the Muppets will get me out of this hideous mood. Yet I'm still furious when we knock on Stan's door and Rainbow, bouncing from foot to foot, lets us into his cottage.

'OMG,' she trills. 'The WHOLE team are in da houzz! Whoop-whoop!'

Stan looks very perplexed. He's sitting on the sofa in pink fluffy socks with an enormous bowl of popcorn on his lap.

'Just in time!' Rainbow says.

'I hadn't expected to see you too, Fay,' Stan notes. 'What a nice surprise.'

I flop down next to him and dip into his bowl of popcorn. 'Massive row with Edie. I've chucked her out.'

'Will she go?'

'I don't know,' I admit. 'I hope so. I mean it this time. I've had enough of her. She treats me like dirt.'

'I've bought WKD for everyone,' Rainbow says. 'Well, not you, Lija, because it's ALCOHOL and you are PREGNANT.'

'This I know,' Lija says crisply.

Rainbow opens three bottles of the lurid turquoise drink, with a flick of a wrist like a pro, and gives one to Stan.

He examines it with a slightly concerned look on his face. 'Lovely,' he says, not sounding convinced. 'What does it taste of?'

'Errr . . . BLUE,' Rainbow decides. 'Blue drinks are the best. My nan loves them. Get it down you, Stan. You'll be breakdancing and EVERYTHING before the night's out.'

Stan turns to me and whispers, 'Is that a good thing?'

'Only in Rainbow's world,' I whisper back.

'No glass?' he queries.

'Straight from the bottle, Stan. It's the modern way.' I plan on doing much the same with wine and vodka in a minute.

'Ah,' he says before clinking his bottle against mine and taking a hearty glug.

'Nice?' I ask.

He licks his lips, savouring the taste of BLUE once more. 'Not necessarily.' But he glugs it again, nevertheless.

If he has a few more of these, he'll certainly sleep well tonight.

'Put your fluffy socks on, Lija,' Rainbow instructs as she hands over a pair of baby pink numbers.

Surprisingly, Lija takes off her boots and slips them on without protest.

'Ooo! Time for MUPPETS,' Rainbow says and, after doing a little dance, rushes to the television to put a DVD, that looks very well-loved, into the player.

I don't want to call Danny as that seems too clingy. I want him to enjoy his evening without him having to reassure me that he's not about to run off with Sienna or some other nubile woman, but I hoped he would have texted me by now. While Rainbow is cueing up the film, I decide to text him. *I love you. Have a great evening. See you tomorrow. Xxxx.* I hope that he'll ping something straight back, but nothing arrives. Maybe he's in a noisy bar and can't hear his phone.

We all squash up on the sofa together. Then Rainbow looks worried. 'I didn't get fluffy socks for you, Fay.'

'I think I'll manage.' In fact, if I drink a couple more bottles of this blue drink, then I won't care about anything at all.

'I rather like mine.' Stan wiggles his toes and gives them an admiring glance.

'Everyone ready?'

As Rainbow is about to start the film, a car pulls up outside the house. Lija stands, goes to the window and draws aside the corner of the curtain. 'Is taxi. Edie is leaving.'

'Good,' I say, ignoring the knot of tension in my stomach. 'Roll the Muppets, Rainbow.'

And a moment later, Kermit is doing his thing on the screen.

'You'll totally LOVE this, Stan,' Rainbow says. 'It's an education.'

So often the little things in life are. I have learned tonight that my sister will never change. She will always be selfish and self-obsessed. At this moment, if you asked me, I'd tell you that I not only don't love her any more, but I don't even like her.

Next to me Lija takes my hand and squeezes it.

As the tyres of the taxi crunch on the gravel, I concentrate on Miss Piggy and my exceedingly blue drink and the love of the people I have around me.

Chapter Forty-Seven

The next morning, I lie propped up in our bed looking out of the window at the canal, the ducks drifting by on the lazy current and the early morning dog walkers on the far bank. My head is still pounding from too many blue drinks. Many, many blue drinks. I stick out my tongue to check whether or not it has turned blue, but I can't see it.

My stomach is still burning with acid after my row with Edie. Not even a lovely night with the Muppets – and I don't mean Rainbow, Lija and Stan – could entirely shake my dark mood. Plus, I still haven't heard from Danny. I keep checking my phone, but nothing.

I think this is the first night that I've spent alone on *The Dreamcatcher* and it feels strange to be without Danny at my side. Turning onto his side of the bed, I hug his pillow. Diggery, sensing that I'm awake, works his way up from the foot of the bed where he's been allowed to sleep and snuggles into the crook of my arm.

'Don't do that,' I mutter to him, 'or we'll never get up.'

A text pings into my phone and my spirits lift as I reach for it. Finally. Danny.

Hi. On way back. Will go straight to boatyard. CU tonight. xx

That gladdens my heart. Though I'm slightly disappointed that he hasn't called me. Only a day apart and I'm desperate to hear his voice. I'm anxious to know how he got on with his old colleagues and whether a job in London is going to be feasible or not. I text him back. *Hope you had good time. Love you. Can't wait till you're home.* xx

Eventually, I manage to muster the energy to dislodge Diggery and head for the shower. The water fails to produce its usual healing powers and I dry myself still feeling out of sorts. I hate falling out with people. I am one of life's mollifiers. I'm not built for confrontation. The urge to phone Edie and apologise is almost overwhelming. Almost. There's still enough of me cross at her for treating me like a doormat.

I go into work, but my mind isn't really on the job. The mince pies today are not going to be made with my usual loving care. I'll just be glad if they end up in the oven and not on the floor. Rainbow chatters on and I let her words flow over me.

'My nan says that Father Christmas is an *actual* saint and EVERYTHING. She said he doesn't even dress in red in real life. That came from drinking too much Coca-Cola or SOMETHING. Who knew? I always thought Father Christmas was my mum and dad. When they weren't divorced. I'm sure I saw them once but I had to pretend I didn't because there's a rule that says if you see Santa then you don't get your presents or WHATEVER. I think I got Heelys that year and you don't want to miss out on Heelys by accidental Santa-seeing. That would be MAD, right?'

'Yes,' Lija and I agree, automatically.

Then Rainbow's off onto something else and we tune out.

Mince pies done, I move on to making the sandwiches – also done on autopilot. Lija is quiet too, but she's concentrating on icing gingerbread biscuits, her tongue sticking out of the corner of her mouth. My mind is not my own today. When I'm not stewing about what I said to Edie and what she, in turn, said to me, I'm fretting about Danny's evening flying solo in the big smoke. Which is ridiculous of me. It was one night away from me and I'm not a jealous kind of person. I know that I could trust Danny with my life. I shouldn't be worried about it. Really I shouldn't.

Yet it's barely lunchtime when I crack and say, 'Can I take some sandwiches down to Danny? He came back from London and went straight to the boatyard, so I'm not sure if he's got anything to eat.'

'Sure,' she says.

'I won't be long.'

'Come back not miserable,' she says.

'Sorry.' I pack some sandwiches into a plastic box for Danny and fill another one with a generous slice of rich Christmas cake. 'This thing with Edie has got me all disgruntled.'

Lija pauses in her icing. 'It is right thing to do.'

'Is it? I feel terrible.'

'Edie will be all right. She always is.'

'I know. She just pushed me too far this time.'

'Go and see Hot Stuff.' She nods towards the door. 'He will put smile back on your face.'

I grin at that.

'See. Is working already.'

Ducking out of the door, I click Diggery to heel and, of course, he's overexcited at going for an unexpected walk. I head over the hump-backed bridge to the towpath and towards the boatyard. There's a nip of frost in the air and there are few boats out on the canal. It's a brisk fifteen-minute yomp to the boatyard and when I get there I ask a whiskered-man in paint-spattered overalls where Danny is and am shown to one of the narrowboats in dry dock.

I find Danny under the hull of a boat scraping off layers of thick black gunge, some heavy indie band blaring out from the radio.

'Hey, handsome,' I shout. 'I have come to tempt you with cake.'

He stops what he's doing and pushes out from under the boat. Brushing himself down, he climbs out of the boat dock and comes to meet me. He looks tired. Hung-over. Sad.

Diggery goes crazy and Danny reaches down to ruffle his ears. 'Hey,' he says, holding up his hands. 'I'm filthy. Again.'

Coming here makes me realise how hard this work is. It's dirty and physically exhausting. Plus he's working outdoors in this weather. The boats may be covered but the rest of the boat dock is open to the elements. I'm frozen to the marrow just standing here for five minutes. It's no wonder that Danny is considering taking a job back in the City.

I hold up my boxes. 'Sandwiches. Christmas cake. I thought you might not have had a chance to buy any lunch.'

'I didn't,' he admits. 'I'd intended to get something at Euston, but I was late and had to sprint for my train.'

'Is there somewhere we can sit? I haven't got long.'

'Let's go back to the Portakabin. I can make us a brew and warm up a bit.'

So we walk back to the utilitarian box that serves as an office and staffroom. There are pictures of Amber Heard and Kylie, scantily clad, Blu-Tacked to the walls. Danny washes his hands and makes us tea. I move a pile of paperwork so that I can sit down and huddle under the two-bar heater that is high on the wall. 'Cosy,' I say.

'Believe me, I'm grateful for any time I can spend in here.'

As he passes me a chipped mug of tea, I touch his arm. 'I know that you're working really hard for us.' Suddenly, stupid tears spring to my eyes.

'Hey,' he says, brushing them away. 'No crying.'

'I had a huge fight with Edie,' I tell him. 'I threw her out.'

Danny laughs.

'It's not funny!'

'I'm not really laughing,' he chuckles. 'I can't imagine you chucking Edie off the boat. What happened? It must have been pretty bad.'

279

'It was. Awful. It's a long story though. I'll tell you later. First, I want to hear how you got on. Did you have a good time?'

'Yeah.' I note that he looks away from me as he says, 'Usual crowd. We went to a couple of bars and then a club.'

'Hardcore.'

He lets out a flat, weary breath. 'Something like that.'

My heart's in my mouth when I ask, 'Everything OK?'

'Sure.' He dips into the box of sandwiches and bites a huge chunk out of one, saying, 'No breakfast', by way of explanation.

'Any jobs on offer?'

'I could be back there next week.'

'Is that a good thing or a bad thing?'

Danny shakes his head. 'I'm still trying to work that out.'

'Want to talk about it?' Clearly something is wrong. I can't put my finger on it and, maybe, it's just a hangover, but Danny isn't his usual self.

'Later,' he says. 'I'm not sure what I want to say yet.'

'OK.' I don't like the sound of that. At all.

So he devours the rest of his sandwiches and starts on the cake. I don't think that he's tasting any of it. Normally, he'd be so appreciative, but he's not even aware of what he's eating. Clearly, he has a lot on his mind and that scares me.

I'm subdued, Danny's subdued and even Diggery, sensing we're subdued, is subdued.

Lunch box finished, he says, 'I should get back to work.'

'Me too. Shall I leave the dog with you?'

Danny nods.

His parting kiss is brief, but he holds my hands tight. Too tight. Diggery follows him back to the narrowboat, keeping close to his side. I walk back to work feeling alone, so very alone.

Chapter Forty-Eight

I worry myself into a lather all afternoon. Even the fact that we've had our best day yet in the café fails to lift my mood. Rainbow, on the other hand, is getting more hyperactive the nearer to Christmas we get. Today, she's wearing a white skater dress covered in smiley Santas and her curls are topped by reindeer antler deely-boppers. I think she frightened some of the customers with her fulsome enthusiasm, though there was certainly a lot of laughter too.

'*Bring us some figgy pudding*,' she sings along with a Christmas song as she stacks the plates into the cupboard. '*Bring us some figgy pudding*.' Then she turns, looking puzzled. 'What is figgy pudding, anyway? LOL. Pudding with a FIG in it? Oh, man. WRONG on many levels. My nana likes rice pudding. What's that about? Pudding made of RICE. BLEURGH. Rice is for curry. DUH.'

It's later than usual when we're clearing up and Lija

looks exhausted. 'Go and put your feet up.' She opens her mouth to protest. 'I insist.'

Rainbow and I finish up. I kiss her as she leaves for the evening and apologise for being grumpy – though I'm not sure that she even noticed. Then I take Stan his supper and sit with him for a while. Stacked on the coffee table is a range of Christmas films on DVD that Rainbow has left him to work through. He's currently watching *Love, Actually* and has *The Holiday* lined up for later. In honour of it, the pink fluffy socks are in evidence again.

'I like these rom-coms,' he says, wiping a tear away as Emma Thompson has just discovered that Alan Rickman hasn't bought the posh necklace for her. I feel a bit choked myself. 'The things these youngsters get up to. It was never like that in my day.'

'I'm not sure that we're better for it, Stan.' I sound melancholy even to my own ears.

He frowns at me. 'Things all right with you and Danny? You seem quiet.'

'Yes, we're fine.' Though I'm not sure that's the truth. 'This thing with Edie has got me very unsettled.'

He pats my hand. 'Edie will be all right. You mark my words.'

'Lija said the same thing.' I can't help dwelling on it though. Where has Edie gone? She has no other friends left here now as she never kept in touch with anyone. Surely she must have checked into a hotel nearby? But she could be anywhere. She might even have jumped on a plane and gone straight back to New York. How would I know?

While it's all churning round in my head, I glance at my watch and am shocked to see the time. 'I'd better go. I'm going to make something nice for Danny's tea tonight and need to crack on.'

'Keep calm. Don't panic,' Stan says. 'It will all be fine.'

I take his tray and hope that he's right.

When I finally head back to *The Dreamcatcher*, I'm surprised to see that the lights are already on. The Christmas lights on the well deck are shining out in the darkness too and the boat looks quite magical.

Danny must be home before me. Most unusual. He's been getting back from the boatyard later and later. Though I have a notion to cook something special, I haven't given the actual menu much thought and, as it's now late, will have to resort to conjuring something up with what's lurking in the fridge.

Jumping on board, I open the door to the cabin. Inside, it is lit up with a plethora of candles and tea lights. There's soft music playing and the scent of something wonderful cooking on the stove drifts towards me. Danny is freshly showered and is looking more handsome than ever. My heart does a backflip and a bit of a somersault too for good measure.

There are fresh flowers in a vase on the coffee table and, for just a fleeting moment, I wonder if they are guilty flowers.

'This looks great,' I say. 'What's it in aid of?'

'Nothing in particular.'

'Well, nothing in particular sounds like a perfect thing

to celebrate.' I go and wind my arms round him. 'What have we got to eat?'

'Nothing fancy. Pasta dressed up with what I could find in the fridge.'

I laugh, a bit too brightly. 'That's exactly what I'd planned for dinner too.'

'Great minds think alike.' He certainly seems a lot more chirpy than earlier, but I can tell that there's something still on his mind. Perhaps I'm reading too much into this because of the situation with Edie, but I feel as if something invisible is hanging in the air between us.

We eat at the coffee table in the cabin. Danny has made a rich tomato sauce for the pasta which is delicious. The bottle of red he opens barely touches the sides, so he opens another and he's matching my one glass with two gulped down. Both of us are going to have bad heads in the morning at this rate.

When we've finished, I go to clear up.

'Leave that until later,' he says, softly. 'Let's go out onto the well deck.'

'It's freezing out there.'

'We'll take some blankets. The lights look really pretty.' He looks away from me. 'Besides, we need to talk.'

My mouth goes dry. What's happened in the short time he was away from me? I can hardly bear to think about it, but there has somehow been a subtle change in his behaviour. I'd be blind not to see it. 'OK.'

So Danny picks up his guitar, which he hasn't played for ages. I grab my fleece and the crocheted blanket off the sofa. We bring some tea lights out too and I arrange them around the well deck. Danny finds the remnants of a bottle of vodka and pours us a couple of shots. We settle next to each other on the benches and I pull the blanket round our knees. Diggery curls up at Danny's feet. It's a beautiful night. The air is crisp and cold and we can see our breath, but the stars are out in force above us. Yet where I should feel warm and cosy, there's only a cold prickle of fear.

Chapter Forty-Nine

We clink our shot glasses together and knock back the vodka in one. The raw alcohol burns its way down into my stomach. I'm *so* going to regret this. Danny rolls a spliff. Something he hasn't done for a long time.

'A present from Sienna?' Last time he had any weed, she'd been the one to give it to him.

He laughs without humour. 'I bought my own this time.'

I feel my throat go tight when I say, 'You haven't said much about your trip to London.'

He takes a toke on the joint and then passes it to me. I think about refusing and then I think, Sod it. Why not? I take the smoke deep into my lungs and try not to cough.

This reminds me of the first proper night that we spent together. Our illicit night when I was still with Anthony. I was high and drunk and we made love all night long on the floor of the boat. I'd never been so reckless before and I revelled in every moment. I also found out just how much love I could feel for one person. If I had my time again, I wouldn't change a thing.

Danny takes another drag and, after a while, says, 'I'm not proud of myself.'

My insides turn to ice and the silence seems to stretch on and on until, finally, he speaks again.

'I went to London thinking that I could dip my toe into that life again but remain above it all.' He leans his head back against the side of the boat cabin. 'I thought I'd moved on, that I was a better person than I'd been then. I thought I had the moral high ground covered and all that shit.' He looks at me with sad eyes. 'I was wrong, Fay.'

He pours us more shots while I try to find some platitudes and fail.

'The reality is that the person I hated so much is right there under the surface.' We knock back the shots in unison and, this time, I'm grateful for mine. 'We went out, trailed from bar to bar, got leery drunk. We ended up at a seedy party. I don't even know where. I did a couple of lines. I don't even know what I was thinking. I *wasn't* thinking. I was right back there. One of the boys again. An obnoxious twat. I behaved in a way I thought I'd left behind.' He stares up at the sky. 'I did things that I regret.'

When he says nothing more, I have to ask the question that's burning in my brain. 'Did you sleep with Sienna?'

It takes him a long time to answer. 'No.' He turns to me. 'But it was on offer. I knew that.'

I'm sure he must be able to hear my heart thumping when I ask, 'And you were tempted?'

Danny nods. 'Yeah. I guess.' He looks at the end of the

joint as if the explanation is there. 'I was completely wasted, out of my head. What can I say? After the party, we went back to her place. I could have stayed at Henry's. I could have made that decision. But I didn't.'

I try to push away the images that start to play out in my head. Danny's lips on hers, his hands on her body, doing the things he does with me with someone else. 'And then?'

Danny blows out a wavering breath. 'Something clicked in my head and, thank God, I had a moment of lucidity and thought of all that I've got here, all that I value. And I didn't. I didn't do anything. I told Sienna how much I valued her as a friend and I slept on her sofa.'

I let out the breath that I've been holding, but my voice sounds shaky when I say, 'That doesn't seem too bad.'

He meets my eyes and I see regret and contrition. 'It scared me how close I came to fucking everything up.'

Danny pulls me close and I take the joint from his fingers and draw the smoke down into my lungs as deep as I can before I nestle into his arms. 'I'm glad you didn't.'

'Me too.' Diggery whimpers in his sleep and Danny reaches out to stroke him. 'I felt I owed you the truth, Fay. I never want to lie to you. I couldn't not tell you.'

'How did Sienna take it?'

He manages a rueful smile. 'Not that well.'

I bet she had a bloody good go at changing his mind, but I don't press him further. He's been straight with me and I'm glad of that. Sort of.

'When we were still relatively sober, Henry said he could fix me up with a job,' Danny continues. 'A six-month contract. Big money. Lots of zeroes on the end of the number. It's more than I'd normally make in a year – maybe even two years.'

After his confession, it makes me nauseous to think that he might go back to that life.

'I can't take it though,' Danny says. 'I'd lose myself again. You have to be in that world to survive. I realised last night that I have the willpower of a fecking *gnat*.'

That makes me laugh and Danny smiles too. 'You have to have a *few* flaws,' I tell him.

'I couldn't bear it if I did anything to hurt you. I like to think that I'm a good man, do the right thing. It's hard to realise that you have feet of clay.'

'You're human,' I remind him. 'We all do silly things sometimes. I wouldn't be with you now if I hadn't lost my head.'

He gives me a slow smile. 'Crazy fool. Look where that got you.'

'It got me the love of a wonderful man and a lifestyle that I love. I wouldn't change it for the world. Maybe we all need to go a little crazy now and then.'

'I love you,' Danny says. 'I don't want to do anything to jeopardise that. This is the type of life, of relationship, I've always yearned for. I don't know why I behaved as I did. I'm sorry.'

'Let's not talk about it any more.' I stroke his arm. 'Call it an aberration.'

'I did learn that I can't split myself between two worlds. I'd end up totally schizo.'

'I just want you to be happy – *us* to be happy.'

'You don't mind if I don't take the job? I'm turning my back on a lot of money and I know how much we need it now.'

'I'd rather have you here and be stony broke than doing something you're not comfortable with.' If I'm honest, I don't want him going back there. 'What we have is too good to lose. We'll manage. Something will come up.'

He cups my face with his hand. 'You know how much I love you?'

'Of course I do.'

'I want to be *us*, here, now, for ever.'

I turn and kiss his palm. 'Sounds like a plan to me.'

'Shall we drink to that?'

I nod. 'Oh, how we're going to struggle to get up in the morning.'

So we do another shot and Danny picks up his guitar and strums. A few Ed Sheeran numbers, then George Ezra and a couple of others that I don't recognise. Then he sings one of my favourite Train songs, 'Marry Me'. His voice is soft and clear and I hum along.

I feel that the crisis has passed and I can breathe again. I have to remember that Danny's young and is going to make mistakes. Who doesn't? I can live with that. I'm sure he's learned a lesson from this. Me too.

When he's finished, he puts his guitar to one side and, before I know it, he drops to his knee in front of me. He takes my hand in his.

'Marry me, Fay,' he says. 'There's no one else that I want to be with. I don't even have a ring or anything. I hadn't planned this. But marry me.'

Tears spring to my eyes. This is the last thing on earth that I expected. All of my life flashes before me, like a time-lapse film, all the hurt, the disappointment, flying away until I'm brought to this moment. Just me and Danny, my love, my soulmate. I feel as if fireworks are going off inside me and the power of speech has completely deserted me.

'Say something,' Danny urges.

I give a teary laugh. 'Are you sure?'

'I've never been more certain about anything.'

The floodgates are thrown open and I start to cry. 'Yes,' I sob. 'Of course I will.'

We stand and hold each other tight in the tiny space of the well deck surrounded by Christmas lights. Diggery wakes up and barks with excitement even though he's not sure why. I feel as if all my Christmases have come at once. The man that I love wants to make me his wife.

Then Danny kisses me and my head spins. The candles gutter in the breeze, the Christmas lights twinkle and the stars in the sky shine that little bit brighter. And I'm in Danny's arms, where I always want to be.

Chapter Fifty

In the morning, I wake up and wonder if I've dreamed it all. Yet my thumping hangover tells me that I didn't. Too much vodka, too much weed, too much love. Everything hurts. I try to lift my head from the pillow and fail. Danny is already awake and looking at me.

My tongue feels as if it has turned into a hairbrush overnight when I eventually manage to croak out, 'Good morning.'

'Good morning, the future Mrs Wilde,' he says with a grin.

'So you did mean it?'

'Of course I bloody did!' Danny says.

'It wasn't the vodka talking?'

He shakes his head. 'I've been awake half the night thinking about it. Let's do it right away. Now. Why wait? I'll call the register office this morning and see when they can fit us in.'

My head is whirring and not just due to the excess of cheap alcohol. 'There's no rush, is there?'

'No need to hang around either,' he says, quite reasonably. 'I want us to be married. I can't have you changing your mind.'

'I think that's highly unlikely.'

'It'll have to be a small do,' Danny says, face frowning in thought. 'Something on here or at the house, if Lija's up for it.'

'That sounds fine to me.' I never thought that I'd be one of those brides with a big church wedding and a Vera Wang dress. Small and cosy sounds perfect to me. I just want our friends to be with us, that's all.

Danny jumps out of bed, all excited. Even in my half-sleepy state I laugh because I've never seen him like this before. 'You'd think it was Christmas morning and you were five.'

He jumps back onto the bed next to me and kisses me again. 'That's exactly what I feel like,' he says. 'God, I could bounce all round the boat. That's how I know this is right.'

I stroke his face. 'I love you.'

'And I'm the luckiest man alive.' Then he bounds away and a moment later I hear him singing 'Oh, What a Beautiful Mornin'' – which I think, if my memory serves me right, is from the musical *Oklahoma!* Wherever it's from, it's now at top volume in the shower. Diggery crawls under the duvet.

When he's showered, Danny brings me a cup of tea and a couple of slices of toast in bed. 'Will I always get service like this when I'm Mrs Wilde?'

'I want to be the best husband ever,' he says.

'Whatever you do, I know you will be.'

He sighs. 'I have to get to work, but I'll phone the register office this morning when I have my break.'

'OK,' I agree, part of me feeling as if I'm imagining all this.

When Danny's gone, I haul myself out of bed too. I get ready for work without really knowing what the heck I'm doing, still stunned by the events of yesterday evening. As I walk up the garden from the boat, the grass white with frost, I have a definite spring in my step.

Swinging through the door, I feel like bursting into song myself. Lija and Rainbow are already there. I note that Lija is rubbing her back and I can see a small bump just starting to show. Brightly, I call out, 'Morning!'

'Fuck's sake,' Lija mutters. 'You sound like Rainbow.'

She's right. I do sound ridiculously cheerful, even to my own ears.

'Is too much for a woman to cope with *two* Rainbows. What are you so happy about, anyway?'

I take a deep breath before I say, 'Danny and I are going to get married.'

Lija stands stock-still and blinks a few times. On the other hand, Rainbow hurls herself across the kitchen at me. 'OMG! I can't believe it.' I'm embraced in her floury arms. 'A wedding! Oh man, you're so lucky and EVERYTHING. Can I be BRIDESMAID? Can I? Can I?'

'I guess so,' I say, feeling overwhelmed. 'We're only going to have a small do, but I'd be delighted if you'd both be my bridesmaids.'

'Squeeeeee!' Rainbow says and tries to squeeze the life out of me before dancing round the table.

'I do not want to be bridesmaid,' Lija grumbles.

'Oh, please,' I beg. 'For me.'

Lija glowers at me and holds up a hand. 'There is NO way I am wearing pink satin dress.'

'I hadn't got that in mind. You can wear whatever you want. Doc Martens. Head-to-toe black.'

'OK,' she says, grudgingly. 'I will be bridesmaid.'

'I'll wear pink satin,' Rainbow says. 'That'd be COOL. I don't mind what I wear.'

'I don't think that will be necessary. We're on a really tight budget though so, the minute I know when Danny's organised a date, why don't we all take a trip to the nearest charity shop and choose something?'

Lija shrugs that my suggestion is acceptable. Then she comes and gives me one of her hug-not-hugs where she tries to embrace you without really touching you.

'I am happy for you,' she says and then bursts into tears. Pushing away from me, she pulls herself a piece of kitchen roll and blows her nose noisily into it. 'I am happy,' she reiterates, crying again. *Flipping* hormones.'

It must be difficult seeing me all excited about my wedding when her man is somewhere out there on the canal not even knowing that he's the father of her child. I should have been more thoughtful. 'He'll be back,' I say to her. 'I know he will.'

'You know nothing, Fay Happyshit.' Her chin juts out defiantly when she says, 'I couldn't care less whether he comes back or not.'

But she does. I know she does. She's like a hurt child herself. 'This will all work out fine. I'm sure of it.'

'You are getting more like her all the time.' Lija tuts and nods towards Rainbow. 'Princes. Romance. Sparkles. Unicorns. Love, love, love. Pah!'

Rainbow is standing there beaming widely, hands clasped, looking all dreamy. I suppress my grin. Lija's probably right.

'When are we having this wedding?' Lija asks. 'I don't want to be fat as house bridesmaid.'

'Soon. As soon as possible. Danny's going to try to book it this morning.'

At that Rainbow lets out an ear-piercing, 'Squeeeeeee!' and does yet another happy dance round the kitchen. It's making me giddy just watching her. 'I've never been a bridesmaid. All my dreams have come true! Can I tell EVERYONE?'

'Yes.'

'Whoop-whoop!' She pushes her hands in the air and circles the kitchen table. Lija and I ignore her. 'Whoop-whoop!'

'We're just having a few friends so we thought it could be on *The Dreamcatcher* or maybe here, if you don't mind?'

'Is your house,' she says, flatly. 'It would be my pleasure.'

'Thank you.' I go to hug her again, but she takes a step backwards. 'I love you. I want this to be fun for you.'

'Is wedding,' she says. 'Of course it will be fun. Have you told Stinky Stan yet?'

'No. I came straight here.'

'He has not had breakfast. You take it. Try not to give him heart attack.'

But Stan will be overjoyed for me. I know he will.

Lija purses her lips. 'You have not told Edie either?'

'No.' I shake my head.

'Are you going to?'

'I don't know.' I've heard nothing from her since she left, so I don't even know where she is. And if I do tell Edie, will she be happy for me or not? That one's going to be infinitely more difficult to judge.

Chapter Fifty-One

When I knock on Stan's door, it takes him a while to shuffle to open it and I stand shivering in the cold.

'How's my favourite girl?' he says when he lets me in.

He's looking very smart today and I love the fact that he does his best to look dapper, even if he's only going to be sitting in the chair all day. Even if, sometimes, he doesn't button up his shirt or his cardigan quite right. And there might be a bit of stray food down the front.

Danny comes by to help him to have a bath a couple of times a week, but I think we should talk about getting him a walk-in shower fitted after Christmas, and maybe a few other bits to allow him to move round his cottage more easily, though I'm not sure that the narrow, steep stairs and low headroom would make a stairlift an option.

He sits down and I give him the scrambled egg on toast that Lija has freshly made. 'Eat it straight away,' I say, lifting the lid. 'Before it goes cold.'

'Lovely,' he says, when he see what it is. 'My favourite.'

I make a cup of tea while he's eating and, when he's finished, say to him, 'I've got some news. Good news.'

'Not another baby?'

I laugh. 'Not this time, Stan. Danny and I are getting married.'

'Oh, how wonderful.' He picks a clean white handkerchief from his pocket and wipes a stray tear from his eye. 'I'm so happy. You make a lovely couple. He's the right man for you.'

'I think so too.'

'That Anthony chap was never your type.'

'I know. Though it took me a long time to realise that.' There's never a day goes by when I don't thank my lucky stars that Danny happened to drop by on his canal adventure. What if he'd just carried on and stopped somewhere further down? I wonder how many people miss their soulmates by seconds, spend their lives never quite meeting the person that they should be with.

'I have something to ask you too, Stan.' For a moment, I think of my own dad and how pleased he would have been that I'm finally settling down with the man that I love. My throat closes with emotion and tears threaten my eyes. He and Danny would have got on famously. I hope he's up there somewhere looking down on me now. I clear my throat and take Stan's hands. 'Would you do the very great honour of giving me away?'

'Oh, my dear girl. Of course I will. The honour is all mine.' Then we have a good blub together and a hug.

'I'll let you know when as soon as we've organised it.'

300

'I'll see if I can clear my busy calendar,' he teases. I give him a kiss on his forehead and leave him with a big smile on his face.

The rest of the day goes by in a blur of sandwiches and mince pies and Christmas cake. Our specials today are chocolate chestnut torte with honeycomb and St Clement's shortbread sharpened with orange and lemon zest. We should have baked double the amount as they've all gone before mid-afternoon.

Rainbow does, indeed, tell EVERYONE that she's going to be a bridesmaid. I think by the end of the day that Lija is sick of the word 'wedding' already and is hankering for non-stop chatter about Christmas instead.

When Danny comes home that night, he's also beside himself with happiness. He winds his arms round me as I'm in the galley scrubbing some jacket potatoes for dinner.

'I've booked our wedding for Christmas Eve,' he says, delighted with himself.

My heart wants to leap out of my chest with happiness. 'So soon?'

'They'd had a cancellation. It's the last booking of the day before they knock off for Christmas. Three o'clock.'

I get the urge to do a Rainbow-style dance around the boat, but somehow restrain myself and settle for saying, 'Sounds perfect.'

Danny looks at me anxiously. 'You're pleased?'

I hold him tightly. 'More than you'll ever know.'

'We've got to go in beforehand and do the paper-work together, but that's it. All sorted. We can do the dirty deed and come straight back here for a bit of a knees-up.'

'It's the wedding I always dreamed of,' I tease.

'If you wanted Westminster Abbey, I'd make that work,' he says earnestly. 'Though we might have to sneak in round the back and tag onto someone else's wedding.'

I laugh. 'I've asked Stan to give me away and he was delighted. Lija and Rainbow will be bridesmaids. One considerably more reluctant than the other.'

'I can imagine.'

I feel myself smiling contentedly. 'Actually, a Christmas Eve wedding sounds very romantic.'

'We'll give it a good go.' He turns towards me and kisses me deeply. 'I can still do romance.'

Then, quite frankly, the jacket spuds go to pot. We spend the evening in bed, our love the only sustenance we need. Though, in fairness, we do get up at midnight to make toast.

Chapter Fifty-Two

'My nana's mate runs the charity shop in WHATSIT.' Rainbow gestures in the general direction of 'Whatsit'. 'It's only ten minutes from here. Nana's just texted me to say that they'll stay open late for us tonight if we want to go and rummage for wedding outfits.'

'Will she? That's fantastic.' I was wondering when we were going to be able to get away from the madness to go shopping for anything. I can't afford the prices in the shops and I can't exactly order my bridal dress online from China when we have so little time to organise everything. Christmas is now hurtling towards us, unstoppable. The food, at least, shouldn't be a problem. We are, after all, a café and a few extra cakes and butties at short notice shouldn't faze us.

'Shall I tell her we'll do it?'

'Yes, please. If we finish briskly at five, we could be tidied away and up there by six.'

'COOL,' Rainbow says and texts that information back. When she's finished she shouts out, 'SHOOOOOPPP-PPIIIIIIING!' And does her now familiar little dance round the kitchen.

I grin and Lija rolls her eyes. 'How are you feeling today?' I ask.

'Fat. Bloated. Tired. Sick. Worried.'

That's quite a speech for Lija who would normally just say, 'Effing awful.'

'We have the wedding to distract us and then, after Christmas, we can start making plans for the baby.' She hugs her arms round herself and I put my hands on her shoulders. 'It will all be fine. You'll see. We're finally getting back on top.'

'Every time you say that, shit falls on my head.'

'Next year will be different. I promise. I can feel it in my bones.'

'I hope that you are right, Mrs Glass-Half-Full.'

We have a lovely, busy day. An office party comes in for afternoon tea and are boisterous and fun. They're all wearing Christmas hats and have party poppers. They order lots of extra drinks and bring their own champagne for toasts. I catch Rainbow making eyes at one of the young men. Her reindeer antlers, and many other parts of her, jiggle even more enthusiastically than usual. The object of her affections doesn't seem to mind a bit.

When they've gone, Lija and Rainbow blitz the kitchen and I sweep up the dining room floor. There are so many coloured feathers floating about, it looks as if a million parrots have been flying around in here.

When we're done, we jump into Lija's car and head up to the charity shop – Lija driving as if we're in a getaway vehicle.

'So,' I say to Rainbow, 'did you get his phone number?'

'OMG! Yes!' She rolls her eyes. 'Did you see him? FIT or what? He looked like Brooklyn Beckham and EVERYTHING.'

'He seemed very sweet.'

'Wait till I tell my nana.' Rainbow punches in a text as we speed down the country lanes.

Even when we hit the city, Lija doesn't slow down and we get to the charity shop in double quick time.

'This is WELL cool, this shop,' Rainbow informs us as we clamber out of the car and head for the door. 'It's done out like a boutique and EVERYTHING. My nan's friend watched that Mary Portas programme on the telly and now she thinks she's running Topshop or WHATEVER.'

The bell jingles as we enter and an elderly lady with cropped red hair greets us. 'Hello, lovelies. I hear you've come to do wedding shopping. Who's the lucky bride?'

'I am.' I put my hand up somewhat coyly.

'Congratulations. A Christmas wedding! How romantic! I've put out our selection of wedding gowns and brides-maid's dresses. We've not too many, but there are some pretty ones.'

Rainbow rushes over to them. On a separate rail, there are three or four traditional 1980s' wedding dresses – confections of lace and big shoulders. She flicks through them squealing with delight.

'OMG! These are AMAZEBALLS! You would look TOTALLY cool in that.' Rainbow holds up something with lots of frills. 'VINTAGE!'

In my book vintage is a close bedfellow to old tat. I make sure the lovely shop manager isn't looking before I grimace. 'I was thinking of something less . . . *frothy*,' I whisper to Rainbow. 'And something warmer. I'd freeze to death in one of these. I don't want to be blue when I say my vows. Sleeves would be nice.'

She puts it back on the rail looking thwarted in her attempt to dress me up like one of those old-fashioned crinoline lady toilet roll holders. I glance at all the rest, but there's nothing really here for me. It's tricky getting married at my age. I'm worried about looking like mutton dressed as lamb. I want Danny to be proud of me. I don't want the first thing he thinks of when he sees me to be whether we've got any Andrex in the cupboard.

The bridesmaids' dresses are predominantly shiny satin in pastel colours. Rainbow gushes over every one. My other bridesmaid and I are less keen.

Lija looks at them with disdain. 'No. *Flipping*. Way.'

Only Lija can say 'flipping' and make it sound exactly the same as . . . well . . . you know what.

'Any good, lovely?' The manager joins us.

'I was thinking more casual,' I tell her. 'The wedding is very low-key, informal, and I'd like to look a bit Christmassy, if you have anything like that?'

'Let me see.' She puts her glasses on and wanders away into the depths of the shop.

'Just go and find what you'd be comfortable wearing,'

I say to Lija. 'I want you to be happy. There's no colour scheme. I don't have a theme.'

'OK.' Lija also wanders off.

'OMG! I, like, totally LOVE this one!' Rainbow holds up a white cotton maxi dress. It has smocking across the bust and long sleeves with smocking at the cuffs. She does a twirl.

'It's very pretty.' She looks like a little angel.

'Nineteen seventies' original,' the manager says as she bustles by. 'Ideal.'

Rainbow jigs with excitement. 'Can I wear this? Can I wear this? Can I? Can I?'

'Of course.'

'I'll try it on.' She dashes for the changing room.

While she tries on her dress, I go in search of Lija. I find her at the back of the shop, rooting through a rail of black dresses. No surprise there.

She pulls one out and gives it a cursory glance. 'This.'

This one is three-quarter length, a heavy material. It's got a V-neck and one of the shoulders has a grey lace panel over the black fabric. When she turns it round, the whole of the back down to the waist features the same lace.

'That's fantastic.'

'It does not say "wedding".'

'No. But it very much says "Lija". I love it.'

Eventually, Rainbow comes out of the changing room. She twirls round and round in her dress.

'You look beautiful,' I tell her, a lump in my throat.

'OMG! I'm not taking it off. EVER.' She admires herself

in the mirror. 'Wait till my nan sees this. She'll blub her EYEBALLS out!'

I think that's probably a good thing in Rainbow World.

A moment later, Lija stomps out of the changing room and glowers in the mirror. 'Is fine,' she says. Which means that she also adores the dress.

'You look wonderful too.'

'Am fat as *flipping* house,' she complains and disappears into the changing room once more.

Now there's just me to sort out.

The manager appears again. 'I've had this in the back for ages,' she says. 'It needs a few repairs. I was going to take it home to do some stitching so we could charge a bit more, but I never got round to it. I'd almost forgotten it was here.'

She holds out a dark red, velvet coat dress. 'I think this is 1970's too. It's lovely quality. A couple of the buttons are a bit loose and the hem's coming undone. If you're not too bad with a needle, that's easily fixed.'

'Oh.' The dress takes my breath away. This is perfect. The material is worn, but luxurious. It's buttoned all down the front with velvet-covered buttons, studded with crystals, as is the collar. It's nipped in at the waist with a broad belt in the same fabric. The sleeves are full, buttoned at the cuff. Very bohemian with a touch of old-school glamour. 'It's gorgeous.'

'That is TOTALLY cool.' Even Rainbow is slightly speechless.

'I can't think of anything better for a Christmas wedding,' the manager says. 'Try it on.'

Taking the coat dress from her, I rush to the changing room. It fits like a glove and when I look in the mirror, there's a beautiful woman looking back at me. I step out of the changing room with a 'Ta-dah!'

Rainbow bursts into tears. 'OMG! I'm all TEARY.' She fans her eyes with her fingers.

Lija nods her approval. 'Nice.'

'Shall I get it?' Will Danny like it? is what I mean. Will I look as lovely as I possibly can do for him?

'Say YES to the DRESS!' Rainbow squeals.

'I wanted thirty pounds for it,' the manager says as if she's asking for a king's ransom. Which she might as well be due to the parlous state of our finances. 'If you buy all three dresses, I'll do you a deal.'

'Done.' I swirl the skirt of the coat, thinking that thirty pounds is a bargain as this dress has made me feel like a million dollars.

Chapter Fifty-Three

I'm still back at the boat before Danny, so I hide my purchases in the small cabin – having a last little peek at my gorgeous dress before I secrete it away. Christmas Eve and the wedding are close upon us now. I'm yet to go into full panic mode, but it can't be too far away until I do. As it is, I'm feeling relatively calm. Lija, Rainbow and I sorted out the catering in the car on the way back from the charity shop. We'll keep it simple – Lija has promised to make her wonderful goulash to her grandma's recipe and her usual mountain of rice. I can make some salads too – the sort of food we prepare every day. We'll do it all together in the morning before the wedding as the café is closed then. I'll take a run to the local trade warehouse in the next few days and buy some cheap prosecco for a toast or two. I still have to give some serious consideration to the cake, and I have to face the fact that if I go for anything too fancy then I'm probably not going to have time to make it myself. For flowers, I'm going plain and simple. I'm not planning to have a formal bouquet, but I'll buy some blooms the day before for us all. Christmassy, if I can. I'm sure the supermarkets will have loads. Job done. I'll become Mrs Danny Wilde with a minimum of fuss and I couldn't be happier.

When Danny finally comes home, he's exhausted and I hate to see him so tired. He takes me in his arms and I rest my head on his shoulder as we sway together for a while.

'It's good to be home,' he says with a weary sigh.

'You're late.'

'We're inundated with work at the yard. Which is great, in some ways. My boss, Tommo, says he's going to keep me on into the new year and for the foreseeable future.'

'That's brilliant news.'

'It's certainly a relief,' he agrees. 'I'm not going to make my fortune there, but it's a steady income and I do enjoy the work even though it's back-breaking. At least we can make some plans now.'

'You'll still manage a few days off over the holiday?'

'Tommo is only planning to close on Christmas Day and Boxing Day. That's it. I asked for Christmas Eve off for the wedding and he even wanted me to work in the morning.'

'You said no?'

He laughs. 'I did. I'm going to have to get Stan and myself ready. That could take for ever. You know how high-maintenance Stan is,' he jokes. 'I'm planning to cook us both a full English breakfast on the boat to start the day.'

'He'll love that.'

'*My favourite*,' we say in unison and then giggle.

I'm assuming that I'll stay up at the house with Lija the night before. We've tidied upstairs a bit after the flood and the leaky roof, but there's more to do to make the spare room habitable again. After Christmas, we need to think about what to do with the roof too – see whether Danny is able to repair it or whether it's a lost cause and we'll have to find the money for a new one. I keep thinking that if we can only get to Christmas, then we can relax. But the truth of the matter is that we've got even more to contend with in the new year.

We eat, chill out on the sofa for an hour and then fall into bed, knackered. The next morning, Danny is up and out before dawn.

I head to the café early too. The air is biting cold, the sky white and heavy with snow. The weather forecasters keep predicting a downfall but, as yet, it's still not appeared. We haven't had a white Christmas for years and it would be lovely. I don't want so much that it grinds the traffic to a halt and our customers can't get to us, but you know what I mean. Everything looks so much more seasonal with a dusting of snow. Proper Christmassy.

We have a busy day, as always. Even though I'm early, Lija and Rainbow are already elbow deep in scones and sandwiches by the time I arrive. The kitchen table is laden with mince pies and Victoria sponges, the icing sugar picking out a snowflake design.

'Morning!' I strip off my coat and welly boots.

'Morning,' Lija grumbles back.

'You two must have been here since dawn.'

They shoot a look between them that I can't quite fathom but, before I can question it, Rainbow says, 'OMG! I was going to put my bridesmaid's dress on and EVERYTHING today. I SOOOOOO can't wait to wear it. I've only got this on because my nana HID it.' She has on a short green dress and red and white striped tights that makes her look like an elf.

'The wedding will be here soon enough,' I say.

'What wedding?'

I turn at the sound of Edie's voice. She's standing in the doorway looking cold and tired. I get a whirr of emotions when I see her but can't really decide whether the overriding one is happiness or sadness.

'My wedding,' I tell her.

'Oh, Fay.' My sister comes to me with her arms open and I stand to be embraced. I accept the hug stiffly but, when I hear her crying, I relent and hold her tightly. Thin at the best of times, there's really nothing of her. I can feel the outline of her bones under my hands. 'I'm sorry,' she sobs. 'So sorry.'

'Go into living room,' Lija instructs. 'I don't want you crying on sponge cake.'

Doing as I'm told, I shepherd Edie into the front room. It's cold in here away from the warmth of the kitchen and Lija doesn't light a fire until the evening, but we sit on the sofa together.

'I've been such a fool,' she says. 'How am I ever going to make it up to you?'

I can think of one very easy way, but that's not going to happen now. The money is gone. I don't even ask how

313

Brandon's 'investment' is going or whether they are back in touch. Instead, I say, 'Where have you been?'

'I'm staying at a place in Milton Keynes. Airbnb. It's OK. Cheap.'

'You're still planning to stay round here permanently?' Edie nods. 'I've nowhere else to go.'

It pains me to see her sunk so low. 'Have you got a job yet?'

'I've applied for a few, but there's not much about now. Everyone's too wrapped up in their Christmas parties to worry about hiring staff. I'll start properly in the new year.' She cries again. Softly, sadly. 'All this has knocked my confidence, Fay. I can't even begin to tell you.'

I pat her gently. 'Hush, hush.'

'I've been so horrible to you. How can you ever forgive me?'

'I'm your sister,' I tell her. 'Whatever happens, we're bound by blood. Even when I don't like you, I still love you. Just about, sometimes.' She risks a smile at that. 'Of course, I forgive you.'

'I'm so pleased that you're getting married. Danny is wonderful. You're so very lucky to have found him.'

I think that every day but I'm not going to share my thoughts with Edie. Not now.

My sister wipes her eyes. 'When is it?'

'Christmas Eve.'

She looks up in surprise at that. 'So soon? I don't suppose you were even going to invite me?'

'In all honesty, I hadn't decided,' I admit. 'I didn't know where you were either.'

'Though you do have my phone number,' she says a little more tartly.

'And you mine,' I counter.

'Let's not fight,' she says, wearily. 'I'm worn out. I haven't slept properly since I left here.'

'You're not eating, either.'

'I don't really have anywhere to cook in my room, so I've been living on sandwiches and fruit.'

'Oh, Edie.' My sister might drive me mad and this situation may be of her own making, but I think what Dad would say if I turned my back on her now. 'You have to come back to *The Dreamcatcher*.'

'No,' she says. 'If you and Danny are newly married, you'll want your own space.'

I remember how badly her brief stay worked out before. My sister isn't the easiest of house guests. As a narrowboat guest, she was a nightmare.

'Do you think Lija would let me stay in the spare room?'

'No.'

'I'll pay her,' Edie says. 'The same as I do at the Airbnb. It's not much but it might help.'

'The room's in a terrible state after the flood. I was only thinking about it last night. It needs a lot of work to bring it back up to scratch.'

'Talk to her,' Edie begs. 'We could clear the room up together, you and me, couldn't we? You can persuade her. She listens to you. I won't be any trouble. I promise. She'll hardly know that I'm here. I've learned my lesson, Fay.'

How I wish I could believe it, though, I have to say, she seems more sincere this time. But I remind myself that I have been burned before. Yet, what do I do? The thought of Edie alone and friendless is too awful to contemplate. It's Christmas. How can I be hard-hearted enough to turn my back on her?

Chapter Fifty-Four

Eventually, my good nature wins over. I can't be Scrooge at Christmas. I have to see if Lija will be kind enough to take my sister in. 'Stay here,' I say to Edie. 'I'll talk to Lija.'

Heart in my mouth, I walk back into the kitchen. Lija is at the cooker, stirring something furiously in a pot.

'Lija—' I venture.

'No,' she says without turning round. 'No.'

'You don't even know what I'm going to ask you yet.'

Now she spins. 'If it involves Sister from Hell, no.'

'She's in a dreadful state,' I persist. 'I'm worried about her.' Lija holds up a hand to shush me. 'She's living in a bed and breakfast place. It's horrible.'

'Tough titty.'

Rainbow comes into the kitchen, quickly spins round again and disappears. Rainbow likes all the world to be fluffy and pink. She hates confrontation of any kind.

'I thought we could salvage the spare room. She can pay you what she pays there. It's thirty quid a night. *Thirty quid*. That would come in very handy, at the moment.' I'm sure I see Lija waver, so I press on. 'I could do with a few hours off before the wedding to organise bits and bobs. Edie could cover my shifts. She'll look for work in the new year, but this could tide her over.'

'She is evil cow.' Lija doesn't mince her words. 'How many times will you let her do this, Fay?'

'She's my sister.'

'She makes *fool* of you!'

'I know. I know. But this will be the very last time.'

Lija glowers at me. 'You say that *last* very last time.'

'That's fine. I completely understand where you're coming from.' Tears prickle my eyes. I only have so much fight in me and Lija is resolute. 'I'll ask her to leave.'

'Do not always be so *flipping* reasonable,' Lija snaps. 'She can stay. OK?'

'Really?' She tuts her displeasure at me. 'Thank you, Lija. Thank you. I do appreciate it.' I give her a hug and she stands rigid. 'You won't even know she's here.'

Lija rolls her eyes.

'We'll go up now and look at what needs doing in the bedroom, then Edie can make a start on it. I'll be down to help you with prep as soon as I can.'

'We have all day,' Lija says sarcastically. 'Take your time.'

'I'd like to echo what Fay said.' Edie, standing at the door, has heard it all. 'Thank you, Lija.'

'If you do one thing to hurt my friend, you will have me to answer to.' Lija waves the wooden spoon in her hand quite menacingly. 'If you were my sister, you would be on *flipping* bike, take a hike. She is too good to you.'

'I know.' Edie hangs her head, cowed. 'I do appreciate it.'

'We'll go to look at the room.' Quickly, I hustle Edie out of the kitchen and rush her up the stairs before Lija can change her mind.

When I open the door to the spare room, the musty smell of damp hits us.

'Bloody hell,' Edie says. 'It smells like someone died in here.'

'I told you it was bad.' It *was* bad and, since I last looked a couple of weeks ago, it's got considerably worse. Edie's childhood bedroom is unrecognisable. The wallpaper is peeling off the wall. It hangs down in great, drooping swathes. The paint all over the ceiling has blistered and bubbled. The carpet is all mildewed. The buckets we've placed round the room have clearly failed to catch all of the rainfall. If the rest of the house was like this, it would be condemned. Once again, I feel terrible that Lija is in this situation. She bought the house to help me out, but I think she's taken on so much more than she imagined. I knew the house needed a lot of work, but now I feel it's crumbling around our ears at an accelerated pace. Plus I still believe it's my responsibility to put it right.

Lija will want this bedroom when the baby is born. It would make a great nursery. It's a light, airy space and has a wonderful view over the garden. There's room for a decent-sized cot and a rocking chair. Perhaps Danny and

I will treat her to one. We'll have to scour the second-hand shops. I can just picture it and get a little thrill thinking about what's to come. Then I have a reality check and simply add it to the long list of Things To Do After Christmas. Sigh. I turn my attention back to my sister.

'You can't stay in here,' I say, stating the obvious. 'You'll get double pneumonia or worse. Let's have a look at the other room. I'm sure Lija won't mind.' I'm not entirely sure at all, but having pushed Lija so far, I think she'll capitulate.

We check the room that was my old bedroom. This has, indeed, fared much better. It smells a bit fusty and there are a few buckets which were put in there to catch drips that are nearly full to the top with water, but it's certainly not as bad as the other room. It's habitable, at least. If it were a warmer day, I'd throw open the window, but it's freezing out there, so I'll bring up a fan heater instead and hope to take the chill from it that way. I should have stripped the bed in here, but we've been so busy that I haven't had a chance. It will need a damn good clean, and dry bedding too, but there's plenty of spare sheets in the airing cupboard.

Edie walks over to the window and looks out. 'It's beautiful out there,' she says. 'All the time I lived here, I never really appreciated it.'

I go and stand next to her. The day is faded grey, the trees like shadows. There's a shroud of mist hovering low on the water but, before we know it, spring will return and the trees and hedges by the canal will be bursting with fat, green buds and unruly leaves.

'I always loved this house.' I look round my old bedroom with its sprigged rose wallpaper that's so terribly out of date and its polyester green curtains and still miss it like crazy.

'I was mad to let this go, wasn't I?' Edie turns to me, eyes filled with tears. 'This was our childhood home. We were happy here.'

'We were,' I agree.

'Why didn't you stop me from selling it?' she says.

'If you remember rightly, Edie, you were absolutely determined – *desperate* – to get rid of this place. You didn't even consult me before you put it up for sale.'

She rubs her face with her hands. 'God. What an idiot I've been.'

'It's too late for that now,' I say. 'We have to make the best of what we've got. Do you want to move back in here or not?'

'As Lija's paying lodger?'

'If you've got another option in mind, then just let me know.'

'No,' she admits. 'There's no plan B. I'm sure I'd be much happier here than where I am now.'

'It's a good, solid room,' I point out. 'You have your own bathroom. There's nothing that a good clean and freshen up won't put right. We can probably move the buckets now. It'll only be a problem if it starts raining cats and dogs again.'

'That's reassuring,' she says, wryly.

'I'll get you the cleaning stuff and you can set to.'

She casts a horrified glance at her perfect manicure and

I hide a smile. I'm not sure that Edie has experienced hard physical work in a long time. 'We have rubber gloves,' I point out. 'It won't kill you. If you want to stay here, you're going to have to swallow your pride and muck in.'

She looks bleakly at me. 'It just feels as if I'm right back where I started.'

'Then use it to turn over a new leaf, Edie.'

'I will,' she says. And she looks as earnest as I've ever seen her.

Chapter Fifty-Five

While Rainbow, Lija and I are busy downstairs serving customers, Edie starts to clean up my old bedroom. She takes a bucket of soapy water, some polish and a pile of dusters plus the all-important rubber gloves. Pink ones, so that cheers her up a bit.

We're run off our feet all morning, so I don't get a chance to pop up and see how she's doing. At lunchtime, when we're in the kitchen, leaning against the counter and eating a quick sandwich from a tray of leftovers, Edie reappears. There's no designer gear in evidence and she's obviously helped herself to a pair of my old jeans and a T-shirt from the wardrobe up there which swamp her frail frame, making her look much younger than her years. She's snatched her hair back in a scrunchie but most of it is escaping and sticking to her face which has a rarely spotted sheen of sweat. There's a rosy glow to her cheeks which has been missing for a long time.

'This is better than a workout,' she puffs, then empties her bucket into the sink. 'To think I used to pay thousands for a high-end gym.'

Behind her back Lija makes a stabbing motion with a butter knife and I bite my lip so that I don't smile.

'Have you changed the bed yet?' I ask.

Edie pushes back a few strands of hair with her forearm. 'Next job.'

'I'll come up and help you.'

So I abandon my sandwich and follow her upstairs. Already the room is fresher, cleaner. She's thrown the window open, despite the cold, and it's given it the good airing it needed.

'You've done a great job,' I say, impressed by her endeavours. For someone unaccustomed to cleaning she's really embraced it.

Together we pull back the fusty sheets and strip the bed. 'I think we should let this mattress air for as long as we can. When you close the windows, leave the fan heater on then we can make it up this evening.'

'Good idea. I think I'm done in here,' she says. 'I've cleaned the bathroom too.' She looks quite proud of herself. 'Do you need any help in the café?'

'I think we're on top of things.'

'I could make a start on the spare room, if you like. I know the roof needs repairing, but I could take the bedding off and take the curtains down. I could even strip the wallpaper.'

Is this really Edie I see before me?

'I know what you're thinking,' she says, snippily. 'But I'm not completely useless.'

'We're going to need to use that room sooner rather than later. We'll check with Lija, but I can't see why not.'

So, that same evening, Edie moves into my old bedroom. She goes to collect her stuff from the bed and breakfast accommodation which, by Edie's standards, is not that much. Thank goodness. I help her to settle in and she looks small and forlorn. My heart goes out to her.

'You can come to *The Dreamcatcher* and eat with us tonight, if you like,' I say.

Edie shakes her head. 'You and Danny don't want me under your feet all the time. I bought a few bits at the supermarket and Lija has cleared me a shelf in the fridge. I've got to start to be self-sufficient.'

I have a moment where I could weep when I think of all that Edie has squandered. But it's no good crying over spilt milk, as they say.

When she's unpacked, I hug her tightly. 'Goodnight, Edie.'

'Thanks, Fay,' she says. 'I won't be a shit this time. I swear.'

'I'll hold you to that.' Then I leave her and go in search of Lija who I find sitting on the sofa with her feet up on the pouffe, eating cheese on toast. She's in the dark apart from the twinkling Christmas tree lights.

'It looks lovely in here.'

'Yeah.'

I flop down next to her and, when I'm close, I can tell that she looks weary. I also notice that the previously tiny bump beneath her loose top is starting to burgeon. 'How are you doing?'

'OK,' she says. 'Tired. Fat.'

'Edie's done a good job,' I tell her. 'She's trying to be helpful.'

'She is *very* trying,' Lija agrees.

I laugh. 'I think this time it might be different.'

'Do not count your horses before your chickens,' Lija observes.

I don't bother to correct her. 'I won't. When she's cleared out that small bedroom we can look at what needs doing. Danny says that he'll get on the roof and see if it can be patched.'

'There is good money coming into the café.' She looks relieved at that. 'Maybe there is some to spare for repairs.'

'We'll help you where we can. You know that.'

Instead of pushing me away as she normally would, she smiles and says, 'Thank you.'

I slip my arm through hers and we watch the twinkling of the Christmas tree lights. 'Even though it's only a few days away, I'm still not sure that I feel Christmassy yet.'

'Am bloody sure *I* don't,' Lija notes. 'I hate Christmas.'

'No, you don't,' I tell her. 'Just think how much fun it will be next year when we have a baby in the house.'

Lija makes a snorting noise. I'm not sure that she's sharing my joy.

'The wedding will be here soon.' I squeeze her arm in excitement.

'I know.' Lija sounds less thrilled.

'It's been so mad busy that I haven't really had the time to think about it.' But now I get a little buzz of excitement.

'Stay here night before,' Lija says. 'Is bad luck for groom

to see bride or some shit. We can have drinks, hen party.'
She shrugs. 'I do not know about these things. Shall we
let Rainbow organise?'

'Oh, Lord.' I laugh. 'We'll all be in pink fluffy deely-
boppers and there'll be blow-up willies.'

'I am seeing no problem,' Lija deadpans.

'You can let her organise it, but on your own head be
it.' I take my chance. 'Speaking of organising, I could do
with a couple of hours off tomorrow to sort out a few
things. Shall I ask Edie to help out? It's another fully booked
afternoon for Christmas teas and I don't want you to run
yourself ragged.'

Lija rolls her eyes and, with overt reluctance, says, 'Yes.'

I'm not sure how good a waitress my dear sister will be,
as she usually likes to be the one waited on hand and foot,
but there's nothing like throwing her in at the deep end.

'I'd better go.' I risk a brief peck on Lija's cheek and
she doesn't wipe it off. 'Danny should be home soon.'

'You've got a good one there,' Lija observes.

'I know. I'm very lucky.' Then, chancing my arm, I
venture, 'You've still heard nothing from the man on the
canal?'

Lija shakes her head and her hand goes protectively to
her bump. 'Long gone.'

'Don't give up on him just yet,' I say.

'Maybe Santa will bring him wrapped up in tinsel,' she
answers, sarcastically.

'Wouldn't that be a sight to see?' I tease.

'Go home,' Lija says. 'Hot Stuff will wonder where you
are.'

I push myself out of the sofa, where I could quite gladly stay all night, and say, 'See you tomorrow.'

On *The Dreamcatcher*, I make a quick pasta dish and, with impeccable timing, Danny arrives the minute it's ready.

I kiss him and wrap my arms round his neck. 'I'm glad you're home. It's been a long day.'

'Tell me about it.'

'Edie turned up again.'

'Oh, man,' Danny says. 'I was hoping she'd gone back to New York. What did she want now?'

'She's still saying that she's back for good. She was staying at some awful B&B place so I managed to persuade Lija to let her use my old bedroom.'

'Are you sure that's the right thing to do?' Danny asks.

'No,' I tell him. 'I can't be hard-hearted, though. She seemed genuinely sorry this time.' He looks about as convinced as Lija did. 'With very little prompting she cleared up her room and made a start on the spare bedroom. She's paying rent too. That'll help us.'

'The jury's still out on whether Edie being back is a good thing.'

'You don't mind her coming to the wedding?'

He shakes his head. 'Of course not. She's your sister.'

'Thank you. I know she's difficult.' Danny yawns and I can see that his face is white with tiredness. 'I hope you're getting good overtime pay for all these hours you're putting in.'

'Sort of,' Danny says, evasively. 'Let me go and have a quick shower while you dish up.'

So he does and I put the pasta in two bowls. We eat sitting on the sofa, the coffee table serving as our dining room.

'I think I'll go and watch some telly with Stan,' I say. 'I'd like to spend some time with him. I haven't had a minute to see him properly for days. I've only caught him coming in and out for his meals and Rainbow has been taking him his supper, bless her.'

'You like her, don't you?'

'She's a great girl. It's always sunny in her world.'

'I'll come to Stan's with you,' Danny says. 'Maybe he'd like a bath before he goes to bed.'

I thought that I might be able to take my dress with me and do the minor repairs that it needs but I'd rather have Danny's company. I'll have to find some time soon though as I'll be walking into the register office in a ragged frock.

'Do you think he's all right now?' I ask Danny. 'I was so worried about him for a while.'

'He's doing great. Due, in no small part, to your tender loving care. He'll want more looking after now, but we're going to be around to do that. It's got to be hard to manage on your own at that age.'

'Do you think we'll grow old together?'

'I hope so,' Danny says. 'I'm planning to give it my best shot.'

'I feel terrible for Stan that he never married. He's still in love with his first girl. After all these years. That's true devotion for you. It's such a shame as he would have been a lovely husband.'

'We'll make sure that he has the time of his life at our wedding.'

'I'm not sure that the delights of Bletchley register office are going to blow his mind,' I point out.

'True,' Danny agrees. 'Still, he'll love the fact that he's giving you away. That was a great idea.'

'I know. I'm pleased he agreed to do it.'

'I want to invite him over here for breakfast on our wedding day too,' he adds. 'I haven't done that yet.'

My stomach flips when he says it. Wedding day. Yikes! 'The countdown really is on now.'

'A couple of days. That's all.'

'I don't even know what you're wearing.'

'Something suitable.' More evasion. 'It's all sorted.'

I don't press him further. I know Danny, he'll look great whatever he wears. 'Lija's asked me to stay at the house the night before.'

'Sounds like a plan,' Danny says. 'Stan and I can have our stag do in peace.'

'No lapdancing clubs?'

'Not on the agenda. Can't have a heart attack the night before the wedding. Stan, not me. Thought we'd have a night in with Jack Daniel's.'

'I'm nervous,' I admit. 'We are doing the right thing?'

'Of course.'

'You're not having second thoughts?'

He takes my plate and puts it on the table, then he holds my hands in his. 'No way. I can't wait for you to be my partner for life.'

'I still can't believe it's happening,' I tell him.

'Believe,' he says.

'This is the best Christmas present ever.' I try out my

330

new name. 'Mrs Danny Wilde.' It seems so strange on my tongue and my head spins slightly. 'This *so* top-trumps my bike when I was five.'

Danny laughs.

As Rainbow would say, 'Squeeeeeeee!'

Chapter Fifty-Six

Over the course of the next few days, Edie works really hard on cleaning up the small spare room. I've never seen her so determined. Or so poorly groomed. Her hair is in a permanent scrunchie, she's devoid of make-up and the polish on her normally perfect nails is chipped to bits. Instead, she's in my old clothes, sleeves rolled up, dirt on her face and seems to be loving it.

After work one night, Danny helps us to lift the soggy, smelly carpet out and we dump it in the garage until he gets time to take it to the local tip. We place the buckets more strategically under the worst of the damp patches on the ceiling. After Christmas – my new mantra – it'll be clear for us to repair and decorate.

In between all the cleaning, Edie quickly scrubs up and helps to cover my shifts when I pop out to run a few errands for the impending wedding. We're so busy in the café that everything has to be squeezed in around it. I'm pleased to say that Edie is getting on better with Lija and Rainbow – I even keep finding them in huddles, whispering. Every time I come into the room, the conversation halts. I'm sure they're plotting something for my hen night. As long as it's not a fireman stripagram – do people even have those any more? I'd die of embarrassment.

Thankfully, this is our last opening day before Christmas. I have all of tomorrow morning to get ready for the wedding. Luxury! While I'm lifting yet another tray of mince pies out of the oven, Rainbow bounces in.

'OMG,' she says. 'Christmas hats or WHAT!'

It seems that Rainbow has bought festive hats for us all. She brandishes them with glee, shaking her hips, boobs and curls for good measure.

'They are *flipping* hideous,' Lija observes.

'It's not even PROPER Christmas without one.' Rainbow jams a top hat fashioned like a chimney with Santa's legs sticking out of the top onto Lija's head. 'LEGEND!'

Lija looks like someone who wishes to commit murder just for the fun of it.

I'm next to receive a festive hat to grace my person. Trying to resist Rainbow in full flight is futile. My hat is a Christmas tree complete with flashing star on top which I actually quite like. She's given Edie one with two candy canes tied with a bow – which is borderline tasteful. Especially when she stands next to Rainbow herself who's sporting a huge Christmas pudding hat over her curls. When we brave the customers in them they, of course, love them. Next year we should definitely sell some here and then I remember that this is Lija's choice, not mine.

'I got my nan a polar bear hat,' Rainbow trills. 'It's MASSIVE! It'll look like it's eating her HEAD.'

This we should obviously view as a good thing.

Our Christmas afternoon tea frenzy is at its peak and, as school has finished for the holidays, we've got even more people in for breakfast every day. There are more canal boats on the move – again, probably due to the festive season – so more are mooring up at the jetty next to *The Dreamcatcher* to pop in to see us and it's nice to welcome back some familiar faces.

After Stan has eaten his breakfast, we make him stay at the table buttering mountains of toast for our hungry hordes. Rainbow hasn't forgotten a hat for Stan either. He's given a snowman decorated with red sequins and lurex holly. He loves it. No doubt it's now his favourite Christmas hat. Though possibly his only one.

Frankly, he's in his element all morning and shows no signs of being in a rush to go home. I'm just happy every time the till chimes as it means more money towards Lija's leaky roof fund.

Rainbow cranks up the Christmas songs and we all sing along. Even Lija. Well, sort of. She somehow manages to replace the majority of festive words with filthy expletives. Still, she enjoys herself and that's what matters. Though I've never heard 'We Three Kings of Orient Are' in quite that manner.

By the time the last customer leaves at five o'clock we're all worn out. I'm glad that we're having a quiet night in before my wedding. I'm not sure what Rainbow has planned for entertainment, but I have my fingers crossed that it's not too taxing. At least she hasn't organised for us to go clubbing in the city. Or maybe she did and Lija talked her out of it.

As Edie's worked so hard in the café and hasn't complained about anything, there's also a slight thawing in relationships between her and Lija. When we've cleared up for the day, we all have a group hug and I'm pleased to see that Lija puts her arm around Edie without any hesitation. Well, not too much. I keep my fingers crossed behind my back. I don't really want to turn up for work and find my sister's blood up the walls. Not before Christmas. Not before my wedding.

'I should go and get my things.' I'm not entirely sure where I'll be sleeping tonight as Edie's in my old room. I could be bunking in with her, if she'll have me. Otherwise, I'll be on the sofa.

'We're not staying here,' Edie tells me. 'I've booked us all a hotel for the night.'

'Is that what you've all been whispering about?' I ask.

'Maybe,' she says.

'It's a lovely thought, Edie, but you don't have any money.'

'I still have my credit card though. Just about. This is my present to you. To you all. It's good to be back and I wanted to thank you for taking me in. Again.'

'Parteeeeeeeeee!' Rainbow shouts and pumps her hands in the air. 'Parteeeeeeeeee!'

I have to smile. Whatever she's come up with, I'll join in with good grace. I've never yet seen Rainbow disappointed and I don't want to be the one to do it.

'What about the food for tomorrow?' I ask. 'I thought we were going to start it tonight?'

'No need to worry,' Lija says. 'We have a plan.'

'Are you going to let me in on this plan?'

Lija looks thoughtful for a moment. 'No.'

Fair enough. There's only a few of us. If it doesn't go according to Lija's 'plan', then we can always knock up something quickly when we get back. We're a café, it's what we do.

'No cooking tonight either. We have a table booked in the restaurant for eight o'clock,' Edie says. 'Better get a wiggle on.'

'OMG!' Rainbow is beside herself with joy. 'I think I might WEE with happiness!'

Me too. I grin, feeling very special. 'I'd better go and pack my things, then.'

Chapter Fifty-Seven

I'm exhausted when I make my way down to the boat to collect what I need for our night out. The air outside is freezing and this is possibly the coldest day of the year yet. The white Christmas that's still being promised by the weathermen seems even more feasible now. On *The Dreamcatcher*, the log burner is roaring away and it's cosy and warm. Danny is waiting for me and takes me into his arms.

'You've finished work early for once.'

'I've got a lot to do,' he says. 'These weddings don't organise themselves, you know.'

'I have no idea how on earth people manage to have parties for a hundred and thirty with all the bells and whistles.'

'Me neither,' Danny agrees. 'Do we even *know* a hundred and thirty people?'

'There are friends that I haven't seen for ages that it

would have been nice to invite.' I've lost touch with so many of them over the last year or so, what with one thing and another. Perhaps it would have been good to make a bit more of a fuss about our marriage. Then I remember that we don't have the type of budget that can run to 'a fuss'. 'Maybe we could have a belated party in the summer.'

'Maybe.'

Danny doesn't seem that keen, so I don't push it. Besides, I have enough to think about now. Even though our celebration may be modest, I'm marrying the man who I love the most in the world and I couldn't be happier.

'We're not staying at the house tonight. Edie's booked us into a hotel.' I can tell by his expression that it's not a surprise for Danny. 'You knew.'

He nods. 'The girls thought it would be nice for you to be spoiled for a change.'

'It's a lovely thought. I can't remember when I last stayed in a hotel. I'm just more worried about Edie's credit card than she is.'

'Let her treat you, for once. You deserve it. Take the opportunity to stretch out in a bath.'

'Sounds like bliss.' I might use all of the complimentary toiletries for the sheer hell of it. 'You're seeing Stan later? I don't like to leave you while I'm out having a good time.'

'Yeah. We're just going to chill out,' Danny says. 'I splashed out on a bottle of JD and some beer snacks. Stan the Man and me are going to get seriously wasted.'

'Don't get so wasted that you oversleep tomorrow,' I warn. 'I don't want Stan staggering down the aisle with me either.'

'As if,' Danny says, but he gives me a worrying wink.

'I won't have time to stop by and see him before I go off to the hotel. Will you give him my love and tell him I can't wait for him to give me away tomorrow? You've got the wedding rings?'

'Everything's under control. I don't want you to worry about a thing.' Then Danny turns away from me. 'One last thing. I picked this for you today.' He produces a basket filled with holly bearing the most beautiful dark red berries which match my coat dress perfectly. There are some fronds of conifer in there too and some pine cones. 'You haven't said what you'd planned for your flowers, but I spotted it on my way to work and thought of you. Can you make use of it?'

'It's gorgeous.' My eyes fill with tears. 'I was going to nip to the supermarket in the morning and buy some flowers. This is so much better.'

On the top of the foliage is a sprig or two of glossy mistletoe. I hold it up. 'It would be a shame not to try this out. See if it works?'

'You know, I can feel it working already,' he teases and holds me close. His lips meet mine, softly, then more intensely. He draws me along the length of his body and his fingers leave trails of tingling pleasure. 'We don't have time for this,' I murmur against his neck.

'We should *always* have time for this,' he counters.

Well, I'm hardly going to be the one to argue the night before our wedding, am I?

So in the time I should be packing, we make love and then, when I can linger in his arms no longer, I run round like a loon throwing things into a case so that I can make the appointed time for our departure to the hotel without Lija giving me a telling-off.

'I'm running late,' I say in a panic.

'I was still right though.' Danny grins at me from the bed.

'Yes,' I admit. 'You were.' I throw my toiletries into the bag. 'You'll make sure that Stan's dressed and ready?'

He gets up and pulls on his jeans. 'We have a breakfast appointment for tennish.'

'Enjoy yourselves.' He takes me in his arms for one last hug. 'I'll see you tomorrow at the register office,' I say.

'Until tomorrow.' As, reluctantly, I move away, he blows me a kiss.

Then, with happiness in my heart, I leave him to go to my hen party.

Chapter Fifty-Eight

The hotel is beautiful. Edie, of course, has really pushed the boat out. I don't think of the damage this is doing to her credit card. That's her problem, not mine. Just as long as she doesn't give me the bill in the new year.

The hotel isn't that far from where *The Dreamcatcher* is moored, but I've never been here before — generally we choose the more modest establishments for our custom as befits our budget.

Tonight we have two adjoining rooms at the hotel. I have one to myself with an enormous king-size bed. Lija, Edie and Rainbow are sharing a family room next door. My suite is all cream and gold and gorgeous with a beautiful chandelier and more cushions on the bed than I thought humanly possible.

Rainbow is totally hyperactive. 'OMG! Look at this. I'm completely INCREDIBLISED. It's all Hollywood and EVERYTHING. I bet the Kardashians stay in places like this. It's so A-LIST!' She runs round opening and closing all the doors, checking out what's in every drawer. 'Kettle. Hairdryer. Ironing board. You could TOTALLY live here!'

Lija lies down on the bed and closes her eyes. 'Heaven.'

'Thank you, Edie,' I say. 'It's wonderful.'

'You're welcome. Nothing too much trouble for my older sister.'

I wonder whether I should have booked somewhere like this for our wedding night but, if I'm honest, I'd rather go back to *The Dreamcatcher* to be with Danny. This is a super treat, but it's not really us.

Rainbow runs out of the bathroom, clutching a fluffy robe. 'Check out the DRESSING GOWNS!' She models hers. 'Totally LUSH.'

'Pre-dinner cocktails, ladies,' my sister says. 'Ta-dah!' She delves into her wheelie case and pulls out a bottle of Bombay Sapphire gin followed by two or three other spirits and cordial along with a bag of limes. 'May I present to you the Laverstoke! Glasses, Rainbow.'

Obligingly, Rainbow finds the glasses in my room and then brings the ones from their room too.

'It should have slices of fresh ginger in it,' Edie says as she mixes, 'but that was too much of a shag.'

'I'm sure we'll manage,' I offer.

'I've got a non-alcoholic one for you, Lija,' she says.

Lija rolls her eyes. 'Joy.'

I want to point out that Rainbow should, at her tender years, maybe have just a small cocktail, but then that makes me feel like The Responsible Adult and I'm going to let my hair down. I'm sure Rainbow has forgotten more than I know about how to handle alcohol in a sensible manner. If two of my bridesmaids have hangovers, then so be it.

Edie mixes us cocktails and Rainbow plonks a big carrier bag on the bed and tips a colourful tangle of knitwear onto the duvet. 'Bad taste Christmas jumpers,' she squeals. 'Courtesy of eBay.'

Lija opens her eyes and recoils in horror when she sees Rainbow holding a garishly bright jumper in front of her. 'I would rather stick pins in eyes. Christmas or not *flipping* Christmas, I am *not* wearing that thing in public.'

'You SO are,' Rainbow says. 'I got this one especially for you.' She passes Lija a black sweater with BAH HUMBUG written on it in big, sparkly letters.

Lija brightens. 'Cool.'

I get a red jumper with a worried-looking turkey on the front. Edie has Santa stuck in a chimney showing his butt crack and Rainbow has one that says, DASHER, DANCER, PRANCER, VIXEN, COMET, CUPID, DARYL DIXON and has a picture of Norman Reedus bearing his customary crossbow and wearing a Santa hat. Even though I don't have a television, I know more about the delights of *The Walking Dead* than I need to, courtesy of Rainbow.

'These are excellent,' I say.

'Put them on! Put them on!' Rainbow urges.

So we all strip off our tops and replace them with the unseemly Christmas sweaters. Edie hands round the cocktails. 'To Fay and Danny,' she proposes and we drink.

'To Christmas!' I offer. We drink again.

'To being a BRIDESMAID,' Rainbow trills.

'To Christmas being *flipping* over.' Lija glowers at her booze-free cocktail.

Edie puts her arm round me. 'I'm the only one who's not a bridesmaid.' She pouts at me.

'Of course you must be a bridesmaid. The girls are just wearing what they want to. I'm sure you've got something suitable in your wardrobe.'

'Great,' Edie says. 'I won't let you down.'

'You'll probably be better dressed than I will be.' Edie's outfit certainly won't be from a charity shop. Which reminds me that I still have some mending to do.

By the time dinner comes round we are less sober and righteous than we might be so, thankfully, they put us in a cosy corner away from the main dining area where we can be noisy. More drink is taken.

Back in the room, on Rainbow's instruction, we take off our jumpers and change into the fluffy robes.

'We're having more costume changes than a BEYONCÉ concert!' she trills, ecstatically, her little cheeks pink with cocktails.

She also produces a bright pink BRIDE TO BE sash for me to wear, along with a pink tiara. Then she makes us all hot chocolate from the hospitality tray, producing a can of squirty cream and a tub of multicoloured sprinkles from her wheelie case.

'You've thought of everything.'

'I've got chocolate COCKS too.' She delves into her bag and pulls out a box of confectionary willies, waving them at us. 'They're only LITTLE ones. Not like PROPER man-size.'

'Cocktail cocks.' Lija regards them with disdain, but eats one with relish nevertheless.

'Pah!' Edie says. 'You won't get Fay putting a cock in her mouth. Chocolate or otherwise. I'm the only one in the family who . . . well, never mind.'

'Of course I'm up for one,' I say gamely and am given a willy to chew on. I consider this getting off lightly, considering how my hen party might have gone.

Rainbow delves into her case once more. 'Secret Santa PRESENTS! WOO-HOO!'

We exchange presents – hastily bought and wrapped in my case as I'd already chosen their presents ready to go under the tree for Christmas day. Rainbow tears into hers.

'Look at me RIPPING this up,' she says. 'My nana folds it all really carefully so she can use it again. She recycles cards and EVERYTHING. She'd go MENTAL if she saw this.' Rainbow gaily rips another strip from her present. 'WHEEEEEE!'

There are face paints for Rainbow and my present is a rainbow-coloured neckerchief for Diggery. Edie gets a wand with a sparkly tiara at the end and, for Lija, a pink, sparkly 'Baby on Board' sticker for her car which makes her cry a bit.

Rainbow insists on painting all of our faces with snow-flakes and I'm relieved we didn't exchange pressies before we went to dinner or I'd have to have eaten my meal looking like Elsa from *Frozen*. When she's finished, she waves a DVD at us. '*Bridget Jones's Diary*. My nan says that NO ONE rocks a Christmas jumper better than Colin Firth.'

Rainbow's nan might have a point.

'But first . . .' She brandishes some red nail polish. 'More beautification. Manicures and pedicures!'

I can't think of the last time I wore nail polish, but I've already learned that I won't get away from this, so I sit back with my hot chocolate, adjust my tiara and let Rainbow attend to my fingers and toes. When she's finished with me, she daubs Edie and Lija too.

'We're all matching and EVERYTHING. This is going to be one SICK wedding!'

When Rainbow starts on her own nails, I slip into the bathroom and sit on the lid of the loo while I call Danny.

'Hey,' he says. 'Having a good time?'

'Yes. I feel nineteen again.'

'That's a good thing?'

'I've had more cocktails than I can remember and a chocolate willy or two.'

'OK.' He sounds a bit unsure about the last bit.

'I've worn a bad taste Christmas jumper and am now sporting a lurid sash and tiara. I have glittery snowflakes all over my cheeks.' Which I'm hoping will wash off by tomorrow. 'I've just had a manicure and my toes painted. You won't recognise me.'

'Sounds as if Rainbow has all the essential hen party bases covered.'

'She's done a great job. And for the finale we're about to watch *Bridget Jones's Diary*.'

'Glad you're having a good time.'

'I'm missing you,' I say. 'What are you doing? Are you at Stan's?' There seems to be quite a bit of background noise that I can't make out.

'Yeah. Having an evening of quiet contemplation.'

'I can hear all sorts of banging and chatter.'

'Must be on the telly.'

'Oh. You're not having second thoughts?'

'Erm . . .' He leaves an agonising pause, during which my heart bangs in my chest. 'No.'

'Don't tease. I'm serious.'

'There's nothing that will make me happier.'

'Good.' I hold the phone closer as if it will bring Danny nearer. 'I'll see you in the morning. I'll be back to get the food prepared.'

'Hmm,' Danny says. 'Maybe talk to Lija about that.'

'Why? What?'

'Relax,' he says. 'I'll see you tomorrow. Love you, Fay.' Then he hangs up.

When I come out of the bathroom, Lija is waving her fingers around to dry her nail polish. 'What's happening tomorrow?' I ask. 'It sounds as if I've missed out on part of the plan.'

'We're all going to have cooked breakfast, then we are going home to make food for wedding while you have relaxing massage.'

'Really?'

'It's all booked,' Edie confirms. 'You can't be making sandwiches and stuff on your wedding day.'

'I don't mind.'

'Well, you should,' my sister says. 'We'll come back and pick you up in plenty of time to get ready and whisk you to the register office.'

'You're spoiling me.'

She kisses my cheek. 'That's what sisters do.'

When we're all filed and painted, Rainbow hands out posh popcorn – even though we've just had a three-course dinner – dims the lights and we settle on the big, comfy bed to watch the film.

I put my arm round her and give her a squeeze. 'This is the best hen party ever,' I tell her.

'Cool.' There's a big satisfied grin on her cherubic face. 'Don't smudge your nails.'

Chapter Fifty-Nine

It's so late when we get to bed. We had to watch the bit where Bridget goes after Mark Darcy in the snow time and time again. Rainbow had a good weep. In fact, she cried so much she made her snowflakes run.

Lija looks a little tired this morning and I wonder if our late night has taken its toll on her too.

'Are you feeling all right?'

'Yeah. Baby may have kicked me for first time.' She places a hand on her bump. 'Or may be trapped fart. Here.' She takes my hand and covers the same spot.

I feel a ripple beneath my fingers. 'Definitely a baby moving.'

'Good.' Lija risks a wary slow smile.

'It seems very real now. It will all be fine, you know.'

'So you keep saying.' Lija sighs. 'But first, we have wedding. Anything you need me to do?'

'Can you nip to the supermarket for some roses for

bouquets? Danny's picked me a basket of holly and fronds of conifer, but it might need a little extra.'

'Romantic bastard,' she notes with a shake of her head. 'He's too much.'

'Some red flowers if possible. Roses would be nice.'

'Sure.' She shrugs. 'I can do this.'

So Lija scoots out and brings back three bunches of red roses for a fiver and I put them in water in the sink in my bathroom. We have a huge cooked breakfast together and then the girls go back to the house and leave me alone. I feel quite teary as I watch them go off without me.

I take myself to the spa and I have a lovely massage – a new experience for me. The lady finds knots in muscles that I didn't even know I had, but I come out feeling relaxed and a little spaced out.

Then I don't quite know what to do with myself, so I try to embrace the concept of 'chilling out'. I shouldn't really call Danny on my wedding day, so I sit around in the hotel lounge – in a slightly blissed-out, slightly stressed state – and flick through all the magazines spread out on the coffee tables in the lounge while eating the last of the chocolate cocks. I listen to the Christmas carols on loop, marvel at the size of the Christmas tree and watch people coming and going. Brisk businessmen and -women in dark suits, families with fractious kids, giggly couples who can't keep their hands off each other, parties of jolly friends here for pre-Christmas lunches. All of life is here.

I go back to the room and, finally, make the few necessary repairs to my wedding dress. I take the bunches of beautiful red roses and arrange them with some of the holly and foliage that Danny collected for me. I tie them with red ribbon that I bought a few days ago. One each for me, Edie, Lija and Rainbow. They look simple but lovely and I hope the girls like them as much as I do.

Before I know it, Edie, Lija and Rainbow are back. We go up to the room and get dressed.

'I'm going to do your hair and make-up,' Rainbow says.

'I'm not really sure . . .'

Yet, before I can protest further, my hair is scraped back and she's slapping foundation on my face. For the next fifteen minutes, she assaults me with a range of brushes, pencils, mascara wands and goodness knows what else. Then she plugs in something that looks like an instrument of torture and sets about my hair with it.

'Is this absolutely necessary?' Rainbow is deep into the zone, tongue out in concentration.

'Be quiet, Fay,' Edie says from across the room. 'You look fabulous.'

When Rainbow's finally finished primping me, I slip into my red velvet coat dress.

'You'll be glad of that.' Edie smooths down the back. 'It's freezing out there. The sky is so low and heavy, it's barely above the hedges.'

I do up the final button and give a twirl. 'What do you think?'

'OMG!' Rainbow does a little excited dance.

Edie whips open the wardrobe to uncover a full-length mirror and, reluctantly, I find myself shepherded towards it. 'Looking good, sis.'

When I bring myself to look in the glass, a groomed

and glossy creature stares back at me. Danny won't even know it's me as I hardly recognise myself. I examine my powdered brows, my full, red lips and come to the conclusion that Rainbow has done quite a good job.

Rainbow has her hands clasped anxiously. 'Do you like it?'

'I think you've worked a miracle,' I say.

'Yaaaaay!'

I run my hands down my dress. 'That's it. I'm ready.'

'Let's get you to that register office then.'

Standing back, I look at my bridesmaids. Lija is in her black dress and Doc Martens looking paler than ever. Rainbow looks like some kind of cute angel. The addition of lacy wings to her white seventies hippy dress only adds to the impression. Edie is rocking the Audrey Hepburn look that she does so well. She's wearing a cream, fitted dress with long black gloves. Her white designer coat is over her arm.

'I wish I had a hat,' she says, pulling on her gloves. 'A black pill box would really set this off.'

'You all look lovely.'

'I bought you this.' Rainbow gives me a small blue box.

'You shouldn't have.'

'It's for now,' she says. So I open it and inside is a silver heart necklace, studded with tiny rainbow-coloured crystals.

'It's Swarovski and EVERYTHING.'

'It's beautiful.' She fastens it round my neck for me.

'Do you REALLY love it or are you doing FAKE love?'

'I really love it,' I assure her.

'I wanted to give you something special on your big day. My nan helped me choose it.'

'She has very good taste.'

'Yeah. I love her to the moon and back. She needs a BOYFRIEND. I don't like her being on her own. Well, except for me, my dad, my brother and the dog. I thought we might pair her up with Stan at the wedding.'

I twist my head to look at her. 'Your nan's coming along?'

She flushes red. 'Er . . . only afterwards. Not to the register office THINGY. I thought that might be OK. Is it?'

'Of course. I hadn't thought to invite her.' If I'm honest, I hadn't really thought to invite anyone. Perhaps we've taken 'small wedding' to the extreme. 'I should have said. I'm delighted she'll be there. I'd love to meet her. You could have brought that young man you liked at the afternoon tea the other day too.'

More flushing from Rainbow. 'OMG. He is soooooo LUSH. If he was in a boy band, he'd be, like, the lead singer or SOMETHING.'

Lija rolls her eyes. 'Stop twittering,' she says to Rainbow.

'Anyway,' I say to take the girl's embarrassment away, 'I'm not sure that your nan is Stan's type. How old is she again?'

'Nearly SIXTY,' Rainbow says, looking horrified. 'WELL old. They'd be perfect. Stan's old too.'

'That fact hadn't escaped my notice.'

'We should hit the road,' Edie says. 'The time slot at the register office is quite tight. You're the last wedding in before they close for Christmas.'

I get a nervous jolt in my tummy. 'I *am* doing the right thing?'

Then they all look at me in amazement and burst out laughing. I'll take that as a yes then.

Chapter Sixty

I check my watch again. It's a scant five minutes before we're due to get married, and of Danny there's no sign. There's a tense hush inside Bletchley register office.

'Ring him again,' Edie whispers.

With a sigh I punch in the number once more. 'It's going straight to voicemail again.' I listen to Danny's chirpy message and, as I've already left several urgent pleas for him to call me, hang up. I give my newly manicured finger-nails an anxious chew. 'He's not coming.'

'Of course he is,' Edie snaps.

'Maybe it's Stan.' I try Stan's phone too, but he's not picking up either. Does that make it better or worse? Are they together? Has something awful happened to Danny or to Stan?

I pace the corridor, fixing my eyes on the worn carpet. We are the last wedding on the list today and the registrar is getting a bit impatient that my intended is nowhere in sight. She's been popping in and out for the last ten minutes, tutting as she does. Now she comes out of her office again and pats her tidy greying chignon. Her mouth is a thin, tight line when she says, 'We're running out of time, Miss Merryweather.' A pointed glance at the clock above the door. 'The office closes for Christmas very shortly.'

It means that she has stuff to do. Christmas stuff. Stuff that doesn't involve hanging around waiting for a bridegroom who may or may not appear.

'It's very unlike him,' I offer.

'Ten minutes,' she says, lacking a bit of Christmas cheer. 'That's the best I can do. If he's not here by then . . .'

She goes back into her office.

'Fucking Scrooge,' Lija mutters at the closing door.

I tut at her.

She shrugs. 'This situation needs more than "*flipping*". Where is Danny?'

'I don't know. Why isn't he answering his phone?' I look at my bridesmaids for support. 'What shall I do?'

'He'll be here,' Edie insists. 'Sit tight. He'll *definitely* be here.'

'He's *never* late.' They all exchange a nervous glance and I know that they are party to something that I'm not. 'What? What are you not telling me?'

'He'll be here,' is all that my sister says through gritted teeth.

I was worried that we should have done something more to celebrate our wedding; now I'm fraught because I wonder if even this has made Danny reconsider his future with me. He's always sounded so sure, but everyone has their doubts, don't they? There's so much going on at the moment, maybe he's thought that this isn't quite the life he envisaged. He wanted to be free and easy, going where the mood took him, unfettered by commitments. Now look at him. There are the problems with the house and the café, Lija's impending baby, looking after Stan, Edie coming back, our constant state of financial embarrassment and probably a dozen other things that I've pushed to the back of my mind. He's a young man, with so many plans. Perhaps he's thought better of saddling himself with all that. With me.

But surely he would have called if he'd had second thoughts? He wouldn't leave me standing here, jilted, like a prize lemon. What if he's had an accident? My stomach turns to ice. Would it be silly to phone the local hospital? Where on earth is he?

It's now past our allotted time and the registrar appears again. Her lips are pursed. 'I'm terribly sorry, Miss Merryweather—'

'It's CHRISTMAS,' Rainbow pleads, eyes welling with tears. 'Have a heart. They are meant to be together and EVERYTHING.'

'If it were up to me . . .'

This woman would clearly be happy kicking Tiny Tim in the shins. I sigh. 'Let's go.'

'We can book you in again, anytime,' she says, thawing slightly.

'I don't think there'll be any need for that.' I let my lovely bouquet of red roses and holly sprigs hang forlornly by my side. It feels as if my entire being has wilted.

357

'We *cannot* just *go*,' Lija says tightly.

'We can't stay here either,' I point out. 'They're shutting up shop for Christmas. What else is there to do?'

As we turn to leave, the door flies open, banging on its hinges, and Danny bursts in. Relief floods through me.

'Problems.' He holds up his hands in apology. 'Many, many problems.'

'I've been trying to call you for half an hour.' I try not to sound annoyed, but I am. I'm overjoyed that he's here and cross that he didn't let me know why he was delayed.

He takes my hands. 'I'm sorry,' he says. 'Really, really sorry. But I'm here now. Let's do it.'

'No explanation?'

'Later,' he says. 'Now I've got a wedding to go to.'

I try not to cry when I inform him, 'The registrar is packing up to go home.'

'Seriously?' Danny goes a bit pale. 'Let me talk to her.'

'She has a heart of stone.'

'I'll give it a go.'

Then I realise that Danny is alone. 'Where's Stan? Is he all right? Nothing's happened to him?'

'No, no,' Danny assures me. 'He's absolutely fine. He's still in the taxi. Do you want to go and get him? I thought it best to dash straight in.'

'I'll go,' Rainbow says and trots out towards the car park.

Crossing his fingers, Danny knocks on the office door and then, before he slips inside, he turns back to me and grins. 'You look bloody amazing, Fay Merryweather.'

That, at least, makes me smile. I'd like to stay cross, but

I can't. Danny only has to flash me one of his cheeky grins and my heart melts. That has to bode well for a relationship, right? It's not the end of the world if we don't get married today, I try to convince myself. He's here. He came. That's all that matters.

'Christ, I can't stand all this drama,' Edie moans. 'There had better be some *seriously* good booze back at the house.'

A moment later, Danny comes out of the office. The registrar is behind him, all smiles and flushed cheeks.

Danny rubs his hands together. 'Let's get this show on the road then.' He turns to the registrar. 'This lovely lady hasn't got all day, she needs to be at home for Christmas.'

'Oh, no hurry,' she says to Danny. 'We're all just relieved that you're here. Aren't we, Miss Merryweather?'

'I've never been more relieved,' I agree. I have no idea what Danny has said to charm her, but it's clearly worked.

Rainbow brings Stan through the door. He's looking very smart in a black overcoat and cap. He has his row of shining service medals on his chest which Danny must have pinned on him this morning – the ones that he gave to me when we left. How wonderful to see him wearing them.

'You look lovely, Stan.'

'Had to scrub up to give my best girl away,' he says proudly.

'It was a close-run thing,' I whisper. Imagine if we'd had to go home and eat all those sandwiches with no cause for celebration.

'I'm all set when you are,' the registrar says.

Danny takes my hand. 'Ready for this, the future Mrs Wilde?'

'Yes. I am.'

We pause to look at each other and Danny's eyes shine with love when he squeezes my hand and says, 'See you at the altar.'

Chapter Sixty-One

My heart does somersaults as Stan takes my arm and we walk slowly down the short aisle to the table at the front of the room. I've never seen this dear man stand quite so tall or beam so proudly. I couldn't have had a better replacement for my own dad. I glance at our small gathering of friends who are like family to me and, for a moment, can imagine my mum and dad standing there with them. They would have been happy for me, I know. They would have loved Danny for a son-in-law and it's at times like this when I miss them all the more keenly.

With all the stress beforehand, I didn't have much chance to look at Danny, not properly. Now I have time to drink him in as we approach. There was a time when I thought that I'd never be married at all, and never in my craziest dreams did I conjure up someone like Danny Wilde to be my husband.

He stands in front of the registrar, the boyish grin that

won my heart firmly in place. My husband-to-be is wearing his signature jeans with a grey tweed jacket and a jaunty red waistcoat. He has a red neckerchief tied at his throat. His hair is as mad as ever and I guess the haircut that he'd planned never happened. I don't care whether his hair is long, short, black or green. I love him exactly the way he is.

I walk in to 'Marry Me' by Train – the song that Danny was singing before he proposed to me – and I think how far we've come in such a short space of time. My rag-tag group of bridesmaids stands at the front of the room waiting for me. One goth, one angel, one channelling Audrey Hepburn. Rainbow is crying already and Lija digs her in the ribs. She remembers that she's our official photographer and snaps some photos on her phone.

Then I'm standing next to Danny and he takes my hand in his. The registrar rushes through her words, still eager to get home for Christmas, but I don't care. The only words that are important are 'I do' and we both say them with conviction and love in our hearts. I feel choked with emotion but, to my relief, manage not to cry. My brides-maids aren't holding up so well. Rainbow is sobbing and sniffing noisily now and even Lija surreptitiously dabs her sleeve to her eye.

Too soon, the ceremony is over and the registrar pronounces us husband and wife. Danny pulls me towards him and gives me a long, lingering kiss. Our few guests clap our union. So we kiss again. And that's it. I'm Mrs Danny Wilde.

Now everyone's crying, including Stan who I see wipe

his tears away with a clean hanky. We leave to Ed Sheeran's 'Tenerife Sea' – another favourite song of Danny's.

Outside, we're showered with confetti and, laughing, shake it from our hair. We kiss again as Rainbow takes more photographs. The sky has darkened now and the air is crisp, cold. It looks as if it might, at long last, snow.

The taxi is still waiting near the door. It's a white Merc and they've tied a red ribbon and some holly to the front of it. The door opens and Diggery bounds out, barking. He's wearing the same red neckerchief as Danny.

'Cheesy, I know, but Rainbow insisted,' Danny says.

'Of course she did.' I bend down to fuss our little dog's ears. 'I'm officially your mummy now,' I tell him and he seems quite pleased with the fact.

We pose this way and that while Rainbow takes some more photos on her phone. Then Lija loses interest and starts to rub her arms, shivering in the cold.

'We should go back to the house now,' I say to Danny.

'Before that, I have a little surprise for you,' Danny says, mysteriously. 'We'll see the others there in a short while.'

'Is this what caused the many, many problems?' He still hasn't told me why he was delayed.

'Not exactly,' he says enigmatically. But he offers no further explanation. Then he waves to the others. 'See you soon.'

By the expressions on their faces, I can tell that I'm the only one who doesn't know what the surprise is. While they all get into Lija's car – Stan included – Danny and I jump into the taxi and speed off. I snuggle in the back seat with my new husband, Diggery curled up on his lap. 'Do you mind telling me where we're going?'

'You'll see soon enough.' He looks very smug.

So I settle back and enjoy the ride out of town and into the country lanes once more. In a little while, we're on familiar territory and it's not long before the taxi turns into the boatyard where Danny works.

I frown at him. 'What are we doing here?'

'I told you. I have a little surprise.' The taxi stops. 'Come on.' He holds out his hand and we clamber out of the car. The driver wishes us good luck and then drives away, leaving the three of us stranded.

Danny grins at me. 'This way, Mrs Wilde.'

I get a thrill at the sound of my new name. 'If you insist, Mr Wilde.'

So we pick our way past the office, me tiptoeing over the discarded cables, pipes and other detritus in my high heels. This is where the *Maid of Merryweather* has been spending her days and I haven't had time to see her in weeks. We head towards the covered boat dock alongside the canal and my heartbeat quickens as we do.

When, finally, we stand at the dock, Danny pulls back the door and we step inside. The *Maid of Merryweather* is sitting in the water. The hull has been freshly painted in her original colours of dark green and red. The roses, so typical of canal boats, have been newly drawn. The boat is festooned with red ribbons and bowers of ivy and holly, rich with berries. They're wound round the boat deck and along the rails on the roof. There's a big red bow tied round the chimney for the stove and a bunch of mistletoe coming out of the top.

'Oh, Danny.'

'You like it?'

'How have you done this? *When* have you done it?'

'All those late nights weren't always overtime,' he admits. 'I've put in a good few hours and I've had more than a little help from the lads here, but she's looking good. We've stripped down and reconditioned the engine. The hull's been repaired and re-blacked and she's watertight again. She's as sound as a pound now.'

'I'm amazed.'

'The inside still needs a lot of work, but I've got more done than I hoped for. Do you want to take her for a spin?'

'Can we?'

'It would be rude not to,' he says.

I can hardly wait to climb on board.

Danny holds out his hand to help me as I step into the well deck. He's right about the inside. Everything has been stripped out, all the fittings removed, so there are just bare walls and floorboards. There are no seats or table and even the kitchen has gone. She's little more than an empty shell, but all traces of the water damage have been eradicated and she doesn't smell like a swamp any more. The *Maid of Merryweather* is ready for a new era.

'A work in progress,' he says. 'I've replaced all the wood inside, so we can start afresh. I've ripped out most of the bathroom too, but I've left the loo. For now.'

'I should be grateful for that,' I tease.

'Another big push and an injection of cash and she'll be as right as rain.'

I stroke my hand over the smooth new wood inside. 'You've done so much and you've saved her.' I turn and kiss him.

'You like your wedding present then?'

'I love it. Surely, it's the best wedding present ever. I never expected this.' For this alone, I'll be eternally grateful to Danny. 'You've worked so hard on it. I can't begin to tell you how thrilled I am.'

'I've one more thing to show you,' he says. He takes my hand and I negotiate the empty cans of paint, tools and dust sheets as he leads me towards our cabin.

Inside, there's a mattress on the floor and clean, white bedding. It's strewn with rose petals. Beside it is a bottle of champagne on ice and two flutes.

'A nice touch.'

He takes me in his arms and says, 'I thought we ought to make our marriage official in style.'

I laugh. Danny cracks open the bottle and pours us two glasses.

'What about our guests?' I sip the cold bubbles, enjoying the fizz on my tongue.

My husband kisses me deeply. 'I think they can wait for a little while.'

Chapter Sixty-Two

I stand on the back of the *Maid of Merryweather*, a little more dishevelled than I was before. I put my hand on my tummy and get a rush of emotion. How wonderful it would be if we'd made a baby on our wedding day. Danny is next to me, arm round my waist, and I nestle into his warmth.

There's a bouquet of red roses tied to the back of the tiller and ribbons festooned around.

'Let's take her out, Mrs Wilde,' he says. 'Easy does it.'

So I start the engine and the boat purrs into life. 'Sounds considerably better than she did last time we had her running.'

'That is entirely down to my skill and patience.' He winks at me, but I know that he is – quite rightly – proud of his achievement. And I am too. With everything else that's been going on, he has still found precious time to do this for me.

'I do appreciate it. You know how much this means to me.' Much more than any fancy wedding, than a honeymoon somewhere hot and exotic, more than anything. Hot tears prickle my eyes. My dad would be so full of pride to see the *Maid of Merryweather* back on the water and shipshape again. As Danny says, there's still a lot to do and, as always, cash is tight, but I feel that we've turned a corner. Danny has saved her from a slow, steady sink into ruin.

Hand on the tiller, I ease her out of the boat dock and into the canal. The water is slate grey today, the sky the same colour. My velvet coat isn't the most suitable garment for the weather, but I hardly feel the cold at all.

Two swans glide out of our way and we head back towards the house. As we do, an icing sugar sprinkle of snow starts to drift down.

'It's snowing.' I lift my hand to catch the flakes. They melt onto my palm. 'A white wedding. How perfect.' It drifts across the canal, speckling the surface of the water as it lands. It will be beautiful if it snows tomorrow too. A white wedding and a white Christmas. What could be more perfect?

Danny pulls me in close and kisses my hair.

'What will we do with two boats?' It's been my dream to restore the *Maid of Merryweather*, but how will we afford to keep them both?

'I've been thinking about that,' Danny says. 'What if we turn her into a café too? We could either keep her moored at the jetty or take customers for trips on the canal. Lija's afternoon teas have been a great hit. Maybe we could do that afloat? If we can make a go of it, we could bring in some welcome cash.'

'Gosh, that sounds like a great idea.'

'We've got a completely empty hull. I can kit her out however we like. We could put tables and chairs in or even refit her as a rental boat. After Christmas we should sit down and thrash out some figures. See what's the most viable.'

'If Edie's staying around, she could maybe run it,' I suggest. 'She's been surprisingly good in the café, but it would be a good idea to keep her out of Lija's domain if we can.'

'All things are possible,' Danny says. 'We're only limited by our imaginations.'

'And money.'

'That too,' he agrees.

'How exciting,' I say. 'Next year is going to be amazing.'

'Whatever we do, we'll do it together.'

I snuggle in again. 'I like the sound of that.'

Too soon, I see the jetty and *The Dreamcatcher* coming into sight. I get a pang of guilt about our waiting guests. I hope they've kept themselves entertained without us. Then I notice a large marquee on the lawn, strung with fairy lights. The sound of music is drifting down to the canal.

'What's that?'

'Ah, that. *That's* the source of all my problems,' Danny says. 'The marquee collapsed just as the lads and I thought we'd finished putting it up this morning. We had to do it all over again. That's why I was late.' He nods towards it.

'I hadn't factored in enough time for a badly behaved tent.'

'Why have we got a tent at all?'

'Because our friends persuaded me that we needed to do a little more to celebrate our wedding than a few rounds of sandwiches in the café. I think they were right. I want everyone to know that we're man and wife.'

My hands go to my chest. 'Oh my, I feel a little over-whelmed now.'

'It'll be great,' Danny says. 'All you have to do is relax and enjoy it. Everything else is taken care of.'

Then I see Rainbow running down the garden, angel wings flapping behind her. 'THEY'RE HERE!' she shouts. 'THEY'RE HERE!' She snaps away on her phone, capturing the moment for posterity, and I'm so glad that they were all in cahoots with Danny's secret plans.

We swing into the jetty and are soon joined by a crowd of friends. I see people here that I've known for years from the local narrowboat club, regular customers from the café, Danny's new friends from the boatyard – who seem to have not only done so much to help with restoring the *Maid of Merryweather* but have also put the icing on this day for us. There are Danny's pals from London too and, for once, my heart doesn't sink when I see the lovely Sienna. I'm Danny's wife now and it's me he's chosen over all the other women in the world. I'm glad that she's here with Henry and Laura to celebrate with us.

One of the lads from the boatyard comes to tie up the boat and, hand in hand, Danny and I jump down from the *Maid of Merryweather*. Immediately, we're engulfed by well-wishers.

'I've organised a little extra ceremony,' Danny says. 'A traditional boatman's wedding. Are you up for it?'

'What a wonderful idea.'

He grins, still very pleased with his subterfuge. 'I thought you'd like it.'

So we walk up to the marquee and there are fire pits burning outside, bringing some much-needed warmth to the winter day. The whiff of roasting pork is in the air and makes me realise that I'm hungry again. Musicians playing fiddles come out of the marquee and join us, serenading us with 'A Thousand Years' by Christina Perri. Hay bales covered in thick blankets are set out in front of a small gazebo to provide seating. Waiting for us is Tommo, the owner of the boatyard, dressed in traditional canal dress. He's wearing a striped linen shirt with a red brocade waistcoat and neckerchief. His bowler hat, complete with red feather, is set at a jaunty angle.

Our friends settle on the hay bales, wrapped up against the cold. The light snow is still falling as we stand in front of Tommo to say our vows.

'Danny has written a few words which I'd like you both to repeat after me,' Tommo says.

My eyes fill with tears once more as he solemnly reads aloud, 'You held my hand and knew my thoughts, you kissed my lips and captured my heart, you looked into my eyes and saw my soul.'

Danny and I repeat them as we look into each other's eyes. Danny's are soft, shining with love. I know that these words have come completely from his heart and they mean more to me than anything in the civil ceremony. They take me back to the day Danny Wilde walked into my life and changed it for ever. 'That's lovely,' I whisper to Danny.

Then our hands are tied together with red ribbon. Two buckets painted with canalware roses are placed with a broom between them and our friends clap as, like canal folk for a hundred years before us, we 'jump the broom' to signify that we're leaving our old life behind, sweeping away our troubles and concerns and are starting out on a new adventure together as husband and wife. It seems like a very good thing to do.

The fiddlers play 'Ho Hey' by the Lumineers while the boaters from our local club hold their brass tillers high to form a guard of honour and we parade through it, being showered with confetti again while everyone cheers.

At the end, Danny picks me up and twirls me round and round until we're both dizzy. When he puts me down, I say, 'Thank you so much for this.'

'You're welcome, Mrs Wilde.'

'I'm not even going to ask how we're paying for it.'

'I borrowed the marquee from the narrowboat club and someone very special has paid for the hog roast and the band.'

'Stan,' I say. It has to be.

Danny nods. 'Our wedding present.'

'He's such a sweetie. How can we ever repay him? I must go to thank him.'

'I bet he's in the marquee chatting up Rainbow's nana.' Danny grabs my hands and pulls me towards the tent. 'Come on, let's get this party started.'

Chapter Sixty-Three

My bridesmaids, who have kept this secret so well, come to hug me. 'You knew all about this! How on earth did you keep it quiet?'

'Danny threatened to kill us and EVERYTHING if we blabbed,' Rainbow says, wide-eyed.

'You're happy with it?' Edie asks.

'Delighted. I could never have imagined something like this. It couldn't be more fitting.'

I can't believe they've been so busy behind my back. The marquee is beautifully decorated with ribbons and swathes of holly. On the tables there are lanterns with glowing candles. There's a band playing a mix of folk and indie tunes. The beer and wine are already flowing. One of the tables is spread with a dozen different salads and breads courtesy, I'm sure, of Lija and Rainbow. In another pergola beside it, the land-lord from the local pub is in charge of cooking and the hog roast smells as if it's just about ready to eat.

Lija comes to stand next to me. 'OK, married lady?'

'Yes. Wonderful.'

'Is nice wedding,' she shrugs. 'Almost makes me feel romantic.'

'Surely not,' I tease.

'I might ask Stinky Stan to marry me,' she bats back.

'It will come right for you,' I say. 'I'm absolutely sure.'

'Yes. But you are loved-up idiot.'

'I saw you crying at the register office.'

'No. *Flipping*. Way,' she says. 'I have heart of ice.'

'Wait until you're a mum, that will soon change.'

'Pah,' she says.

'I've got to go and thank Stan. I believe he paid for most of this.'

'He is kind man,' Lija says. 'He will make very good substitute grandpapa.'

'I don't want you to overdo it tonight,' I warn her. 'How are you feeling?'

'Fat and boring.' She holds up a glass of orange juice.

'No sly vodka in it?'

She looks longingly at it. 'I wish.'

'You don't need to drink to enjoy a good party.'

Lija looks at me with disdain. 'Said no one, ever.'

I laugh and leave her to go off and join the queue that's forming for the hog roast. Meanwhile, I scan around for Stan and see that he's tucked in the far corner of the marquee sitting at a table next to a glamorous blonde. He has a pint of beer in his hand, a flush to his cheeks and a twinkle in his eye. They're deep in conversation and the way she flings her hands around and those curls bounce when she talks, she can only be Rainbow's nana.

I make my way over to them, being hugged and kissed by everyone I pass en route. For someone who doesn't usually like to be the centre of attention, I'm really enjoying the fuss. It takes me a good ten minutes to get to them.

I kiss Stan's cheek. 'This is Rainbow's nana,' he says, clearly taken with her.

'Hello, I'm Fay. I've heard so much about you.' She stands up to kiss me. Rainbow's nana might be sixty next year, but she looks as young as I am. She's wearing a tight-fitting teal-coloured lace dress and lots of fastidiously applied make-up.

'It's lovely to meet you at last. Rainbow always talks about you. She thinks you're wonderful.'

'Rainbow thinks everyone's wonderful.'

Her nan laughs. 'She does. She's a tonic to have around the house. I don't know what I'd do without her.'

'We love her. She brightens our days too.'

'You have no idea how excited she was to be your bridesmaid. I've heard nothing but that for weeks.'

That I can believe.

'Have a nice evening,' I say. 'I'm delighted you could come.'

She lifts her glass of bubbles. 'To you and Danny,' she toasts. 'Rainbow says that you're a lovely couple.'

'They are,' Stan chips in. 'The very best.'

'I understand that I have you to thank for all this.' I gesture at the marquee, the party behind me. 'I really appreciate it, Stan, and fully intend to enjoy every minute.'

'A little token of my thanks,' he says shyly.

'Well, it's wonderful.' I kiss his soft, pink cheek once more. 'Thank you for giving me away today. You did it with great aplomb.'

'My darling girl, the pleasure was all mine.'

'Tell me you'll dance with me later.'

'Nothing will stop me.' He holds up his pint. 'I'm just having a glass or two of dancing enabler. The more I have, the better I move. Or at least I think I do.'

I can see Danny making his way towards me, talking to our friends as he does. When he finally reaches me, he says, 'We should cut the cake now, before we get too drunk and forget to do it.'

'There's a cake too?' I had every good intention, but never got round to making one. Looks as if I didn't need to.

'Of course! I'd be very remiss in my duties as a husband if I didn't provide cake for you. Lija's baked it.'

'You've all been so industrious. How could I not notice? I must have been going round with my eyes closed.'

Lija's already waiting for us beside the three-tier creation and it's the only time I'll feel happy to see my friend with a sharp knife in her hand. The cake is covered in ivory icing and has red bunting dotted with sprigs of holly winding round the tiers. On top is a sugar paste model of *The Dreamcatcher*, with a tiny replica of Diggery beside it. The cake is fabulous and I know just how much effort Lija has put into this.

'Thank you so much.'

She shrugs. 'Is cake. Is what I do best.'

'I think you've excelled yourself this time,' I tell her.

'Bottom is Christmas cake. Middle is chocolate, top lemon drizzle.'

'It looks too good to eat.'

'Cut *flipping* thing,' she says, but I can tell that she's pleased with how it's turned out too. 'I want a piece. Maybe even slice of each. Is wedding. And I am eating for two.'

So Danny and I cut the cake with Rainbow snapping away on her phone. Then the music starts up again and Danny says, 'I've chosen this as our first dance.' He takes me into his arms and we spin round in a circle of our friends to 'Iris' by the Goo-Goo Dolls and I think that I'd be happy to spend the rest of my life dancing in Danny's arms.

When we part, Danny and I grab our friends to join in. I twirl with Lija as they play the song again and we sing at the top of our voices. When they finally stop, we're laughing and panting with exertion. As I try to catch my breath, I look up to see a tall and very handsome man with blond dreadlocks striding up the garden from the canal. There's also an unfamiliar narrowboat tied up by the *Maid of Merryweather*. I peer into the darkness. 'I wonder who this is?'

Beside me, Lija goes very still.

As the stranger comes closer to us, I continue my appraisal. He has a kind face, broad shoulders and a full mouth. His chin sports a neatly trimmed goatee. He's wearing a once-white T-shirt, faded blue hoodie and ripped jeans. There's a necklace of wooden beads at his throat.

'I didn't realise that I'd be crashing a wedding,' he says, apologetically. His eyes never leave Lija's face.

'That's fine,' I say. 'You're more than welcome.'

'Congratulations,' He holds out a hand and I shake it. 'I'm Mog,' he says. 'I've come to see Lija.'

Chapter Sixty-Four

Lija stands like a stone and I'm not sure what to say to intervene. Surely she must be pleased that her boyfriend has come back. They certainly have a lot to talk about.

'You look great,' he says and still she doesn't speak. But it could be worse. At least there hasn't been a volley of F-words. She loves him. I know she does.

'Shall I go?' Mog asks, anxiously.

Lija shakes her head.

He laughs. 'Dance with me then?'

Thankfully – as if in a trance – Lija steps into his arms.

It's an upbeat song yet they barely move. I watch them anxiously, like a mother hen, as first they shuffle awkwardly together then, as the music takes them, they gradually become less wary. Before the song has finished, they relax and sway in time.

This song morphs into the next one and they continue their dance, bodies inching closer, and I can't help but breathe a sigh of relief when Lija rests her head on his chest. This will be all right. I know it will.

At the other side of the dance floor, Stan is throwing some moves. It looks as if Rainbow is teaching him to twerk. For a man of ninety-odd, he's surprisingly good at it. I just hope he doesn't throw his hip out. Danny is dancing with Henry and Laura while Sienna is sitting on the sidelines, narrowed eyes, mouth in a tight line, smoking as she watches. I wonder if she thinks that it should have been her rather than me. However, I'm not going to dwell on that now. This party is going to be the best one I've ever been to and nothing can mar that.

My sister sidles up next to me, glass in her hand. 'Having a nice wedding?'

'Fabulous.'

'Let's hope it's your only one.' There is the whiff of the sardonic in her statement.

'That's my plan.'

'You'll do it,' she says. 'I'm the family fuck-up.'

'It doesn't have to be like that, Edie. We can all have a fresh start. The new year is going to bring big challenges to us all. Danny and I have got some great plans. It would be nice if you would stay and be a part of those.'

'I've got nowhere else to go,' is Edie's reply, which I guess is a guarded agreement.

'You'll make a lovely aunt.'

'I won't.' She glugs at her fizz. 'I can't stand babies.'

'Maybe this is your chance to love them.'

'No bun in the oven yet for you?'

I shake my head.

'Won't be long,' is her view. 'You and Danny will be blissfully happy and will bang out a couple of fabulous-looking kids before too long.' She empties her glass. 'Is there any talent here?' She scans the dance floor. 'I *seriously* need to find someone to shag.'

Before I can say anything else, my dear sister wanders off. It breaks my heart to see her lost and lonely, but changing her life is in Edie's hands, not mine. Still, I hope she settles here so that I can help.

I see Stan making his way off the dance floor and go over to him. 'That was an impressive display.'

He laughs. 'I've worn myself out though.'

'One last dance with me. I promise I won't make you do any hip-hop or anything.'

'A waltz is more my level.'

'A waltz it is then.' I have no idea what the music is, but we waltz to it anyway. Slowly but surely making our way round the floor. At the end of the song, my dear friend pats my hand. 'That's enough for me. I'm off to my bed now, Faye. It's been a fabulous day and I wouldn't have missed it for the world.'

I give him another kiss. 'You're like a father to me, Stan. I can't thank you enough.'

'I need a word with you and Danny,' he says. 'Call him over.'

So I beckon to Danny, then I help Stan as he shrugs on his coat.

'Going, Stan?' Danny asks. 'I'll take you back.'

'I can manage,' Stan insists. 'I don't want you to leave your party.'

'It's no problem,' I assure him.

We each take an arm and help to steer him towards the path that leads from Canal House to his cottage. The music and the noise of the party fade away behind us until the three of us are standing in the peace of the countryside under the starry night. 'I wanted to tell you that I've got a little wedding gift for you.'

'You paid for most of the party, Stan,' Danny reminds him. 'That's more than enough. There's no need for anything else.'

He shakes his head. 'You've been good to me. Both of you. I don't think you know how very grateful I am. But for you, I'd be a lonely old man, limping along. You treat me like family and I won't forget that.'

'We love you,' I tell him. 'You *are* family.'

'I've left you my cottage,' he says. 'In my will.'

'Stan, you can't do that—'

He holds up a hand to shush me. 'I've been to a solicitor and EVERYTHING,' he says, mimicking Rainbow, which makes me laugh. 'I've no other family, so there's no one to contest it.' Perhaps he's thinking of the pain that I went through before with this house. 'When I shuffle off this mortal coil, it's yours and everything in it. You can do whatever you want with it. Live in it, rent it out, sell it. The place is yours with the very best of my love.'

'I don't know what to say.' My legs feel weak and I could do with sitting down.

'Say you'll enjoy it. I hope it will help you out in the future.'

It could be the answer to our prayers.

'I'm sure I speak for Fay too when I say that we're both humbled by this.' Danny looks stunned by Stan's generosity.

'I hope that we don't inherit it for years and years to come,' I tell him. 'I don't want your house to remember you by, I want *you* around.'

'Oh, I'll be here,' he says. 'For a little while, at least. My time is coming, Fay. I know that.' There's a twinkle in his eye when he adds, 'But not just yet.'

'I don't want to let you go.' I seize his hand which feels cold in mine. 'Come back to the party. Let's have another drink. I haven't danced with you enough yet. You can surely manage another waltz?'

'I'm tired,' he says. 'I should go to bed, otherwise I might sleep through Christmas altogether.'

'We can't have that,' I agree. 'I've got you down for table-setting duties tomorrow.'

'I'll be very happy to perform them.'

'I'll send Danny to get you.'

'Thank you.' He sighs heavily. 'This has been a very lovely wedding, Fay. I wish the both of you every happiness in the world.'

'Don't go.' I squeeze his hand tightly, reluctant to see him leave. Tears prickle my eyes. I've become only too aware that one day, we'll say goodbye to Stan and never see him again. I harbour the hope that if I never, ever let him out of my sight then he'll always be here with his kind smile and his words of wisdom.

'You two young things go and enjoy the rest of your wedding. I'll be fine. Really.'

'It's late. Let Danny see you home.'

'No need. I'll take my time.'

I kiss his hand and let it go. Then I watch as he walks off into the night. He looks lighter on his feet than he has in a long time. As he leaves the garden, Stan turns and smiles. Then I think I see a blur of a shadow move beside him as I did before and, if I'm not mistaken, there's a light laugh on the breeze.

Chapter Sixty-Five

Danny sweeps me onto the dance floor again and we lose ourselves in the music, the laughter and the love. 'Are you happy, Mrs Wilde?'

'Deliriously so.'

The night is cold, the stars are out in force and there's still the odd flurry of snow. I can hardly believe that it's Christmas Day tomorrow. I've so much to do, you wouldn't believe it. We're all going to have our Christmas lunch together on *The Dreamcatcher*, which is going to be a right old squash and a bit haphazard, but I think it will work and I can't imagine a nicer way to spend our first day as a married couple. I'm sure we'll manage a honeymoon at some point in the future, take the boat back on the canal for a week or two, but not just yet. Lija needs us here and we're both more than willing to do that for her.

I see her and Mog come out of the house and I wonder if she's been telling him about the baby. I do hope so.

They're holding hands and both smiling. That has to be a good sign. The fiddlers are playing a slow song – 'Open Up Your Door' by Richard Hawley. Lija and Mog take to the dance floor and this time there's no awkwardness. It would be so lovely if he came back into her life and they could be a family. I wonder how he's taken the news that he's going to be a daddy?

They circle the dance floor and, as they pass us, Lija grins widely at me and holds up a thumb behind Mog's back. I wink back at her. I'm so relieved that it looks as if he's going to be back in her life. I guess we'll have another mouth to feed at Christmas lunch tomorrow and I couldn't be more pleased for her. He looks like a nice man and it will be good to get to know him better. It would be wonderful if he was planning on staying here permanently. My loved-up heart likes to think that he will. I want nothing but happy endings from now on.

They pass by us, close enough for me to ask, 'Everything OK?'

Lija nods.

'You're pleased at the news?' I say to Mog.

'Yeah,' he says. 'A bit shell-shocked, but I couldn't be happier.'

'It's good to see you back,' I tell him. 'I'm not the only one who feels that way, I suspect.'

'I would have been back sooner,' he says. 'I needed to make amends for leaving like that, but I got a good job that I couldn't pass up.' That sounds familiar. 'Idiot that I am, I'd dropped my phone in the canal, so have been doing without one. I should have called Lija or let her know or something. I realised as soon as I left that I didn't want to be without her.'

Lija gives me a smug look.

Mog laughs. 'I've had to pluck up courage to come back though. I thought she might chase me off with a knife, if she saw me again.'

'I think becoming a mother is starting to mellow her.'

'Is flipping NOT,' Lija says, but she doesn't look cross at all. Well, not much.

'You're staying for Christmas?'

'I'm hoping to be around for good,' Mog says, slightly bashful. He looks at Lija and I can tell that he's smitten. 'If she'll have me.'

Lija tries to look as if she couldn't care less whether he's here or not, and fails. Phew.

'It'll be good to have another bloke around,' Danny says. 'Me and Stan are seriously outnumbered.'

'Feeling you, bro.' Mog and Danny high-five each other.

As he and Lija dance away from us, I say, 'Wow. That's a relief.'

'Yeah. I hope it works out for them,' Danny says. 'He seems like a good lad.'

'Time will tell,' I suggest. 'But I think you might well be right.'

Behind them, Rainbow is dancing with the young man she's brought. They make a very pretty couple too. She's bouncing all around him while he stands looking slightly bemused and more than a little mesmerised. It's a shame she won't be with us for lunch, but I hope that she'll pop by in the afternoon and maybe bring her nana and dad as well. She's a great girl and has a lot of potential. I'm sure we'll be leaning heavily on her in the new year when Lija's baby comes along and she's more than capable of dealing with whatever we throw at her.

I see that Edie is twined round one of the young men from the boatyard. She looks as if she could eat him alive. With a glance backwards, she catches me watching her and gives me a wave. Then, looking very shifty, she takes his hand and leads him out of the marquee. Off to find somewhere more private, no doubt. Oh, my dear sister. Some things never change. I just hope that this one isn't married.

'Where have you gone to?' Danny asks.

I look up at him. 'Nowhere. I was just thinking of our odd little family and the challenges we've got to face next year. We're going to be busy.'

'I don't want you to worry about anything. We've got each other. Whatever difficulties life throws at us, we'll overcome them together.'

'I like the sound of that.'

He takes my hand. 'Let's walk down to the canal.'

So we leave the party in full swing and stroll down the garden, his arm around me, sheltering me from the cold. Diggery, who has been doing the rounds of our guests, suddenly bounds across the garden to join us. Danny ruffles his ears and the dog gives an excited bark. As we go, the snow thickens into lacy flakes that drift down all around us.

We climb onto *The Dreamcatcher* and sit together in the well deck beneath the twinkling Christmas lights. He's decorated our favourite little spot with holly and mistletoe too and it's feeling very festive. Danny pulls our crocheted blanket round our shoulders and Digs curls up at our feet. Christmas Day is barely an hour away, but I don't want this night to end. I wish we could freeze this moment in time. It's lovely looking back at the celebrations and our friends having a high old time, yet revelling in the stillness on board the boat. Danny reaches for a bottle of Jack Daniel's and two glasses that are hidden away under the bench.

'Well prepared,' he says and pours us two shots.

I accept mine gratefully, enjoying the fiery liquid as it burns my throat and warms me up inside. Danny wraps our crocheted throw around our shoulders and we snuggle in together. Digs settles down at our feet. The seductive sound of Bill Medley and Jennifer Warnes singing 'I've Had the Time of My Life' drifts on the air. Which seems more than appropriate.

'It's been the best wedding ever,' I say. 'Thank you.'

'Yeah,' he agrees. 'It has.'

My heart has never been happier. The moon is shining, snow falls on the canal and love is in the air.

'Merry Christmas, Mrs Wilde,' he says.

'Merry Christmas, my husband.' And when I kiss him, I know that where we were two, we've now become one.

Carole's Perfect Christmas

Christmas Unlimited!

Setting aside all constraints of travel and expense, I thought I'd put together my perfect Christmas day.

I think I'd like to wake up in the Maldives and see the sunrise over the ocean from the veranda of a nice water lodge. My partner, Lovely Kev, and I went there for our first holiday together and it would be great to go again. It's such a peaceful place, nothing to do but look out at the ocean. It was the inspiration for my novel *A Minor Indiscretion*. We sat one evening on the beach and saw a pod of dolphins jumping across the horizon beneath the setting sun. Beautiful. That would be a Christmas day treat.

Then it would be off to The Ritz hotel in London for a full English breakfast. We spoiled ourselves and stayed at The Ritz a little while ago which was gorgeous. We booked their Christmas shopping weekend and were treated like royalty – especially when we were whisked down to

Clarence House in a big shiny Jaguar, plied with champagne and warm mince pies then let loose on lots of sparkly goodies from Prince Charles' Duchy range of products. It cost an arm and a leg, but was well worth it for the experience.

Christmas lunch would be at Jamie Oliver's house, cooked by Jamie with his usual bish-bash-bosh flair. I followed his advice for cooking my own Christmas lunch last year and it came out fabulous. His roastie spuds are amazing. He does 'proper' food. I don't like my Christmas dinner too faffed about with. Traditional all the way suits me. On Christmas Eve, I often make Mary Berry's fish pie which apparently features on her menu at home too. I do love cooking my own Christmas dinner, but I'd be happy to give this pleasure over to a celebrity chef for one year!

Then we'd pop over to Buttermere in the Lake District for a stroll after lunch to walk off all those calories. This is my favourite place on earth and I don't need an excuse to go up there. To my eternal shame, we've never been in the winter and it would be lovely to see it in the snow. Then we'd be spirited to Chesters at Skelwith Bridge, my favourite café there. In my dream Christmas, they'd open specially to make us a restorative hot chocolate and some of their fabulous cake at the end of our walk.

In the evening we'd go to see the Kylie Christmas show at the Royal Albert Hall in London. We went last year for the first time and it is the most fabulous party atmosphere. Ms Minogue certainly knows how to entertain her crowd – there were Santa hats, glitter balls, confetti and all the Kylie hits. You can't help but feel Christmassy.

After that we'd head to Hong Kong and take the Star Ferry across the water to have cocktails at The Peninsula enjoying the amazing neon-lit skyline of Hong Kong island.

To top it off, we'd scoot up to the Arctic Circle and finish our day in the original Ice Hotel at Kiruna. We stayed there for research for *Calling Mrs Christmas* and it is a magical place. We were lucky enough to see the Northern Lights and stayed out until three o'clock in the morning just in awe of the spectacular display – even though the temperature was a cool thirty-six degrees below zero. We got to sleep in one of the stunning ice rooms on a bed of reindeer skins. How wonderful!

Sigh.

OK, back in the real world! I'll probably do the same as I do every year – stay home, eat too much, watch rubbish telly with a tin of Celebrations and love every minute of it.

Merry Christmas, everyone!

Join us at

The
Little Book
Café

For competitions galore,
exclusive interviews with our lovely
Sphere authors, chat about
all the latest books
and much, much more.

Follow us on Twitter at
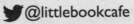 @littlebookcafe

Subscribe to our newsletter and
Like us at **f** /thelittlebookcafe

Read. Love. Share.